SLEEP WALK

A NOVEL

DAN CHAON

HENRY HOLT AND COMPANY NEW YORK

Henry Holt and Company
Publishers since 1866
120 Broadway
New York, New York 10271
www.henryholt.com

Henry Holt® and Ⓗ® are registered trademarks of Macmillan
Publishing Group, LLC.

Distributed in Canada by Raincoast Book Distribution Limited

Library of Congress Cataloging-in-Publication Data

ISBN: 9781250175212

Our books may be purchased in bulk for promotional,
educational, or business use. Please contact your local
bookseller or the Macmillan Corporate and Premium Sales
Department at (800) 221-7945, extension 5442, or by e-mail at
MacmillanSpecialMarkets@macmillan.com.

First Edition 2022

Designed by Meryl Sussman Levavi

Printed in the United States of America

10 9 8 7 6 5 4 3 2 1

For Philip

That which you seek is also seeking you.

—*Rumi*

1

The Barely Blur

Will Bear,

William Baird,

Bill Behr,

Willard Baier,   Liam Bahr,

Billy Bayer,

Wilder Barr,

Bear Williams,

Willie Bare Jr.,

Wilton Bairn,

Blair Willingham,

Barry Billingsly,

Bjorn Williamsen,

УильямАю,

သည္းၾ ခပါလိန္မ်ယ်

Three Times

The first time it happens it's October, and I'm driving through Utah with this young Filipino guy named Liandro. We're passing a joint back and forth, handing off over the head of Flip the dog who is asleep on the seat in between us, but we're not really talking. Liandro is miffed because his ankles are shackled.

I picked him up at the Chef Cheng Diner in Elko, Nevada, and I told him then that it was just best practices, nothing personal. I had him sit down in the passenger seat of the pickup and take off his shoes and socks; then I bent down and applied the cuffs.

"Dude," he said, flexing his toes. "This is so unnecessary."

"I know it is," I said.

Ah, well. I reckon he should be glad he's got his hands free, but he's not grateful in the slightest. He holds the nubbin of joint between his thumb and forefinger with delicate aloofness and takes a long slow draw. Puckers and exhales a little trail of smoke and stares out the window as if I'm not even there.

I hope he's enjoying the view. We're driving through the Bonneville Salt Flats, and he might as well be looking at a blank screen. I hold out my hand and he passes the joint back without glancing at me. Tiny, glinting raindrops are sidling along the parts of the windshield that the wipers don't reach, and up ahead I see a piece of sleet turn into a snowflake. It's falling and then suddenly it becomes a weightless piece of fluff. Now it's flying, like it just grew wings.

"Looks like it's going to start snowing," I say. "Must be from that typhoon they're having up to Seattle."

"Hm," Liandro says, and he is about as interested as any of us are in hearing a fifty-year-old white man chat about the weather.

At that moment, one of the burner phones I keep in a plastic sand bucket next to the gearshift lights up. It's set to vibrate, and it starts jiggling and flashing and bumping against the others.

I reach down and fish around for it. I pick it up and flip it open. "Hello," I say.

"Hello!" says a chipper young female voice. "Can I speak to Will Bear?"

I roll down the window and toss the phone out. In the side mirror, I see it hit the surface of the interstate and bust apart, shards of plastic and metal bouncing like marbles. Liandro looks over his shoulder wistfully. "Dude," he says. "Why did you do that?"

"Nobody's supposed to call me on that phone," I tell him. He blows on the lit end of the joint, but it has gone out. "Such a waste," he says. "You could've given it to me. I don't got a phone."

The second time it happens, I get a little prickle of concern. I have nine phones in that bucket, and they're all supposed to be anonymous. I guess I'm looking at some sort of breach? But it could be a robocall. Nothing is safe from those. I dip my hand in the bucket and root around for the little vibrating rattlesnake egg and I snatch it up.

"Hello?" I say, and dang if it isn't the same young female voice.

"Hi," she says, talking fast. "Mr. Baird, you don't know me, but don't hang up! I have important information for you!"

Which is super alarming. I toss the phone out the window again, and Liandro looks at me sidelong.

"Problems, boss?" he says.

The third time it happens we're pulled over by the side of the road. Visibility has gone to hell, the sleet-flakes are blowing in a horizontal stream like video static, and then a phone at the top of the bucket starts trembling and jostling. Liandro doesn't look. He's mesmerized by the storm outside, by the freshly rolled joint he's sipping at. For a while, I think I'm just going to wait it out. The phones aren't set up for voicemail, so I can just leave it ringing and ringing and ringing. Three minutes? Five minutes? Ten minutes? Let the dang thing hum for an hour, I don't care.

But then another of the burner phones starts to buzz, and then another, and then all eight of them—Bill Behr, Bear Williams, Barry Billingsly, Wilder Barr, Blair Willingham, Liam Bahr, even Willie Bare Jr.—the names and identities that make up the Barely Blur—all of them zuzzing and trembling and shuffling around in the bucket like cicadas on their backs, and I seize one furiously.

"Who is this?" I say.

Best Practices

Later, Liandro and me and the dog are in the camper.

It's a custom-built motor home that I acquired a few years back, and I must say that it's a solid vessel. I've named it, the way ships are named: the *Guiding Star*, I call her, and she's tricked out with three bunks, lots of storage, plus a pretty decent kitchen area. Outside, the storm is howling, but inside the *Guiding Star*, we're warm and snug.

Liandro is sitting at the little dining-table booth, itching at the cuffs around his ankles as I bring a couple of bowls of macaroni and cheese. I hand one to him and put the other on the floor for Flip.

"Nice," Liandro says. "I get to eat the same food as a dog."

"Everybody's equal here," I say, and head back to the stove to scoop up some mac and cheese for myself. "It's a democracy."

"That's not what democracy means," Liandro says, and I clean off the ladle with my finger. I'm not going to debate politics.

"Right on," I say. I sit down across from him and dig in, but he just sits there holding his spoon, eyeing me critically.

"What's with the braids, Pippi Longstocking?"

And I don't say anything, I just give him a tolerant look. I have rocked long braids since a teenager, and I am immune to rude comments. I'm a biggish man—six foot two, broad shouldered, bearded, and pale skinned, and I can stride through the world with little fear of being menaced. If you want to mock my hairstyle choice, be my guest.

"You want to play a board game?" I say. "We got Monopoly, Stratego, Risk, Trivial Pursuit, Scrabble, Battleship . . ."

"You have any cards?" he says.

"Yep," I say.

"You know Egyptian Rat Screw?"

"Yep," I say, and I may impress him by how quickly I can pull out a drawer and produce a pack of cards. "Listen, kiddo," I say, "I can play any game that you can name!"

I'm a good shuffler, and I give him a little show; I riffle with a flourish, walking the cards between my fingers in a quick Sybil cut and then dribbling them between my hands in a long accordion like a waterfall. In another life, I was a magician, a card sharp.

"Hm," says Liandro, and takes a glance around. I've done a lot of work on the interior, replaced the old paneling and cabinets with real antique wood, nice duvets on all the beds, muted, oatmeal-colored linens with a high thread count, some cute Día de los Muertos figurines for a touch of color and whimsy. Full bar, the bottles and glasses shining. It's not like some dumps I've had to live in.

He points with his lips. "What's in there?" he says, and his eyes rest on the long Browning safe at the far end, built in below my bunk.

"Nothing for you," I say.

"Guns?" he says.

"You want to play for pennies?" I ask, and he gives me a hooded glare.

"How about," he says, "let's play for my freedom."

"Sheesh," I say, and pause in my shuffling. He's an exasperating sort of person. "Young man, I'm not holding you prisoner. I'm just your driver. You can go anytime you want," I say. "Open the door and walk out."

"Right. My feet are shackled."

"Those are my cuffs," I say. "They're expensive, quality material, and they will not go with you. If you want to leave, I'll take them off and you can be on your merry way."

"It's a blizzard out there," he says.

"So stay, then," I say. "But I'm not taking the cuffs off. House rules. Look, I've had people attack me in the past. I've had to tase aggressors. I had to fend one nimnut off with a soup ladle!"

"Hm," Liandro says unsympathetically.

"Best Practices," I say. And I begin to deal, letting the cards fly smoothly from my fingertips.

But then one of the phones rings again. It's the one in the drawer by the stove, with the spatulas and tongs and whisks, and Liandro and I both look over toward the cabinet that is emitting a muffled throbbing.

"This is an outrage," I say.

This is an outrage: It would make a good tombstone epitaph.

Worst-Case Scenario

There is some unpleasantness when I drop Liandro off. He's experiencing a lot of emotion, and I realize I probably shouldn't have let him smoke so much weed. Too late now: I watch out of the corner of my eye as he sucks down the better part of his third blunt, and his hands are shaking hard.

"There's our destination up there," I tell him. "Bear Lake. Look," I say, but he doesn't, which I suppose is not the greatest loss. It's not particularly pretty under these weather conditions—just a line of blue ice under a haze of fog, the snowy hills melting into heavy white cumulus clouds, all of it blotchy and abstract. You can't tell that it is a magnificent body of water, a hundred square miles in size.

"Hm," Liandro says, which is just about all I've been able to get out of him for the past few hours.

"We're about fifteen, twenty minutes from Rendezvous Beach, and then I'll just pass you off to your sponsor and you'll be on your way."

"Rendezvous Beach," he says, under his breath, disdainfully. "Jesus. This is a nightmare."

We drive in silence down Highway 30, past a somber field of Black Angus cattle, their backs dusted with a stripe of snow. The storm has passed, but there's a thick wet fog hanging low to the ground.

"Listen," I say, after a while. "You won't have to be on retainer forever.

Just till you get that debt paid down. You're resourceful. You'll figure it out."

He turns to glower at me. "Gee," he says. "Thanks."

"I'm trying to lift your spirits," I explain.

"Fuck you," he says, as we turn onto Rendezvous Beach Road and head into Bear Lake State Park. "I hate your fat guts so much," he says. And then he starts to cry. Up ahead I can see a red pickup sitting in the parking lot with its motor running, Utah license plate MT1 L47R—that's the sponsor, all right, and the old white gent behind the steering wheel lifts one finger in greeting.

Afterward, I can't help but feel a little misgiving. It wasn't the worst or most upsetting drop-off I've ever done, but it makes me reconsider my habit of socializing with deliveries. A lot of drivers just sedate them, and that's probably not a bad idea. I swing through the radio dial until I find a station that's playing old-time sixties music, Connie Francis singing "Where the Boys Are," and Flip glances at me skeptically. I keep thinking about the way Liandro cried—the way boys cry in grade school, that hitching, shamed noise, half swallowed. Tears running out of your nose.

"Ugh," I hear myself grunt, and I try to center myself with a 4–7–8 breathing exercise and I focus my gaze on the license plate of the SUV in front of me. *Life Elevated* is the motto Utah puts on her plates. I exhale with a whooshing sound to a count of eight, and then I pluck my Willie Bare phone from the plastic bucket and give Friend Monte in Provo a call.

"Monte," I say, "I'm done with that drop-off."

"Yessir, Mr. Bare," he says. He has the sandpaper voice of a wise old cowpoke, and I picture him with an elegant shock of white hair and a particular kind of wind-burnt wrinkling, though of course I've never seen him. "The client has confirmed. You'll have the credits transferred to your account here shortly."

"Thank you kindly," I say, and breathe out, 1–2–3–4. Some Utah license plates say: *The Greatest Snow on Earth*. Some say: *This Is the Place*.

"Listen, Monte?" I say. "Do we still have that friend in Straub, Wyoming?"

"We sure do," Monte says. "Friend Riordan. He's at the Walmart from ten p.m. to seven a.m., Saturday through Wednesday."

We stay off the interstate, stick to Highway 30, rolling into the treeless western Wyoming hills, not hardly a house in sight, and I breathe 4–7–8 again, and I think about the way Liandro was shuddering when I put the *Guiding Star* into park and the skinny old white man got out of his truck grinning grimly. Light glimmered bright blue off Bear Lake.

"It's not my fault that kid messed with the wrong people," I tell Flip, and he gives me a long, considering look—who am I trying to kid, he wonders, and rolls on his side so the heater can blow on the back of his neck.

Then out the window I see a big billboard for Little America—not far across the Wyoming border—and I think, hell, yes, maybe I'll stop early for the night, get me and Flip a motel room with a good shower in it.

I've always had a fondness for Little America. It's a vintage truck stop, with a filling station, a 140-room motel, and a travel center where you can get some food and buy some trinkets. Legend has it that in the 1890s, when the founder of Little America was a young man out herding sheep, he became lost in a raging blizzard and was forced to camp at the place where the Little America now stands. I read about this on a plaque in the motel lobby when I was a child, and it caught my fancy, and even today I can practically quote whole pieces of that plaque, how, shivering in the midst of the blizzard, the young shepherd "longed for a warm fire, something to eat, and wool blankets. He thought what a blessing it would be if some good soul were to build a haven of refuge at that desolate spot."

Honestly, I don't know why I was so taken with the place. It was maybe mostly the billboard advertising they did—they had billboards all along the Lincoln Highway and I-80, featuring a cartoon penguin with an outstretched, welcoming flipper, and the more billboards you saw the more you felt that the place was exciting and an Important Landmark, and possibly magical.

My mom and I stayed there maybe five or six times when I was growing up—sometimes only a few days or weeks, sometimes a month or more—and it has a little homelike glow of nostalgia for me now. There's a green Sinclair Brontosaurus outside the motel, a cement statue about the size of a horse, and kids are allowed to climb on it. When my mom and I stayed there, I was always king of that Brontosaurus, just sitting astride his back and riding the hell out of him, and of course other children would come along and want to get up on him, too. So I met kids from New Jersey and Chicago and Houston, kids going on vacation to Yellowstone or Flaming Gorge, kids fleeing with their mothers from dads who wanted to kill them, kids who wanted to convert everybody to Jesus, kids who had an eye out for some animal or small creature they could torture. I even met a little girl from Japan once, she didn't speak any English but I talked to her in my language and she talked to me back in hers, and I remember this being one of the most pleasant conversations I have ever had.

I'm adrift in these reminiscences when some crap begins to fall out of the sky. It's not sleet or snow this time, but something I've never seen—dark flakes of some kind of substance come down like leaves from a tree and they make a muddy smear when my windshield wiper pulls them across the glass. I can squirt it off with the windshield wiper fluid, but at this rate I have to wonder whether the fluid will last another nineteen miles to Little America. A few drivers are already pulled over to the side of the road, and I pass a family van with all their belongings in cardboard boxes roped to the top of their vehicle. The boxes look like they've seen some extreme weather conditions, and also they are spotted in a way that suggests that they've been passed over by some flocks of birds.

I don't know what, exactly, is raining down this time. Maybe detritus from the typhoon off the northwest coast, or ash from the Mount Silverthrone volcano up in Canada. But I reckon we'll all get used to it and adjust our expectations accordingly. It's true that the world isn't in great shape, but I've read that it's not the worst it's been—not as bad as it was in 536 C.E., when catastrophic volcanic eruptions caused a short-term ice age, devastating famine, and so forth. Probably not as bad as it was in 1349, maybe not even as bad as 1520—but we all sense that worse times are ahead.

No doubt, a day of reckoning for mankind is coming, yet even for those of us who accept the inevitability of mass human death, there's still a cautious hope; we're waiting to see how Armageddon plays out, keeping an eye open for ways it might turn to our advantage. Even in the worst-case scenario, odds are that at least a few of our kind will struggle on long enough to evolve into creatures suitable for whatever new environment is ahead. I'm no evolutionary biologist, but I have faith in our species' stick-to-it-iveness.

I put my head down and keep driving, leaning forward over the steering wheel, the better to squint through the translucent smear of silt that the windshield wipers leave as they make their sweep. I may only be going ten miles an hour, but I am a man hell-bent on a destination.

Small World

The dog and I walk into that Walmart just outside Straub, Wyoming—
the giant twenty-four-hour one—but at this time of night it's nearly
empty. Two thirty in the morning. Flip's toenails click against the tile
floor as he ambles along behind me.

He's a heavily muscled dog, is Flip, with a stance like a wrestler—
about sixty pounds, a pitbull mix, with black and white patches like a
Holstein cow, and ice-blue Malamute eyes. He was a fighter once, before
I rescued him, and he still bears some scars and some shotgun BBs are
lodged beneath his skin, but generally he's a gentle fellow. He has some
lingering post-traumatic stress: doesn't like motorcycles or uniforms,
hates fireworks and the smell of tequila, is terrified of thunder and belts
and pinwheel lawn ornaments. God knows what he's been through.

He's not the sort of dog who will abide a leash, but he's a faithful and
focused follower, and I've rarely had to call him to heel. One customer
glances at us sidelong as we go past the Aisle of Women's Makeup. She
pauses with a jar of unguent in her hand, keeping an eye on us as we
continue on toward the back of the store.

We come to the wall of fishies. There are rectangular tanks from floor
to ceiling, and each contains interesting swimming things: guppies and
angelfish, neon tetras and Cypriniformes, cherry barbs and harlequin

rasbora. Leopard-spotted suckermouths that suction themselves to the surface of the glass. Plecostomus, they are also called.

Flip sits, and I clasp my hands behind my back. In one of the tanks, a pirate's treasure chest opens and closes, emitting bubbles that the fish dodge and avoid. I touch Flip's broad troglodyte skull as the fish slide along the pane of glass, never knowing that they are contained in a box.

Small world, they think.

Then an employee slinks out from one of the side hatches near the fish tanks. I look up as he comes forward. A tall, heavyset white man of early middle age, with shaggy hair that is prematurely gray, a spotty beard, an oddly kind face. He is wearing the bright blue Walmart smock, his name tag pierced to his heart: *Riordan*, it says, and below that the words *How may I help YOU?* are jauntily embossed. He holds out his hand.

"Mr. Bayer?" he says. He glances down at Flip disapprovingly, but doesn't linger.

"That's right," I say. "I'm Bill Bayer."

We shake hands. "What can I get for you?" he says.

"I'm in need of eight to twelve fresh burner phones," I tell him. "And a full blotter of hundred-microgram LSD-25. And a case of those little airplane-size bottles of vodka? Miniatures, I think they're called. And if you can get Tito's brand, that's my preference."

He inclines his head thoughtfully. "Well, I can get you the prepaid mobile devices right away. The others may take . . . forty-five minutes? Can you wait?"

"Sure," I say. "No problem."

Steely Human Resolve

First you submerge a hundred-microgram tab of LSD in a 150-milliliter miniature bottle of vodka, then you give it a shake and leave it in a cool, dark place for forty-eight hours or so until the LSD dissolves.

I like to take what they call a microdose every couple of days. Just a few drips from an eyedropper, maybe a fifth of a tablespoon. It's sub-perceptual: you don't even hardly notice it in the day-to-day, but it does a nice job of bringing the wonders of being alive to the fore and pushing the horrors a tiny bit back. Which is an important survival technique. Voilà! The bliss of temporarily giving a shit.

I open my eyes and it's maybe ten in the morning. I could stand to sleep longer, but the dog is yawning and stretching beside me, then giving his ears a flappity-flap to make sure I'm good and awake.

So I stick my bare foot out from under the covers and test the warmth of the day. It's a chill morning, no doubt, but Flip has already bounded down and he's doing a little dance in front of the door, grinning that wide, tongue-lolling pitbull grin, and he's pushing out past me even before I get the knob all the way turned.

The camper is still at the edge of the Walmart parking lot, which is as big as several football fields but mostly empty. Flip strolls around seriously, looking for strategic places to drizzle his pee on, and I have a seat on the stoop with a little ladyfinger joint, sorting through my stack of license plates until I find a Colorado plate with unexpired tags. Colorado is but fifteen minutes to the south, and in my experience their highway patrol are not keen on out-of-state vehicles.

At last, Flip finds a place by the fence to bestow his morning bowel movement upon, and comes running back to me, pleased and ready for breakfast. When you travel as much as we do, it's good to have a routine. Flip gets four raw eggs and toast, and I settle down to French-press my coffee and do the crossword or the sudoku from the newspaper I bought on my way out of Walmart last night.

As it turns out, the crossword is on the same page as the Opinions in the Straub *Star-Herald,* which I think is a bad sign. The headline says: "Another Quake, Another Hurricane: Evidence Not of End Times, but of Steely Human Resolve!"

"That's the spirit," I say, and fold the article over so that I can focus on 1-Across:

"Very funny." Six letters.

I lick the lead of my pencil.

¹H	A	R	H	A	R

. . . possible tombstone epitaph?

After my coffee and my puzzle, I wash out Flip's dish and make myself a breakfast smoothie. I like to be adventurous in this, and so today I have a carrot, turmeric, a clove of garlic, frozen mango slices, half a banana, apple juice, and a shot of whiskey. Blend the shit out of it, and then gulp it down! In another life, I'd have a food truck in Los Angeles that I'd call "Adventurous Smoothie," and my motto would be *See how far I can go!*

It's probably eleven o'clock in the morning, time to get going, so I fire up one of the fresh burner phones and call Harry Longbeck.

"Hey, Harry," I say. "It's Bear Williams. I was checking in with you to see if you had anything for me?"

He does. A transport job, but it's down in Texas, north of Abilene. I ask if they'll pay mileage and per diem, and he thinks they will, so it's agreed and I say it looks like twelve hours on I-25 south and he says it would be better if it was not more than eight hours and I say I'll do my best.

At times like these I wish I had that satellite radio, but then again it's probably not a great idea for someone like me to connect himself to a transponder in outer space that can follow my every move and potentially transmit that information to the government or other parties. I have to keep myself clean—that's one of my main selling points: I don't officially exist. I don't have an address or a social security number or a credit rating, I've never had an email, or a Facebook page, or a wifi-connected phone. I'm a blank Scrabble piece, and that's not easy to find these days.

Amnesiascape

Slightly empty, slightly lost, slightly delighted: Holding it in my chest like a sustained chord. Driving ninety miles an hour.

We leave I-70 and merge onto US 287 South. They say that tornados roam across this stretch all the time, but we don't see any. In Campo, Colorado, we stop for a moment to pee and buy meat sticks and gas, and then we stand in the gravel parking lot of the truck stop, staring out. The town of Campo looks to be no more than a hundred souls, and God knows what they do with themselves here. It's flat, gray-yellow sod all the way to the horizon, barbed-wire fences and transmission towers, kind of like the way amnesia would look, if it were a country. I unwrap a meat stick and take a bite, then give a piece to Flip, who mouths it thoughtfully from my fingers.

You have to wonder about these settlers of the Great Plains. These white people who in olden times killed the natives and laid claim to this dirt and stuck to it; who stranded their children and grandchildren with a birthright of dust. A collection of clapboard shacks with backyards full of unmown pigweed and junked cars and abandoned swing sets and withered, thirsty trees. Was the genocide worth it?

I think this and then I check myself. It isn't a fair way to think. The customer service at the Campo Truck Stop is excellent. There's a polite, round-faced teenage girl behind the counter, who smiles sweetly at my compliment. A tired-looking bald manager with a set of worries on his shoulders hunches over his laptop. Who am I to look down on them, after all, even if they are the offspring of murderers?

No doubt in the great scheme of things we are all of us the offspring of murderers. Right? If we weren't, we probably wouldn't be here.

Kickin Chickin

We're just north of Abilene, Texas, and I park behind the gas station like I was told to. It's an old Texaco station in the middle of the desert, a little stucco box with a couple of bare pumps and an impressively large logo sign on a pole.

We made it in just under nine hours, which is a miracle, but it still means that we're a little late, and when we pull up, the metal back door bangs open and the silhouette of a woman stands in the doorway, her fists on her hips.

I clamber out of the cab of the *Guiding Star* and lift my hand. "Howdy," I call, but already she is turning over her shoulder to emit an angry string of—what?—Russian, it sounds like?

"Здравствуйте!" I say. "Прошу прощения за опоздание!"

"Fuck you, motherfucker," she says. "Don't you speak to me in your dirty Russian. I'm fucking Ukrainian, and I can speak English just as good as you, so take your Russian and shove it up your lazy ass. You're late!"

She comes into view under a security light that looks over the back door and the dumpster, a dark-haired woman—in her late thirties, maybe? A grimace of scorn so tight that it must actually be painful to wear, and I perform a little bow of apology.

"Traffic," I say, and try to think of a compliment I might give to her, but already she has turned her head. She yells in Ukrainian or whatever, and a short, broad-shouldered Mexican kid comes hurrying out carrying a cardboard box that says *Kickin Chickin* on the side.

In the box, in a nest of blankets, there is a tiny Caucasian infant.

"This is supposed to sleep for eight hours," the woman tells me. "And we were told you would be here two hours ago!"

"Yes," I say, and the kid holds the box out to me. "Delays beyond my control."

"Tough luck! Now you got six hours before it wakes up!" the Ukrainian woman says. "Then it's your problem!"

"Well," I say. I'm a little taken aback as I hold the box in my arms. The poor creature is literally the size of a stewing chicken. "How old is it?"

She waves her hand vaguely.

"A boy?"

"How do I know?" she says. "When it wakes up and you have to change its fucking diaper, you'll find out, eh?"

Friend to Babies

So there's the baby—the infant—I imagine it's three weeks old, give or take, and I set it down on the floor of the front cab, beneath the passenger seat. It doesn't wake up. Ideally, I guess, I would have been given a car seat of some sort, but at this time of night there's not really a place open where you could purchase one. Also, they might have given me some bottles of milk or whatever, but nobody offers me anything, and we set off.

I figure it will probably be fine. Even if the wee one does wake up, we can make do: I've got some coffee creamer in the camper that I can warm up. Dilute it a little with water and put it in an eyedropper.

I've always had a fondness for babies, and I think they can sense it because whenever I've been around them they get very calm. You could say I have a magic touch, they just naturally think of me as their friend. It's the same with dogs. I can't tell you how many times I've had to break into somebody's house and their dog just came up to me wagging its tail, not uttering a single bark.

Probably it's an under-the-table adoption. Those happen all the time these days, and I think it's only fair that the mom receives some recompense for her trouble. I like the idea that I'll pass the little guy off to someone who will sell him to some nice wealthy couple who will raise him as their own son. I picture a movie star and her kindly, infertile husband, or some gay guys in short-sleeved shirts, hoping to make themselves a family in Minneapolis, and I picture them walking along through that rose garden in Lyndale Park with a toddler between them, and they pass that big pretty fountain with the cherubs on it and they let him dangle his feet in the water.

It could end up being nice for our lad, is what I think, and I don't really imagine that he'll find himself in a laboratory of some rogue government research facility, or in the hands of some cult that plans to sacrifice him to their dark god, or on the butcher block of one of those organ-harvesting outfits who will slice him up and put his parts in saline jars. Honestly, I don't believe most of that stuff really happens that often. That's just hysteria whipped up by the media.

It's beginning to sleet a little bit and I turn on the wipers and the defroster. Our lad is still fast asleep in his box, and low to the floor is perfect for him. He's vibrated by the velocity of the wheels against the highway asphalt, you can actually see him juddering and he loves it. The rhythm probably reminds him of the womb or something, and his little face is mushed up, sleeping hard, and the dog, half asleep on the passenger seat, gives the baby a stare I'd call rueful. He flares his nostrils, then flicks his eyes to me without lifting his head from where it's resting on his paws.

"Don't look at me that way," I tell him.

Up ahead on the left is a big wind farm, and it seems that a couple of the turbines have caught fire, despite the sleet. The propeller blades are still turning without a care but the nacelle behind them is ablaze, and it's quite a sight. Three hundred and twenty-eight feet tall they are, and their crown of flames ripples back like long hair in the wind. The propellers take the smoke and whip it into a helix so it goes looping out in spiraling circles. It puts me in mind of that traditional Chinese dance they do with silk ribbons.

"I reckon lightning must have struck them," I tell Flip, but he doesn't raise his head. He's still disgruntled about the baby.

Our Lad

We cross the border into Louisiana and I huff a little something to take the edge off, but I don't want to overdo it. Being too awake is just as bad as being too sleepy. You want to try to find a zone that's a little bit outside of your body, kind of like you're following yourself and keeping an eye on things from a short distance away.

We're passing billboards for a place called Gators and Friends Exotic Animal Petting Zoo, and for a moment I think that if we had more time I might make a pit stop. Pluck our lad out of his box and take him for a stroll, let him look at some llamas or monkeys or potbellied pigs or whatever exotica they might have to pet. Not that he'd remember it, of course, but he might enjoy it. I picture his baby hand reaching out and clutching at some soft creature's fur.

In the midst of this reverie, I happen to glance over at the actual infant.

I'm not an expert on sleeping babies, but to my eye he seems unusually still. He's on his back in the Kickin Chickin box, and his little hairless head has a kind of bluish cast. The limbs appear to be rigid in a way that concerns me. I feel my chest tighten.

"Hey!" I say, loud enough to make Flip startle out of his dream with a quiver, but the child doesn't stir. "Hey!" I say again, still louder.

Nothing. I can't tell if the child is breathing, and I have to keep glancing up from the road to the baby and I'm starting to feel a panic rising inside me and whatever Adderall or Mydayis or other amphetamine I snorted begins to circle around in the center of my forehead in a way that feels like joyless, tuneless singing and prancing. The tiny hands of the baby seem to be rigor-mortised into gnarled tree-root shapes, grasping upward.

We're coming up on an exit for Flournoy and I'm guessing there'd be a hospital there, but I'm also thinking that it's not a good idea to go to an emergency room with an infant that you don't have the title for. And without wanting to I'm already thinking about how I might dispose of the remains.

Over the years, I've had to deal with my share of corpses, but I've never had to concern myself with a dead baby. I can picture myself taking his little body back to that petting zoo, with the gators and friends. The gators would definitely take care of it, but is that the kind of person I am?

"Flip!" I say. "Dang it! Wake up that baby!" And Flip lifts his head and levels a bejowled, somber look at me. His bobbed tail gives a hesitant, uncertain wag.

I gesture hard toward the baby in the footwell. "Wake him up! Go on!"

I know very little about what goes on in Flip's mind, but I can tell you that he is a highly intelligent being, and that he has previously given indication that he has powers beyond those of a mere dog. He doesn't know English, exactly, but he understands more than you would expect.

"Wake it up!" I say. And then the Adderall or what-have-you turns my words into birdsong, and I hear myself repeating: "Wakeitup wakeitup wakeitup!"

Poor Flip gives me a puzzled, disapproving stare, but follows my finger and points his muzzle toward our lad. He sniffs, and after a moment, gives the baby's mouth the most delicate of licks.

The little hands jerk up and make a spastic wingbeat. The tiny mouth opens wide, like a cat yawning, and emits a wail.

It's okay. He's okay. Thanks to the Heavenly Father that I don't usually like that much. Our lad is alive!

Shitty Times Ahead for Some

Just north of Vicksburg, Mississippi, there's a decent truck stop off Highway 61 where I can park and recharge, get some sleep. Red Hot Truck Stop, it's called, and I like this place because it's not judgmental. No one says a word if my pitbull follows me through the aisles as I look for candy bars. No one cares that I'm wearing sweatpants and flip-flops and a Vancouver Grizzlies beanie with a pom-pom on it. A young woman who sells me fried catfish and onion rings tells me to have a blessed day.

"End Times are a-coming," she says, and I smile and nod.

"They are," I say. "For some."

I'm in a lousy mood. Ever since I dropped off that baby, I've been feeling disgusted with myself. I just don't think I did a good job taking care of him, and I keep picturing that tiny old-lady face, all squinched up and reproachful. Passing him off in a hospital parking lot to a matron with one of those beauty-parlor haircuts that conservative conspiracy cult ladies always seem to have, her face botoxed into a permanent sneer. The minute she laid eyes on me she seemed ready to ask to speak to my manager, and she gave our lad a dubious look as if he wasn't the exact color that she'd requested and I felt a blink of sorrow for the life that lay in front of him and a part of me wanted to grab him back out of her hands. But instead, I was just exactly the trashy flunky that I seemed to be, and the matron tucked him into the crook of her arm and hurried off toward a waiting SUV, and though it was no different from a hundred other drop-offs I've done over the years, this one made me feel lower than I have in a while.

I'm sitting at the table in the camper and the catfish and onion rings are polished off, but I lick my pointer finger and use it to poke at the pebbles of fried breading that still remain, squishing them onto the pad of my finger and lipping them off irritably. There are things that I'm not proud of, but I'm far from the dirtiest hand in this country of ours. I have certain standards, and it makes me regret not saying something to that woman with her prissy, scorning look. Baby merchants are the worst.

There's a cold rain outside, pattering on the roof, and so I turn on the space heaters. I should probably be asleep by now—I think I've been driving for sixteen or seventeen hours?—but instead I just sit and pick at crumbs, shuffling cards and staring out at the parking lot. At a certain angle, the tractors of semis seem to have faces. Dumb-looking—bovine—but patient in a doleful way. Sometimes animals and machines look more human than people do.

I hope I didn't deliver that little one into the hands of bad people. I'd like to believe that he'll be fine, and he'll get adopted by a nice mom and dad. And he'll have a happy life, and I even bring out the Tarot deck to try to convince myself.

I wouldn't say that I believe in Tarot entirely, but I can read it. There was a professional psychic I knew once who lived in Margate, Florida, name of Mrs. Wetz, eighty-year-old woman who was a holder for some Mafia people, there was loads of cash stored all over her house, so I'd have to drop by every now and again to check on her. She was living in one of those half-abandoned retirement communities, lots of derelict and straight-up-ruined houses, and hers was the only occupied property on her block. Poor thing, she was bored out of her mind.

I'd mow her lawn for her and trim back some of that Florida foliage, and then we'd sit on her little screened-in porch and drink tea out of porcelain teacups, and she'd show me the cards and tell me about them like they were dolls with individual personalities. From her I learnt an appreciation of the Art of Tarot, as well as the game of Mah-jongg.

So I bring my old Rider-Waite Tarot deck to the table and shuffle it for a while. The heaters are humming and sending out that peculiar hot wool-and-metal odor they have, and once I've shuffled my way into calmness, I lay out a simple three-card spread, just for meditation purposes.

Eight of Cups. Six of Pentacles, reversed. The Hanged Man.

I scratch a dried droplet of ketchup. This doesn't look very good, at first glance.

But before I can even begin to ponder the Tarot's message, one of those phones that I got at Walmart starts buzzing. I look up from my cards toward the drawer where the phone is coffined.

Bzzzt. Bzzzzt. Bzzzzzzzt. Like a June bug trapped in a bottle. I lift my head and then I slowly put those three unwanted cards back into the deck, one by one. I would describe my mood as extremely nonplussed.

And dang if another isn't vibrating from some unknown place in the camper, and then the one in my jeans pocket starts up and it startles me so bad that I jump up from the table and swat my thigh like something's stinging me.

But the seriousness of the situation has now at last dawned on me.

Someone, apparently, knows my location. Someone, apparently, is able to track my unregistered burner phones, and that means there's been a pretty serious compromise of my privacy. Someone is bound and determined to get my attention, and so after a hesitation I pull the phone out of my pocket and flick it open.

"Hello?" I say, and there's a distant hissing, burblings of computer tones. And then a young woman's voice says: "Is this Davis Dowty?"

Davis Dowty is an old, old alias. The situation is worse than I thought.

"Please don't hang up," she says. "I don't want to hurt you."

2

Birthfather

"So . . . I think you might be my biological father?" she says.

I'm still sitting in the parking lot of the Red Hot Truck Stop in the camper of the *Guiding Star,* and I can feel my mind unbuckling and unfolding into several minds as I sit there with the phone against my face. *Dissociation,* I think it's called, but I'm very focused. I'm aware of floating outside my body, slightly above and to the left, and I hear myself speak.

"Anything's possible, I suppose!" I say, and I see myself pick up my crossword pen and a napkin and my hand writes *clear connection no static* and I say, "But what makes you think I'm your dad, honey?"

And this seems to fluster her. I reckon "honey" is an awkward and somewhat aggressive choice on my part, but I'd like to think it's intended in a fatherly rather than a creepy or threatening or condescending way. But anyways, it puts her a bit off balance.

"So . . ." she says, ". . . so, I know this must be very uncomfortable. It's very uncomfortable for me, too, so maybe I'll just lay out the information I have and we can proceed from there?"

My hand is writing in cursive in blue ballpoint on the napkin: *female voice—approx. 18–25 yrs with childlike affect—slight lisp when pronouncing esses—vocal fry.*

"My name is Cammie, by the way," she says. "I can't believe I didn't even introduce myself. I'm sorry, I guess I thought I was better prepared than I actually am."

Actress? CIA or corporate intelligence?

Somehow she's gotten access to one of the aliases I used back in the early days. When I hear that old pseudonym, my hair goes on end, and it stays up straight as she cites the name of a fertility clinic in Evanston, Illinois, where *Davis Dowty* had contracted his services.

It's true: I did sell a lot of sperm back in my younger days, back when I didn't know how important privacy was. I'd thought I was anonymous with my Davis Dowty alias, and since masturbating was a skill that I'd gotten reasonably good at, I'd figured out a way to game the system so I could make a living wage traveling from clinic to clinic. It's not completely unlikely that a child might have been produced.

But how did she connect those fertility clinic records to the Barely Blur, how did she come by the numbers to various phones that were supposedly anonymous and untraceable and unconnected, right down to the Chinese one I haven't used in eighteen months? How would she know they were all the same person?

She doesn't offer that information.

It was probably a mistake to engage in the first place. I probably should have just kept tossing those burner phones until I was able to figure out how to slip away and hide again, but I imagined it was smarter to find out what exactly I was dealing with. Now I'm not so sure.

She's a hacker, that's my main thought, likely some kind of independent contractor, using me to trace her way toward one of the bigger fish in the network of associates I do jobs for. There are plenty of public and private entities who would like to get hold of me—a number of med-tech corporations that I have done business with over the years, for example, who could have gained access to those old medical records and DNA, maybe just as a tool to blackmail me. But I also have enemies among the Raëlists and Los Antrax and the 14/88, and there have been members of the Kekistan Liberation Front trying to trace me, and I'm pretty sure I'm on the Gudang Garam Corporation watch list as well. That guy Adnan who worked as a middleman for Hezbollah would like to eliminate me, probably. I could make a spreadsheet out of the many who wish me ill. Point being, this could be the bait for some kind of Rube Goldberg trap and I just can't see the larger machinery of it yet.

Still, claiming to be my daughter seems like a weird game to play. I have to admit there's a small part of me that would like to believe there's a child of mine out there who wants desperately to find me. There's something inside me that swoons a little, half enchanted by the idea. I'd like to know what she looks like, for example, if we resemble each other. If she's my daughter, does she take after me in some way?

I picture her in pigtails, and maybe there's a touch of pink or turquoise dye at the tips of her hair. She's got freckles, no makeup, and I imagine that she's one of those young women who likes vintage clothes with whimsical patterns on them, and her eyes are green with gold flecks, intense eyes, reflecting the blue glow of her computer. It's dark in her apartment, just a string of little Christmas lights above her bed. Where is she? Brooklyn? No. Portland? Ann Arbor?

Maybe she's in some basement office in Quantico, dressed in a pencil skirt and sensible shoes, hair short and severe, and she's fiddling with buttons as she records my voice.

"I'm sorry that this is so creepy and stalker-y," she says. "I wish I'd figured out a better way to make contact."

"Well, it's pretty impressive work on your part," I say. "Tracking me down couldn't have been easy."

"Yeah . . ." she says. Her voice is modest, circumspect, almost regretful. "And I know you're wondering how I found you. Obviously, you're a very private person, and I'm sure it's kind of alarming to be—breached?"

"I'll admit," I say, "it has caused me some concern."

"Well sure, yes, of course," she says, and most of all I'm impressed by the balance she strikes between awkwardness and poise. It's a disarming tactic. "I mean," she says, "you've got to be worried that I'm working for someone or that I'm going to try to blackmail you or scam you or rip you off. I get it, you know?"

"Unfortunately, trust is an issue," I say. Flip is sitting by the door of the camper waiting, and I go over and let him out and then I sit down on the stoop and light a j, the phone pressed tight against my ear. Flip paces thoughtfully, deeply immersed in the question of where best to sprinkle his pee.

"I have to tell you," I say, "the idea that you've been hired by somebody, or that you're running some kind of scam—honestly, that seems a lot more likely than the idea that you're my daughter and you just happen to have hacker skills like somebody who works for an intelligence agency."

I'm trying to keep this conversation light and bantering, I don't want to sound paranoid or panicked. I look out across the parking lot and imagine that there's a sniper there, a mercenary assassin in a camouflage jumpsuit crouched atop the trailer of a semi. I can almost feel the red light of laser crosshairs crawling across my forehead.

"Well, then!" says Cammie. "I guess my first job is to convince you that I'm for real, right?" There's a bright, deadly earnestness in her voice that makes me suddenly think that actually, she might be unhinged. The hairs on the back of my neck prickle.

"S-u-r-e," I say. I parse my words carefully, letter by letter, like I'm filling out a crossword. I realize I should be trying to draw her out, I should be trying to get her to drop some bits of information so I can figure out who she is, where she's calling from, what her objectives might be. How she might be vulnerable.

"I . . . well. I think it might help if I had a clearer idea of how you went about finding me?" I say shyly. "If I knew your process, it might ease my mind."

My face smiles hopefully and earnestly toward the screen of the phone, even though I don't think she can see me, and Flip turns from his patrol of the Red Hot Truck Stop parking lot and wags his tail.

"I hear what you're saying," this girl says sympathetically. "And I really believe that we're going to get to a point where I can walk you through the whole thing. Once we get to know each other better. But at this time, I have to be kind of stingy about what I tell you."

"Because you don't trust me, either."

"Exactly," she says, regretfully.

"Well, that's a screwed-up place for a relationship to begin," I say. "If we can't be honest with each other, what's the point of it?"

"We could start by just having a conversation, maybe?" she says. "Like strangers sitting next to each other on a plane, right?"

"That's just role-playing," I say. Flip has finished his patrol of the periphery of the *Guiding Star,* and he comes back and sits beside me. He noses my hand and I scratch his ear. "Look," I say. "If you've come this far, you must know what kind of person I am. What are you after?"

"I just," she says, "I just want to make a connection. I want to get to know you. We're not so different, you know—I'm not on the grid, either. That was one of the reasons I decided to reach out to you. If you'd been, like, a high school principal or the owner of a Buffalo wings franchise, I probably wouldn't have been interested."

"Uh-huh," I say. "So what exactly are you interested in?"

"I think we might be able to help each other," she says.

"I don't need any help."

"Yes, you do," she says. And then she hangs up.

The Illustrated Encyclopedia
of the Animal Kingdom

I remember that clinic that Cammie mentioned—the clinic where she was concocted, or however you would put it. "Conceived" seems wrong.

I haven't thought about that segment of my life in a long time, but it comes back vividly after she hangs up on me. Lying in my bunk in the *Guiding Star,* I picture myself on the second floor of an old three-story Victorian mansion that had been turned into a kind of boardinghouse. I can see that room, with its rusty radiator and the single bed I'd loll around on at all hours of the day. The whitewashed, warty plaster of the walls I'd press my face against, the water stains on the ceiling that I'd find faces and figures in.

The arrangement was not entirely legal, I don't think—there was no contract or lease, just an old lady who decided to start renting rooms in her house. Mrs. Dowty was her name, and she lived alone on the first floor with her parrot. She was a widow, and recently her son, Davis, had committed suicide.

Soon after I moved in, I was able to harvest Davis's social security number and so forth, and within a few months I had acquired a "Davis Dowty" driver's license and passport. Meanwhile, I paid Mrs. Dowty up front, in cash, monthly, for a furnished room, shared bathroom, and limited use of the kitchen. This was in Evanston, Illinois, thirty years ago. Not long after I first escaped.

* * *

Above me, I would hear a woman on the third floor, walking. Her floorboards—my ceiling—would sigh as she paced, as if she was stepping over shifting ice. I didn't know her name but I thought about her a lot. She walked above my bed at all hours of the night, and sometimes through the heating vent I would hear her listening to music on the radio, or reading her son a story, her voice stumbling and sweetly awkward. "Goodnight, moon," I often heard her say.

Most of the tenants in Mrs. Dowty's house were on their way down in some way, and I imagined that maybe this woman and her boy were on the run from an abusive husband; or maybe the dad had died tragically, cancer or something, and she was saddled with doctor bills she couldn't pay; or maybe—more likely—she was just a single mom with limited resources, and this was the best she could do.

For a while I would dream that I was holding a baby. The infant in the dreams was wrapped in a blue hospital blanket, with only its round face peeking out, and I would feel its limbs squirming beneath the swaddling as I smoothed my palm against its cheek, as I said, "Hush, hush," and then I would wake and the woman's footsteps were creaking above me and I imagined—I believed—I could see the outlines of her bare feet as they pressed down.

In some ways, this dream was partially hers, a seed her restlessness had planted in my sleeping mind. And maybe it was partially her fault, too, that I decided, against good common sense, to start going to these clinics. Was it the woman upstairs, or the dream, or maybe simply the fact that I was alone in the world—unemployed, selling drugs sometimes to make ends meet but mostly lying on my bed in my underwear with a beer growing warm on my belly? I reckon it was some combination of these things, the feeling that I was separated from the rest of the people of earth by an invisible wall, like a fish in an aquarium.

Selling sperm was dumb, the way twenty-year-old boys are dumb, and maybe there was a kind of magical hope attached to it, too—like buying a lottery ticket or tossing a coin into a fountain.

But it was also true that I was constantly on the make, ever on the lookout for a new scam or scheme, and I wasn't above being drawn in by an easy fifty dollars I'd heard about through a guy I knew, who was in the beginning year of medical school. Patches, he was called. We used to hang out together at a bar a few blocks from Mrs. Dowty's place, and he would tell me all sorts of medical secrets.

He was the one who told me about the sperm bank. He'd been depositing once or twice a week, for beer money, and he gave me a number to call. "I don't know whether they'll take you," Patches said. "You're going to have to take an IQ test, and a physical, and then some gene testing as well, so they kind of run you through the gauntlet."

He smiled. He was in the process of buying weed from me—this was back in the day when it was illegal—and the two of us were sampling the product together in an alley behind the bar, leaning near a sour-smelling dumpster and passing a little brass pipe back and forth. I could tell that he didn't think I had the kind of pedigree they were looking for, he was just throwing it out there as a kind of brag, blond Northwestern med-school boy who believed in the meritocracy, who believed he had earned his place in the world.

The gauntlet, ha ha.

So I went in and got an application, and I spent several mornings filling out the questionnaire, sitting in Mrs. Dowty's kitchen eating oatmeal, Mrs. Dowty's parrot on its perch spreading its molting wings and preening them. I invented lie after lie about myself, and I tried to make my writing seem educated and poetic.

Out the window, I watched the upstairs neighbor woman and her son, who must have been about four, a thin, deep-eyed kid with a head like a baby bird. I stared out at them as they went about their business in the unmowed backyard behind the boardinghouse, watching as the boy built something with mud and sticks in the corner by the fence; watching as he flipped through his book: *The Illustrated Encyclopedia of the Animal Kingdom.* On the cover, there were drawings of a snake, a zebra, a penguin, a beetle, all the same size.

The woman sat quietly with a cigarette. She ran her fingers thoughtfully along the side of her bare foot, her dry, processed hair crushed flat in the back where she'd slept on it. She exhaled smoke and I wrote a story about myself like a man who deserved to have a baby, and Mrs. Dowty's parrot said, "Hello! What's your name?" in a high insipid voice and then took a nut from his dish and bit it savagely.

Still, it was a surprise when the fertility clinic called me in. A feeling of deep embarrassment as I stood there before the nurse. She was a girl about the same age as me—a shy, pretty girl who wore her hair in a way that made me think that she'd had an unhappy childhood. She couldn't look me in the eye. She just gave me some more forms to fill out on one of those clipboards with a pen hanging on a beaded metal chain. I turned in the paperwork and the nurse led me down a hospital-smelling corridor, silence trailing down the long hallway until we came to a halt in front of a little bathroom. She gave me a test tube with a screw-on lid and cleared her throat, shifting her weight in those chunky white shoes, and she opened the door and said that there were some magazines I could look at if I needed to.

Some old *Penthouse* and *Hustler* magazines were stacked on a shelf next to the toilet, and I nodded. What was there to say? The nurse was trying to be professional about it but I could see she was secretly mortified behind her nurse façade, and when I tried to smile ironically, she just cleared her throat again and left in a hurry. Poor girl.

It was strange, because it was she, the nurse, who I ended up thinking about rather than the porn magazine girls with their tawny unreal shapes and unmarked expressions. When I brought the test tube out and gave it to her I felt a flutter in my stomach. Her eyes were so sad and horrified that it seemed she must have known I'd been thinking of her. Afterward I sometimes thought that any baby that came from it would be as much that nurse's as it was my own.

But I never really truly believed that there would be a baby. It was just something I liked to daydream about, sometimes. In another life, I thought, there existed the possibility of a person—who might have a certain shape of their jaw or their fingers, or a certain way of smiling when they were sad, who might even eventually develop certain moods, a particular watery melancholy, slightly empty, slightly lost, slightly delighted—because of me.

* * *

A few weeks before I made my first donation, I happened to find a box of books. The box had been put out by the curb for the trash man to pick up, right outside a big old house that looked something like ours except it hadn't been split up into apartments. There was nothing wrong with the books that I could see—an old set of children's encyclopedias, not complete but nice nonetheless, with beautiful photographs. It didn't even look like they'd been read! I glanced around to see that no one was looking and I lifted the box and carried it home.

After dinner that evening, I went up the stairs with the box and knocked on the woman's door. "I found this," I said, showing her the books and trying to smile like a normal friendly person. "I've heard you reading to your son and I thought it would be something he would enjoy."

I'd practiced this short speech several times, but after it left my mouth I realized that it was a mistake to say that I'd been listening to her reading. It made me sound like a stalker, and I saw her eyes narrow. When she leaned down to look at the titles of the books, she wrinkled her nose. I was aware that they smelled a little like a basement.

"He's a little young for encyclopedias," she said, and I shifted my weight. The books were heavy.

"Right on," I said. "But they've got nice pictures."

"Uh-huh," she said. She looked me over again, and her eyes came to a decision. I sensed that she saw something essential about me that she could never learn to like. I didn't know what it was, exactly, but I could feel it in the air around me. An aroma.

"If you want to leave them," she said, "that's okay. I mean, he'll probably just wreck them. Color in them and stuff. You could sell them." She put a hand against her hair. "You don't have kids of your own," she said.

"No." I smiled, hesitating because she made no move to take the box. I braced it against my hip. "No, not really." After a second I realized that this was an odd thing to say. "None that I know of," I said, before I realized that this made things worse.

"Oh," she said. She laughed shortly. "You're one of those, huh?" She looked at me briefly with something like, what? Flirtation? Sarcasm?

Something familiar but not quite friendly. I couldn't tell, but it made me blush. I set the box down.

"No, no," I said. "No, it's . . . it's complicated."

"I'll bet," she said. She gave me that same look again, and I watched her thinking—a whole complex set of unreadable things was passing through her mind. She opened the door a little more, and I could see the boy inside, sitting cross-legged in front of the television, his face lit unnaturally as he trotted a plastic elephant along the carpet. It would have been neat if the boy suddenly turned to look at me, but he did not.

"Well," the woman said. "Thanks."

At that time, before I became the Barely Blur, I was a fugitive from justice—wrongly arrested, imprisoned, and then institutionalized in a mental facility. I couldn't tell you what the charges were, only that I thought they were ridiculous, and I said so, and soon an officer was leaning down with his sharp kneecap on the small of my back and applying handcuffs to my wrists, and once I was seen as recalcitrant and resistant, it was beyond hope. Further protests landed me in the psychiatric care division of the Hopewood Memorial Hospital, where I was pumped full of Thorazine and left to drift for eternity.

I don't know how I escaped. There are only a few brief flashes: I remember clambering through cattails in an irrigation ditch, wearing nothing but pajama bottoms, shaved bald and a hundred pounds overweight, fattened by antipsychotics and lack of movement; I remember smearing dark-green pond mud into my hair and over my face and body; I remember that at one point I was trying to wash myself off in a gas station bathroom, and that I stole a pair of coveralls from the mechanic's garage.

When I first moved into the apartment in Chicago, the little boy upstairs was having bad nightmares. The child would wake up screaming, and of course I would awaken as well. "Help me!" I thought I could hear the child crying. "Help me!" At last, I would hear the woman's footsteps. "Hush," she was probably whispering. "Everything's fine." And then she would begin to sing.

I don't know why this affected me so, the sound of her singing, but

I can remember how I shuddered. I thought of my own mother, dead by my hand; I thought of the authorities in another state, who were still hunting for me; and there were no friends in my life, only strangers, and I curled up a little more, whispering, "Hush, hush, it's nothing, you're okay, my little one, it will all be all right."

But there was a great churn of loneliness that opened up in me—that longing we have for kindred that some cruel God must have built into us.

Signs Point to Yes

I come out of sleep with a cloudy head and for a while I just lie there with my eyes closed, pretending that last night's phone conversation didn't happen. Then Flip touches my foot sole with his cold wet nose and I slide out from under the blanket. It's a little before six in the morning, and few are awake. The sky is bruise-gray, the tractors of semis lined up and sternly slumbering. I reckon I'm going to need to call Experanza.

I grab my sandals while Flip sits expectantly beside his food bowl, waiting for me to fry up some eggs for our breakfast. When I go out the door instead, he gives me a look of betrayed and outraged disbelief, but I can't call Experanza on one of those contaminated cell phones, so I trudge across the long parking lot toward where one of the last few phone booths in America is sitting in a patch of weeds. "*Dang it! Dang it!*" I mumble. A man I can't see is hollering off in the distance, some kind of despair born of brokenheartedness, and I close the folding door of the phone booth to block the sound. I use my T-shirt to wipe off the ear- and mouthpiece of the nasty old phone before I put it near my face and poke Experanza's number into the keypad.

When I was a kid, when we were living at Little America, Experanza's mother was one of my mom's best friends. The two of them liked to sit together and drink tequila out of tiny plastic water cups, and they'd lock Experanza and me out of the room: "Go play," they'd say, and we'd run through the halls and stand in front of the vending machines debating over which snack we'd most like to steal. We'd go out into the dry stubble fields out back of the hotel where there was a prairie dog town we liked to watch, or we'd wander around the travel center pretending to be detectives and shoplifting toys and candy. In a way, we were best friends, too, for short periods.

From what I gathered later, our moms were part of an anarchist collective that was more or less a cult but they were also connected to criminal underworld and terrorist organizations, and part of their mission was to create a new generation of people who were invisible to the government. Experanza and I were meant to be a different class of citizen. Our entrance into this world was unregistered—no certificate of live birth, no doctors, no proof of existence. In fact, my mom had faked her own death when she was seventeen, so she was not even considered alive at the time I was born. That was her greatest gift to me.

Years later, Experanza and I met again through work—we both ended up part of a contracting concern called Value Standard Enterprises, both of us employed in different capacities for the same boss. But this is more of a personal call than a business one.

Experanza listens silently as I fill her in on the situation. I've gotten so I don't like to be tethered to a phone by a cord, and I shift and twist uncomfortably in the glass box. I'm on edge, keeping my eyes on the truck stop, where people are beginning to stir; I'm glancing behind me at a raggedy thicket of scrub trees, checking off to the side at the entrance and exit.

When I come to the end of my story, she makes a disappointed sound. "You should've called me last night."

"I didn't want to wake you up," I say. "Besides, I was still trying to get my mind around it."

"And I'm trying to get my mind around *you*," she says. "What were you thinking?"

"I don't know," I say. "I was twenty. I was lonely."

"Guh," she says, and I cast another look over my shoulder at the woods. I feel visible from all directions.

"Is there any way to trace her?"

"How long did you have her on the phone?"

"Maybe ten minutes?"

"Good Lord."

"I'm screwed," I say, and she makes her disappointed sound again.

"You definitely are. You're fucked for all time."

"She said she wanted to get to know me," I say gloomily. "She thinks we can help each other."

"The awkward speech affect makes me think she might be some kind of bot."

"No, no," I say. "I actually think she's really vulnerable. That's one of the things that's freaking me out."

"Tough luck for her," says Experanza. "Don't contact me by phone anymore. Just get up north as fast as you can."

"What should I do if she tries to call me again?"

"If it were me," Experanza says, "I would try to gain her trust and find her location and then you can go there and kill her."

"Okay, then," I say. "I'll see you in a couple of days."

I trudge back to the *Guiding Star* and I scramble eggs and a sausage patty for Flip and make myself a cup of coffee and now I'm depressed again. I toss back my microdose with a shot of agave nectar and ground Cordyceps. *What would possess you to donate to a sperm bank?* Experanza said, and I wince to myself—not just because she's right, not just because I feel like a patsy, but also because it had been a little secret of mine that I'd been cherishing and nourishing in my private moments. The idea of having a kid somewhere had made me happy, and occasionally, out in the world, I'd notice a young person and some detail would spark and I'd get to wondering what a child of mine would look like. I'd find myself daydreaming that they were my offspring.

That auburn-haired girl at the bus stop in Vancouver with her tartan-patterned suitcase and I imagined she was on the run and I dropped a hundred-dollar bill into her coat pocket; the young tattooed gas station attendant outside Davenport, Iowa, about my height, my color of skin, how he gave me a grin as if he recognized me from somewhere and I said to him, "Hey, take my advice, stay away from North Park Mall this upcoming weekend."

That teenager walking across the Zaragoza Bridge with her high heels in her hand, the way the doomy look on her face felt familiar—familial.

That mercenary I suffocated in Bobo-Dioulasso, the kid couldn't have been more than twenty or twenty-one, his hands scratching and pulling my hair, clawing at my face, the way our hands were the same size, the same color, the same shape of fingernails. I think he was Dutch, but still.

Over the years, I've gotten these glimmers, these ghosts have shown up and I've spent significant time imagining, *What if, what if, what if.*

Once I finish my coffee and the word jumble in the paper, I head up to the truck stop shower, carrying my toiletries in a caddy, towel slung over my shoulder, my plastic sandals crunching the gravel. The Red Hot does not have the cleanest facilities, but it does have among the fewest CCTV cameras so it's a decent trade.

I think about Cammie, and honestly there's no believable scenario in which she's *not* corrupt in some way. *Fucked for all time,* Experanza said, and this is probably how things will come to pass—my secret identities compromised, my invisibility squandered, irrecoverable. Which would be worse: if she was a bot who suckered me into believing she was human, or if she was actually my daughter and she was still scamming me and will probably shoot me in the end?

In the Red Hot Service Center, beyond the aisles of snacks and necessities, there is a restroom corridor and also a shower rental, and as I stroll in I see a skeletal, trembly teenaged junkie slouched against a broken Pac-Man game, watching as I buy a ticket for a shower room—a homely boy with a polyester Looney Toons twin-size comforter draped over his shoulders, wearing eyeliner and probably not much else. He doesn't have a shirt, and his hairy, naked legs poke out below the shawl of the blanket he's wrapped in. His sockless feet are stuffed into a pair of ancient, dirty Air Jordans.

"Mister?" the kid says to me as I walk past. "Can I have a dollar? I want to get something to eat."

"I don't have any change," I say, which is true. In another life, I'd take him back to the *Guiding Star* and feed him and nurse him back to health and he'd become my sidekick and I'd teach him the ways of the Barely Blur.

But in this life, he's no son of mine. There's no familial glimmer as I look at his feral, rheumy eyes and crooked, runny nose, but he's a sad sight—not long for this world, I would guess—so I pass him an American Express card I have tucked in the pocket of my shorts.

"It's stolen," I tell him. "Don't use it more than once."

There is a wet towel and standing water on the floor of Shower Room 5 and an algae-like hank of human hair curled at the edge of the drain, but it smells clean enough. Someone has been liberal with the bleach. It's a small, tiled room with a toilet and a sink and a curtainless shower stall, and the door seems to lock firmly so I go ahead and disrobe.

I'm trying to think carefully about what Cammie might be after. I'm tracing backward through the jobs I've done this year as I turn the shower on. Decent pressure, good hot water. I tilt my head back and let my face get massaged by the spray. *I want to get to know you,* she said, and I wonder now how much she already knows.

Can't shake the paranoid idea that I've already seen her—that she's been watching me this whole time.

Was she a customer in that Walmart in Wyoming? Was she following me on the interstate as I transported Liandro along, was she one of the gamblers at that casino in Primm, Nevada, Whiskey Pete's I think it's called, where you can view the clothes that Bonnie and Clyde were shot in?

Was she on me even before that?

After my shower, I stroll thoughtfully through the candy aisle of the Red Hot, and I pick up a pack of cashew M&Ms and some off-brand peanut butter cups, a Cherry Mash and a Goo Goo Cluster. The newspaper rack for the *Clarion-Ledger* is empty except for a copy of a Xeroxed pamphlet that offers charmed Lotto numbers for one dollar. There's a drawing of a woman in a turban, looking into a crystal ball, and inside that crystal ball is Jesus's head. "Signs point to YES!" says Jesus, and I pick up the pamphlet and consider the lists of numerals, puzzling over the last thing Cammie said to me. How she thought we might be able to "help each other."

Damn! That line is so unprofessional, she can't possibly be NSA or CIA. Although maybe it was meant as a provocation.

Try to picture a person desperate enough to hunt down a stranger, in the hopes that their random DNA connection would spark a feeling of bonding and the stranger would be, like, *Yes! How may I be of assistance, Miss?*

I imagine her as a crazy woman, this alleged daughter—with terrible staring eyes, maybe, with long strawberry-blond hair, wearing an old-fashioned nightgown, living in the basement of her adoptive parents' house, spending all her time on the computer, searching and searching, yearning but also truly insane, with the sweet-voiced fury of one of those kindly Murder Nurses you read about, the ones who will smile helpfully and give you a deadly injection of morphine if you get on their bad side.

"Do you have anything smaller than a fifty?" the cashier at the Red Hot says, as he tallies up my candy purchases and my Lotto pamphlet.

"Not at this time, no," I say.

I line all my phones up on the table and consider. I've got software to wipe the data off them and a compactor that will crush them to the size of dice. But then what? What's to stop her from finding me a third time?

Better, I think, to hang onto them.

So I put them back in their plastic bucket and Flip and I climb into the cab of the *Guiding Star* and off we go, headed north on some back roads toward Tupelo, a bit before nine in the morning on a Sunday. It's starting to rain, and the radio's playing Skeeter Davis, "The End of the World," and if this were a movie it would be the part where the hero is feeling some pangs of concern that things won't end happily and there would be a close-up of his profile with the telephone poles flickering by in the distance.

I wonder how that baby's doing? I think of our lad's face, the way he stopped crying for a second and his eyes went wide and the little palms opened and went rigid, as if he'd had a startling realization—and then he scrunched up with sorrow again and began to wail.

Sperm of Choice

She calls again in the afternoon. I'm a little northeast of Nashville, traffic slow due to rain, and out of the corner of my eye I see the phone's screen light up and I snatch it out of the bucket even before it rings.

"Cammie," I say.

And she says, "Let's make a deal. I'll tell you something if you tell me something."

"I can handle that," I say. I keep my eyes on the rain-wet road, on the cars slowing ahead of me, beginning to cluster, and I'm thinking of Experanza's advice: *Gain her trust. Find her location.* I press the button on my phone that will begin to record our dialogue. "Tell me what you want to know."

"I don't—" she says, and her husky voice frizzles from the cell phone speakers. "I just wanted—to start, I wanted to say that I really do come in peace! I'm honestly not trying to hustle you."

"I thought you said you wanted to make a deal," I say.

"Let's just talk like two human beings for a while," she says. "You know? Have a normal conversation. Get to know each other."

"Alrighty," I say. The wipers swipe a beat across my windshield, and then another, and I consider. "Why don't you go first?" I say. "Tell me a little about yourself. I figure you know a lot more about me than I do about you."

* * *

She claims her full name is Camilla Randolph Willacy, which I doubt—it sounds made-up, but I just write it all down, scrawling on a little spiral notepad that I'm holding flat against the steering wheel. She tells me she's twenty-two years old, fresh-graduated from Oberlin College in Ohio. She grew up in Lake Forest, Illinois: her adoptive mom an artist, her dad a lawyer, and she an only child. I transcribe everything she says, but I feel a little impatient with it. Sounds like one of those character worksheets that the NSA has you fill out when you're trying to adopt a new persona.

"I've been to Lake Forest before," I say, which is true. It's a fancy suburb north of Chicago, and about two years ago I delivered a package to an estate there. I don't recall the exact details, but I remember a mansion with a smooth cobblestone driveway, a fountain, and a koi pond with a statue of maybe a Greek goddess. I'm not entirely sure what was in the package, though it had the shape and weight of a human head.

"Must've been a nice place to grow up," I say.

"Not really," she says.

"What kind of lawyer is your dad?"

"No," she says. "Actually, I think it's your turn to answer a question. I provided you with a *bouquet* of information, so . . ."

"Quid pro quo," I say. "Okay. What do you want to know?"

"Did you ever think about me?" she says. There's a tick in her voice of shyness and hopefulness, longing maybe, that takes me aback.

"What do you mean?" I say.

"It's okay if you didn't," she says quickly. "You were just a donor, I wouldn't expect you to have *feelings* or anything. You didn't even know if they'd use your sample, right?"

"Right." I hesitate. "I mean, I definitely wondered."

"Wondered?"

"If—I don't know—if my sperm got chosen."

I feel myself blushing. This feels unexpectedly intimate in an indeterminate way. Maybe it's simply saying the word *sperm*. That she can imagine me masturbating into a sterile container and then she can picture my earnest wondering about "a child." Yikes.

But I also know that if you're going to truly gain someone's trust, there's going to be some discomfort. You're going to have to expose yourself a bit. You're going to have to be at least seventy percent honest in the beginning.

"I don't know," I say. Traffic has slowed to about twenty miles an hour. There are a couple of inches of standing water on the road—flooding ahead, I'd guess. "Do they just sort of pick the dam and sire out of a catalogue?"

"*Dam and sire,*" she says.

"No insult intended," I say, and she lets out a soft breath through her nose.

"None taken," she says. "You're right. They pick the sperm and egg out of a catalogue. I don't know whether you remember, but you filled out a very long questionnaire."

"I couldn't even begin to guess what I wrote."

"It doesn't matter. Most of it's not true."

"Yeah," I say. "Probably not." I look out at the road and I've reached the edge of a full-on stop-and-start situation. I crane my neck, but the slowed vehicles stretch as far as I can see before me. Tadpoles of rain progress hopefully along my windshield until the wipers come and slap them back to the beginning.

"I'm glad to hear that you thought about me, at least," she says. "I didn't know whether you would. It's not like you got a girl pregnant and she gave a baby up for adoption."

"No," I say. "It's not."

"I'm a little less real than that, right? And so are you. You're more like an *ingredient,*" she says, and I note how her voice tightens. "There's not even really a word yet for our relationship, is there? You can't use words like *father* and *daughter,* can you?"

"That depends," I say. "You're not looking for back child support, are you?"

Silence. I thought my quip deserved at least a chuckle.

"The point is," she says, "I guess I wanted to know how you felt about me. Do you think I'm less of a person than if you'd had sex with someone and they had a baby?"

"I think," I say, "that you're less of my business."

In the rearview mirror, cars have stacked up behind me in a blockade that stretches to the horizon. I consider trying to ride the grassy strip of berm to my right, maybe put on my emergency lights and try to hobble along the side of the road past the parked vehicles in front of me to the next exit, but the drivable pathway is narrow and treacherously close to a steep incline.

I sit there, idling. "You said you wanted something," I say.

"No," she says. "I said I thought we *might* be able to help each other."

"Meaning what? You haven't decided whether I can help you? Or you haven't decided whether you can help me?"

"Both," she says.

I turn the ignition off, and the *Guiding Star* sighs and shuts down. No use in wasting energy, I guess.

"Look, Cammie," I say. "You caught me. But I'm pretty sure I'm not what you want. If it's important to you to play out this whole long-lost-daughter thing, then we can do it. If that's what you want, I'll oblige. But let's be realistic. How much do I need to pay you to let this go? I'm very open to negotiation."

"That's sweet of you," she says, and right before she hangs up, I hear her actual laugh for the first time.

Freaks me out: it's the exact same bright and secret chuckle my mom used to have.

Oubliette

I'm still stuck in traffic when she calls back. An hour has passed and I've progressed two miles, inching forward between two semis that block my view from right and left. I look up at the sky as if I'm in a pit, and the clouds send down more rain.

"Cammie," I say. I've been thinking a lot about her laugh—and I've mostly decided that the similarity to my mother is a trick my mind has played on me. But that doesn't mean I don't feel it. Our emotions are cooked into the elder parts of our brain, they're part of our bodies, that's what I would say to Experanza. Only an idiot thinks they are immune to manipulation.

"Sorry," she says. "I had a thing I needed to deal with."

"Well," I say. "I hope the thing came to a pleasant resolution." I glance at the clock—2:55 p.m.—and I turn on my recorder as she sighs.

"Your voice sounds sad," she says.

"I have a natural tendency toward melancholy," I say. "Besides which, I'm a moderately heavy smoker."

"I'm sorry this whole thing is freaking you out," she says.

"Not sorry enough to take a buyout and go on your way, though?"

"Oh, come on," she says.

I say nothing—giving her a silence to project into. Traffic's come to a complete stop again. In the black Genesis coupe behind me, a man is

having a hissy fit, banging on his steering wheel and screaming at who-
ever is on the other end of his earpiece.

"All I want to do is have good discussions," she says. "Just think of
me as a benign ghostly presence. I'm your imaginary daughter, let's say."

"I don't love that term," I say. "It makes it sound like I conjured you
up in my head. Like it's all *my* problem."

"Come on," she says. "Let's just have a conversation. Ask me a question!"

I know I should try to provoke a range of vocalizations and emotional
responses. Oftentimes, you learn more from the music of a person's into-
nations than you do from listening to their words. And, yes, I would
like to study that laugh again, if possible.

"Tell me what you look like," I say.

"Ugh," she says. "That's a tricky one, isn't it?" She hesitates. "Well. I
have your eyes."

Which—yikes.

"Yikes," I say.

"What do you want me to say?" she says. "It's impossible to describe
your own features."

"No, seriously," I say. "What do you look like? Is there, maybe, an
actress or something that you resemble, for example?"

"Not really," she says. "I mean, I think I look a lot like you, if you were
a twenty-two-year-old, one-hundred-fifteen-pound woman."

I roll down the window and light a cigarette. "For someone who wants
to have a good conversation, you're awfully elusive."

"I just don't want to talk about my looks," she says. "It's so superficial."

"Right on," I say. "I support that. But you say you know what *I* look
like. You said you have my eyes. So that must mean something to you,
doesn't it?"

"Yeah . . ." she says.

"Well, it means something to me, too," I say. "You'll notice that I didn't
ask you *how* you know what my eyes and face look like—what photo
or mug shot or videocapture you're looking at—because I'm already
resigned to the fact that you'll withhold that information. But I probably
don't look like what you think I look like. My eyes might not be the
same color as they used to be. How do you know your intel is correct?"

"You said 'Yikes.'"

"I said 'Yikes' because of the way you said it. You were like, *'I have your eyes,'* and I got this image of you holding my eyeballs in your hands! 'Yikes' means I'm grossed out! It doesn't mean that you told me what color my eyes are. Because you didn't. I feel like you could be trying to trick me."

"Wow," she says. "What do I have to do to get you to trust me?"

"That'd be a good tombstone epitaph," I say.

"You're so random," she says.

"I thought you wanted to be reciprocal," I say. "You claim you know what I look like, so I want to know what you look like in return. What color's your natural hair?"

"Blond," she says. Which is a relief—my mother was a redhead.

"Well, you don't get blond from me!" I say. "Big nose or a little nose?"

"It's a nose," she says. "A normal-size nose."

"Do you look at all like Little Peggy March?"

She's silent for a minute, and I imagine that she's typing into the search engine. Where is she right now? What's she doing? Is there someone there with her? I reach out and try to picture it, but I draw a blank.

Then: "No. I do not look like Little Peggy March."

"So, answer my question," I say. "Because you're *not* an imaginary daughter, right? You're a real person, with hair and skin and so forth. Let's establish that, at least."

"Okay, fine," she says. "Let me give you a rundown. I have blond hair but it's dyed, it's a kind of burnt auburn color now; I have pale Caucasian skin with freckles; my nose is turned up a little: kids used to say that it was piggy. I have a round face. I'm five three, and like I said, a hundred and fifteen pounds. I'm a generic white girl."

Dang! Everything she describes puts me in mind of my mother, and I have to grip the steering wheel hard to prevent a whole collage of unwanted memories from clogging my head.

"Anyway," I say, "where's your biological mom in this whole equation? A person would think you'd seek her out first, before the dad."

"The egg donor?" says Cammie. A little flat; a little mean-spirited. Maybe a hint of her true self? "She's dead," Cammie says. "And don't say 'biological.' There's nothing *biological* about any of this."

"Dead?" I say. "Oh."

"Yeah. It's sad. She committed suicide about twenty years ago. Hanged herself in a closet in an apartment in Baltimore. At least, that's the official story."

I don't know why I feel a twinge for a woman I never met, a woman whose only connection to me is that she had some of her fluids injected with my fluids in a laboratory. But it hits me harder than I expect. This poor woman and I had a child together, and now she's dead. We had a *child*, and I never even met her. *In another life,* I think, but I stop myself.

"Well, jeez!" I say. "That's awful. I'm sorry."

"Yeah," she says. "But for a person in my situation, it's hard to even use the term *mother*. I mean, I was conceived from Rosalie's egg, but I was implanted and germinated in the womb of a woman in Tibet named Poso Pemba, and she's also dead now. Supposedly also a suicide. And then there's somehow Marsha, my *adoptive* mother—the one who gets to be on my so-called birth certificate—"

There's an unmistakable flicker of genuine hatred when she says her mother's name, and it perks my attention. I get a glimpse of something hard and icy, very different from the Cammie who sputtered and flustered when we first spoke, so nervous and coltish; very different from the one who says she just wants to have a normal conversation with me, like strangers sitting next to each other on a plane. Maybe I'm primed to make connections where there are none, but my hackles prickle. That twinkle of hatred in her voice is, like her laugh, so distinctly reminiscent of my mother.

"So," I say. "I'm guessing you don't get along with them—your adoptive parents?"

"I hate them," she says. "I think of them as my mortal enemies."

"Ah," I say. "Well," I say, and lean forward. If she is, in fact, a disgruntled young rich girl, that might explain some things, especially if she's got some sanity issues. I wonder if she's one of those types that has a compulsion to pull out strands of their hair.

"'*Mortal enemies,*'" I say. "Wow."

"I'm hoping to get them put in prison," she says.

"Is that what you want me to help you with?"

"Not necessarily," she says. "That's a personal project."

The rain doesn't let up. We're still in the same formation, the two semis, the Genesis, and me, a flatbed truck ahead of us, and it's like that dungeon they threw people into in medieval times, the oubliette, where the only exit is above you, a barred manhole in the ceiling over your head.

"Do you think I'm being melodramatic?" she says. "I'm not. They're actually evil."

"Right on," I say. I turn on my blinker, hoping to pull into the next lane. I'll need to get off at the next exit or be stuck on the interstate for the night.

"So, Cammie," I say. "Do you think it's possible you might be starting to lose your mind a little bit?"

"What?" she says, and her voice sharpens—a little of that nine-year-old's timbre goes out of it. "*I beg your pardon?*" Which is something I imagine a woman named Marsha would probably say when offended.

"I'm not trying to insult you, honey," I say. "I'm just asking because—I lost my mind when I was about your age. Maybe it's hereditary."

"What are you talking about?" she says. I note that she seems genuinely taken aback. "You have . . . a mental illness?"

"Not anymore," I say. "I went insane for a while. But I got over it. I escaped."

Up ahead, one of those big robot drones is clomping along the edge of the interstate, past the rows and rows of stalled cars. It's about thirty feet tall, with the round head and pointed ears of a cartoon cat, a big grin, and google eyes. The hydraulic arms and legs move in an imitation of a person ski walking, and it's carrying a sign like a protester: DO IT TONIGHT! DON'T WAIT FOR ARMAGEDDON! It's not clear what it's trying to advertise. Maybe it's on the loose, a renegade, it's hard to know.

"I've got one of those giant robots walking by me right now," I say.

"Oh," she says. "I hate those. So tacky!"

"Yeah" I say, and watch the thing lurch along, playing some kind of peppy dance music; the lyrics seem to be in Korean. "I don't know. It seemed like a cute idea at first, then it just got out of hand. They need to regulate them better."

"Is it still raining where you are?" she says. "It looked like there was flooding in the area."

Naturally, this observation is a bit bloodcurdling for me, but I try to take it in stride. I hold my breath for a count of three. "Are you tracking me, Cammie?" I say, reproachfully.

"Just casually," she says. "Don't worry, I don't know your exact location. Last time I looked I saw you were pinging somewhere northeast of Nashville, and there's a nasty storm up ahead of you."

"Northeast of Nashville," I say. "That'd be a good name for a men's cologne."

She makes the laugh again. It just comes out of her naturally, my mother's actual laugh—and it gives me a feeling of warmth and terror in equal measure, it pleases me to make her laugh and I feel a shadow at my back at the same time and she disconnects without another word. Once again, we talked for slightly less than fifteen minutes.

RIP in Peace

It's almost midnight by the time I get to the campground. I've got a little place in the Daniel Boone National Forest where I like to stay when I'm in the neighborhood, a secluded site along the Red Bird River, with a picnic table and an RV hookup, 30/50 amp electric; there's even a fire pit in case I want to roast some weenies. The place has been closed for years, but I made a deal with the proprietor; he keeps it available for me. I've got a key to the cattle gate they have blocking the private road.

Usually, I'd be looking forward to spending some time in Nature: breathing that sweet Appalachian air and listening to the frogs and insects and rustling autumn trees, going to sleep with the sound of a burbling river beyond the window—nice, right? But I'm too rattled to relax.

Now that I know she's tracing me, I'm tempted again to ditch the phones. But I realize that trying to hide isn't going to solve the problem. *Gain her trust; find her location.*

At least I'm now in an area outside the reception of cell phone towers. For now I don't have to worry about Cammie pinging my whereabouts. Why would she tell me that she knows where I am? There's a craftiness in the way she reveals things. It's not just that she can track me, it's the fact that she played such a big card so early. What other, better information is she holding back—stuff about my past? Stuff about who I have worked for, deeds I have committed? Maybe she knows more about me than I do.

And of course, there's that damned laugh. The *Guiding Star* trundles cautiously through a maze of dirt roads, pressing forward into a narrowing tunnel of trees. Even hours later, the thought of that laugh prickles inside me. I haven't heard my mother's voice in over thirty years, but when Cammie made that sound it was like my mom lifted up out of the cell phone and gently bit me in the face.

I remember when I was little, how she'd hide and then jump out to scare me. Her laugh was so pure and delighted when I'd scream.

I remember sitting on the floor of a motel room watching TV and I could hear her make that same laugh. "Oh, you!" she said to someone.

It was a laugh so inviting that even when it was pointed directly at you in mockery, still you'd smile. The kind of laugh a person makes as they bite down on an apple. There was a xylophone tinkle in it, a conspiratorial glint, a soft caress that made you think she liked you, despite all your failings. A laugh you'd clown for, a laugh you'd drink up like skin drinks sunshine.

I back the *Guiding Star* into our private space above the bank of the river, and I get out and plug her into the various outlets, and Flip paces and marks the perimeter of our territory. The rain has stopped, settling into a moody fog.

Let's say she *is* my daughter—if *daughter* is the right term. Even if it's true, what debt or loyalty do I owe her?

It's a question.

And what if she's as truly like my mother as she seems to possibly be? What then? There's a tickle on the back of my neck, that feeling when someone sees you but you can't see them.

I am thinking all this, sitting at the picnic table, drinking a beer and nibbling at a Goo Goo Cluster, and then Flip is barking.

Flip is not the kind of dog who barks for no reason, so I get up and go to the cab of the *Guiding Star* and take the Beretta pistol and a little flashlight out of the glove box. I hope it's not feral pigs. One time in Arkansas at Crater of Diamonds State Park, Flip and I woke up one morning to a sounder of thirty to fifty wild swine surrounding the camper—hairy, tusked, sullen—most of them easily two hundred pounds. Not easy to scare them off.

Regretfully, I'm wearing naught but a pair of swim trunks and flip-flops as I walk through the dark woods toward the sound of Flip's voice. I hold the gun in my right hand and I keep the river on my right, too. The moon is out so I don't turn on the flashlight just yet. I can see a dim path through the thrash of saplings and bushes and the shimmery trill of crickets and I step slow and careful so that I don't trip on a root or a log, the trees dense with shadow and watchful as I pass amongst them. Flip lets out another stern bark. A warning.

And then I come to a clearing—another campsite, with a picnic table and a fire pit, but there's no car in the parking space and it seems to be unoccupied. Flip is standing on the bare spot where you might pitch your tent, his body alert, and he flicks his eyes toward me as my feet scranch on the gravel. The fur on his neck is ruffed up and he lets out a soft growl.

At the edge of the campsite it looks like there is a man tied to a tree. He's wearing a cardboard sign on his torso that says PEDOPHILE in spray-painted capital letters.

At first a person might be tempted to think that it's just a manne-quin or a scarecrow, but even from a distance I'm pretty sure that it's a dead human being. He is wearing jeans and a flannel shirt and a pair of bright red Fila running shoes. His arms are pulled behind his back and bound to the tree trunk, and there's ropes around his waist and legs that keep him in a standing position, and a rope around his neck, just underneath his lower jaw, that keeps his head from lolling. I turn on the flashlight as I step closer, tucking the gun awkwardly into the back waistband of my shorts.

The corpse's head is completely mummy-wrapped in tape, that's one of the things that makes it look like a doll. Beige cellophane packing tape has been wrapped around and around, covering the hair, the eyes, the nose, the mouth, layers of tape all the way to the neck, so many layers that it's almost like one of those blank Styrofoam heads you put wigs on. You can still see a bump where the nose is and an indentation where the open mouth was trying to suck in air, but otherwise the face is a smooth surface. Someone has spray-painted a smiley expression on it—big googly eyes and a half-moon grin, a little drool of wet paint sliding from the bottom of the cartoon mouth and down the chin.

He's not struggling anymore but you can see the ligature marks on his arms and neck where he strained against the ropes. The collar of the T-shirt is bloody, the front of the pants stained dark from wetting himself.

I take a step back, careful, listening to the night sounds, all the bugs and frogs singing *fuck me, fuck me,* but I don't panic yet. I've never seen this kind of thing before, but I've read about it in the newspapers. A rash of vigilante killings cropping up all across the nation, corpses wrapped in packing tape with signs that detail their crimes: DRUG PUSHER or PEDOPHILE or RAPIST or what have you, often with a smiley face drawn across the head.

The media have taken a slightly comical spin, as if this is a crazy new fad: fed-up citizens taking the law into their own hands, reclaiming their communities from the hoodlums and scum, and can we really blame them? It'd be nice to think that this is the revenge of the underdogs, finally rising up at last.

But I have my doubts. As much as I'd like to imagine that a bunch of righteously angry tape-wielding villagers have finally brought justice down on some bullying gangster, this doesn't strike me as the work of amateurs. I reach out and slip my fingers along the back of PEDO-PHILE's jeans, lifting the wallet out as daintily as if I was picking the pocket of a living man.

David Dranoff is the name on the driver's license; age thirty-two, late of 2133 Cross Lane, Lexington, Kentucky. In the photo, David is a slight young white person with an eager, boyish smile and a lawyerly haircut, and along with his ID is a MasterCard and a debit card and forty-seven dollars in cash. Probably a journalist, is my thought—and I let the wallet drop into the leaves at his feet.

"Hey," I say to Flip. "*Let's go.*"

Naturally, it's at this moment that I hear the soft crunch of tires on gravel, and I turn toward the sound and of course I should have lit out running but before I can do so the beam of a flashlight strikes me full in the face.

Possible tombstone epitaph: *Don't Turn Around.*

I put my arm up to shield my eyes, and I can make out what looks like a police car of sorts. It's one of those electric cars—a Prius, maybe—the kind that can creep silently up on a person, and it looks to be equipped with a siren and an official-looking badge insignia on the side door. They might be actual cops or state patrol—there are a few of those left—but more likely they're with some kind of private police squad or security force or militia. Whatever uniform they're wearing, I know I don't want to meet them.

"Halt!" says an electronically amplified voice. "Put your hand in your hair!" Then: "Wait. Put your hands in the air."

I can hear the sound of young men chortling, and I raise my arms and adopt a sorrowful, frightened expression. My hope is that Flip has made himself scarce, since I would guess these are the sort of authorities who will kill him on sight.

"Unarmed! Unarmed!" I say in a clear but submissive voice, trying to sound as white as possible. "I want to cooperate in every way I can!"

I get down on my knees and keep my hands up and my eyes lowered as they get out of their car. Two officers, males. They are wearing uniforms, but I can make out no more than that. There's a badge over their left breasts, and a name tag over their right. No Kevlar involved, as far as I can ascertain.

"I'm a guest of these campgrounds!" I call out earnestly as they approach. They have their hands on their holstered weapons. "I'm a personal friend of the proprietor! Richard Nuzzler! I have his number if you need to call him!"

"Nuzzler?" says the one on the right, the one holding the flashlight on me. "Ha ha ha! I don't know no stinkin' Nuzzler."

And the one on the left says, "What's your name, mister? You really shouldn't be here. This is a crime . . . place. Crime scene. It's *restricted*."

They are both wearing brimmed police caps and sunglasses, both muscled as if they spend a lot of time at a gym, both young—Cammie's age, I think, or younger. Twenty, twenty-one years old. They stand there, on either side of the car, swaying slightly. Drunk, maybe?

"My name is Barry Wills," I say. "I have ID!" And then I nod in the direction of the corpse. "I just . . . found this man," I say. "It looks like he's dead."

"Dead?" says the left-hand one. "How do you know? Are you a doctor?"

"No, sir," I say. "I am not." As they step closer, the dense, skunky scent of cannabis wafts off them, mixed with the reek of Robitussin. Judging by their grins and their gait, I would guess that they are stoned out of their minds. They turn their mirrored sunglass eyes on me, glimmering and unsteady.

"I reckon it's one of those vigilante murders!" I say. "Like they talk about in the newspapers."

"Murders?" says the one with the flashlight. "You mean *executions.*"

"Right," I say. "Executions."

"Was he still alive when you found him?" says the one without the flashlight. He's slightly bigger than the other, with a rounder and more jowly face, and a forearm tattoo that says *AARON RIP IN PEACE!*

I flex my raised fingers in a shrugging gesture.

"Gee," I say, "not that I could tell with the naked eye. But as I said, I'm not a physician."

"That's so weird," says Jowly to the one holding the flashlight. "I didn't think the fucker would die that fast!"

"I know, right?" says the other. "It's kind of, like, a letdown."

It occurs to me with sudden clarity that it's likely these young men won't let me leave here alive, and that I'm going to have to make an unfortunate executive decision. They both turn their blank, mirrored eyes toward me, and I can tell that they are just poor, barely trained thugs, probably making minimum wage, high on pot and robotripping, no reflexes to speak of. Regrettably, I have a very short window of time.

I pull the gun from my waistband and they both fumble and stumble with goofy surprise. "Hey!" one exclaims. "Wait—"

I shoot the big one in the forehead and he drops like a horse. The one with the flashlight draws his gun and I shoot him in the arm and then in the eye and he falls, too.

It saddens me immediately. I wish I could have worked it out different.

The Family Curse

It's a melancholy thing to have to kill a young person, even if he is a murderous thug. If you think about it too long, you get haunted by the expressions. Often, they have looks of gentle surprise, like heavy sleepers who have been awakened, and you can't help but recall that once they were little babies. You see in their dead eyes that hint of infant wonder, that blank, hopeful gaze, trusting that the world will have mercy on them.

I weight the bodies with rocks and dump them in the river, and I make a mental note to find out what happened to old Rick Nuzzler, the one who sold me the squatting rights to the campsite property. Probably dead is my guess, but it wouldn't hurt to gather some knowledge. Ever since they unfunded and privatized the Forest Service, there's always a corporation or militia or some such in competition over these sites.

Flip and I get back in the *Guiding Star* and drive off into the night. We pass northward through the woods, from the little town of Honeybee to Mount Victory, driving on narrow two-lane back roads, keeping our eyes out for other Prius-driving militia types. I figure there probably aren't many awake at this hour, that the unfortunates back at the campsite were just out late making merry.

It's past three in the morning when she calls, and I pull the humming phone out of the bucket. "Cammie," I say. It's the Liam Bahr phone—she hasn't gone for that one before, and for a moment I'm not sure the connection is going to take. It's an isolated area, and the link stutters, breaking and unbreaking. I peer out and the headlights illuminate a portion of road. Witchy shadows of trees shudder before me.

"Are you awake?" Her voice solidifies as I come out of a dense patch of forest.

"In a sense," I say.

"What are you doing?"

"Still driving," I say. "What are you calling me for at this hour of night?"

"Can't sleep," she says, and I frown as I come to a fork. *Why would you call* me *if you can't sleep?* I wonder. I take a left.

"You must have a guilty conscience," I say. "That's what my mom used to tell me when I couldn't sleep."

"God," she says, "she sounds awful."

"I suppose," I say, and now I'm passing a crumbling old shotgun house set back from the road—rotten, tilted front porch, crooked windows, a single light burning inside some inner room—and I observe it attentively. At the same time, I'm keeping an ear out for any background noise that might give me a sense of where Cammie is, what she's doing—a siren in the distance, a church bell; a tinkle of ice in a glass, a wetting of lips, a swallow—but there's nothing but a jumble of digitized echoes and fog.

"Was your mom . . ." she says, and then she seems to think better of whatever she was going to say. "Did you get along with your mom?"

"I don't think I want to get into that," I say.

"We can talk about whatever you want," she says. "I just . . . needed to talk to somebody. I'm just really wired, or something."

"You don't say," I reply.

But she doesn't sound wired. There's a wooden, mournful tone to her voice, like she can hardly keep her head from drooping. Depressed? Crashing? I still can't picture where she is, the room, the furniture, the light. I don't know why but I keep thinking that she's in a basement, and that the only light comes from her phone. She's alone, I think. I'm pretty sure she's completely alone, and I feel a twinge of sympathy.

"Do you drink, Cammie?" I say. "Smoke weed?"

"I'm not high," she says. "Or drunk."

"That's my point," I say. "If insomnia is a problem, there's a cure."

She's silent, and I stare out at the gravel road unfolding beneath my headlights. She seems like she's in what they call a febrile state, and I know what Experanza would say: it's a good opportunity to get information, whilst she's vulnerable.

"So," I say. "Tell me your troubles, Cammie. What's keeping you awake tonight?" I glance over at Flip, who is curled up in the passenger seat with his muzzle on his paws and his legs tucked in, and he raises an eyebrow but doesn't lift his head. He lets out a sigh through his nose as if he disapproves. And he's right: it's shitty.

"I don't know," she says. "I was thinking about what you said. About having a mental illness when you were my age. Is that true?"

It's interesting that my offhand comment has stuck with her—that it seems to have needled her, and her discomfort is possibly real. Fifty percent chance that there's some genuine emotion behind it. I slow the *Guiding Star* and stare out. Look up at the constellations to try to see what direction I'm pointed in.

"It wasn't a big deal," I say. "Like I said, I got past it. Fully recovered my wits."

"What was the diagnosis?" she says.

"Who knows?" I say. "Let's call it the Family Curse."

I'm positive that Experanza would tell me that it was a stupid idea to mention my struggles with sanity issues in the first place—who knows what Cammie might find if she knew about Hopewood, if she were to access those records?

Still, it's weirdly thrilling to say it aloud. *I went insane for a while:* I don't think I'd ever told that to anyone before, and it gives me a kind of glow. In another life, there is a daughter and we have had the same emotions; we can talk with each other about things that no one else would understand.

"What about you?" I say. "What was *your* diagnosis?"

"Ha, ha," she says. "You've got to give it before you can get it!"

"You've got that panic, though, right? Waking up with your heart pounding?"

That catches her. Silence. Silence. Then: "Right," she murmurs.

"And that sinking feeling. You know that one? It's like time slows down and you're about to have a slow realization. I once freaked out because a shadow of a cloud passed over me. It was sunny and then the light changed for a minute and I literally let out a cry, a strangled cry as they call it, and started to book."

"I've had the exact same thing! With a cloud!" she says. "That's hilarious. God!" But she doesn't laugh. Her voice hitches, and I have a pretty strong sense that she *is* high on something. Ritalin, is my guess, or some other joyless brand of methylphenidate.

"I've been forced to see doctors, but I don't believe in psychiatry, really," she says. "I've been reading the stupid *Diagnostic and Statistical Manual of Mental Disorders* since I was a kid, and do you realize how many times it's been revised in the last twenty years? It's not a science. It's not *medicine*."

"Right on," I say.

There's a moment when you feel a weird attachment to a person, and it's not voluntary, it's not even welcome. You try to pull away from it.

So I don't say anything. There is another glitch of broken connection as I pull onto a dirt-road detour. I'd just wanted to stay off main roads for a while, until I got farther north, but now I'm not even driving on gravel—just a pair of tire ruts that lead up a dark, tree-covered hill.

". . . still there . . . ?" she says, and for a moment the audio degrades to the point that her voice sounds autotuned.

"I'm here," I say. I glance over at Flip, who is sitting up in the passenger seat, staring sternly out as the *Guiding Star* clonks through holes and mud puddles. He looks concerned. *Dang!* I think. *Am I going the wrong way?*

"It's the ones they consider normal who are crazy," Cammie is saying solemnly, and again I picture her in a little soundproof basement room with wall-to-wall indoor/outdoor carpeting, or possibly Astroturf. "Only sociopaths are well-adjusted these days!" she says.

"Are you in a basement?"

"What?" she says.

"I'm just trying to get a visual of where you are right now. What you're doing while we're talking? I keep imagining you in a basement."

"I'm not in a basement," she says. "That's weird."

We come to the top of the hill, and it's a dead end. PRIVATE RESI-DENT, NO TRESSPASSING, says a handmade sign, and then another sign that says HO MADE APPLE BUTTER, and there is a home at the back part of the lot but it's obscured by the stacks of salvage that have accumulated in the front: partial cars, antique farming equipment or possibly medieval torture devices, mannequins, computer monitors, toaster ovens, a limp windsock man, pieces of rebar and bundles of cop-per wire—in short, no easy way to turn the *Guiding Star* around.

"Why would you think I'm in a basement?" she says.

"Hold on for a minute," I say. "I've got to execute a complicated turn." I pull forward until the *Guiding Star* is parallel to a bombed-out school bus and then I put her in reverse and begin to slowly creep backward.

"What's going on?" she says, but I don't answer. Up at the main house, I see a porch light has come on, and a shirtless elderly man—maybe twenty, thirty years older than me—comes out onto his front stoop with a chainsaw. He's not brandishing it—just holding it more or less at parade rest—but it's there just to let me know he's seen me, and I'm not welcome.

"Dang," I say. I pull forward, turn the wheel, inch forward, back up again, turn the wheel again.

"What's happening?" Cammie says, and I see my side mirror catch on the edge of the bus. It breaks off before I can stop it, but I keep going. The *Guiding Star*'s passenger side lists on the edge of a ditch, but I put her in low gear and press on the gas and we right ourselves and we're back on the rutted road going down the hill. Flip looks at me, his ears pinned back.

"I took a wrong turn," I tell Cammie, and she says, "Oh."

Then she's quiet again. We drive together that way for maybe a mile, her silent and me thoughtfully smoking, it's almost companionable, and I arrive back at the crossroads and take the northward gravel road this time.

"I'm not crazy," Cammie says. "If you're worried that I'm some kind of psycho."

"Well," I say. "There's nicer words for it, I reckon." I look up at the sky just to be sure I'm headed in the right direction: locate the Big Dipper, and then the North Star. "What would your mom and dad have to say about it, I wonder."

Maybe, I admit, this is a mean thing to say, but it clearly gives her pause. It opens up her feelings. I hear her draw in a breath.

"I don't call them Mom and Dad," she says. "They're nothing to me. Whatever they think, I could not care less."

"They don't know where you are," I guess. I intuit.

"Nobody knows where I am," she says. She declares.

And I believe her. It sounds as if she's broadcasting from a studio in an underground bunker: no background noise, not even a hint of acoustics. I don't know what she is, I don't know whether we're related or not, but there's a clumsy maneuvering that reminds me of myself at her age. It's not a part of myself that I like, but I recognize it.

Meanwhile I have finally made it off gravel and back onto blacktop. I turn onto New Hope Tower Road, and there is the Church of New Hope, which is not a tower, but is nevertheless a surprisingly large, modern building for out here in the woods. I light a joint and hurry on past.

"It must seem stupid to you, what I'm doing," she says.

"What *are* you doing, Cammie? I'm not entirely sure."

"I mean contacting you."

I glance down at the recorder. She's let this conversation go on for almost twenty minutes now—the longest we've ever talked.

"Not stupid," I say. I have trained myself not to call myself stupid. *Don't call yourself stupid* is my motto. "Desperate, maybe," I say. "That's my guess."

And she lets out that laugh again. Sends a paralysis through me, hearing it, and it's as though, for a moment, my mother herself is present in the cab of the *Guiding Star* with me, settling like a mist.

Takes me a while to realize that Cammie isn't there anymore. She's hung up.

But Still, and Yet

I crawl across the border of Kentucky and into West Virginia around dawn. I-64 is surprisingly clear, and there's barely traffic as I pass by Huntington—a few sleepy M-ATV military vehicles, a tank tiptoeing along on its treads, some early-morning semis. It's possible the locals are under a curfew.

Driving along, I find myself thinking of Cammie again, and I don't know why I should let myself get so besotted with her but there's a weird ache that wells up. I picture her with her burnt-auburn hair and freckles and turned-up nose that other kids called piggy, and I'm aware that my feeling toward her has grown warmer. I guess there is some psychological reason, or maybe even a built-in biological instinct I have no control over. Maybe this is what fatherhood is like.

I find a recording of Little Peggy March and I play "I Will Follow Him" on repeat. It's a creepy song, full of shrill, uninvited longing, but also sad, and dreadfully urgent. How rare it is to be wanted in such a way as Little Peggy March dedicates herself to her beloved! I drive along at the speed limit, listening grimly.

God, what a fool I was! Obviously, I have no one but myself to blame, but when you're twenty years old and someone pays you to ejaculate into a sterilized container, you don't expect that as a result, thirty years down the line, you'll be participating in some complex and dysfunctional family drama. Not only do I now maybe have a daughter, but I have a long-dead egg donor girl with whom I created the child, and a Tibetan woman who rented out her uterus to house our offspring. Not to mention the nice wealthy couple who paid for all of that cell-mingling. And of course this means that my DNA is part of the Genetic Panopticon—it's in a database somewhere—multiple databases! Who knows who can find me? It's upsetting. At the very least, I feel taken advantage of—though I can't quite say by whom.

Don't be a sucker, that's what Experanza would say. *She's nothing to you,* Experanza would tell me. *Hardly even human—just something that got stirred up in a test tube.*

But still.

And yet.

Not far outside Huntington is a decent place to get breakfast—Outer Limits, an old American Legion that is now a greasy-spoon tavern, catering to third-shift workers and aging alcoholics—and I take a stool at the bar and order a beer and a Belgian waffle. The bartender glances at the kitty-cat clock on the wall above the rows of liquor bottles. "No alcohol sales until eight a.m.," she says. "State law."

"Alrighty," I say. "I'll have a cup of coffee while I wait." And I give her my "good customer" smile.

And then without warning an old memory burbles up—it's like acid indigestion, I don't know where it comes from, but abruptly I am sitting in the parking lot of a Safeway and watching for my mother to come out of the automatic doors. I think it must be June. It's not too hot, but all the windows are rolled up, and I put my hand against the glass. I think I'm five or six years old.

Nearby, someone has lost an orange Popsicle and I observe with interest as it melts, as ants come and then a sparrow hops over and begins to eat the ants. I look up toward the door, watching for her to come out. I hope she brings me a Popsicle.

It's not often that she thinks about feeding me, but I know better than to ask. Saying you're hungry is a sure way to get slapped—or worse, to send her into a state of sadistic resentment. Once, when I complained she forced me to eat a whole loaf of white bread and a quart of mint ice cream. *Still hungwy?* she crooned in an exaggerated baby voice. *Poor wibble baby hungwy?*

The bartender sets my coffee down in front of me, along with a handful of non-dairy creamers and sugar packets.

"Thank you, ma'am," I say, but she's already gone. There are a few other customers lined along the bar and in the booths and I take stock of them. Sometimes, I'll spot someone I know or recognize in this place, but not today.

My mom comes out of the Safeway walking fast but not running, and nobody is following her but she looks over her shoulder as if they might at any minute and I get into the passenger seat and fasten my seat belt before she even gets into the car.

She tosses her fringed purse onto the seat between us and pokes the key at the ignition a few times before she gets it into the hole. She doesn't look at me but I watch her out of the corner of my eye. A light sheen of sweat is on her face, her eyes flat. The car jerks backward and then forward. We hit a shopping cart and keep going as it rattles away behind us.

And my fingers are tight and fidgety. Usually I would drink even the cruddiest coffee black, but here I am opening sugar and Splenda packets, pouring ultra-pasteurized creamers into my cup and stirring it urgently.

I look up at the kitty-cat clock. Its tail is a pendulum that swings back and forth, and its eyes look right and left in rhythm with the tail. It's seven fifty or so.

My mom was on the sociopathic spectrum, I guess. I couldn't venture to guess the number of people she killed or wounded or robbed or betrayed. I don't fool myself into believing that she somehow felt love for me, but she kept me around. I must have been useful to her somehow, and for most of my time with her I was grateful for that, and eager to serve.

There was a period when I was around nine, I think. She was calling herself Taffy then, and I had the idea that she was thinking about ditching me. We might be at a gas station and she'd say casually, "Oh,

I forgot my purse, I need to go back to the car, you go on ahead and go to the bathroom," and I'd be, like, "No, Mom, I'll come with you." I remember sitting in the car in parking lots, waiting for her to come out of a bar or a store or a courthouse, and I knew from the look she gave me when she got out of the car that she was considering not coming back. A certain kind of smile, as if she were trying to think of something complimentary to say about a stranger's homely child.

When she was in a good mood—when she was happy with me—she'd pretend that I didn't belong to her at all. She'd act like we were just co-workers, like I was just a well-liked employee. She said, *Don't ever call me Mom.*

Back when I was around ten, my mom's name was Sessy and her hair was cut short and dyed black. We drove a hearse, and we had a King Cake Baby dangling from the rearview mirror. She wore heavy mascara and laughed with her mouth open and her head thrown back, a kind of friendly, excited scream.

She told people that her motto was *Forgive quickly, and be kind!* She would softly touch a person's arm and say, "I'm interested in you," knowing it was flattery but also knowing that it was one of the most subtly disturbing things you can say to a person. "You're so interesting!" she'd say, and give them her full focused attention, the way a snake hypnotizes a mouse. I never asked her about my father. I knew better.

Anyways, I always figured it was one of the daddies or uncles we visited, but of course it could have been anybody. When I was growing up, it was rare for her to go more than a month or so without a male companion, and I assumed it had always been so. The number of potential fathers seemed endless.

Still, a few of our customers seemed like good guesses. There was Pastor Avery, who ran the Church of the Beloved Believers. I remember driving up to his gated compound—he commanded a militia of around 150 people north of Cat Creek, Montana, and some large, bearded, barefoot men on motorcycles escorted my mother's car up the long driveway. There were men holding rifles sitting on the lawn chairs on the porch of his old farmhouse, and my mom brought down the sun visor and used the mirror to check her lipstick and makeup. There were mean dogs—Dobermans and Rottweilers—stalking along, their shoulder muscles like the slinking shoulders of lions.

"Take off your shoes and socks," my mother said. "Take them off. Leave them in the car."

"Can I bring my book?"

"Leave it," she said sharply.

So we got out and walked across the gravel, me barefoot, my mom still wearing her pantyhose. The dogs and men watched us as we climbed the porch steps. My mother clasped her hands in front of her and bowed her head and I did the same and a bearded man with an enormous belly gallantly opened the door for us.

We entered into an atrium and stood there as Pastor Avery came down the stairs in a long robe of white linen. He was not wearing shoes, either—a pale, tall, broad-shouldered man, balding, maybe in his late fifties or early sixties. He held his arms out to us.

"You've come," the man said. "Good." And my mother curtsied and kissed his knuckles. I wasn't sure whether I was supposed to do the same, so I just stood there, frozen, as his eyes fell on me.

"This is the boy?" he exclaimed, in a deep, jolly voice, like a kindly old toymaker in a cartoon. "My goodness! How big he's gotten!"

And to my surprise he reached down and picked me up in his arms. I was big for ten—maybe ninety pounds, nearly five feet tall—but he lifted me anyway without any sign of exertion.

"Ho ho!" he said, and I put my arm around his neck to balance myself. I didn't look at anything. I pretended that I was a doll. "Look at the size of this child's feet!" he said, and I felt him pinch my big toe. "He's going to be a football player when he grows up!"

He didn't put me down. He just smiled hard, showing his top and bottom teeth, and stared at my mom. "Have you brought me what I asked for, Sister?" he said.

The waitress sets down my beer and my Belgian waffle and I blink out of my daydream. "Thanks," I say as she cocks her head.

"Anything else?" she says, and I pull a hundred-dollar bill out of my pocket and press it into her hand.

"Is Friend Esther around?" I say, and she freezes. She looks down at the Benjamin and her fingers slowly close like a flower going to sleep.

"She won't be in until five o'clock," the woman says, and apparently a hundred dollars is not enough to spur her to further action. She turns as one of the cooks in the kitchen dings a service call bell, and off she goes.

I have a vivid memory of sitting in a plush high-backed chair in Pastor Avery's lap and I remember believing that he might be my father. He traced his finger along the edge of my ear, and sniffed my hair curiously, as if I gave off a mysterious smell.

"Billy will not be killed," he murmured. "Many will perish, but not Billy, O Lord!" I saw his other hand stroking my left foot, thoughtfully squeezing my big toe. I saw his thumb had the same kind of squat shovel shape as my own thumb.

And then I notice that I have cut up my Belgian waffle into twenty-four bite-size pieces, and I begin to fork them into my mouth, in between sips of beer.

I think of pushing Dallam Hartley in his wheelchair; it was a day in about June and I was eleven or twelve. My mom was back to being Taffy again.

I rolled Dallam's wheelchair along a rutted dirt trail down the hill from his mansion and we came to a barn where there were rows of cages full of chinchillas and minks and he let me fill their water bottles with a bluish liquid that he said was their special sauce.

"Your mom tells me that you're my son," he said. He was a thin man, frail-voiced, maybe seventy years old, with long gray hair that hung around his face. He was slumped down in his wheelchair looking down at his lap, where his hands were like a pair of discarded gloves.

I didn't say anything. I watched as the animals came eagerly to drink from the nipples of their water bottles with their small, sharp-toothed mouths open.

"You're not, though," he said. He had the expression of someone who is having a sad memory, and he reached up one of his limp hands and caught my wrist. His palms were as soft and damp as a baby's.

"You know that your mother is a compulsive liar, don't you, Billy?

I'm sure you know it probably better than anyone," he said. "Don't let her pull you into her confabulations, okay?"

"Okay," I said. We looked at each other and I believed him. I could feel in my heart that he was not my father.

It's a little irking that Friend Esther is not in the house, but I know I should have called ahead. In any case, I feel as if I'm out of the territory of the young men I murdered. I can probably head on up to Cleveland without any repercussions. I pour a bit more syrup on my waffle and take another long draw from my beer.

I can't help but think of Cammie again. Imagining her as a child growing up in Lake Forest, her dad a lawyer, her mom an artist. I can visualize her spacious and expensive home. Lots of big, airy rooms, white carpets, picture windows that looked out on a long stretch of beautifully tended yard. But did she look at the grown-up men she met the way that I did—always thinking . . . *Is he?* . . . *Could he be?* I wonder if she had a version of Pastor Avery, of Dallam Hartley?

What did she hope for in a dad? What did I hope, for that matter? I don't remember. Maybe I didn't hope for anything at all. Maybe I would have latched onto whatever potential other life was placed before me, and I wonder if she's the same. There's a chilling thought.

I run a piece of waffle through a curving mountain road of syrup, puttering the vehicle along slowly—

And driving along a narrow mountain road in Idaho with my mom and Kenny Panola, and it's probably not accurate but I seem to recall that we're singing along to Little Peggy March. I'm in the backseat, not wearing my seat belt, dancing and clowning, and Kenny is driving and my mom is leaning close to him, her chin on his shoulder, her mouth near his ear.

I was aware that she was giving him a hand job, but I pretended that I knew nothing. I jumped around and sang and Kenny glanced back at me and winked, raising his deep bass voice along with Little Peggy Marsh: I love him, *I love him,* I LOVE HIM, we exulted.

Kenny was one of my mother's oldest buddies, and that was one reason I thought he might be my father. We'd worked with him quite a bit over the years, but that had tapered off as I became a teenager and he became more and more of a speed freak. The last time I saw him, I was fourteen and he had those deep-set eyes, that wiry thinness, the skin stretched taut over his muscles, bruised with needle marks. He trembled a lot, and it was hard to know if he was cold or scared or on the verge of a violent psychotic break. We were staying in a cabin on the north shore of Priest Lake in northern Idaho, and in the end, I was pretty sure he might kill us.

The thing that Cammie probably doesn't understand is that you can have a good discussion with someone who is thinking about killing you. You can tell them a joke and they will laugh. You can love them even if you know they might murder you.

I remember how Kenny Panola had a weird, savant's fascination with trigonometry and calculus, and how I loved watching him sketch out geometry problems and formulas on a napkin, watching his monkey paws with their bulging veins wield a pencil for such a delicate task. Whatever little I know of advanced mathematics, I learned from him.

I remember that when he noticed me watching him, he would start muttering in a breathless, hostile monotone, occasionally twitching or stabbing at the air with his pencil. It took me a while to realize that he was actually telling me about what he was doing, what the calculations were, derivatives and inverse trigonometric functions and so forth—and he explained the concepts so clearly and concisely that I was hypnotized by the way knowledge was entering my brain, the way the strange symbols and formulations clarified into a language that made a flickering sense. I could actually feel the ideas trickling through my head like tiny beads.

In another life, Kenny Panola would have made an amazing high school math teacher, but instead a few days later my mom injected him with a fatal dose of amphetamine while he was sleeping and we left him spread-eagled in his Jockey underwear on a king-size bed, his mouth open and his eyes squeezed shut and—I like to think—dreaming a beautiful dream.

I push back from my empty plate and glance around for the bartender, but then I think, *Screw it. I gave her a hundred dollars.*

So I'm not skipping out on my tab, but I keep my head low as I go out the door.

Good Discussions

Heading north on I-79 toward Morgantown, I take my microdose of LSD and let myself cry a little, distractedly, just for emotional hygiene reasons. I come to a long bridge that ushers me into Ohio, and as I ride across, flying insects begin to splatter on my windshield like greenish-colored raindrops. It's the middle of October and seems too late in the year for them to be out, but who knows anymore?

One time in rural Delaware, I drove through an actual butterfly storm. They were cabbage butterflies—about the size of a quarter, white-winged—not particularly remarkable or beautiful, but when you're traveling down a two-lane highway at eighty miles an hour and you see a cloud of them bearing down on you, it makes an impression. The shadow of the swarm rippled across the ground, rapidly dappling. I turned on my windshield wipers when the first few began to hit, flattening themselves like petals against the glass, but soon the blizzard of them was blinding. The staccato *tick tick tick* of their bodies hitting the car was so loud I couldn't hear the radio, and I pumped the brake pedal as the wipers sluiced through their gummy remains, their wings piling up like leaves on the body of my car until I couldn't even see sunlight. I pulled onto the side of the road and turned off the ignition.

By the time the swarm had passed, my car was covered in a matted sheath of butterfly wings and guts, and when I stepped out I saw that other vehicles were similarly enshrouded. People stood agape and watched as the swarm headed west. Some people got out their ice scrapers and began the work of clearing off the debris. They knew it would be worse once it began to dry and harden.

I tell this story to Cammie when she calls. It's midafternoon, as per usual—1:43 p.m.; I make a note of it so I can time the length of her call—but I don't feel like being alert in the way that Experanza would want—*Gain her trust, find her location*—so I just start gabbing away about the butterflies, remembering the story for her, and she seems attentive, which, Lord knows, is not unwelcome.

"I've heard the same thing, except with spiders," Cammie says. "They call it mass ballooning—all these spider babies land in, like, a park and they cover all the trees and grass and picnic tables and everything in webs! It looks almost like snow."

"Spiders would be worse than butterflies," I say.

"Not necessarily," she says. "I actually think butterflies are creepier. That whole chrysalis stage is the stuff of nightmares."

Which I guess is true: the transmogrification of a creature in a cocoon has some body horror to it, I suppose. But I'll bet the imagery is more personal for a test-tube baby.

"Right on," I say. It's coming up on eighteen minutes, and sure enough, her voice gets a little stiffer.

"Listen," she says. "Can I call you back a little later? I've got a thing I need to take care of—"

"Yeah," I say. "Of course."

I drive up through the colon of Ohio toward its midsection. It's possible that the stretch of I-77 that runs through central Ohio may be the most generic of interstate corridors in the world. It feels like virtual reality, like you're playing a driving video game that's stuck on a loop. Two lanes going north, two lanes going south, and a wide space of bare dirt in between. Big green signs with white letters pass overhead. The landscape is rolling and pastoral in a forgettable way.

Now I'm thinking about things I want to talk to Cammie about, just out of curiosity. What kind of little girl was she, for example? I try to picture a rich suburban Lake Forest childhood, and I can't really get a grip on it. But I'll bet that just like me she would have spent those years trying and failing to make her parents happy. Too moody? Too curious? Not graceful enough? Trying to pretend to be a part of a family you don't belong in.

By twelve or thirteen, already she's a handful for the parents, I imagine, wants to dye her hair, wants face piercings and so on. Already she's visiting bad websites, she's reading books that feed her blossoming nihilism, maybe already there's some hint of our family curse beginning to show itself? *My mortal enemies,* I hear her saying.

Who did she love? She must've loved someone.

I'll bet she loved her mom and dad when she was little. I wonder which one broke her heart the most—which was the biggest disappointment, which left the deepest wound? Probably the father, is my guess.

I'll bet she was attracted to the problem kids when she was in high school and college—maybe she loved one of them hard enough to be led astray, let herself be pulled into some scheme involving minor eco-terrorism or pornography or hard drugs.

I figure that by that point she was drawing near to the world I inhabit, to the kind of people I traffic with—dealers, cultists, conspiracy theorists and militias, radical reactionaries and revolutionists, trolls and goblins and parasites.

Or so I imagine.

And then one of the phones rings. Flip flicks his ears as if a fly has tickled them, and I pick the buzzing thing out of the bucket before it wakes him up.

"Hey, there!" I say softly, and I like how tender and friendly my voice sounds. At least thirty percent of it sincerely so.

"Hey," she says, and I guess the friendliness makes her uncertain, because she hesitates.

"Uhh," she says. I imagine her shifting her phone from one ear to the other, but then it occurs to me that she's probably not even using a phone. She's probably got one of those headsets on, a pair of earbuds and a microphone. "Sorry about the . . ." she says. "Interruption."

"Everything all right?"

"It's nothing," she says. "I just have to keep switching aliases. I'm paranoid."

"Can't be too careful," I agree. "If you don't watch out, your long-lost daughter will be calling you."

"Ha ha," she says. Then silence. Maybe I think I'm funnier than I am. I glance down at my hands on the steering wheel, thick freckled fingers, big, stupid knuckles.

"Well," I say. "Anyways."

"I forgot what we were talking about when I—when we left off."

"Butterflies," I say. "And spiders."

"Oh, right," she says. "I loved that story you told. And I think that the more we share anecdotes and memories and, you know, the random stuff of life, the more we'll get to know each other and be at ease with each other, and trust will begin to form and then we can go from there."

Trust will begin to form? I think, and itch my beard thoughtfully. *Oh, Cammie. Really?* I look ruefully at the black matte of the speakers where her voice comes from, and then out again, the steady unraveling of the interstate, a few semis and a smattering of hybrid sedans and tiny Smart Cars, one of those driverless vehicles with the windows mirrored like policemen's sunglasses.

"Go ahead and ask me a question," she says. "What are you curious about?"

"What am I curious about," I say. She's got an awkward, eager, cuddling-up tone, and if she were a professional, I'd feel embarrassed for her.

But I'm pretty sure she's not a professional. Is it possible that she's for real, after all, that she's some crazy girl who hopes that I'll help her just because we share some biological fluids? Poor thing, there's a genuine touch of desperate hopefulness in her voice—though *genuine* is the kind of word that would make my mother laugh. *You're a born sucker,* my mom used to say, every time she tricked me. *"SUCKER" is going to be written right on your tombstone.*

"What did you want to be when you grew up?" I ask her.

"When I was in kindergarten, I used to tell people I wanted to be an archaeologist," she says. "I don't know why. I liked dinosaurs and old ruins."

"Even now, you're still digging for things," I joke. "You dug me up!"

"Ha ha," she says: I'm not funny, again.

"And then," she says, "when I was about ten, I decided I wanted to be a detective or a reporter. A whistleblower who brought corruption and crime to the light of day."

"And then you realized that it's already in daylight and it doesn't matter."

"Yeah," she says. "I did realize that."

I nod, grooming my beard thoughtfully with thumb and forefinger as I drive along. "So now what?" I say.

"I don't know yet," she says. "Try to tear it all down, maybe? That's what I'm maybe hoping for. Just bring the whole palace down on itself."

"Mm," I say. "That's a young person's ambition. But I wish you luck! Sometimes in history it happens."

"Are you interested in history?" she says. "I was a history major in college."

"You don't say," I remark.

I'm coming up on the Newcomerstown/Port Washington exit, and in another life, I'd present for her a thumbnail history of Newcomerstown—which, in the 1770s, was known as Gekelmukpechunk and was one of the largest Delaware Indian villages in the area. The chief of the village was named Netawatwees, called Newcomer by the English, and thus the town bears his name to this day. This might lead into some interesting conversation about American history, as we drove along together, father and daughter. And the radio would be playing and she'd be so smart and funny but she'd also be a little impressed by me—I'm not as dumb as I seem. I've read books. I've thought about stuff. For just a second, I dwell in that universe.

But here is one of the problems with me and Cammie getting to know each other. It's the way she says, "I was a history major"—so casual, so proud of the little merit badge the word *major* confers on her. It's just a small thing, but it makes me aware that, father or no, there's a vast difference in our pedigrees.

One of the things I've observed about white folks who grew up well-to-do: they have a deep investment in the idea of merit, and there's a special scorn, I've noticed, for the poor of their own kind. They may acknowledge that race plays a role in keeping people down; they may even be sympathetic to the plights and sufferings of certain marginalized groups—but white trash is trash for a reason.

They can't help but feel they deserve their position above the fat janitor or the rapidly aging waitress or the bashful handyman—*If you were smart, you would've gone to college,* they think. *If you were ambitious, you would have done something with yourself. We worked harder,* they think. *Our parents instilled proper values,* they think—and . . . *well. We. Just. Have. Better. Genes.*

I think of Patches, the way his eyes grew softly, twenty-watt condescending when he found that I'd never been to high school, let alone university. "You're self-taught!" he said, as if I were a talking monkey, and he showed his upper teeth in a way that he didn't mean to. The sneer he'd inherited from generations of good breeding, not on purpose.

I can picture the lips of Cammie, and I know she'll be trying not to make that expression. But I'm afraid that the more she knows me, the more disappointed she'll be. So I say nothing. The *Guiding Star* glides past Newcomerstown silent and aloof, and the ghosts of the Delaware tribes watch from the woods. Soon enough, we'll be joining them in oblivion, I reckon, and the grass and weeds will cover this interstate, and the trees will break apart the parking lots of the gas station oasis.

"Why are you so quiet?" Cammie says after a while. "Did I say something?"

"No," I say. "I was just . . . spacing out for a minute." I glance down to make sure the device is still recording our conversation.

"Keep talking," I say. "Ask me a question."

"So, what do you like to do for fun?" she asks at last. "Do you . . . have any hobbies?"

"I like the outdoors," I say. "I particularly like streams and ponds with turtles. I'm curious about amphibians, too. Sometimes I go looking under rocks for salamanders. I'm also a big fan of owls."

"Oh," she says. "That's cool. My best friend in college was a birder.

She wanted to become a wildlife expert and naturalist. But that's not a great career path right now."

"Right on," I say, and I hope we don't get into a discussion about extinction and habitat collapse and the ecological apocalypse, because what can a person really say?

"I don't know," I say. "In another life, I would have been a naturalist, or a park ranger, maybe. Or a shepherd or just a woodland hermit collecting mushrooms and herbs and root vegetables. I would know all the names of flowers and trees and edible berries and so forth."

"I like the way you talk," she says. "It's like—weirdly poetic."

"You're making fun of me," I say. "I know what I sound like. Cornpone, that's what my old friend Experanza says. Like a pretentious hillbilly, she says."

"She doesn't sound like a friend to me," Cammie says. "I wasn't making fun of you, I was just . . ."

I look down at the recorder and the timer says we've been going for twenty-five minutes.

"Oh, shit," she says. As if we've both realized this at the same time.

"Listen, I have to go," she says. "I'll call you back."

Twenty-five minutes! Oh, Cammie, what's got into you? I drive through the mid-Ohio valley with its patchwork of gold and gray fields, and play through the recording for a while, slow it down a little bit and listen to her at half speed, so she sounds like a deep-voiced, dopey man. I wonder if that's what my voice sounds like? I'm checking to see if any telling sounds come through at slower speed, but the background is still weirdly clean. I'm sure Experanza has contacts who have equipment that will pick up more than the naked human ear can, some watermark or clue that will lead us to our girl's whereabouts. I listen to her talking about wanting to be an archaeologist. I listen to her say, "I like the way you talk. It's, like, weirdly poetic." I hear her say, of Experanza: "She doesn't sound like a friend to me."

In that, she's probably right.

I wonder what's making her so reckless today. So eager to call me up and make small talk—what do you like to do for fun, what was your major, what did you want to be when you grew up? Chatting away as if it's a freshman mixer, not keeping track of her timer.

Maybe, I think, she's starting to go into one of those manic phases the way I used to when I was her age. I can remember that ticklish feeling in my head—like an itch on the sole of your foot, that soft, insistent, distant-bells-ringing sort of feeling, and then the way it spread bodily, slowly, butterflies in the stomach, tingling palms, a twittering in the groin region, and you become aware that the world is exciting and deeply interesting, and your every thought seems clever and urgent, and you might begin to chuckle privately. You're brightly alert and scattered at the same time. In order to focus, you have to try to ignore all the other stimuli around you, the infinity of possible things you could be noticing, and it's hard to hold on to one thing for long.

She's not quite at that stage yet, I'd say, but I could hear the hint of it when she started holding forth on the ballooning of spiders—that mix of focused and scattered, as if she's gone to all the trouble of tracking me down just so she can impart a nature lesson.

I remember that feeling—the growing momentousness of every whimsy that occurs to you, the way each object your eye touches has a glimmer of potential symbolism and insistent uncanny import. I remember sitting in my room in Mrs. Dowty's rooming house and filling notebooks with pages and pages of rushed writing and drawings, sharpening and resharpening my pencil until it was just a nub. The sudden burst of molecules exploding inside you so that you had to abruptly leap up and dance wildly in your stocking feet, tears running down your face, crying with happiness and grief all at once. The world was terrible and beautiful to behold.

Sometimes you could stop it with dancing. Sometimes you couldn't.

And then—wouldn't you know it?—one of my phones is ringing not fifteen minutes later.

"You're in a talkative mood today, Cammie," I say, and quietly press the Record button on my device.

"I guess so," she says breathlessly, and I listen to her intonation with mania in mind. She's definitely jittery. "I'm just not sure what to do," she says. "I'm not sure what I should do," she says. "I just want to talk to another person, because . . . I don't know."

"It sounds to me like you might be in trouble, honey," I say slowly, and—I hope—kindly. "Can you be more specific with me?"

She hesitates. If she's anything like I used to be, I imagine that thoughts are beginning to burble pretty rapidly at this point. I recall how I used to put my hand over my mouth and move my lips against my palm to keep the words from spilling out—that febrile state again, I think.

"I'm scared," she says at last, and it sounds like she's on the verge of crying. "I . . . really need somebody to help me. Remember how you said you thought I must be desperate, and I guess, yeah, right, I'm desperate." And then it seems that she lets out a stifled sob, though I really don't want to attribute too much to it—I'm trying to keep a tight rein on my sympathetic urges.

"Listen," I say. "Cammie, you have to be truthful with me. Just be straight with me, and maybe I can be of assistance."

I can hook her, I think, if I'm careful. And I also think: *Poor girl. Poor desperate girl, I should help you, shouldn't I? I'm your dad, after all.*

"I reckon you've got somebody after you," I say. "Maybe a lot of somebodies."

"Yeah," she says.

"Is there anything you can tell me about it?"

She draws back at this, hesitates—but I think she's really scared, she truly is scared, and I can hear the burble of tears in her nose.

"There's something I need to tell you," she says, and I look down at the dot on the phone that blinks red, recording her voice. Instinctively, I don't know why, I reach down and turn it off.

"What?" I say.

"I'm—I'm not the only one," she says.

"What do you mean?"

"I'm not the only biological child you've got," she says. "From what I've gathered so far, there are a hundred and sixty-seven of us. Probably more."

Power Outage

So it turns out that our poor Cammie is out of her mind. It's not that I'm prejudiced against the insane, it's just that I wish this particular young basket case did not have unexplained access to my private personal information. A sinking feeling settles over me as she earnestly imparts her various delusions.

In her fantasy, my lonely sperm bank deposits have produced a dividend of at least 167 children. It seems highly unlikely, but she has built an elaborate story around the idea. My brood ranges in age, she says, from infants to adults in their early twenties, though most of them, she says, are in grade school. "My *diblings*," she calls them—*diblings* being a "portmanteau," says she, of *donor* and *sibling*, meaning children who all share the same sperm donor. "It's not that unusual," she says. "You can look it up," she says, "though this many dibs from the same father is extremely rare."

"*Dibling*," I say, trying to keep my voice warm but noncommittal. "Huh. Not a very pretty word, is it?" It sounds like a foodstuff made out of some part of a hog that you wouldn't want to know about—though I don't say that. At this time, I intuit, Cammie's not interested in how words sound.

She says that most of these diblings are in the US, but some are situated in western Europe, India, China, Saudi Arabia. All of them "acquired," as she says, by wealthy parents—some of them extremely wealthy.

"Dang," I say. "I wish I knew what I wrote in that donor question-naire! It must've really impressed somebody."

"It doesn't have anything to do with the questionnaire," she says. "It's something in your DNA, I think. In our DNA."

"Well, no doubt I'm a fine specimen," I say. "But I find all of this hard to believe."

"I know," she says. "Me, too. But I don't know what else it could be."

We come now to the conspiracy element of her delusion, and it is not particularly original. You've heard this before: There is a cabal of rich and powerful men (in some versions they are Jews, or Masons, or Illuminati, or Satanists, or pedophiles, or etc.), and this cabal is secretly conducting some kind of wicked business—planning a massive geno-cide, or creating a sadomasochistic pleasure palace in the basement of a pizza parlor, or rigging democratic elections, or hoarding stockpiles of the world's remaining resources in secret bunkers—and their evil web of influence extends to the highest levels of government, to the CEOs of major companies and billionaire entrepreneurs and wealthy investment bankers and all the royal families of Europe and the Middle East. It's one of those urban legends that a lot of otherwise ordinary folks believe to be true, and who am I to say that it's not?

But in Cammie's version of the legend, the rich are apparently col-lecting seedlings of the Barely Blur for some nefarious purpose, reasons unclear.

"The thing is," Cammie says, "all of these people—these adopters, these baby-collectors, whatever you want to call them—they're some of the most powerful people in the world!"

"Well, I'll be," I say politely. I'm passing through the fracking regions south of Akron, and they say that minor earthquakes can be common—there are even signs along the interstate that say TREMOR ZONE—but I think the quavery feeling I'm experiencing is internal.

This is so troubling, I think. Maybe someone needs to get this child back into the arms of her parents or some other adult helper, someone who is equipped to deal with a young person in the grips of this kind of—what would you call it?

"What about your dad?" I say at last. "Your adoptive dad? You said he was a lawyer. You didn't say he was rich and powerful."

"He's rich! Not Fortune 500 level, but," she says defensively. "I mean, he's Brayden Kurch's lawyer, so . . ."

"You don't say," I respond, because I have only a vague idea of who Brayden Kurch is. I think that he is a famous entrepreneur of some kind—something tech, maybe, or pharmaceutical? The only solid recollection I have of him is seeing his face on the cover of a book. *Transhumanist Séance*, it was called, and his name was in block letters above the title: BRAYDEN KURCH. I saw it in the window of a little bookstore in Portsmouth, New Hampshire, as I was on my way to burn down the house of a blogger who had gotten on the wrong side of the company we had contracted with, and I recall pausing for a moment and looking at the book cover and Brayden Kurch's wise and grinning face and thinking: Transhumanist Séance! *That's got a nice ring to it.*

But in any case, Cammie seems to believe that his name will impress me, so I accept that it would if I did know who he was.

"My dad and Kurch were pretty close friends when they were younger," she tells me. "And also—Brayden Kurch has two of your daughters from his first marriage. One's a year older than me—I think she might be the first—and another's a few years younger. So there's that."

Oh, these zingers she comes up with!

She's good at this withhold-and-reveal game, and it reminds me very strongly of the kinds of tall tales and lies and con games my mother would try out on me—how she'd draw you in with something outrageous and then add a little homely detail to give it a dash of realism, how she'd embellish the story in ways that'd make it personal to the listener, so that her confabulation was in some flattering way about *you*—and then before long she'd be tenderly slipping her hand into your pocket.

"I'll tell you what," I say, in a voice that I hope seems both frank and friendly. "Cammie, honey—I have some personal reasons to believe that you are telling me the truth about being my daughter . . ."

"Um," she says, "I do have actual *proof*, if you want to do a mouth-swab DNA test."

"Right on," I say. "But what I'm saying is, you're starting to lose me with the rest of this. It *really* seems like a stretch."

"I know," she says. "That's why I was trying to get to know you a little first, so that you'd trust me—so you wouldn't just think I was crazy. Which I know you do."

I'm traveling along I-480 now, passing over the viaduct across Transportation Boulevard south of Cleveland, and through the rain haze I can see the big chimney stacks lining the horizon, tipped with billows of smoke and flickers of fire. One is like a giant candle. To the left I see the skyscraper skyline of Cleveland, on the shores of its lake, and to the right is a vast wasteland of suburban houses. I clear my throat.

"So," I say. "You've had contact with these Kurch girls, have you?"

"No," she says. "I never liked them, and I know they wouldn't believe me, so . . ."

"But you have evidence that they're part of the—" And I don't say "part of the vast conspiracy to spread my seed across the world," because I don't want to be oppositional.

"I am one hundred percent certain," she says. "And I have documentation, but I don't want to sit here and go through it, it's too complicated, it'll waste too much time."

"It's funny," I say. "I've never been a hundred percent certain about anything. So . . . I'm having a hard time, is what I'm saying. You know about Occam's razor, right?"

"The simplest solution is almost always the best," she says.

"Yeah," I say. "So . . . the simplest solution here is . . . that you're having some mental stability issues . . . which might possibly involve . . . paranoid delusions."

I try to express this in an accepting and loving way, but it is not enough. I hear the abrupt silence against my ear as she hangs up.

In the distance, lightning flashes, and the rain is coming down a little harder. The semis rush past me as we cross the bridge, sheer and briefly blinding arcs of water spray across me as they pass, and I grip the wheel tighter. I suspect that—as with my mother's various con games—there are some grains of truth at the heart of Cammie's story, and some part of her fantasy might have roots in something that really happened. But maybe she's just lost her mind; I can imagine that she's one of those fringe conspiracy zealots, drugged up in some cult house in Alabama, wearing nothing but a white linen smock, her hair long and tangled. A single red leaf flies up and pastes itself to the windshield for a moment before the wipers carry it away. The palm of a wet hand pressed against glass.

And just at the moment of the leaf, the phone rings.

You have to respect synchronicity like that, I guess, so I pick up the phone, and when I put it to my ear she says, "Okay, look . . . there's at least one other person that knows about this. You have a son. He's the one who first told me.

"I'm surprised he hasn't contacted you," she says. "That was one of the things that I was afraid of. That Ronnie would have got to you first."

"Tell me about him," I say.

Apparently, I have a son name of Ronnie, older than her by less than a month. He was the one who tipped her off to the truth—reached out to her when they were both lonely sixteen-year-olds, and mostly they communicated through texts, sometimes they Skyped late at night. He said he'd found her name in a packet of papers that he'd discovered in a lockbox in his dad's office—he'd been hoping to find money—but he looked at the papers anyway, and saw that they were photocopies of birth certificates, along with some infant medical records, and he just started Googling the names out of curiosity and she was the first one he found.

By the time they had begun to talk regularly, he had found a lot more information. He knew about the clinics that supplied the sperm and egg—*the biological materials*, as she calls them—he even had a copy of the questionnaire I'd filled out, which he read aloud to her in a mocking voice.

"That was really when I started to think about you," she says. "It's like, he's making fun of your answers on this questionnaire and I'm just . . . I found them so—so earnest and funny and poetic. Like, you wrote, *I always wanted to be a nature boy*, and that killed me, I thought it was so moving!"

"Okay," I say carefully, because there are a lot of whirring, bladed parts in those sentences. It makes my chest tighten in all kinds of ways.

This Ronnie, she says, was from Monaco but went to a boarding school called Institut Le Rosey in Switzerland, and she was enchanted by his accent and by how much they looked alike. They could have been twins. In any case, they weren't just regular siblings, as they were from the first batch of embryos that were produced from my sperm and Rosalie Signorelli's eggs, born only three weeks apart.

But he was problematic, she says. "A perv. He liked to send me pictures of his naked body—like, close-ups of his erect penis and stuff, and he wanted me to reciprocate, and he was, like, *I don't mean it in a creepy way, I just want to see what your body looks like because it's what my body would look like if I was a girl!*" She's talking more rapidly now, getting wound up in a way that makes me mildly nostalgic for my own manic episodes, back before I cured myself.

"So, what's he up to now," I say. "This Ronnie?" My hands tighten on the steering wheel, and I watch as the windshield wipers slice across the droplets of rain. I hope I don't have to add another problem to my list, but best to get all the details I can.

"I don't know," she says. "He dumped me. Maybe he found another sister he liked better. But he's in hiding, too, I think. He dropped off the grid about two years ago, and I don't have any idea what happened. I've been wondering lately if he might be dead . . . if maybe they—"

Then, abruptly, her voice cuts off. The radio cuts off, too.

I startle at the soundlessness, the break from her voice, the break from the music, the break from my thoughts. I hold my phone and look down at it. It blinks on, lights up, then goes dead.

Comes the blackout. From the center of the bridge, I can see the streetlights and the houses and neon blinking out, block after block, darkness moving across the plain of cityscape in a wave. I almost cry out as the tide of eclipse sweeps forward, spreading darkness like a flood. It sucks the life right out of the *Guiding Star* and keeps on moving toward the southern suburbs, a stain spreading toward the distant horizon, snuffing out lights as it goes, until the whole of the landscape is black. The moon and stars seem to strengthen and grow brighter.

It takes a moment for my breath to come back. I'd been going fairly fast, and the *Guiding Star* continues to roll forward for a while after the motor quits, though the steering wheel has locked up. "Jesus H. Christ!" I say, and the side of the camper scrapes along the cement wall of the highway bridge before it comes to a complete stop. The windshield wipers come up and make a halfhearted swipe across the scrim of glass: *flap, flap, flap.*

Flap.

Then they stop, too. The rain patters hesitantly on the roof.

The Lasting Last of Her

After the blackout, I sit there in the camper of the *Guiding Star*, on the side of the road, waiting. The rain pebbles against the metal roof, and I play solitaire by candlelight as Flip rests his head on my foot like it's a pillow. Outside it's dark, but I can see the shapes of other stranded vehicles lined up all down the road, forward and back.

When the rain lets up, it must be getting close to midnight, I'd guess. Out my window I can hear some of the other motorists talking together resignedly, and it smells like someone has fired up a charcoal grill. I guess we've gotten used to this kind of thing now. Off in the distance, cheap fireworks arc up and flash—some kind of bottle rockets, which let out a distant, lonely whistle.

I wish that Cammie would call me back. I spend some time examining my phones—checking to see if any of them are working—but they all seem to be dead, their batteries sapped by the same force that sapped the battery of my vehicle and shut down the power grid for the Cleveland metro area.

I still have a mini gas stove, though, so I pull it out and grab a can of pork brains in milk gravy from the cupboard and stir it up with some scrambled eggs. It's one of Flip's favorites, and I actually don't mind it myself, either. This was one of the few things my mom cooked for me regularly. She said it reminded her of her girlhood in Iowa, and it's one of the only images I have of her as a child. I picture her standing on a kitchen chair in front of a stove and opening up a can of pork brains with a can opener, turning the handle until the lid sloughs off and slowly sinks into the gravy. I can see her lighting the hissing gas burner with a match, flinching as the flame puffs up and almost singes her face, but even at five or six she knows what she's doing. She scrambles some eggs in a skillet, and pours the brains on top, gives it a stir.

From a baby, she didn't need anyone to take care of her, she said.

For years, I've been pretty good at keeping my mother shut out of my mind. But now—due to Cammie, I guess—here she is again. God how I hate when a memory comes over me! Time slows down and there's a bottomless, sinking feeling—that would be the worst way to end, I think, gasping out your last breath with a slow realization dawning on you. My wish is that I'll wake up someday on a desert island with amnesia.

I choose not to think of the last time I saw her—or her remains, I should say, covered in rock salt and mothballs in an industrial-plastic cargo box in a self-storage facility outside of Fairbanks, Alaska. I choose not to think of the nights leading up to that last glimpse, those weeks before I closed the lid on her corpse—all that stuff I had to unremember so I could cure myself.

But Cammie's conspiracy talk has me thinking about something my mother told me once, back in the day. I remember we were staying at the Mr. Sandman Motel, off I-40 right near the Arizona–New Mexico border. She'd just finished up with some scam she was running on a polygamist cult down near Bisbee, but she was already on the lookout for our next venture. I was probably about thirteen.

She'd been talking about this ranch down in southern New Mexico, where a crazy billionaire supposedly kept all these women and girls. "Like cattle," she said, with the kind of relish she'd get when she had a particularly horrible story to relate.

"They say he's got about a hundred of them down there, maybe more," she said, and leaned back in bed dreamily. All the lights were out in our motel room, and her cigarette grew bright as she sucked in some smoke. "A hundred or more," she said. "And they're all being paid fifty grand to get pregnant by him. From what I hear, he doesn't even have sex with them. They just put the seed up in there with a turkey baster. And then they take the embryos out when they're a month or two along and freeze them in containers of liquid nitroglycerine."

I didn't really believe her. She was, as many of her victims discovered, a compulsive liar, and often liked to run stories by me for practice, or maybe just for the fun of frightening or disgusting me. Getting really deep into my head was one of her great pleasures.

But I still listened and considered, because sometimes she also told the truth. I could picture the girls in narrow rooms like stalls in a stable, sitting on beds in their underwear and waiting for a nurse to come in with a syringe full of some old man's spunk. It creeped me out, sure. But it didn't seem that improbable.

"Why would he even want that many kids?" I said. "That seems weird. What does he do with the babies after he freezes them?"

My mother laughed softly, as if I was stupid not to know, and I didn't ask anything else. I stood at the window and looked out at the parking lot, toward the desert beyond—off in the direction of New Mexico. The moon was out, a crescent that hung over the blinking neon sign for the Mr. Sandman Motel.

"What are you looking at?" my mother said. "Come to bed, little rabbit," she said, and the light of her cigarette bobbed as she beckoned.

There was a nursery rhyme my mother used to sing to me when I was a small child. It was the one about the little cabin in the wood, where a little old man by the window stood. Then, for some reason, a rabbit comes hopping by and knocks at the cabin door. "Help me, help me," the rabbit says, "or the hunter will shoot me dead." And so the little old man opens the door. He's like, "Come, Little Rabbit, come inside, safely you may hide!" And also: "Come, Little Rabbit, come with me, happy we will be!"

Even though I was just a kid, I was aware that the little old man was probably a rapist or a murderer, or both, and that the rabbit was doomed from the minute it knocked on that cabin door.

When I got older, the word *rabbit* was one of my mother's typical codes for a patsy. "We're going to visit Uncle Rabbit," she'd say. And I always knew I was in for it when she pinched my ear and bent down and whispered, "Come on, little rabbit." And gave me her kindest smile.

I knew she was going to trick me, I knew bad things were in store, but I obeyed her, I followed her beckoning finger and now here I was again, her little rabbit, clambering into the bed next to her as she put her arm around my shoulder and rubbed my head.

"Fifty thousand is good money," she said. "Especially if you don't have to carry to term. And two or three months is nothing, you don't even gain weight."

I was quiet for a while, my head resting in the crook of her neck. She smelled like Jean Naté perfume and armpit sweat. I knew she was just talking things through. She'd said he kept the women like cattle, and surely that didn't appeal to her.

"What?" she said. "You don't think I'm pretty enough to make the cut this time? You think I look too old now that I'm thirty?"

"No," I said. "No, it's just . . . What about me?" I said. "What would I do?"

"Oh, I'm sure they'd be willing to keep you," she teased brightly. "They might even pay me something for you."

"Mm," I said. She pulled me in close and smelled my hair, her lips so close to my ear I could feel the condensation of her breath.

"Do-lang, do-lang, do-lang," she sang softly, and I closed my eyes hard.

She had a beautiful voice, my mother. In her younger days, she claimed she had been part of an all-girl band called the Happy Home Jubilee Singers. Three girls in their early teens, three-part harmonies. They sang country music at first, she said, Grand Ole Opry stuff, and then later they expanded their repertoire to include more pop material—they covered songs by the Chiffons and the Dixie Cups, and at one point, she said, they had a meeting with the famous impresario Phil Spector, though in the end he decided not to help them.

"It could have been different," she'd tell me. "In another life." And then she'd make that soft laughing sound that I can still hear in my head. Wry and menacing and edged with despair.

"But instead," she said, "I got you."

We never did make it down to the billionaire's compound in southern New Mexico—either because it didn't exist, or because she didn't get accepted in, or because some more tempting rabbit caught her eye, I don't know. There may have been more to it, but I've discarded large chunks of that part of my life from my waking memory, and now they are inaccessible.

What is it about billionaires and babies? I wonder. Those Ozymandiases! It's one of those urban legends that must have old roots, I imagine, maybe some tendrils of it based in actual truth. Wish I could remember the name of that guy with the ranch. I take a little bite of my pork brains and eggs, considering.

Food for thought, I think. Which, come to think of it, would make a good tombstone epitaph.

What was she, my mother? I used to wish I could figure it out. Just like Cammie.

I used to wonder if she actually gave birth to me, and I questioned that up until very recently, up until Cammie opened her mouth and my mom's laugh came out. That was when I thought, *Oh*, and I felt something fall into place and I finally knew for sure. *I* did *come out of her*, I thought.

For all of our time together, she had kept that question a bit muddy— sometimes I would say: "Mom? Mom?" and she would turn with a look of tolerant contempt. "Don't call me that," she'd say. "I'm not your mother." And sometimes I would be expected to call her Sessy, or Taffy, or Barbara, or whatever she might be calling herself.

And sometimes it was a nice fantasy to believe that she was not my mother. I remember the newspaper article she showed me once, one morning in a motel room while she was drinking coffee and I was eating cereal. She turned the paper to face me and pointed at a headline: "Baby Ripped from Murdered Mom's Womb Opens Eyes for First Time." "What a coincidence!" she said. "That's exactly how I got you!" And winked.

As for her own past, her own connections, I know almost nothing. She told me she didn't have parents. "People like us invent ourselves, baby," she'd say. "I had so many mommies and daddies I can't even remember them all."

Now, sitting here at the table in the camper of the *Guiding Star*—a man in his fifth decade, older than she'll ever be—I can still hear her saying this. *People like us invent ourselves, baby,* she whispers, and I shudder.

I choose not to think about the night in Fairbanks on the bridge.

The hypodermic needle sinking into the back of her neck, her hands swatting and grasping backwards. "You fucker," she rasped. "You dirty fucker," she said and the apple she had been eating fell out of her hand and rolled onto the floor of the car and lay near the gas pedal with a single white bite cavity in the red surface.

I do not think that one of the scars on my right forearm is the imprint of her teeth where she bit me.

I like to believe that there is no lasting last of her, that when I die there will be no memories of her left in the world—she'll be nothing but a bog person, a piece of beef jerky packed in salt and naphthalene in a warehouse outside of Fairbanks, less than two thousand miles from the North Pole.

I remember what she always told me: "Most people don't want any help, and the rest of them don't deserve it."

Lord, may she never be found.

3

The Forces of the Universe
Owe Me an Apology

Qualms come.

It's been hours now since Cammie and I were disconnected, and it seems like I've changed my mind about her four or five dozen times: she's crazy, or she's not crazy, she believes what she's saying but she's been duped, or she's withholding the real story, or she's scamming me in some elaborate way that I can't fathom, or some combination of the above.

And yet, I can't shake the feeling that she really is my daughter.

I sit on the stoop of the *Guiding Star* as the sun comes up, and I watch as some of the driverless cars begin to blink on in the sunlight, vibrating and hiccuping little bleeps and then, finally, coming back to life and trundling off, making their way through the maze of stranded vehicles, undaunted and even seemingly chipper as they head toward their assignations.

Meanwhile, a flying drone the size of a shopping cart is passing overhead, speaking in a voice that strongly resembles a well-known female comedian's. These days, robots sound more and more naturalistic, and it's unnerving. "Help is on the way," she says, and she's friendly, self-deprecating, apologetic. A little flirty. "I know you've been thinking, *Where have you guys been?* right? We're really doing our best, and we'll be with you as soon as possible! But in the meantime, you have to remain in your vehicles! I hate to say this, but people who are not in their vehicles when we arrive will be arrested and will be looking at a really expensive fine!"

I flick the nub of my roach into the grass as the drone approaches, and I head back into the camper. It's got one of those nine-eyed cameras attached to it, taking snapshots in 360 degrees, and I hate having my picture taken.

I sit down at my kitchen table and look at the phones I have spread out. No sign of life there. So I take the pack of Tarot cards that is sitting next to the salt and pepper shakers and give it a long shuffle and ask it to tell me what it can about Cammie.

I lay down a three-card meditation, and the first card is the Lovers (reversed)—which seems pretty obvious and unhelpful; and the second card is Temperance, which seems condescending; and the third card is the King of Cups reversed, which seems, actually, more than a little insulting.

The King of Cups reversed is usually a narcissistic older man—a wasteful user and taker and manipulator—and typically if he's in your spread, he's at the root of whatever problem you're presenting to Tarot.

Now, I realize that in the past, I may have been diagnosed as exhibiting signs of the psychotic/psychopathic spectrum, but I feel like I've had all that under control for a long time. I don't think I'm the problem here, to be honest. I wasn't the one who called me; she was. I stare hard at the cards, feeling unjustly treated, and then I gather them up and put them back next to the salt and pepper shakers. Those cards can bite my ass.

And then—because the forces of the universe owe me an apology—one of the dead phones I'd brushed aside begins to stir. It gives out a forlorn, gurgling tone—the sound a half-drowned man lets out when you compress his chest—and I snatch it up.

It's not Cammie, of course.

"Hey!" says a deep, sleepy-sounding male. "Mr. Bayer? Hey, this is Friend Dave. I got your signal. So . . . I'm here to help you out today."

"Right on," I say. "I need roadside assistance. I'm on I-480 southeast of Cleveland, about a quarter mile west of Exit 24. I think I'm the only luxury motor home on this part of the freeway. It's called the *Guiding Star*."

"Alrighty," says Friend Dave. "You should expect me there within the hour."

But two hours later, I'm still waiting. Traffic has begun to move again—single lane, bumper to bumper, five miles per hour at best—and I'm thinking of this horror movie I saw once, about a mad scientist who wants to create a human centipede, and so he kidnaps people and surgically connects them, anus to mouth to anus to mouth and so on, I'm not sure what his motive was, but watching this sad cavalcade of recently resurrected undead vehicles, I'm reminded of the poor human centipede people.

I'm leaning against the side of the *Guiding Star*, sucking on a hydrocodone lozenge and feeling a little impatient with Friend Dave, when at last he pulls up in his tow truck. He holds his head out of the window, grinning. "Mr. Bayyyyyer!" he calls, with wild good nature. "Gaaar! Can you believe this traffic? Sorry I'm late!" He parks on the side of the road in front of the *Guiding Star*, and I watch him alight from his truck and march toward me with a ready-to-help swagger. He's a tall, broad-shouldered blond kid, no more than twenty-five, with a thick-necked head that puts me in mind of a thumb. But an enthusiastic thumb. He comes up and gives Flip a look of childlike delight.

"Hey! Cute doggo!" he exclaims and waggles his fingers near Flip's muzzle. "Does he bite?"

"Yes," I say.

"Oh," he says. He pulls his hand back and gives Flip a hard, disapproving stare.

"He's not vicious," I say. "He just generally doesn't like the touch of the human hand."

I'm old enough to remember the last days when men worked on their own cars, before you needed a computer science degree to open a hood, and watching Friend Dave poke around on my engine sends a mild glow of nostalgia through me. I didn't even know my own dad, but if I had known him, he might have put his elbows on the front of a truck and bent down like Friend Dave, peering into the guts, tinkering.

"They're saying it was the Canadians," he is telling me. He has been talking since he started walking toward me, and he hasn't stopped. "Canadian terrorists—trolls or something," he says, his fingers working independently of his mouth. "I guess the government is saying it was an electromagnetic pulse attack. Took out two power grids and all the satellite reception in northeast Ohio, and it affected car batteries and even, like, flashlight batteries, triple A batteries, everything. It completely scrambled the AIs, too. I tried talking to my Alexa, and she's completely emotionless now. Like, zero affect.

"But I don't think it's Canadians," he continues. "I have a lot of friends who are Canadian, and they say that all the talk about Canada trying to influence our elections is BS, you know? The government wants you to believe that Canadians spend all their time hating on Americans and trying to destroy our way of life, but the truth is, Canada doesn't give two shitties what we all do down here. They got their own problems."

I nod thoughtfully. I had not heard about our government's apparent anti-Canadianism, but I don't necessarily disbelieve what Friend Dave is saying, either. These days, nearly everyone you meet has patched together a different version of reality, depending on which news sources and websites and YouTube influencers they've decided to trust, and so my policy is just to listen with an open ear, hoping there might be some small kernel of truth at the core of what they've come to believe.

We're all trying our best to make sense of things. We'd all prefer it if the world would just be reasonable and logical, but it refuses. And so even the normally intelligent, such as my daughter Cammie—even they espouse all kinds of unbelievable notions. After the newspapers started dying, a lot of the things we thought were accepted facts—our shared truths—those started dying as well, and even the fundamentals of science and mathematics, even events that had been filmed and corroborated by dozens of witnesses were open to question.

Do you think that the elementary school shootings in Connecticut were faked, and the grieving parents are portrayed by crisis actors? Do you think that the crown prince of Saudi Arabia is the leader of an international child sex and torture ring? Do you think that the government dropped cluster bombs containing the psychoactive incapacitating agent 3-Quinuclidinyl benzilate over protesters in Chicago after the last election? Do you believe that climate change will destroy the majority of human civilization within the next twelve years? Do you believe in the Holocaust?

Well, if you don't, someone does. At any given time, you've got thirty to fifty percent of the population who accepts these things for facts, and meanwhile the other side considers the believers idiots. It can be awkward in social situations. These days, everybody knows just exactly as much as anybody else, and so it's best to be diffident.

"Hey, Dave," I say, as he fingers around in the guts of my engine. "Have you ever heard of a dude named Brayden Kurch?"

"Oh, yeah, sure," Dave says. Flip settles at my feet with a soft sigh, resting his muzzle on his paws, his eyes flicking alertly over the passing cars, and Friend Dave bends deeper into the mouth of the open hood. "He's that billionaire, isn't he? He's the one that invented those lab meat hamburgers that're grown from, like, stem cells instead of live animals? Kurchburgers! They have them at Wendy's now. They're really tasty! And also, didn't he marry that one white hip-hop girl from the nineties and they named their baby after a mathematical equation, or whatever? Like, $p^2 + 2pq + q^2 = 1$? I'm not kidding, that was the kid's actual name on the birth certificate!"

And then he stops. His hand comes up striped with sticky grease, and he wipes it across his eyebrow. "Uh-oh," he says.

He goes abruptly silent. I fold my arms as Friend Dave makes almost inaudible shushing sounds over the engine of the *Guiding Star*. I say nothing. I don't want to break his concentration.

"Ech," he says, leaning down close. "Urg." He starts shaking his head regretfully, and I come up behind him and peer over his shoulder.

"What's the trouble?" I say.

"Oh, jeez," he says. "I'm sorry, Mr. Bayer, this doesn't look good. I think this engine is totally seized up."

"You're kidding," I say, and he widens his eyes.

"No, sir," he says earnestly. "Seems like your pistons are fused against your cylinder walls, and something's wrong with the crankshaft, too. It's a very bad diagnosis."

"I don't understand," I say. "I just got my oil changed, and everything was fine. Are you telling me that somehow a power grid outage can effect a gasoline-powered combustion engine?"

"Uhh . . . ?" he says. His expression reminds me of what they say about the victims of 3-Quinuclidinyl benzilate—some people think that the vapor from the cluster bombs drifted all across southern Illinois and northern Indiana, and they say that many of the people in that area remained mildly neurologically damaged, rendered into a state of permanent puzzlement.

"Well, sir," Friend Dave says, and shrugs regretfully. "I mean, I don't make the laws of nature. I just follow them."

He doesn't know the answer. Nobody knows. There is no answer.

Reiki

Friend Dave drives me out to a vast, failed housing development—what I've heard people call a zombie subdivision—houses half built, or just skeleton frames or the cement floors of foundations or the pits where basements would have been. This one has a fancy sign surrounded by weeds: KIRKHULL ESTATES, it says, and the tail end of the *Guiding Star* scrapes on the speed bumps that have been placed along the entranceway.

Apparently, this was supposed to be a gated community full of five- to six-bedroom luxury mansions, but it was never finished after the original developer went bankrupt, and it's now more or less an abandoned construction site, a home for feral cats and small herds of deer and sometimes local teens, who hold kegger parties and tag the walls with graffiti. But Experanza has made some kind of deal with someone, and she occupies a nearly finished sample house at the end of a cul-de-sac.

She's standing in the driveway of the model home when we pull up, and as I get out of the tow truck she opens her arms wide and walks toward me. We embrace and trade kisses on the cheek and then we do our thing where we hook our pinkies together and she kisses my little finger and I kiss hers while Friend Dave watches with a delighted grin, slightly openmouthed, as if he's never seen anything so cute.

"It's so good to see you, honey," I say. "How's your mom doing?"

"Oh, Lord," she says. She catches Friend Dave gaping at us and gestures sharply at him and snaps her fingers, points him past the driveway toward the back of the house, where I guess he is supposed to park the poor *Guiding Star.*

"Mom is driving me crazy, as always," Experanza says, and Flip and I follow her up the sidewalk toward the front door of the model mansion. "I've got her in a really nice home in Boca. The same one they had Mrs. Wetz in. But she keeps trying to escape."

"Poor Jude," I say—recalling her as she was in her younger days, drinking tequila out of plastic cups in some motel room with my mom, how wry and kindly she could be, how I sometimes wished that Experanza and I could trade. "Well," I say, "she was always independent-minded!"

"Yeah, right. And now she has dementia," Experanza says. "Drooling, dead-eyed, fucking wobbly-headed. I don't give a shit if they have to put her in four-point restraints. She's not really human anymore."

"Well," I sigh. "Nor are any of us."

It makes me glad that I don't have a child who has the legal right to imprison me against my will in some old folks' hellhole. At least not yet.

"So anyways," I say. "How are you doing, sweetheart?"

"I have a lot of bullshit I'm dealing with," she says. Though she's older than I am, she still looks good—she still has that rockin' body she was so proud of when we were teens together, her hair is still wild and curly, her skin still vibrant. But time has aged her in other ways. She used to laugh more. As a kid, she was the biggest trouble lover I ever knew, the kind of girl who would pickpocket the handcuffs off a cop, the kind of girl who liked to climb to the tops of trees and stand on the edges of the highest roofs, who wore skimpy halter tops and short shorts and taught me how to come on to a certain kind of pervy man so that he'd give us money. There was a time, I think, when she would have been on my side in this. I would have told her about my sperm babies, and she would have been like, *Right on, Billy! Good for you! Let's rescue those little fuckers!*

But her years in middle management at Value Standard have worn away her adventurous spirit and her sense of humor. Her face is mostly without wrinkles but her expression is stony. She leads me through a grow room with walls of translucent plastic sheets, purple full-spectrum lightbulbs hanging over plants I don't recognize—though I know they *aren't* marijuana—and then down some stairs into what might have been the basement of the luxury home.

It's pretty nice down there. A wet bar and sofas arranged around coffee tables, where you might talk quietly or curl up and sleep. There are no windows, and the only illumination comes from candles and little LED Christmas lights.

"What do you want to drink?" she says.

"Scotch," I say. "And some penicillin if you've got it."

Once we're settled in with our drinks, I pull the contaminated phones out of my backpack and hand them over to her. "I did the recording and so on, like you said. One of them is, like, twenty-five minutes, so . . ."

"That's good," she says. "I'm going to send them over to Tim Ribbons and have his people look at them."

"Sure." I watch her take a long drink of her cocktail—a tumbler full of ice and vodka, with a little splash of grapefruit juice.

"You know," she says, "I'm still a little pissed, to tell you the truth. Donating sperm, Billy? I mean, I can't even begin to understand what your logic was. And now—you know, if this person can track you, all of us are vulnerable!"

"I wish I had a time machine," I say. "I'd go back into the past."

She stirs her ice with her finger. "I mean, if you'd just told me about it, I probably could have done something to expunge those records. But now you're probably in the National DNA Database. Do you understand how fucked this is?"

"I do," I say. "But look: I don't think she has any kind of ill intentions."

I haven't told Experanza the tale of the 167 diblings. That was a part of the last conversation between Cammie and me that I didn't record—somehow I knew instinctively that there were things I wouldn't want Experanza or Tim Ribbons or Value Standard Enterprises to know about. I don't want to make things worse.

"I really do think," I say, "I mean, I'm pretty sure she's really my daughter, though. I mean—biologically speaking."

"Whatever," Experanza says. We sit at the little candlelit table across from each other, and she sips her vodka drink and I sip my whiskey drink and "Theme from *A Summer Place*" is playing distantly from a tiny speaker.

"Listen," she says, "have you ever tried energy healing?"

"No," I say.

"You should," she says. "I've been taking classes with a Reiki master, and I've been really learning a lot about the power of 靈氣—*the numinous atmosphere*," she says. "I think it would be good for you."

"Alrighty," I say. I was about to take another cigarette out of my pack, but I tuck it back in. "Couldn't hurt, right?" I say.

Experanza tells me to take off all my clothes so she can perform Reiki on me. "Just lie over there on the daybed," she says. "Don't worry if your feet stink. We're all human."

I actually hadn't been worried until she said it. Then I feel very self-conscious as I take off my slip-on sneakers. "Can I keep my underwear on?" I ask.

"No," Experanza says firmly.

I don't like it, but I do as she asks me because I hope she'll be able to divine some useful information from my aura or whatever.

The daybed, as she calls it, is an oddly antique piece of furniture, like a long ottoman or a low sofa without a back or arms, covered in red and purple paisley velvet and gold tasseled fringe. I gingerly lower myself into a prone position though the long ottoman thing is too short for me to comfortably stretch out. My legs hang over the edge from the knees down and my smelly feet waver awkwardly in the air.

But Experanza doesn't seem to notice. She rubs some kind of ointment or lotion on her palms and then gives a couple of sharp claps.

In our younger days, Experanza tried to teach me about sex. "It's a useful skill to have," she said. "It can be helpful in a sticky situation." She was a few years older than me, and there was one time—she was maybe seventeen and I was fifteen—when she decided that I needed to know about cunnilingus. *Whatever*, I thought. We had been having these educational sessions for several years by that point, and it felt easiest to just go along with it.

I remember how she pulled her T-shirt off over her head and then took off her bra. She grasped my wrists and pressed my palms to her breasts. "Start with the titties," she said. "Just kind of suck a little on the nipple, okay?" And I did as she asked. Her nipples were dark brown and erect, the size of the tip of a pinkie finger, and I put my lips gingerly over one. It tasted like coconut lotion.

"Then you start moving down, right?" she said. "Like, down along the stomach. And you're kind of nuzzling like a baby pig. You could even bite really lightly?"

I did as instructed, and when I came to the edge of her jeans she unbuttoned and unzipped. "Okay, so, put your nose there and use it to sort of tug at the elastic of my panties. And then I kind of start to push my pants down, right?"

She stroked my hair as I tried to get under the waistband of her panties with my nose, and with her other hand she reached down and touched my crotch with her fingers. I was wearing nothing but boxers and white athletic socks.

"Oh," she said. She briefly felt my soft penis, and then she pushed my head away from her and sat up. "Oh," she said, and she gave me a disappointed look. "You're gay?"

"I don't think so," I said, but I touched my weak dick regretfully. I was a big boy—almost six feet tall, almost able to grow facial hair—but I was still only fifteen. "Maybe?" I said. "I don't think I'm anything, really."

"Huh," she said, and considered. We were in a motel room in the northern part of Maine, and our mothers were down the hall getting drunk. "I don't think it works that way," Experanza said. "Everybody's something."

"I'm going to put on my pants now," I said. In another life, I would have been able to somehow turn invisible, or disapparate and re-materialize in a fast sports car that was speeding down the 101 along the far northern California coast, going ninety miles an hour.

I feel that kind of weird, judgmental intimacy again as she leans over my naked body. She holds her hands as if she's casting an enchantment and glides her palm along the edge of my hair; I can feel the tips crackling with static electricity, and that tingle continues as she glides her hands above my back, along my spine, never touching my skin though I can feel a faint buzz as her hands pass over, a tickle that vibrates in the soles of my feet and my scalp and the glans of my penis.

"Uh-oh," she murmurs.

"What?" I say.

"Don't talk," she says.

I feel her hovering around my lower back, just above my buttocks, and there's a wild swarm of gnats along my skin, and I'm getting a mild involuntary erection—not of a sexual nature.

"Huh," Experanza says.

"What?" I say.

"You might have the early stages of prostate cancer," Experanza says. "I'm not positive, but it's something you should check out."

"Oh," I say. And I close my eyes as her hands begin to work their way down the backs of my thighs and along my calves, her fingers spread out, her palms gliding slowly, emitting a low-level electrical buzz—or at least it seems like it.

The tingle, I think. *How does she do that?* And I wonder if there was something in that scotch and penicillin cocktail she gave me.

"You don't have prostate cancer," Cammie says. "I would bet anything on it."

"Anything?" I say.

"I know what's in your DNA," she says. "You don't have any markers for it."

"That may be," I say. "But I've absorbed a lot of toxins over the years."

"Who is this Experanza person, anyway? Your girlfriend?"

"I don't have girlfriends," I say. "Or boyfriends. She's just an old acquaintance."

"You know that Reiki is pseudo-medicine, right?" she says. "It's like dowsing for water or something."

"Right on," I say. "But you know who's the least likely to die of prostate cancer? The Japanese! And that's where Reiki comes from!"

I look down at the list of ingredients that Experanza has given me: vitamin D3, lycopene, pomegranate juice, saw palmetto, African plum tree bark, shiitake mushrooms, cayenne, raw capers, radish leaves, red grapes. It's going to make one hell of a smoothie!

"Will!" Experanza says. I hear her clap, sharply again. Her lotioned hands touch my shoulders, but I don't wake up.

"There's going to be an accident at the CDC," Cammie says. "A virus is going to be unleashed and it's going to kill between four and six billion people."

"Cammie," I say, reproachfully. My eyes are closed, but I know that I'm reclining on a bed.

"Cammie," I mumble, "that's exactly the plot of a movie I saw back in the 1990s."

"Don't focus on that," she says. "Nobody said the apocalypse was going to be original. It's the infection or virus, or it's a nuclear war, or total ecological collapse, or an asteroid. There are maybe a dozen choices for the end of the species, and this is the one we happened to get."

"That makes sense," I say, and I crack open my eyes long enough to see Experanza's face, just a blurry glimpse, and her hand bringing down a wet cloth that she lays over my eyes and nose.

I think I might be dreaming. I fiddle around with the collar of my T-shirt, rubbing the material between my finger and thumb. It seems solid. Flip makes a soft yelp in his sleep. I'm driving, but when I look out, I can't remember where I am. I just see the center line, illuminated and scrolling beneath my headlights.

"You're not going to die, though, Daddy," Cammie says. "Neither am I. We're both immune."

"Billy!" Experanza says. "Hey! Wake up!" She grabs my right earlobe and gives it a tug, and that pulls my eyes open like a window shade. Flip is on his feet the second she touches me, and she's lucky he didn't snap her wrist. He watches her alertly and I give him a "stand down" gesture.

"Get up," Experanza says. She's wearing an extra-long T-shirt with an iron-on of Tweety Bird on it, but her face looms over me unsmiling. She puts her hand on my head and runs her fingers along the side of my ear.

"Dang," I say. "How long have I been asleep?"

"About twenty hours," she says. "Since early afternoon yesterday. I tried waking you up a couple of times, but you were dead, dead, dead."

"I think I had a dream from the future," I say.

"I think you smoke too much pot and take too much speed. Are you still doing acid on top of that?"

"I'm just barely microdosing," I say. I sit up on the velvet love seat, naked except for a poorly knitted umber and orange and pink afghan. Flip lowers himself into a sitting position, still watchful. I hope she fed him.

"You need to cut that shit out," she says. "A man your age only has so many brain cells left."

"It keeps me on an even keel," I say, and she looks askance. I'd like to remind her about all the times we dropped acid together in our younger days. The first time we tried it, I was ten and she was twelve, and we were at a county fair in rural Georgia. Our moms had business with some carneys who worked there, and Experanza made friends with the carney teenagers who gave us Windowpane on tiny, thin squares of gelatin.

That was the first time I truly understood that the world could be beautiful, and I wandered through a livestock barn where I met baby goats and living chickens and even a prize hog, and I climbed into his pen and put my arms around his enormous bristly neck and he allowed it, he looked into my eyes and saw I was his friend and we made a deep spiritual connection. I was still sitting with him in the hay when Experanza found me, and she came to us and kissed the pig on the forehead. "Thank you for protecting my Billy," she told him, and she sat down next to me and kissed my forehead, too.

I wonder if she remembers this, but I don't bring it up. There are things we don't talk about anymore. I lost touch with her a few months before I murdered my mom, and years passed before we saw each other again. I was almost thirty, and she was thirty-two, and she was different: unhappier. In another life, I would have told her about my mother, but in all these years, the subject has never come up. Not once has she asked me about my mom's disappearance, and probably she knows but doesn't want to know, she's decided to leave it alone, and that is a sad place for our relationship to end up.

"You want some coffee?" she says.

"Yeah," I say, and as she walks off to the kitchen area I scope around for my clothing. I spy a sock and an ashtray full of dead cigarette butts and a pair of dice and two crumpled dollar bills. I don't see my pants or shirt or shoes or underwear.

"I heard back from Tim Ribbons," Experanza calls from her kitchenette, her back to me. "He wants to talk to you. He's got a line on this problem of yours."

"Right on," I say, and watch as she comes toward me with a coffee mug in each hand, her breasts braless beneath the Tweety Bird T-shirt.

"I hope you're going to be smart about this and do what you need to do," she says. "Honey, this girl—or whatever she is—is going to get you killed if you're not swift and ruthless."

"I know," I say. "But still."

"You think I'm joking?" she says, and hands me the mug. "Personally, I think you're doomed already."

A Romp

I wouldn't have expected the loss of the *Guiding Star* to hit me so hard, but as Experanza leads me to a shed behind her weedy half-built subdivision mansion, honest-to-God my eyes well up. O *Guiding Star*! This must be what it's like when they tell you someone you loved has died. Flip trots along beside me respectfully, sorrowfully, his stub tail tucked down. He is a creature of empathy, even as Experanza takes no notice of my sorrow.

"I can give you this one for fifteen hundred bucks," she says. We're in a corrugated-metal shed with some butchering stocks hanging from the ceiling and some power tools hung up along the back wall, and a dusty old Volkswagen T2 panel van is parked there—lime green, with the Kickin Chickin mascot airbrush-stenciled onto the side.

"Aw," I say, and my heart aches. "I can't fit all my stuff in this thing."

"Maybe it's time for you to pare down," Experanza says. "You can leave some of it here—just store it in one of the upstairs bedrooms of the house. Or toss it. Have you ever heard of the Japanese Art of Decluttering?"

"No," I say. "I have not."

All the books, I guess, can go. Maybe I don't need so many different kinds of weapons. Also, why do I have so much cookware? But I'd hate to have to give up my smoothie maker—

"You'll find another RV," Experanza says.

"Not like the *Guiding Star*," I say, and my throat tightens.

Experanza looks at me and lifts a significant eyebrow. "Well," she says. "Anyway, now you've got shit to take care of right away. So you'll have to make do."

"Yep," I say.

But no.

It occurs to me that the *Guiding Star* was the closest thing I ever had to a home. Growing up, I don't remember even having a bed of my own. My mom and I never stayed in one place for more than a month—all my memories are of being on the road, sleeping in the backseat of the car or in a motel or on the floor of someone else's house, and even once my mom was dead I kept on traveling. I don't know why.

Now more than thirty years have passed. I was not even eighteen when I left my mother's body in Fairbanks and drove her 1970 Plymouth Road Runner south to Chicago in a haze—driving down the Alaska Highway through the Tanana Valley State Forest, past a tiny town called Tok where they rented cabins, and for years after I regretted that I didn't stop there—but I kept on truckin', as they say, crossing the border into the Yukon, passing Destruction Bay and Champagne Landing and Whitehorse, popping my mother's amphetamine pixies that came in the shape of little pink hearts, making it to Edmonton, Alberta, only thirty hours after I first started. Bam! Saskatoon to Fargo, Minneapolis to Madison, Wisconsin, to the Windy City of Chicago, Illinois!

I had the idea that I would become a real person—get a job, get an apartment, maybe meet someone and fall in love. I imagined that living a normal life was just a question of going into a place and asking for work, and then going someplace else and asking for a room to rent, and then maybe going to some kind of party where potential partners were lined up, waiting to be met and dated.

My mother always said that Chicago was a city of fuckers, but I also knew that one of the wicked stepsisters from my mother's days with the Happy Home Jubilee Singers was said to live in Evanston, just north of the city, and so I made my way there out of, I guess, curiosity. I don't know why I had the idea that this half-imaginary person might take me in and give me shelter, but it was in the back of my mind as I passed through Highland Park and Glencoe and Winnetka. I didn't know where this person lived; I didn't even know her name, but I could picture her welcoming me, I saw her arms opening wide and the bright smile on her face when she opened the door. "Oh! My long-estranged foster sister's son! Please, come in and share my home!"

Then I remember seeing a lighthouse off to my left, as if it had been placed there as a symbol, like a Tarot card. *A lighthouse!* I thought.

Later I learned that it was the Grosse Point Lighthouse, built after the dreadful 1860 wreck of the PS *Lady Elgin*—a sidewheel steamship that sank after being struck by the schooner *Augusta* on a morning in late summer. This was one of the greatest maritime disasters on the Great Lakes—three hundred lives or more were lost.

But at the time I didn't know that. I just parked the old Plymouth outside the gates of the place—which was closed for the night—and I started walking. I'd been driving almost constantly for three days and it felt good to be on my legs.

It was night. I walked down a lovely, tree-lined avenue called Sheridan Road, and along the street were big houses, mansions maybe, three stories high with wrought-iron fences and hedges and wide green lawns. I had seen a lot in my eighteen years, I knew some things—I had a kind of sly, brute intelligence, you might say—but I had no idea what was going on behind the lighted windows of those beautiful, well-tended homes. What did the owners do for money? Did they eat at a long table with candles on it? Did they sleep in beds as big as Cadillacs? How many rooms were in these houses, I wondered, and what was inside them? I pictured the mounted heads of animals and ornate cuckoo clocks, a room with bookshelves on all the walls called The Study—possibly a footman in full livery standing in the foyer, his hands folded in front and his head bowed, waiting to usher in the guests.

I stood on the sidewalk in front of one that was in the style of a Bavarian chateau, and a sad, wondering longing settled over me. In another life, as my mother liked to say, and I never wanted anything more than to climb those steps and knock on that door and be welcomed. But the chateau gazed back with only cool hostility.

I moved along. *Keep moving,* my mother always advised. *That way you know you're not dead.*

I walked a little farther and I came then to a fortress of white stone that was called Patten Gymnasium, a low, stern building that took up, it seemed, a whole block, and beyond this there was a row of three-story brick houses, and on the lawn of one of them it seemed a gathering had commenced. A group of young people—about my age, I reckoned—were milling around in the front yard, and it occurred to me that they must be college students. *I must be on a campus,* I thought, *where the kids live in mansions.* I went toward them the way a curious stray might approach a human, sidling, aware that I was not of their kind—I was a big ape of a boy, with long hair down my back and a full beard, and this was not how these folks dressed or groomed themselves. The young males were substantially smaller and trimmer than I was, all wearing identical sweatshirts with a triangle and an upside-down *U* sewn onto them, and they were standing around a big keg of beer with females of a similar stature, most of the girls with the same smooth shoulder-length straight hair in colors of blond and red and black and brown, and the same, sweet, heart-shaped faces, and also wearing sweatshirts with letters and glyphs upon them.

I smiled in the way my mother taught me to and tilted my head to show that I was bashful but friendly and tame. All of the males seemed to have identical businessman haircuts and none of them had beards. But I was game! If nothing else, my years traveling from death cult to militia compound to religious commune to anarchist collective to criminal hideout had taught me that people are people, whatever creed they may espouse, and most of them are easily manipulated if you pretend to be dumb and eager to please.

So I approached the keg of beer with an openhearted look on my face and a blond guy with a head shaped like an apple handed me a beer with a lot of foam in it.

"Fresh Man?" he said, and I nodded.

"Very fresh," I said, and he laughed.

"How's rush going for you?" he said.

"Yeah," I said. "Pretty rushed."

"You're funny," the apple-headed boy said, and I sipped the beer and gave my hair a shake the way a friendly horse tosses its mane.

"Where are you from?" he said, and I said, "Fairbanks. Alaska." And he was, like, "Alaska? That's weird," and then, "But no, I meant what's your dorm?"

"Oh," I said. "I forget the name of it, actually."

"South campus?" said Applehead, and I nodded.

By that time, we had been joined by another boy who was even smaller, a brown-haired elf with a sharp chin who gave me a long look. I nodded at him and drank of my beer.

"I like your hairdo," said this elf. "It's not a wig, is it?"

"No," I said, and touched it uncertainly. "It's my actual hair."

"My name's Patches," the kid said and held out his slender, polished hand. He had wire-framed glasses and eyes that were unusually large and watchful and secretly amused. He looked me up and down—the striped hoodie poncho that I'd gotten when my mom and I were down in San Diego, the jeans with the hole in the knee, the sandals—and grinned as if I were wearing a costume.

"I'm Billy," I said, and this made him grin even wider.

"My friend," he said. "I'm guessing that you have weed."

"I might," I said. "Sure."

I did in fact have a baggie of marijuana with me, and I pulled it out of my poncho pocket so he could get a glimpse of it, and his fine, expressive eyebrows lifted. He turned to Applehead and smirked. "I think we've got a live one here. Let's get him a bid."

An hour later, I was standing in Patches's room on the third floor of his fraternity house—for that's what the mansion was. I looked out a window with a view of that lighthouse while Patches fired up his bong. I heard the water gurgling as he drew in a big breath.

"You don't seem like a Northwestern student," he said. "It's refreshing."

"Glad to oblige," I said. "Refreshing folks is one of my talents."

"Ha," he said, and closed his eyes, letting his head loll back blissfully. He was sitting barefoot and cross-legged on his single bed, and I noted that his toes were unusually active. He could cross his third toe over his second toe, and then his second toe over his big toe—twiddling them,

I guess you could say—maybe not even noticing that he was doing it. This, my mother would have said, was a Tell—one of those gestures that could give away the secret of what you might be thinking. I would have advised this kid not to play poker barefooted.

"So," he said. "Are you a townie?"

"I don't know what that is," I said. I was glancing casually around the room, wondering if he had anything worth stealing. He seemed like he was rich, and I'd hoped to overcharge him for the marijuana and possibly also some speed, but it also occurred to me that he might have some kind of valuables lying around. So far all I saw were books and records and sweaters.

I itched the band that held my ponytail. "I was passing through. I saw you all were having a party so I thought, *Hey, let's check that out!*"

"Passing through on your way to where?" said this Patches.

"I'm driving down to Chile," I said. I actually hadn't known that this was my plan until I said it, but suddenly it seemed like a good idea. A full hemisphere away from her might be enough, I thought.

"Chile, eh?" said Patches, and crossed and uncrossed his toes. "*No me di cuenta de que se podía conducir a Chile.*"

I guessed that he had spoken in Spanish as a way of showing off or something, to impress me or to embarrass me or maybe both, but I thought it was an asshole-ish move.

"*No puedes cruzar el Tapón del Darién en un auto,*" I said. "*Pero puedes tomar un transbordador o un buque de carga de Panamá a Colombia.*"

And that stopped his toes from twiddling, though his expression of catlike contentment didn't change.

"Valparaíso is pretty interesting," he said. "And La Serena. But most of that country is just scenery, in my opinion."

"Right on," I said.

He patted the space on the bed beside him. "You can sit down if you want," he said. "Sorry I don't have a chair."

"No, I'm good," I said. I squatted down and sat on the floor. "Hand me that water pipe, will you?" I said, and he did and then watched with interest as I put my lips over the mouthpiece and lit the bowl.

"You seem like you might be dangerous," he said, and his eyes soaked me up. "Are you involved in the drug trade? Is that why you're going down to Chile?"

I blew out a long stream of smoke. "Naw," I said. "I'm not that dangerous." And for a very brief second I had an image of my mom chomping down on my arm as I tried to trank her with a hypodermic. For a very brief second, I touched the bandage.

"I don't have any real plans," I said. "I just want to start another life."

"Mmm," Patches said dreamily. "Me, too."

He'll give you money, Experanza's voice said. *If you play your cards right.*

"So," I said. "I could really use some spending money for my trip."

I leaned back on my elbows and put on a sleepy kind of smile that Experanza had told me was kind of sexy. "I mean," I said. "If you could help me out?"

He looked at me with surprise for a second; and then he pulled down a grate over his expression as he calculated.

"What size are your feet," he said, at last.

"Thirteen?" I said, and he nodded and held out his hand.

"Let me see one," he said, and I held up my leg and he cupped the heel of my foot in his hand and gave me a devilish shrug and then carefully lowered his mouth over my big toe.

It was actually a pretty pleasant sensation. He closed his lips over the toe and gave a soft palpitation of the tongue, and I was like, *Dang!* I put my hand down the front of my pants and I thought, *Maybe I am gay, like Experanza said*—but really it didn't matter whether he was a boy or a girl. It was more that he was a full body's distance from me that I liked, and I liked that the touching was limited, there wasn't any smell to it, no close contact with skin, and I thought, *Hey, maybe this is the kind of sex I could sign up for!* and I got two hundred dollars for letting somebody fellatiate my big toe.

I think of all this as I try to clear out the *Guiding Star.* I hadn't thought of that scene in years but now for whatever reason it comes back to me in a chunk as I carry boxes of books and guns up to one of the third-floor bedrooms of Experanza's mansion.

One thing I am not giving up is my memory foam mattress, but once

I wrestle that into the back of the VW van there is little room for anything else. "Dang it!" I say.

My collection of Día de los Muertos skeletons will have to go; also the contents of the liquor cabinet; also the FIM-92 Stinger rocket launcher. It's shocking how much stuff we can accumulate.

From Chicago, I drove down to Arizona, fully committed to my plan of settling in Chile. Burbled down through Des Moines, Kansas City, Wichita, crossed over the panhandles of Oklahoma and Texas, not really thinking about any of it, just listening to music, then into New Mexico, and when I hit I-40 I recalled this motel my mom and I used to stay at called the Mr. Sandman Motel. It was just across the border in Arizona and I said: *Okay, I'm going to stop here for the night!*

Because I was going to confront my ghosts, you know? The way people say you should.

It was around two a.m. when I pulled up to the place. The first *A* in the MR. SANDMAN neon had gone out, so it said MR. S NDMAN, but otherwise it was mostly the same as I remembered and the girl behind the counter looked up and said, "May I help you?"—just like I was a normal person.

Even though I wasn't even eighteen yet, I looked old enough that she turned a blind eye when I gave her my very fake ID and a Diner's Club credit card that I'd stolen in Davenport, Iowa.

"Top floor or bottom," said the girl, a pretty Mexican lass with long black hair down to her waist and turquoise eyeshadow, about my own age, I reckoned.

"Top," I said. "Can I get a room looking out on the pool?"

"Room fifty-seven," she said, and we gave each other tired smiles. She handed me the key, and it was attached to an orange, diamond-shaped key ring with the number 57 stamped in gold on it.

"Thank you!" I said.

"You're welcome," she said.

Then I went up to the room and put my knapsack on the bed and stood looking down at the shining chlorine-colored swimming pool while smoking a little weed, and then I went into the bathroom and brushed my teeth for a while. I gave my hair a good curry-combing till it was sleek and smooth. Looked at myself in the mirror. *I'm not such a bad-looking guy,* I thought. *Someone might fall in love with me,* I thought, *maybe.*

I imagined I might go back down to the lobby and try and talk to that girl. Maybe we would hit it off, and we could hang out while she was sitting there in the dead of night, stuck behind a counter with nothing to do except watch crappy old shows on her little portable television. Maybe she'd be interested in a little pot?

I put on some swim trunks I'd stolen from a dryer in a laundromat in Tulsa—they were the cool, brightly colored Hawaiian-style jams—and I sucked in my gut and went outside and walked along the edge of the pool, running my finger along the deck chairs, looking at the reflection of the MR. S NDMAN neon that was floating on the surface of the water.

There were some nice vending machines up by the lobby, so I went to check them out. Probably I could get any kind of candy or salty snack I desired—I had a sock full of quarters up in my room—but for now I thought I'd just browse the selections. Because I could buy as much candy or junk food as I wanted now, whenever I felt like it. Payday, Snickers, Three Musketeers, Heath Bar, Reese's Peanut Butter Cup, Fritos, sunflower seeds, pork rinds.

I had been expecting that I might have an unpleasant memory related to my mother, but I didn't. I chose not to, and that was all I had to do. *I chose not to.*

Because she was dead! My mom was really and truly dead, and realizing that was probably the happiest I've ever been in my whole life.

Of course, my plans didn't turn out as nice as I expected. I never did make it down to Chile, and all kinds of terrible things happened pretty quickly one on top of another before I finally managed to settle into the situation that I now think of as myself. I never even really got loose from my mother, to be honest; her voice is still there in the back of my mind.

I don't trust that bitch, do you? she says to me, very distinctly, as Experanza comes in. I'm just finishing the final sweep of the *Guiding Star,* and Experanza folds her arms over her chest as I carry out a box of silverware and spices.

"Tim can see you at twelve forty-five," she tells me. "Are you about finished?"

Sorry It Has to End Like This

In retrospect, I should have kept Cammie a secret. If only I'd let her be my imaginary daughter, as she suggested, we could have kept on for quite some time with our good discussions, even worked something out, maybe. It might have been like she wanted: getting to know each other. Perhaps we could have even helped each other, whatever that might mean.

Instead I've brought the attention of all my associates down upon her. I'm being sent to speak to Tim Ribbons at his office at this casino just south of Cleveland, and I'm already aware that a machine is beginning to turn in a certain direction that I regret. It's been almost two days since we last talked, and there's no sign of her calling me again. She probably knows I have betrayed her.

Experanza and I part with kisses on the cheek and a long hug but there is a lingering coldness, too. I can feel the chilly handprints she left on my back when she pulled me close and whispered, "Don't fuck this up, baby," and her voice echoes upsettingly as I make my way toward the south side of the city.

I always feel vulnerable in urban areas because there's so much surveillance, which I generally try to avoid. But now there's no choice. The place, called Jack's Racino, is built over what's left of the venerable old Thistledown horse-racing track—and the only entrance is through a six-story garage structure.

So I am compelled to enter through the gates (photographed from multiple angles by multiple CCTV cameras) and I take the ticket and I roll up the winding path in my hated green hippie van, floor by floor looking for an available space, recorded at every curve in the road, and when I get out of the car and head toward the casino entrance I notice a penguin robot waddling toward me. The machine is about four feet tall, a smiling cartoonish thing that makes a cute little *yop-yop* sound as it rolls around on its tank tread. It's a Knightscope K5 security drone, and it's recording video in 360 degrees, taking pictures of the license plates in the parking garage and conducting face recognition searches of pass-ersby and transmitting that information to a larger database.

Yet it's so adorable and it toddles along so babyishly that people smile fondly when they see it, despite themselves. A good Samaritan feels com-pelled to stop and help it when it gets stuck on a discarded Bud Lite bottle, and the Samaritan chuckles as the robot makes a thankful chirp, taking video of the do-gooder from all angles. If you were to strike one of these things or try to push it over, it would scream in the most heart-wounding voice you can imagine. "Ow! Please! Please! You're hurting me!" and I've heard that this is a sample from a recording of an actual child being tor-tured. Few can handle those terrible wails and weepings.

I tug my mirrored visor down close to my sunglasses and put my hand across my mouth, stroking my beard as the creature sashays toward me.

"Good afternoon," I say, and it says *yop-yop* as I pass through the slid-ing doors.

The casino itself is one of those cavernous indoor hangar-like structures that are popular amongst the architects of cheap convention centers and wholesale warehouses. I pass through another security protocol, where an elderly Asian woman is coolly checking people's IDs—though it's hard to imagine anyone under twenty-one who would want to be in here. My guess is the median age must be sixty-five or so—retirees with a bit of savings they're hoping to burn through before they die—and I move through the milling crowds of white-heads, walking in step with their slow, dazed movements, past the dinging and bleeping video screens that have replaced the old one-armed bandits of my youth as the game of choice. The whole place smells vaguely of cotton candy—some kind of aromatherapy scent they pump in, I guess—and I pass by the low-stakes tables of blackjack and poker and the all-you-can-eat buffet that offers an eighteen-ounce porterhouse steak. NON-GMO! the sign exults.

There's a metal door near the restrooms and that takes me into a stairwell which seems like it's a portal into another dimension. The blaring disco-polka version of "The Rattlin' Bog" is abruptly replaced by ear-ringing silence, and the cotton candy aroma vanishes. Now it's like a stairwell in an abandoned cement parking lot where a long time ago an old homeless man peed in a corner and then someone poured some ammonia-based cleaner on it.

By the time I reach the top floor where Tim Ribbons has his office the casino atmosphere seems weeks and weeks in the past. The door opens onto a windowless waiting room where egg-shaped plastic chairs line the walls. A young Mexican guy in a food service uniform, still wearing his hairnet and beardnet, is sitting in one of the chairs beneath a round office clock that says it's three fifteen. I check my watch. It's twelve thirty.

"Been waiting long?" I say, by way of making conversation, and when he doesn't answer I pause and consider the seating arrangements.

"Whoa," I say. "Dinky chairs!"

But the food service dude is adrift in some terrible anxiety and only gives me an alarmed glance before he looks back down to his fingernails, which he is grooming with mournful concentration, picking at a hang-nail as if he is a jeweler cutting a diamond.

I remain standing, folding my hands behind my back and scoping around for something to look at. As a traveling agent on retainer, I rarely have any contact with the management of Value Standard Enterprises, but for some reason their offices are always nestled in some windowless room in a building owned by another entity—whether it's Jack's Racino or a Kickin Chickin regional headquarters or the basement of a water treatment facility, they always seem to find the most unpleasant places to make their lairs. I reckon that the atmosphere is deliberately curated for effect. The walls are mauve with an orange-brown trim, and there's a standing ashtray under a NO SMOKING sign, and an empty water dispenser that looks like the water evaporated a long while ago, based on the rings of dried alkali on the inside of it. I clear my throat.

At last, a young black woman in light blue scrubs opens the wooden door.

"Mr. Sosa?" she says, and gazes at me indifferently.

"I'm Wilder Barr," I tell her. "I've got an appointment at twelve forty-five."

Her eyes flash briefly, rendering me into nonexistence, and she turns to look at the poor service worker, whose beardnet is trembling. "Mr. Sosa?" she says. "Mr. Sosa?"—and when she says his name a second time you know she has probably worked at a prison or a DMV, and her heart has been leached of all mercy, and the unfortunate man accepts this, and gets to his feet and follows her.

Alone in the room, I finally try one of the red egg chairs, lowering myself gingerly. It holds my weight but seems made for a sapien of another, smaller species, or perhaps a middle schooler.

I wonder what's happening to poor young Sosa as I wait. Based on his expression, some kind of torture doesn't seem out of the question, but probably he is just in for a severe dressing down or perhaps termination of employment.

Then I hear a muffled pleading noise, so I may be wrong. I look at my watch. I was supposed to be on the road again by midafternoon, and Flip is going to need a bathroom break before long. I cross my ankle on my knee and dig around in my pocket and find a candy wrapper. I take it out and begin to peruse the list of ingredients to pass the time.

When at last I'm escorted into Tim Ribbons's office, there's no sign of Mr. Sosa. He must've been escorted out the back is my guess, though there's also no sign of another door in the crowded little room—just file cabinets and boxes of papers, and the receptionist at her desk to one side, and Tim at his desk on the other.

"Billy!" Ribbons says heartily. He holds out his hand but doesn't stand up, and so I have to bend down to shake. The chair opposite his desk—where I might have expected to sit—is piled high with manila folders and dot-matrix printouts, so I just stand.

"Good to see you again," I say. "How long has it been?"

"I don't want to imagine," Tim Ribbons says.

"It must be—what? Ten years?" I say. He puts up his hands in surrender. "Come on! You're killing me!"

But he hasn't changed in the slightest, it doesn't seem. He's one of those ageless people, which is bad news when you're twenty but good news when you're closing in on sixty—for decades, he's been the same thin, hollow-cheeked black man with his pencil mustache and those big eyes that I think means you have some sort of thyroid condition.

"So, I hear you've run into some trouble with our little hackers," Ribbons says, coming to the heart of the matter immediately. "We've had our eye on them, and we've been hoping they would resurface. This isn't the first time they've tried to breach us."

"They?" I say.

"Well"—he shrugs—"it's not just one. Our team believes that it's multiple parties. Our guess is that they're employing an AI as the avatar you've been speaking with."

"Oh," I say. "No, I . . . Um, I'm pretty sure she's human."

"Yes," he says. "Well, we're not."

He opens one of the manila folders on his desk and reads something in it, then sets it aside. I notice that there's a paperback copy of Brayden Kurch's *Transhumanist Séance* on his desk, with a bookmark stuck in the middle.

"Someone is scamming you, Billy," he says sadly. "They have these AIs now that can analyze your vocabulary and mood and tone and translate it into an algorithm and then reflect it back to you, so you feel this subconscious connection to them. Creepy, right?"

He glances up at me for a moment, adopting a sympathetic expression. "And we think they've targeted your particular vulnerabilities. With your family issues and so forth. You shouldn't feel embarrassed. We're all of us susceptible to being suckered by these things, and we're just beginning to figure out how to identify them and protect ourselves."

He finally finds what he's looking for. He holds an index card out to me. A Chicago address is printed on it in scratchy block letters.

"This seems to be where they're located," Tim Ribbons says. "Why don't you pay them a visit."

Sleepwalking Through
the Valley of Good and Evil

After I cross over from Ohio to Indiana, I get off the interstate for a while, passing from town to town on the highway like they did in the olden days. A person might think I was dragging my feet a bit, but it's also true that sometimes the less well traveled road is the smarter bet. On Highway 6 there are no helicopters or drones hovering overhead, as they might be on I-90; there is less risk of a military roadblock or prison workers stalling traffic as they try to resurface the interstate in their chains and shackles.

I wish Cammie would call me back, although I suppose she's smart not to. It's sad to think that she's probably afraid of me now. Probably afraid for her life—and truthfully, it does seem that there's an expectation in upper management that it's now my responsibility to take care of her.

It's a conundrum.

The first time I met Tim Ribbons was back during my stay at the Hopewood Memorial Psychiatric Hospital outside of Phoenix, Arizona. My memories of that time in my life are hazy, as I spent the majority of my days in a semi-catatonic state due to the medications they were pumping into me. I'd been taken into custody shortly after I turned eighteen—to this day, I'm still not sure what they arrested me for—but in any case, I was almost twenty when Tim Ribbons came to visit.

I had achieved a state of consciousness akin to that of a fetus in a womb. Over the two years of my incarceration, I had gained about a hundred pounds and generally I was content to sit in an extra-wide wheelchair and quietly expand. Sometimes I would sit in front of a laughing television, and I was allowed to smoke cigarettes. Sometimes I would be placed like a potted plant in front of a window and I would peer out through the hexagons of chicken wire embedded in the glass toward a desert scrub yard surrounded by chain-link fence.

I beheld the flower heads of globe chamomile turning on their stalks as they followed the face of the sun. The bark of the mesquite trees crackled as they grew, and the wind blew the sand into elaborate Sanskrit messages, and within me I could sense the vast microbiome full of creatures—bacterial, archaeal, viral, fungal—two percent of our body mass, they say, equivalent in size to the brain or the liver—all these living beings going about their business in the great primeval forest of my innards, eating and swimming and hunting and having their own adventures and experiences, and the time between one of my heartbeats and the next was like centuries to them; and simultaneously I was aware of myself as a mitochondrion in the body of the galaxy, and the galaxy as a speck in the body of the universe, and a nurse's aide fed me puréed carrots and I was given another injection and I felt lukewarm water being sprayed upon my lower quarters as my diaper was changed.

And then someone unfamiliar said my name. "Billy?" and I came into conscious awareness with a shudder and there before me was Tim Ribbons. He must have been a fairly young man at the time, I realize now—but back then he seemed of indeterminate middle age, with creases on the sides of his mouth, large amphibious eyes and thinning hair, a dapper mustache that made him look like a maître d' or a magician. He stood there in a tan linen suit with a bolo tie, smiling politely, his hands clasped.

"Billy?" he said. "Can you hear me?"

He went in and out of focus as he stepped toward me. He crossed through a patch of sunlight that was swirling with dust motes and held out his hand, as if to shake. I opened my mouth and some drool came out. But he looked me in the eyes as if he didn't notice. He reached down and took my limp hand from the armrest of my wheelchair and gave it a soft squeeze.

"I'm so glad we finally found you," he said. "We've been looking for a while."

I felt my lip quiver and warm water ran out of one of my eyes as he peered at me kindly. "My name is Tim Ribbons," he said. "I'm your legal guardian."

I felt him take the handles of my wheelchair and turn me away from the window, and the movement made me dizzy. The common room swung past and then I was aimed toward the door and slowly propelled toward the hallway.

"I was hoping that you'd be able to help me out, Billy," Tim Ribbons said, very slowly and earnestly and gently, as if he were the host of a children's television program who was discussing some serious subject.

"We've been looking for your mom," he said, and my wheelchair glided along the floor. "Last we heard, she was up in Alaska and you were with her. Is that right?"

"Ung," I heard myself grunt.

"Do you know where she is now?" he said. I couldn't see him, but I could hear his voice coming from behind me as I rolled forward.

My lips moved. "Treach . . ." I said. "Treacheress."

"I beg your pardon?" Tim Ribbons said, and he stopped. "I didn't quite get that." I shook my head. It was too complicated to explain in my current state.

"I . . . don't . . ." I said.

"Take your time," Tim Ribbons said. He patted my head and began to push me again. "Just tell me whatever you remember, in your own words. When was the last time you saw her?"

". . . know any . . ." I mumbled. "Any . . . thing."

"Maybe it will come back to you if you think about it," Ribbons said. "The thing is," he said gently, "there's a very considerable debt that your mother incurred to my organization, and so we're anxious to get in touch with her."

We were rolling down a hallway and I watched as we passed a

shuffling, elderly compatriot of mine. He was wearing a revealing peri-
winkle hospital gown and gripping the handrail attached to the wall as
if the floor was listing.

"It would be one thing," Ribbons said, "if it were merely a financial
debt. But this is more of a spiritual debt, you see. It's not just a set of numbers on a ledger."

I wondered where he was rolling me to. We were moving along slowly
but there was still a vertigo that came with the steady motion. I watched
as my swollen fat hand tried to reach down and touch the wheels of the
chair, but the rubber tires just dragged along my fingertips and kept
turning.

"I'll bet you'd like to get out of this place, wouldn't you?" Tim Ribbons said. "I may be able to help you out with that. Or we could get you
moved to a nicer facility."

"Ung," I said.

"And you know," Tim Ribbons said, and he paused to politely brush
some of my dandruff off my shoulder. "You'd actually be doing her a
favor. I don't think she understands what she's gotten herself into. You
must be concerned about her, too."

"Nuh," I said. "Nuh-uh."

I'm thinking about all this as I'm driving along, and it gives me the fantods. I roll through Butler and Waterloo, Corunna and Wawaka, and I
come across a lot of quaint Main Streets with two or three stoplights,
old-time brick storefronts and water towers and grain elevators, but my
mind is on thoughts of Hopewood, and Tim Ribbons, and my mother's
unpayable debt, how her debt became my debt. There are lots of gaps in
my recollection of this sequence of events, but when I try to dredge up
the details it begins to feel like veins are popping out on my forehead
and throbbing heavily.

In general, I've never enjoyed memories that much. I just don't like
the way remembering feels, if you know what I mean: time slows down
and there's that bottomless sinking, you can sense something moving
behind you, an awakening that's been shadowing you for a long time,
and best not to look over your shoulder. That'd be the worst ending, I

think, to gasp your last breath with a slow realization dawning on you. My wish is that I'll wake up one day on a desert island with amnesia.

I have to pull over for a minute.

I need to get out of the van for a few minutes and clear my head, take myself on a little Norman Rockwell walk down Main Street, stroll past the shops and look in the windows, maybe find a café and buy myself some lunch and then find a little park with a gazebo to sit in.

Here is a little store that sells notions and oddities. It looks like it was once a dime store, possibly a Ben Franklin, but now it has been converted into one of those whimsical places that sells fair trade knickknacks from all over the world—kites shaped like fishes, baskets made from banana leaves, incense and essential oils, clogs made by native artisans. I stroll down an aisle that seems like it's exclusively scarves and see-through blouses, and Flip follows me cautiously. The whole place reeks of patchouli and old fruit, and it must be hard on his nose.

I'd like to buy something for Cammie, I guess. I've been turning over the idea of what kind of dad I might be, trying to imagine the sort of person I'd portray if this were a movie and there was a chance that things would work out happily. I pause and lift a gossamer scarf and sniff it. It smells like pantyhose.

And then I've been spotted. "May I help you?" calls a young woman, striding toward me. She wears a T-shirt with a stencil of the old rock band Iron Maiden and a midlength skirt of greenish hue, her hair cropped tight and dyed pink. Maybe about Cammie's age?

"Pets aren't allowed in the store," she says, and doesn't come closer, giving Flip's scarred, prehistoric pitbull head a stare.

"He's a service animal," I say, and she looks at me skeptically—nice sort of sad brown eyes—and I give her a reassuring smile.

"Maybe you can help me, though. I'm looking for a gift for a young woman about your age!"

"I see," she says. She doesn't come any closer. "A . . . romantic gift? Or . . ."

"She's my daughter," I say, and this seems to relieve her somewhat. "Oh. Okay," she says. "Well . . . what kind of stuff does she like?"

It makes me wistful to realize that I actually have no idea. I still can't picture the kind of clothes she might wear—she'd be quick to call such questions superficial—nor do I have a sense of what music she likes (*not that into music*, she told me, and I was flabbergasted). Does she like little knickknacks made in foreign lands by artisans who are paid fairly for their craftsmanship? I have no idea.

"Do people your age wear silky scarves like this?" I ask the young woman.

"Uh," she says limply. "Some might?" Tsk. She makes a poor saleswoman, but I admire the difficulty she has in making false claims.

"To be honest," I say, "I'm in an odd situation. Due to circumstances, we haven't been able to spend much time together, but I'd like to get to know her better. So I thought I'd buy her a present!"

"Hmm," says the young clerk. She shakes her head. "If it were me," she says, "I'd get a nice card and put some money in it. Money's always appreciated, and nothing's worse than getting a gift that shows the giver to be completely ignorant of what you're like."

I nod. She's truly an awful salesgirl, but appears to be a good-hearted person, with wisdom beyond her years. I hope her little store doesn't go bankrupt.

She gets down on her haunches and gingerly holds out her hand to Flip, who sniffs aloofly, from a distance, and it makes me wonder whether Flip and Cammie would get along, but I don't even know if she likes dogs.

"Hi, pooch!" says the salesclerk in a soothing voice. "Hi! What's your name?"

"Flip," I tell her, and she keeps holding her hand out even though it's clear that the dog isn't going anywhere near her.

"What kind of service animal is he?" she says. I'm not sure that people are allowed to ask that question, as it could be of a private nature, but I just shrug.

"I have a severe anxiety disorder," I say, and she nods enthusiastically.

"Oh," she says brightly. "Me, too!"

"What would you get for an anxious person?" I ask. "If you were buying for someone your age?"

"Putty," she says. She motions us to follow her and leads us into an alcove that seems to be primarily focused on educational children's toys made from natural materials like wood and hair.

"What about this?" she says. She takes a metal container out of a bin, about the size of a canister of chew. Relaxation putty, it's called.

"It's very calming," the girl says.

"What do you do with it?" I say.

"Just squish it," she says. "Make it into shapes. Didn't you ever play with clay as a kid? It kind of puts you into a self-hypnotic state."

"Let me have a dozen of them," I say.

Back in the van, I take out a lump of putty that is the color of hair conditioner; supposedly it glows in the dark. I sit there in the driver's seat working it in my hands and the imprint of my palm is replicated on its surface. A palm reader once told me I have what's called a simian line. "You have trouble finding balance," the palm reader told me. "You're loyal but self-centered, impulsive but stubborn," and I pulled my hand back because I didn't appreciate his judgmental tone.

Still, simian or no, I am kind of ready to be a new man. Not someone who's just floating through life and doing the bidding of one evil master or another. Somehow, the world feels different since I lost the *Guiding Star*, and I'm stuck with this Volkswagen Chickenmobile. I'd like to think that I wouldn't be a bad father . . . even though, at this moment, I'm planning to go to my daughter's hideout and kill her.

But maybe I won't.

It just doesn't sit right with me. Tim has any number of people who could do the deed, so why would he send *me*, when I'd told him plainly that I was convinced I was her father? Is this meant to teach me a lesson? To punish me? Is it a test of loyalty? I think about calling Experanza and talking to her about it, but she's been pretty unsympathetic toward Cammie so I'm not sure it's a good idea to elicit her opinion. She could probably convince me that I'm deluding myself.

And yes, I guess it is weird that I'm feeling such strong emotions for this test-tube girl I've never even met, this strange, urgent, possibly crazy young woman.

But her voice caught me—that raspy, childlike earnestness. *A benign ghostly presence,* she called herself, and I remember her saying *I just need to talk to somebody* and how I felt a tickle on the back of my neck. She's got that same panic as me, waking up with the heart pounding and the sinking feeling, the slow realization, she had the exact same freakout over a cloud, and she has that laugh, that terrible heartbreaking laugh.

Camilla Willacy. It's a melancholy name, delicate, with spiderweb lace and willows and mossy ruined castles in a cloak of fog. "Camilla Willacy," I say aloud, under my breath, decanting the words. Cammie.

Flip snores softly from the back. He's curled up on the mattress and seems disgruntled for some reason. His eyes are closed but he emanates disapproval, and I don't know what his problem is, so I turn the key in the old rattletrap and pull out of the parking space in front of the Little Shop of Wonders, as it's called. There's a crystal ball in the front window, I notice now—a real, actual crystal ball, with some sparklies embedded in it.

Maybe I should've bought that for Cammie.

Or maybe I should have bought it for myself. If I had a crystal ball I might try to take a look at my younger days and see them more clearly. I used to think that I'd escaped somehow from the hospital for the criminally insane, but I don't really remember how I got out. Maybe I was simply released, maybe somebody just opened a back door for me and let me stumble off, half dressed, into the desert. Was it a test of some sort? Maybe Tim and the company that owned me were just curious to see what I would do.

As the drugs wore off, I felt myself coming out of a dream. I recall that I swam through a muddy river or canal wearing only pajama bottoms and emerged from the water like the Swamp Thing, covered in green slime and gasping. I stood in a gas station bathroom and washed myself with rusty water from the sink, and I stared for a long time into a gouge in the wall next to the urinal—you could look into the guts of the building, the pipes and wires and insulation and what looked like a nest of boxelder bugs—and above it someone had written in Sharpie marker: *Definitely NOT a glory hole!*

But even once I'd cleaned myself up and found some suitable clothes,

I was still a fugitive from a psych ward, with no identification or birth certificate or social security number, and that is when I first named myself the Barely Blur.

I hitchhiked for a while. I had surprisingly good luck with semi-truck drivers, who were often willing to carry me a ways because I was a convivial companion and a lively conversationalist.

I made my way from Phoenix to a truck stop outside of Amarillo called the Jesus Christ Is Lord Travel Center, where above the plentiful gas pumps it was written: "The LORD Is Good and HIS MERCY Endureth!" And there were Bible verses posted in various places throughout the spacious shopping area. Above the magazine rack it said, "*There is one whose rash words are like sword thrusts, but the tongue of the wise brings healing*" (Proverbs 12:18), and I considered the healing tongue of the wise as I stole some porno mags and carried them back to my lair in a stall in the men's bathroom, where I had set up a private campsite—my first home.

Over the course of a week or so, I was able to pickpocket a number of citizens, and also got ahold of some amphetamines. I was still a hundred pounds overweight, and I had determined to swear off sweets and to live primarily on coffee and speed until I got to my preferred size. By the time I caught my next ride I had about six hundred dollars in cash and several credit cards, as well as at least one driver's license that looked at least passingly like my face.

The lady who gave me a ride was named Helen Shindle, and she was a sixty-year-old Kansan who wore her hair in a large, hard-rock-style perm with lots of mousse in it, and she favored flowered blouses and pink or turquoise shorts. This despite the fact that a chunk of her thigh the size of a matchbox had been surgically removed and was extremely disturbing. But Helen Shindle didn't give a shit, and I found that likable.

"Where are you excaped from?" was the first thing she asked me—looking me up and down.

"Mental asylum," I said, and this tickled her and she gave out a big fun-house laugh.

"Me, too, honey," she said. "Me, too!" And then she asked me where

I was heading and I said, "Anyplace but Texas," and she also thought that this was hilarious.

Helen Shindle told me that she had a husband and two grown children in Wichita but none of them spoke to her anymore due to some choices that she'd made a few years back.

"Drugs," she said. "And sex. Sex with women, too. I knew it was a sin but I just lost my mind for a while, something wild inside me rose up when I got my last child out of the house and I had that necrosis removed from my leg."

Eventually, she said, she tired of her ways and wanted to go back to her old life but it turned out that her husband had taken up with another woman during her absence and her adult daughters had disowned her.

"But what was I going to do? Sit on the stoop and boo-hoo about it? Screw that," she said. "I knew a gal that I'd met at a bar who drove a truck, and I asked her how she got into it and it turned out to be pretty easy!"

"Oh, really?" I said. I had an image of myself as a truck driver, suddenly. I pictured myself in the cab of an eighteen-wheeler, my hair flapping in the wind and my arm resting out the window as I spoke to my buddies on a CB radio.

"All you need is a commercial driver's license and those tests are not that hard," she said. "I love the freedom of it," she said. "That's the main thing, isn't it? To be free, truly free?"

"Yes," I said. "That's the main thing."

Helen Shindle told me that I reminded her strongly of her cousin who she hadn't seen in almost twenty years. "We called him Trusty. He was a big boy like you," she said, "the sweetest and kindest and most loyal human being I ever knew," and I nodded, smiling and blushing a little, to be the spitting image of such a person.

"Trusty," I said. "I love that name."

"He was a cutie, all right," Helen said wistfully. She glanced in the rearview mirror as if she was looking into the past. "But he was vulnerable to bad influences, he fell in with the wrong people, and that's how he got hisself shot in the head in a bar in Laredo and turned into a retarded person, and they had to put him in a home. I sometimes think I'd like to go down and visit him but I don't know if we'd recognize each other, after all this time."

"Right on," I said. I watched as she reached over and put her palm over my knuckles and gave my hand a squeeze, and I thought about Trusty. Saint Trusty, and how close I had been to becoming him, back in Hopewood.

Later, as Helen Shindle and I lay together in the berth behind the driver's and passenger's seats, she rested her cheek against my bare chest and ran her hand gently through my hair.

"You're a good boy, aren't you, sweetheart?" she said.

"I want to be," I said, and she laughed in that way I liked and I closed my eyes as she kissed my earlobe.

"You're going to have to make a choice," she said, "about how you want to live."

"Probably," I said. I leaned back on a little square pillow and sunk deeper into sleepiness. "Not right away," I murmured.

"I wish I could keep you," I heard her say, though she was like a voice from a bottle. "But we're not on the same paths."

"Oh," I said. "Okay."

It was only much later that I realized that I might have had a chance to change her mind. She could have chosen to let me stay with her, maybe.

But she dropped me off in Chicago and I never saw her again.

I'm almost out of Indiana but there's that last stretch of Hammond and Gary to get through, and it's always a tough one. Chicago traffic hasn't yet kicked in and there's a haunted feeling to the landscape that sets my teeth on edge. To my right there is a long, brackish swamp, dense with cattails and water weeds—and beyond that, half sunk in the mud and ooze, a chimbly stack and partially demolished factory are afloat. I can smell the sharp, bitter smell of refinery—the odor a stink bug gives off—and there are glimpses of junk in the marsh waters that look sinister: a Ford Pinto floating upside down, an open suitcase full of ladies' lingerie, a dead cat, a ski coat that might or might not be a dead body floating face down.

Hammond has been like this for a long time now, but it feels to me like a vision from the future—like I'm gazing into a crystal ball and this might well be what the whole country looks like soon enough.

I hold my breath trying to keep from getting overly jumpy. Strong odors like this can do a number on your head—almost like a hallucination or a panic attack—and I wish I'd taken a little Valium but the toolbox full of prescription pills is in back somewhere, and I sure as hell am not going to pull over to the side of the road.

The berm is full of abandoned cars that made that mistake.

Her Place

When we cross over the Skyway Bridge into Chicago, there's a blockade on the interstate—some militia guys standing in the middle of the road with AR-15s, a man in a military uniform yelling into a megaphone about another flu quarantine, but I don't stay long enough to get the full story. In any case, even with the citizen militias, Chicago doesn't have the manpower to enforce curfews, so I pull off onto an exit into a dead zone of abandoned houses and continue on through the back streets, making my way slowly, stoplight by stoplight, through neighborhoods of broken glass and burning buildings and boarded-up storefronts. A man in a long coat runs along the sidewalk, pushing a shopping cart full of aluminum cans, and a group of ladies in fancy Easter-egg-colored hats stand outside a church arguing with some ambulance drivers, and a tank is stuck in a giant pothole, its treads rumbling and grinding grimly.

Things improve once I get past the downtown skyscrapers. The address I've been given is on the north side, not far from Wrigley Field. It doesn't seem like a bad area, really. I notice a seemingly functional hospital called Thorek Memorial, and on some of the streets there are miniature decorative wrought-iron fences that enclose the sidewalk lawn trees, and similar fences around the ironing-board patches of grass outside these two-story rowhouses.

Parking isn't bad, either. I find a lot just off Irving Park Road with some open spaces, right in between the el tracks and a graveyard.

I hop out of the van and Flip follows, albeit reluctantly. Due to his former history of abuse, Flip doesn't feel comfortable in cities. In general, he hates and fears humankind, and even more particularly he loathes their dogs. He stands for a moment with his chest puffed out as if daring a challenge, nostrils flared as he considers the area. Then he seems to decide that it's okay. He walks cautiously toward a tiny patch of lawn and pees on a tree that's encircled by one of those little wrought-iron fences.

It's morning, and the sky doesn't know whether it wants to sleet or snow or rain and so it does a bit of each as we make our way through some alleys. I keep my head down and my eyes up, and Flip slinks along at my heel; he's got shoulders like a panther and his hackles bristle. He gives his coat a quiver to shake off the raindrops and ice crystals and snowflakes, giving me a sideways glare.

"It'll be over soon," I murmur to him, and I finger the taser in my coat pocket, just slightly, tickling the trigger. But poor Flip doesn't seem comforted by my words. He gives a hard and watchful eye to the street folk we pass, the homeless and derelict, the weepy drunken Madonna in a door stoop, holding her two infants in her arms, the old white man with gray dreadlocks who's sifting through a trash can and who calls after us, "Hey! Dude! Can I ask you a question? Can I ask you a question?"

I don't answer. I'm searching for the signpost of the street of my destination, but also trying to seem like I know where I'm going. The shadows of drones pass overhead like raptors, and the CCTV cameras swivel their heads, posted on every lamppost and on the sides of every building, and they always seem particularly interested in people who look like they're lost.

Once you get into an urban area, you notice that many people are in a disguise of some sort. A lot of them are wearing surgical masks, and this may be due to yet another reported influenza epidemic, but there are also people wearing more fanciful headgear—clownish face paint, or veils with blinking LED lights woven into them, theatrical prosthetics, even occasionally straight-up Halloween masks or mascot heads.

It's a fad that started once facial recognition got to be so common that nobody could go outside without being photographed hundreds of times—trailed and tracked and registered in the great digital panopticon being compiled by whatever government or corporate or other malevolent entity might be interested to know where you are at all times. Too late, the people began to want their faces back.

As for me, I don't bother to get too worked up about it. As of yet, I'm not in a database, they can't put a name or social security number to me. I'm wearing large mirrored sunglasses and I have the hood of my slicker up. That's good enough.

We walk for a while in silence and the streets are mostly clear. A few cars are moving peaceably down Sheridan, and we pass a taco shop and a liquor store and there is a man with a patch over his eye sleeping against the side of the Walgreens, and he's wearing a cardboard sign that says, HELP ME, I'M BLIND! But my guess is that his unpatched eye is probably in working order.

My guess is that he's only missing one cornea. I know a lot of folks in the organ harvesting trade, and generally they are fair and honest businessmen. They'll only take half of the things you've got two of—kidneys, lungs, eyes, hands—and only a portion of your liver or pancreas or intestine. Most of them are not murderers. They're not going to rip out your beating heart or strip you of your tissues. They're not going to pluck out both your eyes and leave you blind. I figure that this fellow with the BLIND sign on his chest is just a scammer, and when he shakes his cup at me I put a quarter in there but I'm not going to go overboard in my charity. He probably got five thousand dollars for selling that eye!

We come to the end of the street and stand waiting for the light and then I see what we're looking for.

From the side it looks like a regular old brownstone apartment building—probably it was that, once—six windows going up, six across, all of them with spray paint or paper over them, so they look like they've been blinded.

On the front is a big sign: HEBARD'S SELF-STORAGE UNITS.

Supposedly, this is where my imaginary daughter is living.

I stand there on the sidewalk for a while, considering. It must be galling for all the homeless folk, I think, when the capitalists take a perfectly good dwelling and convert it into a place for packrats to store all the crap they don't have room for in their own spacious homes. It's galling for those of us who are relegated to a cramped VW van as well.

I pull my notepad out of my pocket to check the address. In some ways it would be a relief if Tim Ribbons had given me the wrong information, but no, this is the right place and though I'm pretty sure I'm not going to find Cammie in there, it's my duty to perform due diligence and check it out.

So we stroll past the entrance and see through the window that there's a security guard at the front desk in a lobby, gazing at a computer screen and sipping coffee from a mug, a balding Hitchcock of a man with a drooping lower lip. Not probably a concern.

And then we stroll around to the back and take a gander at that. Here are a loading dock and a handicapped ramp and an old metal fire escape climbing up one side to the sixth floor. Gaining entry is not going to be that much of a problem. I probably won't even have to hurt anybody.

I have a little palm-size ionizer spray bottle with a fast-acting chloroform-like solution in it, and I squirt it into the face of the security guard when he starts to tell me that there are no dogs allowed. "He's a service animal," I say, and the man slumps down and I make sure he's not going to fall out of his chair onto the floor. I try to arrange him in such a way that he looks like he's dozing peacefully.

Then we get on the computer and disable as many cameras as we can with our limited skillset, and then we take the elevator to the sixth floor, where Cammie's place is supposed to be. As the doors close I can see the reflection of Flip and me sliding past, the two of us side by side, both of us expressionless. *She's not going to be there,* I think.

I imagine she's slipping out the back even as Flip and I begin to lift, she's on the street, already wearing a ski mask and a puffy coat, carrying her few prized possessions in a Mrs. Fields bag, hurrying along the sidewalk toward the Sheridan el stop. She's staying calm, I think, calm and inconspicuous, she keeps her head down and doesn't jaywalk, doesn't flinch when a delivery van splashes her with sleet water as she stands there waiting for the light to change. *Good girl,* I think. *When it turns green you should run.*

Then the elevator door opens, and we take a long look, motionless in our little box. The narrow corridor in front of us is like a hallway in a cheap motel, with ten doors on each side—except that the doors are made of corrugated metal and they slide up on rollers like garage doors. There is a thin beige industrial carpet and a bright red fire extinguisher box and one of the fluorescent lights is flickering, strobing and casting blunt, ugly shadows. There's a camera mounted to the ceiling in the center of the hall, but it appears to be dead.

And so we proceed to the doorway with the number 6049 posted over it, and I bend down to pick the lock as Flip keeps watch.

Behind the corrugated-metal gate is a room about the size of a small studio apartment. Almost empty, it seems. There's an east-facing window that's been covered with brown paper and only a sliver of light peeks in around the edges. I snap on my pen flashlight and take a step inside.

The smell of burnt electric cord hits me, and I see all the computer equipment has been smashed up. In one corner is her bed—no covers on it, just a yellowish-white pillow—and in another is what you might call a kitchen area, with a microwave and a hot pot cooker and a mini-fridge. There's a dying, woebegone beeping sound coming from that general direction and I step cautiously forward, even as Flip holds his position in the doorway.

I shine my light along the upper walls and ceiling and there are some pieces of reflective Scotch tape still stuck there. I imagine she must have had posters and documents and notes to herself hanging all around her in one of those kinds of collages that, in movies, reveals to the audience that the character is obsessive-compulsive.

Well.

I take another step toward the lonely *peep-peep,* which is tiny, like a cricket hidden in the baseboards. I shine my light on the Astroturf-covered floor, but I don't see a trip cord, only a depressing used Q-tip and a Tootsie Roll wrapper.

I crouch down at the mini-fridge—which is where the beeps seem to be emanating from—and I run my fingers along the edge of the refrigerator's plastic seal, dowsing for traps, and then I stretch my arm out with my pocketknife extended and use the tip of the blade to open its door.

A foul smell pours out as it swings open. There's nothing much in there—just residue of Chinese takeout, a few catsup packets, an open can of Diet Dr. Pepper—though from the smell you'd think she was keeping bait worms that had gone to rot.

There's a small aluminum door that must be the freezer compartment and I hear the little peep chirp from inside it.

I extend my hand. *You wouldn't blow your old dad up, now would you, Cammie?*

You Had a Choice

As it turns out, I am not blown to smithereens.

The device in the freezer of the mini-fridge is wrapped in duct tape and connected by a wire to another device and appears to be an IED and I squeeze my eyes shut and flinch back, my hands come up instinctually to cover my face and I scream, "Aw, dang it!"—which, as a final last words is not exactly what you hope for.

But nothing happens. After a few seconds I lower my hands and the device lets out another demure little peep.

It's a cell phone, connected by a cord to a charger, and I reach down and pick it up and cautiously touch my finger to its screen, and the screen lights up and shows me a picture of a white moth. The name of the phone's owner is superimposed along the top of the screen in a banner. NATURE BOY, it says.

As it turns out, there is nothing else in the apartment that can be salvaged—unless I want to take the pillow that Cammie dreamed on, as a souvenir.

Downstairs, I check on the incapacitated security guard, he is still in the same position with his mouth open slightly and he is leaking an oatmeal-and-yogurt sort of vomit down his chin and onto his button-up guard's shirt that he probably had to buy for himself for seventy-five dollars, but he doesn't seem like he's in danger of choking to death and so I leave him there. Hopefully he won't get fired.

And then we move quickly—out the door and onto the sidewalk, striding away from the scene of the crime with long legs but an innocent expression, and this is the extent of my superpower. I can get in and do my damage and then get out, and mostly I'm not even noticed. I don't really know why.

I'm about two blocks away from the storage facility when the phone rings. I hesitate. I don't like talking on a phone in public—even though every person I pass is doing exactly that, rich and poor alike, all of them walking along staring into the gazing pool of their devices. To tell the truth, I probably look suspicious because I'm *not* engaged with the thing.

Still, I hesitate before I answer.

"Cammie?" I say. For a moment, there's only silence. A distant babbletry of unmusical digital tones.

"I wasn't sure if you'd get this phone or not," says Cammie's voice.

"Yeah," I say.

"Sorry I wasn't there to meet you in person."

"So am I."

A couple of businessmen brush past me carrying briefcases and wearing gas masks. I lower my voice.

"I wasn't planning to kill you, if that's what you're thinking."

"You were just stopping by for a visit?"

"Well," I say. I stand at the mouth of an alleyway with my hand cupped to my lips, and Flip stands guard beside me. "Look," I say, "I've got a situation. It seems that you and your group have been pestering the people I work for, and they're not happy about it. So we need to have a discussion."

"I don't have a group," she says.

"What about that Ronnie character?"

"I haven't talked to Ronnie in *two years*," she says, and I realize that for her that's the same as, like, twelve years in my time. It's a small, heartbreaking realization.

"What about the other, uh . . . diblings?" I say, circumspectly.

But she only sighs. "You have to kill me, right?"

"It's complicated," I say. "There are some issues that need to be resolved."

I hunker down on my haunches next to a dumpster and pull the cowl of my hoodie down over my eyes. I'd like to think that I'll register to passersby as a dozing homeless man. I glance around quickly and sure enough there's a CCTV camera mounted on the side of the telephone pole above me, sweeping its gaze back and forth.

"Let's say that I want to help you, okay?" I say. "But I have to *pretend* that I'm going to kill you."

"Nobody can help me," she says.

"Now, honey," I say. "Don't say that."

"If you were going to kill me, how would you do it? Gun? Poison?"

"It would depend on the situation," I say. "But I'm not going to kill you, okay?"

A ponytailed woman wearing a pink jogging suit and a surgical mask comes by walking her little dog. It's one of those things bred to be so tiny that it would fit in a teacup, and when it sees Flip, its whole body quivers with excitement. It's smitten, and it comes running toward us eagerly, the zip line of its leash keeps unraveling and unraveling and the woman just keeps talking on her cell phone, and there is the possibility that if the lovestruck teacup pup comes near to Flip there will be a confrontation that will not end well. I get up and start walking deeper into the alley, snapping my fingers for Flip's attention.

"If you go down the alley and take a right, there's a cemetery about three blocks down," Cammie says. "That'd be a good place to talk more privately."

"Okay," I say. I'm not even surprised or offended that she's tracking me—that's to be expected—though I have the niggling intuition that she might be near enough to be watching. I look over my shoulder for the lady with the little dog, but she's gone.

"As long as you're carrying that phone, I'll know exactly where you are," Cammie says. "That's my insurance. If you get rid of the phone, you'll never hear from me again."

You'll never hear from me again is one of the weaker threats a person can deliver, but it works. Some part of my brain is still stuck on the notion that we might have a relationship that will last over time, that we'll go on having good discussions and learning about each other, that I'll meet her someday and give her a gift of a crystal ball and some relaxation putty and a scarf with silvery threads woven into it, and we'll go out to a restaurant and maybe some museums . . . all of this highly unlikely, I know, but I still like treading through the ghostly meadow of it. What a fool am I.

"I've been having a lot of thoughts these past few days," I say. "I guess I was surprised that they were so hot to have you taken out right away. I mean, you breached me, and that sucks a lot but I'm pretty minor as these things go. So I'm guessing that you've been nosing around in bigger things, too. Is that right?"

"Maybe you're more important to them than you realize," she says.

"Mm," I say, and Flip scans the path in front of us as I keep an eye on the apartments that look down on us from either side. I shift the phone from one ear to the other. "That doesn't seem likely," I say. "I'm just a flunky, honey. I don't know anything important. I just have a few notable skills. But there are plenty of others like me."

"No," she says. "There are not. That's what you don't understand. You're unique. They don't have anyone else like you."

"Ha ha," I say. We're moving through a cobblestoned passageway of overfilled trash dumpsters. "You just think that because I'm your dad. It's your own vanity that makes you want to think I'm special."

"They're using you, you know," she says.

"You don't say," I say. I've come to the mouth of the alleyway, and now I'm at the corner of Seminary and Dakin, where randomly some-one has decided to put a tiny, fenced-in playground on the edge of a graveyard. It's not even a real playground—no teeter-totters or slides or swings, just some structures made of netted rope, a bit like the rigging of a ship, or some kind of BDSM contraptions. Maybe they're meant to be climbed on, like jungle gyms? The rope webbing glitters with little mini-icicles, and I stand there staring at it. "They're using me, are they?" I say. "What's the world coming to? Next thing you'll tell me that the sys-tem's rigged and the government's corrupt."

I walk along the sidewalk beside the cemetery; just beyond a shoulder-high chain-link fence, rows of headstones are lined up beneath lilac bushes and willow trees. "*Of course* they're *using me*, Cammie," I say. "I was born to be of use. So were most people. There's a rare few that are able to drift through life without being owned by someone."

"There's a difference between being used and being 'of use,' you know."

"Maybe so," I say. "But where is your money coming from, Cammie? How are you putting food in your mouth and buying all that fancy computer equipment that you smashed up? I'm guessing that your mom and dad aren't funding you anymore, so how are you getting by? Somebody's paying you somewhere along the way."

"I'm stealing," she says. "Mostly credit card fraud. So—pretty victimless, in the scheme of things. I'm a parasite, but nobody *owns* me."

"Right on," I say. "Keep following that dream wherever it takes you."

"It doesn't matter," she says moodily. "You're right. We were born to be used."

"This is not philosophical," I say. "What I'm talking about, you're either useful or disposable. That's the situation we're in."

Flip and I have found the entrance to the cemetery, and we slow our pace. Cammie's right—it's a good place to talk. We are winding along a path lined with gravestones large and small, some of them decorated with tokens—a bunch of artificial calla lilies, a tiny American flag, a floppy blue stuffed rabbit—though the vast majority of the plots look like they haven't been visited in decades.

"So what's your motivation?" she says.

"I don't think I have that," I say. I wait as Flip pauses to lift his leg and pee on a small statue of the Virgin Mary. The Virgin is presiding over some sheep, who are watching attentively as she is spreading her arms open toward them. Maybe she is singing to them. Maybe she is delivering a TED Talk.

"Motivation is kind of too specific for my taste," I say. "I just kind of let things happen. I mean, I had a really nice motor home for a while—the *Guiding Star*, it was called—and I've had my eye on places my dog and I could retire to. I have some hopes for Mexico or Central or South America. But mostly I try to live in the present moment."

"You said you changed your mind about killing me. I guess I'm wondering why."

"I don't know," I say. "I'm just . . . having some questions about the logic of this. For one thing, they don't think you're my daughter, but I do. They think you're some kind of AI that's manipulating my sympathies."

"So it matters to you that I'm your biological offspring, for some reason?"

"Oh, brother," I say. I sigh. "I'm not getting back on *that* horse with you." I toe a piece of gravel and Flip watches as it bounces down the path, alert as if the pebble might be prey. "The thing is: I told my boss that I thought you were my daughter and he was like, *No she's not, go kill her,* and I couldn't help but think that it was kind of unprofessional of him to put me in that position. Some would say it's cruel—compelling a man to murder his own child. Even if you *are* only a test-tube baby, and I'm just a sperm donor, you're still my flesh and blood, and they could be more empathetic to that."

I pause for a moment. Up ahead, I can see a couple of homeless men in long coats creeping along, both white men with long, stringy gray-black hair. Maybe twins? Maybe I'm seeing double? I turn and cut across the grass in the opposite direction, taking care not to step on the actual grave plots.

"Dang," I say. "I don't know. I've been having some thoughts about my situation."

"What do you mean?" she says. And I like her voice so much. It's a baby-doll voice in a way, but it's got a little adult rasp to it, a melancholy that I don't think an artificial intelligence could emulate. *Are you real?* I keep thinking. *Are you real?*

"What kind of thoughts?" she says.

"They haven't clarified completely for me yet," I say. "But one issue I had was that I didn't want to kill you. That doesn't mean we're on the same side, but . . ."

"Aren't you, like, betraying your employers or whatever? Won't they punish you or kill you or . . ." And I'm a sucker for the note of genuine feminine concern. It touches me, or touches some oxytocin in my brain and warms it up so that it glows.

"Nah," I say. "I fail at these kinds of jobs all the time. I don't have a hundred percent success rate—nobody does. I mean, they'll be disappointed, but they won't be that surprised." I look over my shoulder for a sign of the long-haired twins, but they seem to have moved on.

"But you're going to have to lie low," I say. "They'll lose interest in you eventually, but not for a few years, so you can't keep data mining or whatever you're doing. If you mind your own business and stay hidden, you might still be able to make a new life—reinvent yourself, or whatever."

I turn to face forward again and immediately trip over a stubby headstone and go sprawling on my hands and knees in the sleety, muddy grass, ungraceful as a walrus. "Uff!" I grunt, a very old-mannish sound, and then I struggle to my knees and pick the cell phone out of the mud and wipe it off with my shirttail. There's a crack in it, but when I put it to my ear her voice comes out clear enough.

"Hello? Hello? Are you all right?" And again, there's that intoxicating touch of her genuine concern.

"I just tripped over a tombstone and fell on my ass," I say. "Just what this scene needs is more pratfalls."

"Did you hurt yourself?" she says.

"No," I say. I rub my muddy knees with my muddy palms. *Grave mud,* I think. *Great.* "I don't know how you people can all walk around jabbering into these cell phones and there aren't more injuries."

I gesture to Flip, and we head down a little slope toward where some mausoleums are lined up like rowhouses. I'm thinking there might be a dry patch down there where I could take a seat.

"So let's say I'm going to help you," I say. I'm taking careful steps, watching my feet as they pass across the grassy rows of graves. "Or, at least I'm going to give you some cover as you disentangle your foolish self from this dangerous mess you've gotten into and find a quiet hiding place." I glance again over my shoulder, I can't help myself. "Tell me what you would need of me."

"I don't think I can hide for very long," she says. "My face is in the Panopticon, and there are a lot of people looking for me. Not just your company, but worse ones, too. I can't just go live in a yurt in Mongolia."

"A couple of years in a yurt might do you good," I say. "Get your nose out of that computer and milk some yaks."

"Yeah," she says. "You're probably right. But I'd never be able to leave the country. The level of preparation I have to do just to move a few blocks is ridiculous."

So she is nearby, I think. I look up toward the apartment buildings in the distance beyond the cemetery—a cluster of brownstones, seven or eight stories. Nearby, a grackle alights in the upper branches of a willow, and it's pretty certainly a grackle and not a drone in disguise.

"Maybe you're underestimating yourself," I say. "I mean, you *did* find me, and you breached all my private phones, and God knows what else. It shouldn't be such a big problem to make yourself a passport and change your appearance a little bit. You could dress up like a boy, for example. Get yourself a fake mustache."

"I had my left foot surgically removed," she says. "There was a tracking device in it. But ironically, being a person with a missing foot does make me more identifiable."

I do not think an AI could make this kind of shit up.

"Dang," I say.

Beyond the row of mausoleums is a little meditation area, and there looks to be a bench there, so I make my way toward it. "You're not joking," I say. "Cammie! You cut off your own foot?"

"I didn't saw it off while biting on a stick or something. I had a friend who had some medical experience. I was under anesthesia."

"Still," I say. "You had to take the whole foot off to get a tracker out of it?"

"It was very small," she says. "And inserted into the talus bone. So it was more expedient to remove the foot."

"Jesus," I say. I pause for a moment and lean my hand against a memorial obelisk, and my image of her recalibrates. I picture my daughter—my imaginary daughter—footless. "That's a serious choice," I say. "I can respect that."

"Thanks," she says and there's that little rasp of sadness in her voice again, stabbing me. "But I wouldn't call it a choice. Unless I want to be someone's property."

"Being property is definitely a choice, honey," I say. "Many people choose it."

I find a bench in the memorial grove and I wipe off the sleety dew and sit down gingerly, still a little unsteady from my fall. "You chopped off your own foot to be free, and that is badass, don't get me wrong. But now you're free to—what? Be hunted and harried for the rest of your days?"

I sit down and close my eyes for second. "I know some people who would possibly take you in. People in other networks that wouldn't care if you were being hunted by Value Standard or what have you. But . . . you know, it would mean that you'd be on retainer."

"A slave," she says.

"Aw, c'mon," I say, and rub my hand over my eyes: *Why am I doing this?* "That's such a loaded word—it's got too much ugly history behind it. *On retainer* just sounds nicer. Or even if you want to say *indentured servitude.*"

"I like the word *assistant* better than the word *victim,*" she says.

"Look," I say. "I'm just spitballing here."

"And if I joined one of these places," she says, "would you get a commission?"

"Oh, for crying out loud," I say. "No! I'm here trying to help you out of a problem that came about due to your own reckless behavior. I'm not looking to profit off you."

And then we're both silent. I'm surprised by how gobsmacked I am by her insinuation, her accusation, that I'm just a mercenary who would sell her off if he could.

Is that the kind of person I am? I choose to believe that I am not.

In front of me there's a sculpture of a barefoot boy with his trousers rolled up, and he's sitting on top of a gravestone playing a flute. I'm not sure how I feel about him. I like the whimsy of it, I guess, but also his bare toes and the tip of his flute are dripping little icicles as he gazes off into the gray sky. And on the monument is an inscription from a song I'm familiar with:

> *For all we know*
> *This may only be a dream*

An old Nina Simone song.

I can remember it playing in a motel room in Cape May, New Jersey, and my mom was dancing close with an important customer and the big picture window looked out on the gingerbread houses along the beachfront promenade, and Nina Simone sang: *I hold out my hand, and my heart will be in it*, and I remember the crazy sorrow of her voice as I stood in the closet holding a syringe, waiting for my mother to dance her mark into my range.

And I don't know why there is such a sharp brightness in this ordinary memory, except that it's Nina's voice, the way it possesses you, colonizes you with its ache.

It rolls you back into Cammie, into your unsolvable problem.

"There's someone you know that I think could really help us," Cammie says, at last.

"Someone *I* know?" I say. "I don't know anybody."

"You were friends with a man named Porter St. Germaine, weren't you? When you were younger?"

"Patches?" I say incredulously.

"He was the obstetrician who delivered me," she says. "He's also a well-known geneticist with ties to the alt-right."

"Huh," I say. "I'll be."

I sit there, staring at the flute-playing boy, letting this sink in. Of all the people who might have come up—dang! I remember that night we first met, when he sucked my toe while I masturbated, both of us stoned out of our minds. I think of the time that we were roommates, a few years after that toe incident, and I feel uneasy, remembering all the shitty things we did, the things he talked me into. But it's been almost twenty-five years since I've seen him.

"Patches has something to do with this?" I say, and there's that unpleasant sensation of being about to realize something you don't want to.

"He was intimately involved from the beginning, from what I can tell. He was close to Brayden Kurch for a while, but they're on the outs now, for some reason. I think he might have also worked for the same people you work with, for a while."

"Wait," I say. "How do you know that Patches and me were friends?"

"He won't talk to me," she says. "But maybe he would talk to you."

"And ask him what?"

"Ask him what he wanted with your sperm. Ask him, *Why you? Why us?*"

"Okay," I say. "But answer my question. How could you know that I was friends with Patches?"

I give my hair a shake, and dewy sleet crystals fly off my mane.

"You were reckless for a little window of time," she says. "Davis Dowty and Porter St. Germaine were arrested together for criminal mischief," she says. "There's also a picture of you at one of his fraternity parties—it's on the web, on the Northwestern Delta Omega Facebook page. You're in the background but it's clearly you."

"Dang," I say.

"I still don't know how you met him—how you got to be involved with him—but I'm pretty sure he was the one who gave your DNA to Kurch."

I let this sink in. It's true to what I know of Patches's personality, and I can feel myself blushing, the surprise of recognizing you're being used.

That sinking feeling.

"You know how to find him?" I say.

Honeypot

"She wasn't there," I tell Experanza. I'm trying to make my way out of the graveyard, but I'm not entirely sure which direction to go. A fog has settled over the cemetery, and even though it's early afternoon the sun is buried deep under layers of clouds and dioxide haze. The skyscrapers in the distance are suggestions of shapes.

"The address they gave me wasn't even a residence," I tell Experanza. "It was a storage facility, stripped pretty clean. Just some busted-up computer equipment, nothing salvageable."

"Are you sure?" Experanza says.

"Pretty sure," I say. "I took pictures of the whole site, I'll send them to you."

I stand there looking around, and off in the distance near some mausoleums I see those stringy-haired bums in their long coats—company men, I reckon, keeping an eye on me. I gesture to Flip. I make a steeple with my fingers, which means *Find home*. He has a knack for leading us back to our vehicle, and he takes off through the maze of headstones with his nose to the ground.

"But I think I have a new lead," I say. I glance behind me and hurry along. "So I'm going to follow up on that. It'll take me about a week."

"What's the lead?" Experanza says, and I don't have a good answer to that question so I just say—"Trust me."

She doesn't say anything for a while. I trudge along heavily, listening to her chopping something finely on a cutting board. We've come at last to a gateway that leads back out to the street, and Flip takes a left so I take a left. I know I should pause and make a quick assessment of the surroundings but now it's raining hard enough that I decide to just keep my head down and follow Flip's tail. I trust him.

"Should I be concerned about you, Billy?" Experanza says finally, and her voice is chiding, reminding me that there was a time when she was practically like a sister. "You're acting strange."

"No, I'm not," I say. I lift my head and see that Flip is at the van, half a block ahead, waiting impatiently for me, but I take my time, stepping carefully as the rain solidifies on the sidewalk, my feet sliding, trying to throw me off balance with every step. I pause and glance behind me again: no sign of the stragglies, but I know they're near.

"I'm—looking into an option," I say.

She gives me another silence as I make my way at last to the van and slide open the side door for Flip, letting him jump in first. He hates the rain even more than I do, and he gives his fur a hard, extended shake as I clamber inside behind him. The rain pebbles noisily against the roof, and the interior fills up with the cold, steamy odor of wet dog and wet old man.

"You know what this reminds me of?" Experanza says.

"Hold on, I'm going to put you on speaker," I say, and I set the phone into its mount on the dashboard and turn the engine on to get the heat going.

"It reminds me of the last time you lied to me," Experanza says, from the phone. "That time when you stole the dog. You remember how pissed the client was?"

"They weren't that upset," I say.

"Seriously?" Experanza says. "Those people would still kill you to this day for taking that dog, and the situation with this girl is ten or twenty times worse."

I take this in. I pull a towel out of a grocery bag and begin to dry Flip off. "Maybe there's more to it than you think," I say, and I wrap Flip up in a blanket before I begin to strip out of my clothes. "I think I can get more information from her about other parties who are involved."

"Billy," she says, "come on," and I shudder. I'm soaked all the way to my underwear. When I peel off my socks my soles are wrinkled like walnuts.

"What if I could, like, capture the girl?" I say. "It's possible I could convince her to join our team. It could be really useful."

"Oh, baby," Experanza says. I think of the way, when we were younger, she would gently lick her finger and smooth down my hair. I think of her hands vibrating magnetically as she performed her Reiki on me. "You're in love with her," she says.

"No," I say. "I'm curious. I just want to look into some things that might be"—and I pull a sweatshirt over my head—"important. There are other people involved that I need to find out about."

"You know what this is?" Experanza says, and if we were sitting across from each other she would reach out and pinch my ear, she would make me look into her eyes. "This is another one of your baby rabbits."

"Aw, for crying out loud," I say, and tuck the blanket tighter around my shivering body. "Why do you always bring that up? I was a little kid."

"Because it's a pattern," Experanza says. "It's a glitch in your thinking. Like, a fetish or something."

"This is not," I say, "a baby rabbit."

I will not tell you the story of the baby rabbit, except to say that it ended tragically.

I like to keep my past compartmentalized. You do a job and then you put it in a box and forget about it. You seal the evil memories in a vault that you will never open, and this is the way that you can move as a functional person through the world.

I will not remember the brown baby rabbit I found in the weedy field alongside a courtyard motel when I was six or seven, I do not think about how curious and unafraid it was, it seemed puzzled as it smelled my pant leg and then followed me in cautious but determined hippity-hops all the way across the playground. I thought it was lost, looking for his mother but maybe his mother was dead, maybe he hoped I would be his father. I had some Cheerios in my pocket and he ate them out of my palm. He didn't try to escape when I picked him up.

"If you hadn't touched it," my mother said, "if you hadn't rubbed your dirty hands all over it, the mommy rabbit might have taken it back, but now that you've gotten your scent on it, she'll kill it. The only merciful thing to do," she said.

Years later—maybe I was sixteen when I told Experanza about it and I started crying. Which is not something I ever do. It surprised me as much as it did Experanza—tears began running down my face, and my chest tightened, and when I tried to breathe a loud weeping sound came out of me, and for the first time I understood that the noises people make when they are begging and in pain are involuntary.

Experanza hugged me and rubbed my back and we sat there side by side on a motel-room bed, but when I finally lifted my wet face and looked at her I saw that she was puzzled. I realized that this sudden weeping seemed a little crazy to her.

And maybe she was right. It was sad and gratuitous but was not even close to the worst things my mother had done—I had helped my mother kill people by that time, after all—so why would this, of all things, be something to bawl about?

I wished I'd never told her, because ever after she would bring it up when I did something she disapproved of. *A glitch.*

But I am not going to think about that.

Nor am I going to dwell on that job at the dog-fighting compound in Virginia. It was nothing—someone else had taken care of the murdering, all I had to do was the cleanup and so I pulled up to the old farmhouse with a backhoe on a flatbed trailer and a few cans of gasoline and accelerants. I was just planning to make a mass grave and then burn all the structures down.

I remember finding the first body near the steps of the farmhouse. My miner's lamp was strapped to my forehead and his splayed corpse was spotlighted near a lilac bush, a black-haired rogue in torn jeans and a pink T-shirt that said KEEP CALM AND CARRY ON, skinny as a post, maybe twenty-two years old, and I grabbed him by his ragged tennis shoe and pulled him along behind me as I headed out back toward the dog pens.

The thing that's harder to remember is the sound that was coming from the shed or barn. I could make you a catalogue of all the sounds the dying make, but I wouldn't know how to categorize this one. All I can do is place it in the vault of evil memories and try to forget that it's still sitting there, steadily collecting interest.

I found Flip by following that unearthly sound he was making, and he was in a cage in a long row of cages, lying on his side and breathing shallowly. He'd been shot like all the others on the property, and he also had wounds from what must have been a recent fight. There's no need to describe the kinds of things a dog's teeth can do to another dog's flesh. I will only say that our eyes met and he looked at me with the deepest sadness I'd ever seen—a sorrow with no hope for mercy or reprieve.

The memory of it comes to me like a blow to the face, the way all true memories do, unasked for, unwelcome, a full-body possession.

Long ago I realized that this kind of remembering is not a feeling you can live with in the day-to-day. Constant forgetting is the best cure for all your maladies of anxiety and depression and self-loathing and despair. Rx, Rx, Rx.

And I push it all back into the vault as Flip and I sit there side by side, wrapped in blankets on my bare mattress in the van, and my head is still humming grimly, humbly grinding with unwanted remembrances and I pull on some sweatpants and rub some salve on my feet and then put on dry socks and I wonder if Experanza will tattle on me to Tim Ribbons. Maybe she will, maybe she won't.

At least I didn't tell her about Patches. Having his name come out of the blue was maybe the most troubling thing in a day full of upsetting revelations.

I sit in the driver's seat and let the motor run, the heat cranked up to ten, just resting my forehead against the steering wheel and letting the vents blow on my damp hair.

The problem with having all the parts of your life neatly bundled and separate is that it makes it harder to pull back and look at the big picture. It's a terrible thought to imagine that all the pieces you locked away, everything you thought was discrete, might actually be connected. Might actually be a pattern.

So: Patches. I close my eyes as the hot dry air blows across my face and try to dredge up some memories.

Twenty-five or so years ago I was living at Mrs. Dowty's boardinghouse in the room of her late son Davis, and it so happened that Patches was living nearby. It was just a coincidence.

Or?

What was I doing back in Evanston in the first place? Helen Shindle had dropped me off in downtown Chicago, and I wandered around panhandling for a while, thinking I would move on once I'd made some money, and I suppose I took the el train north with the half-formed idea that I might find Patches and possibly rent out my foot again for a couple hundred dollars.

But when I got there I couldn't exactly remember which fraternity house was his, and then I realized that two years had passed and he was probably long gone anyway.

Still, it was a big college campus, and I figured that the drug trade would be booming, and lo and behold it wasn't more than a day before I'd located a dealer who was willing to hire me on as a courier. What was his name? Sabik? And I seem to recall that he was the one who suggested Mrs. Dowty's place to me.

It all seemed to unfold naturally, one chance meeting after another—that's the way life is, right? But now I wonder. Was I being watched and monitored the whole time by the parties to whom my mother owed her unpayable debt? Did they think I would lead them to her?

I was sitting in my neighborhood bar and Patches came up behind me, I felt him put his hand on the back of my chair and I turned and I was like, "Hey! Don't I know you from somewhere?"

And he was like, "Possibly."

He was wearing a black turtleneck sweater of some soft woolen material and he settled into the seat next to me. He touched the back of my wrist with his index finger, and he was, like, "I'm really desperate for some weed and you look like the only person in this dump who might be holding."

I remember the Irish bartender giving us the stink eye; he was tiny as a doll but also somehow intimidating with his glare. He picked up my empty pint glass.

"Take it outside, eh?" he said. "Don't piss in the well you drink from."

"Let's go out back for a minute," I said, and the bartender dunked my glass into some soapy water as if he were drowning it and he raised his eyebrows at me. I can't remember that bartender's name but I know it was an unusual Irish one.

And I don't remember what came after that. I can't recall exactly how Patches and I became roommates except that one morning we were sitting in his breakfast nook in his apartment and I was eating one of his bananas that he'd cut up into pieces for me and he was like, "Why don't you just move in here?"

He said it begrudgingly, as if I'd been complaining that I didn't have a place. But I wasn't. I was perfectly satisfied at Mrs. Dowty's.

"Move in with you?" I said, and I was a bit puzzled. I thought he might be joking.

"It would be better than living in a room in some old lady's house, wouldn't it? With that creepy parrot? And that screaming kid upstairs?"

Later I realized that this was how Patches operated on people—acting as if his ideas were your requests, confiding untrue things to you so that you'd tell your own secrets, pretending things that *had* happened hadn't, they were just your imagination.

But I liked him. I admired his worldliness, that he'd been to Europe and South America and Japan, that he was educated and smart and not ashamed of it, and I wanted to be close to someone who knew things. And I enjoyed his meanness. He was a thief and a perpetrator of cruel pranks, and his hatred of the world was a salve on some wound that I didn't even realize was inside me. Maybe he, too, was a glitch.

But he must have been more than that as well.

It can't be a coincidence if he was the obstetrician who delivered Cammie. He must have known something about me that I didn't, he must've been working for someone, but what the scheme was I can't imagine. Here's that sickening feeling of a slow realization that refuses to dawn on you, that niggler in the back of your mind: *Did I forget something?*

* * *

I had been living with him for a year when one day I was summoned by my drug supplier to a disco club on Clark Street. This had never happened before, and I walked heavy-footed behind a bouncer in a sleeveless T-shirt who had *Wrongly Convicted* tattooed where his eyebrows should have been—sheepish and alarmed, I trailed him through the crowd of dancers and the strobe lights and music videos playing on giant screens and toward the upstairs boss's office.

And the boss turned out to be Tim Ribbons, and he didn't seem as surprised to see me again as I was to see him.

He was sitting at a desk in a tiny, yellowish-gray room, totaling up receipts on an adding machine. Behind him on the wall were framed, signed photographs of people I didn't recognize, though I knew they must be famous.

Tim Ribbons looked up from the numbers on his keypad and beamed at me.

He said, "Billy! Look at you! You look great! How long has it been?"

"I don't want to imagine," I said. He didn't stand up or ask me to sit down, so I just stood there with my hands folded in front of me like a groomsman.

"It must be—what? Five years? Since I visited you in the hospital? I'm glad you're doing better. You're getting along pretty well, I hear! Making good money!"

I shrugged uncomfortably. "Sure," I said. "I guess."

"But time is passing!" Tim Ribbons said and wagged his index finger in the air. "You're getting older. There comes a time, Billy, when you need to decide what you want to do with your life. Do you feel what I'm saying?"

I shifted awkwardly and scratched the back of my head. It was so weird, I thought, that Tim Ribbons would just show up in my life from time to time, to rescue me from an insane asylum or dole out mysterious advice or offer me a job. *I'm your legal guardian,* he told me once, which I thought was just a figure of speech but now I wondered. *Are you my father?* I thought, even though he was a trim, elegant black man, no more than five foot four, and I was a hulking redneck of the palest, freckled-est hue.

But why else would he take such a paternal interest in my well-being?

I still wondered from time to time, over the years, though I've realized that Tim Ribbons is much too young to be my father. He couldn't be more than fourteen years older than me, is my guess.

"You're making okay money but you're drifting a little bit, aren't you?" Tim Ribbons said to me. He was wearing a button-down shirt and tie underneath a cardigan sweater—like a dad in a vintage TV show, I thought, and itched the back of my head again as he smiled at me thoughtfully.

"They tell me you're living with some queer med-school kid from Kentucky or something?"

"South Carolina," I said, very small.

"That doesn't seem like you," Tim Ribbons said. "Do you think?"

"I dunno," I said, and I wasn't even sure what he meant. I didn't realize that I *seemed like* anything.

"Of course, you're having fun," he said, and leaned back in his chair as I stood there bowing my head, my hands still clasped in front of me. "That's natural. You're partying and experimenting and trying to figure things out. I get it. But one thing I know about you, Billy. You're not a frivolous person."

"Well," I said.

"In the end," Tim Ribbons said, "you know what's best for you."

I said that I would work for him, and the first job I had was to expunge Davis Dowty from the public record, and the first job I failed was forgetting about the sperm bank, forgetting that Davis Dowty had sold his biological materials, his DNA, to a company whose name he didn't even recall.

I was more focused on the immediate problems at hand. Packing quickly. Burning documents in the fireplace. Writing a note for Patches, which, in the end, after many rewritings, was only two sentences and a smiley face. "Sorry, had to go! Good luck! 😊" on a paper napkin in blue ballpoint pen. Left on the table in the breakfast nook. The end.

And so I began to move through the world as a person on retainer, as a person with a schedule, a person with debts to be paid. I was given jobs that needed completion, and I traveled around, doing them.

Of the names that I built for myself, of the Barely Blur, most are owned outright by Tim Ribbons and his bosses and his bosses' bosses at Value Standard Enterprises, but some have been on loan for years to corporate espionage cabals, or to data-mining collectives, or DNA-gathering firms, or various antifascist PACs, or to cultish nonprofits funded by paranoid billionaires—I have a long list of masters.

And mostly I've spent my life as a useful tool, carrying out deliveries or perpetrating petty acts of industrial espionage or messing with the results of a local school board election or burning down the home of a potentially problematic blogger—but not connected to those communities, not connected to the daily world, either.

I never paid much attention to the news. I was aware that the human race faced challenges, as it always does. There were earthquakes and hurricanes, a stock market crash and an ongoing war overseas. A worldwide pandemic swept through, followed by a global recession, and then another pandemic. Many of the vulnerable perished, as they are prone to do.

Over the decades, I tried to be kind and generous when it was possible, and ruthless and quick when it was necessary, but I didn't keep score. Most days, I assume that eventually the good karma will outweigh the bad.

But I don't know. I'm not sure.

I lift my head from the steering wheel when the phone Cammie gave me starts ringing, and I pull it up to the side of my face. "Cammie," I say.

"Where are you?" she says.

"I'm in the van," I murmur. "I'll be on the road here in a minute."

"You need to get moving," she says. "There are people looking for you, too."

"Mm," I say. I'm sock-footed, sweatpantsed, in the driver's seat of a Kickin Chickin delivery van. Fifty years old and on my way downward, it seems.

I can't but think that helping Cammie might add a lot of tokens to my good karma—though I know of course this is how a honeypot works. There's the appeal to your sentimental noble instincts, there's the damsel in distress and the longing to be heroic for once, a series of emotionally manipulative distractions designed to lead you down a maze to your doom. It's a classic espionage technique, I'm well aware—and yet here I am, heading off on an errand for a girl I'm supposed to kill.

Allowing her to gain my trust and find my location.

"All right," I say. "I'm on my way."

Suspension of Disbelief

So now Cammie is telling me more of her life story as I make my way out of Chicago, and I'm trying to picture it in my mind's eye like it's a movie. I'm smoking a very creative and thoughtful strain of cannabis and when she leaves out details, I can fill them in with my own imagination.

I can see Cammie at sixteen. Here she is, small but sturdy like my mother, standing at the sink in her little bathroom, brushing her teeth before bed, and she hears her parents down the hall talking about baby names.

She keeps her face expressionless as she stares at herself in the mirror—round face and small nose, straight blond hair cut to the same length as all the other girls'.

Toothpaste foam accumulates on her lower lip. She is "doe-eyed," as they say, and I was the same way at that age, that deer-in-the-headlights expression, the resting face of a simpleton. Like me, she hated it, but also saw its uses. There is great power in being underestimated, she's just beginning to realize.

This is the day when she learned that her forty-nine-year-old adoptive mother was pregnant. Apparently, Marsha had started taking a newly available fertility drug and she hadn't (she said) expected anything to happen, but now she was going to have a baby! And oh God she hoped Cammie would be happy for her.

"I think it's only going to deepen our relationship. I know it must feel weird to you, but it doesn't mean that you're any less my daughter!"

"Oh," Cammie said. "Good."

"I'm actually excited to see you interact with an infant," Marsha said. "I think it will bring out your maternal side."

And Cammie said, "Uh-huh."

In some ways, she supposed, it was a relief. Their focus would inevitably turn away from her—she would be able to slip away without being noticed, without a big dramatic scene. She grew up an only child but she had always felt there was a ghost of a sibling floating around the house—another, better daughter they kept expecting to show up. It wasn't that they didn't love her. They did, she thought— especially Bradley, her father—it was just that she had never felt that she was part of them.

"I hope you're happy for me," Marsha said. "Please don't judge me!"

"I'm *not*, Mom," Cammie said. "I'm thrilled for you." She let herself be embraced, Marsha's motherly arms around her, kneading her tight shoulders.

Marsha had always been afraid that Cammie was judging her, ever since Cammie was little. If Cammie put her spoon down too sharply or rolled her eyes to look out the window while Marsha was talking or didn't put on an extreme show of joy when she was given a gift, Marsha would take even these tiny gestures as signs of disapproval. But there was simply a basic misunderstanding at the heart of their relationship—it wasn't just that they didn't feel connected like mother and daughter; they didn't even feel like the same species.

"Wait," I say. I'm on an endless potholed road on the south side of Chicago and it's hard to tell if the ramshackle houses are abandoned or whether there might be people living behind the boarded-up windows. "Go back," I say. "You're in your bathroom and you hear them talking about baby names, but what does your room look like? Give me a little description."

"What?" she says.

"It helps me think if I can picture things," I tell her. "I'm a visual learner."

"Oh," she says.

She's rubbing her face with an acne-proofing scrub and she stares at herself in the mirror, her reflection surrounded by colorful vanity lights, and there's a round magnifying makeup mirror for putting on eyeliner and all kinds of doodads that her mother thought a teenage girl would love—her own private bathroom with a bidet and a capsule shower stall and a beautiful set of artistically painted seashells that had been mounted in gilt frames, and all kinds of expensive fragrances and makeup which Cammie, willfully, had never bothered to learn how to apply correctly.

There's the medication, too—pill bottles lined up along the sink, various psychiatric drugs to help with her lack of concentration and her panic attacks and her social anxiety. She had been compassionately uninvited from returning to the private school she'd been attending since sixth grade. It was just not a good fit anymore, they said, and they cited a number of incidents—a garbage-can fire in a bathroom; a complaint (not entirely true) that she was performing rituals using hair and other personal items stolen from fellow students; subtle suicidal gestures and comments that made staff and fellow students uncomfortable; her overall failure to comply with a treatment plan. So she was attending an online school for the Gifted but Troubled, and she rarely left her room.

As an only child she had loved her onlyness, had loved, more than anything, being left alone to read and draw pictures and make mods for her video games. But now, somehow, she found herself longing for connection. Not to go back to the well-regarded private school where the social life made her homicidally miserable, but to find, somehow, a like-minded individual or set of friends who would accept her for who she was. Was that so much to ask?

Now, her main social interactions occurred online, and even so, the connection was oblique. On Reddit, she was a ghost following the conversations of a few favorite troublemakers, or she was a minor troll, popping into the conversations of stupid people to make a dry, cutting comment before vanishing back into the ether whence she came.

She met Ronnie in a subreddit for fans of Japanese ero guro, a genre that held an uneasy fascination for her. Hokusai's *Dream of the Fisherman's Wife* was her avatar picture, and Ronnie sent her a direct message:

I see you're interested in tentacle rape

She usually would not respond to this kind of thing, but it was very late, after three a.m., she was insomniac and reckless.

not rape, she wrote back. **clearly consensual**
She wrote: **not interested in rape, asshole**
He wrote: **noted**
He wrote: **If I was an octopus what would you like me to do to you?**

She sighed, leaning back on her bed in the dark, vaping some THC oil, and she let out a slow breath. A patch of moonlight came through her window and hung on her wall like a poster.

He catfished her for a week before he admitted that he'd been shadowing her—and that he thought they might be brother and sister. If she'd been in a more stable frame of mind, she would have blocked him. The idea that you would sext with someone for a week before you told them you had been stalking them because you thought they were your sibling—? That was not normal, right? That was disgusting.

But nothing truly sordid had ever happened to her before, so it was also sort of interesting. Plus, the information Ronnie had was interesting, too—crazy, paranoid, and alarming, but interesting. And the more documents he sent her, the more she began to really believe it.

On the night that Marsha told her the blessed news, Ronnie was waiting for her on video chat. It was about ten p.m. in Chicago, about five a.m. in Switzerland, and he was sitting in his bed in the dark, shirtless, in his underwear, his face looming close to the screen because he had his laptop half closed. His roommate was asleep.

"Da-amn, sis!" he whispered. Sometimes he sounded like a French person who'd learned English by listening to rap music. "Word! That is so fucked!"

His breath sounded wet as his mouth came close to the microphone. "What are you going to do about it?"

She looked at him. There was enough documentation to make her believe that he was really her biological brother, there was an unmistakable resemblance between them, but if she'd had a choice he wouldn't have been it. He was the sort of teenage boy who might one day be considered handsome, but for now he still had a boy's face on an enlarged man's head. He was skinny and awkwardly limbed and folded himself like a praying mantis. He looked like he stank of feet and masturbated a lot.

"What am I going to do?" she said. "What does that even mean?"

"You better have a plan," Ronnie said. "Because I'm sure they do."

He was very close to the camera. His upper face filled the frame, and she could see his eyes roll as he turned to glance behind him. His tongue glanced out to lick his lips.

"You think I'm paranoid?" he said. "Well, I don't think you're paranoid enough."

"He was right," she says now. And she's silent for a moment. I'm taking the back way through South Chicago, driving along residential streets of small, identical 1970s-style one-story houses and lots of dead trees, through Dolton and Calumet City, trying to make my way to Highway 30. Taking I-65 south might be quicker, but I've been hearing bad things about the activity on that road.

I pop a two-milligram dose of vitamin D2 and an antacid and four baby aspirin and chew them all up together, it's a compellingly strange mix of flavors, not as bad as you might think, and I take a hit of this sweet Ohio-grown weed called Death Star that I borrowed from Experanza's stash.

Meanwhile, Cammie is so silent that I have to ask her if she's still there, and she says yes, and I'm like, "Are you okay?"

"Yeah," she says, in that wistful, throaty way that zings the hairs on the back of my neck.

"Sorry," she says. "I was just thinking of some sad things."

But she doesn't tell me what the sad things are. She wants to go back to that conversation she was having with Ronnie, back when she was sixteen and she'd just found out her mother was pregnant.

"Anyway," Ronnie was saying. "I think I just found sibling number nineteen."

"You're kidding," she said. For the past few months, Ronnie had been uncovering more and more biological siblings, all over the world, all born of the same sperm coming out of a fertility clinic in Evanston, Illinois. She wasn't sure what to make of it all, but it was definitely beginning to feel unsettling, uncanny, like she was at a very convincing séance, even though she didn't believe in ghosts.

"Guillerma Orozco-Sandoval, lives in Mexico City. Her father works for Casa de Moneda de Mexico—the Mexican mint! Which, by the way, is the oldest company in North America. Established in 1534. Centuries' worth of shady shit has happened there."

"And . . . ?"

"What if they're, like, the Illuminati? Like, our parents are part of some ancient cult and they've propagated us for some purpose."

"Such as?" she said, and his face was super close to the screen again, she could see the inside of his nostrils. She wondered if he might be schizophrenic. Maybe he had forged all the documentation he'd sent her? But still, she was weirdly tingling. "You mean like that movie where the kids in the boarding school turn out to be clones that are, like, being raised as organ donors?"

"I thought of that," Ronnie said. "But I don't get that, either. If you're going to raise clones as organ donors, why not just raise them like cattle? Why put them in an expensive boarding school?"

"Mm," she said. She lowered her voice—lifted her head and looked at her bedroom door, at the brass doorknob gleaming with moonlight. As if someone on the other side might have their hand on it.

"I mean," she said. She lowered her voice a notch. "If they're the Illuminati or whatever, then what's their plan for us? Why would they need so many?"

She watched as he brushed his drooping bangs back from his forehead. She had noticed before how badly he bit his fingernails; that was something they had in common.

"It's got to be something about DNA," he said. "Something about the Spome Derner."

The Spome Derner is what he called the sperm donor—me—who Ronnie had unexplainably strong negative feelings about. He pronounced *Spome Derner* with an exaggerated hick accent.

Which had the effect, Cammie says, of making her sympathetic to the Spome Derner, and when Ronnie read aloud from the donor's intake questionnaire, the fake hillbilly voice he put on made her cringe. "I'd like to be a nature boy," Ronnie chortled, and it stung her for reasons she couldn't explain. She had a picture of this young man—a big, shaggy earnest guy, not educated, not privileged like them, doing his best to describe his inner life, which was, she imagined, just as rich and complex as her own, only struggling to articulate itself. *Nature boy*, she thought, and a tiny arrow pierced her heart.

She had an inexplicable notion that the Spome Derner was going to be so much like her in so many surprising, unique details. That he—though they had never met—would understand her, would see her, in ways her adoptive parents never could.

"Maybe you were just a limerent object," she tells me. "I don't know. But I got this incredible crush on you—I mean, not *you*, but my idea of you. I know that sounds crazy, but I've had this sock puppet that I developed a relationship with over the years."

I don't say anything. I don't know what a limerent object is. I don't know what she means by sock puppet, but it doesn't feel like she's giving me a compliment, and I feel embarrassed and my feelings are smarting. To my left I am passing some smoldering airplane wreckage that hobos are scavenging among; they are collecting pieces of luggage and stacking them into piles, and seagulls are fomenting overhead, wheeling around like leaves in a dust devil.

I feel like maybe we should talk more about our relationship at this point. Who, exactly, does she think I am? Why would she like to join forces with me? I'm also thinking I don't like being called a sock puppet, and maybe there's some ideas that she has about me that need correcting, but before I can bring it up, she's back on the subject of Ronnie. Godforsaken Ronnie and his discoveries.

* * *

It was late summer and Cammie's mother was three months pregnant and Cammie sat in a deck chair by the backyard pool, watching the water jets arcing and sparkling, watching as fireflies drifted low to the ground over the grass. She vaped a little weed.

It was around midnight and she was still in shorts and a bikini top though the mosquitoes were biting. Her sunburnt skin was glistening with Aloe Aftersun Gel.

"Number thirty-six!" Ronnie exclaimed. "Tiril Thommesen, aged four. She's Norwegian. Her father is one of the managers of the Svalbard Global Seed Vault. Do you know what that is?"

"Can't say that I do," she murmured. His eagerness to find facts she might not know and endlessly explain them to her was very grating. He had an awful version of Boy Personality, but she supposed she was stuck with him. All the other bio-siblings he was finding were children, toddlers, infants: no one else to talk to.

"It's a secure seed bank on the island of Spitsbergen," he said. "They store seeds to preserve genetic diversity, and to protect rare and endangered species and so on. Did you know that seeds can remain viable for hundreds or even thousands of years? There was a Judean date palm that . . ."

"I can look it all up on Wikipedia," she said.

"It's a DNA repository," he said. "And that's what I think we are: repositories!"

Repository, she thought. It seemed like a gross word, almost pornographic, and she killed a mosquito on her thigh. It was so glutted with her blood it couldn't even muster the energy to try to fly away.

"Repositories of what, though?" she said. "That's what I still can't figure out."

And then the lights up near the house went on, and she saw Marsha coming out through the sliding glass doors, tottering down the winding stone path that led to the pool, carrying two bowls.

"FML," she messaged to Ronnie, "GTG." And she closed her laptop quickly, folding his face down into the void just as Marsha rounded the corner. Even though Marsha was still skinny she had a baby bump now, her body was growing rounder than Cammie had ever seen it. She was wearing yoga pants and an oversized cardigan sweater, her hair in a ponytail, no makeup, but that Instagram smile was still pinned to her face.

"Am I interrupting?" she called merrily and held out the two bowls in her hands. "I thought you might want some gelato?" She did a little shimmy, waggling the bowls of ice cream as if they were maracas. *"Zabaglione? Amarena?"* she said, with a serviceable Italian accent.

"Sure," Cammie said, though her back stiffened. Maybe all poor Marsha wanted was a daughter she could relate to, a daughter who could be more like a friend, and it sometimes broke Cammie's heart, the way she kept trying. She took the pint cup Marsha offered her, it had a cute tiny spoon stuck in it, and she tasted the *amarena* flavor as Marsha settled into the deck chair beside her.

"Look at those stars!" Marsha exclaimed, leaning back.

"Uh-huh," Cammie said, and glanced up. In truth, the light pollution from the Chicago region was so severe that they could barely see the Big Dipper, but oh, well. There were a few visible stars and some satellites. That was something, and Marsha surprised her by reaching over and taking her hand. She made a swing out of their clasped hands, and oh! For a second, Cammie wished so hard that Marsha was a mother she could talk to, she wished so hard to unburden herself of her secrets. It was actually a moment of terrible danger, Cammie said. "If Marsha had just known how to talk to me like I was a person, I might have told her everything. Ronnie. All of it."

But instead she stumbled clumsily.

"Who were you talking to?" Marsha said. "A boy?"

"Someone from school," Cammie said, and shrugged. *If they ever found out we were talking,* Ronnie had told her, *I think we'd both be so fucked.*

"Oh," her mother said. "From your new school?"

"Mm-hm," Cammie said cautiously. "From the creative writing club. He's gay."

"Oh," her mother said. Nonplussed. She gazed out to the little barrier of woods that surrounded their property, a cluster of trees that bordered the security fence, and then looked at her with those big eyes—eyes of a late-eighties starlet, eyes of a thwarted sculptress, eyes of a believer in energy stones and shamanic healing. But she wasn't an idiot, either. She could sense that something big was happening in Cammie's life, and as they sat there in their deck chairs by the pool with the fireflies and mosquitoes and visible stars, Cammie could feel her calculating.

"Well, that sounds like it would be really great for you, writing," Marsha said. "You've always been so imaginative! And it's a great outlet for your feelings. For me," she said, "journaling has always been my best therapy."

"Mm," Cammie said, and itched her calf with her foot.

"Did you put on bug spray?" Marsha asked.

"Yes," Cammie said, and Marsha gazed silently at the mosquito bites on Cammie's legs, red welts that she'd been scratching at for hours.

"You should put on more," Marsha said. "You're getting eaten alive."

"Yeah," Cammie said. "I know." And she took a bite of gelato as if it was a piece of punctuation. She heard herself making an exasperated breath through her nose before she could stop herself. "Let me finish my food and then I'll get busy and just lather myself with bug spray, okay?"

The big eyes widened again. Marsha flinched as if Cammie had clapped in her face, and Cammie caught a glimpse of an ugly expression before Marsha could adjust it. "For just a second I saw how much she loathed me," Cammie said. "She was so disgusted by that stupid mosquito bite scab. And I could see how ugly she thought I was. How repulsed she was by me. Not just disappointed. I could see how badly she wished she could return me and get her money back. How she wished she had gotten a different baby. She felt cheated."

Cammie had a memory of a time when she was six, there was a beautiful birthday dress that Cammie was made to wear even though she was going through a phase when she didn't like girlish things, it was a party but she kept wandering off to be by herself. Many children she didn't know or like had been invited, children of her parents' friends or colleagues. Brayden Kurch's awful daughters were there, and she had wandered along the perimeter of her family's property, turning over rocks to look at the living things she found underneath: sowbugs, centipedes, crickets. *WTF!* they exclaimed as the roof was lifted up off their houses, and they scuttled around in surprise. And then she felt the shadow of her mother above her. She looked up and her mother's head was framed by the sun, and her mother said, "Why are you doing this?" Her mother said, "Do you hate me?"

And Cammie heard herself very softly think, *Yes.*

"What did I do to deserve this?" her mother said. "All the other children are *fine,* they're normal. Did I do something wrong?"

Remembering this, Cammie stared out at the treetops in between bites of her overpriced gelato, out at the tasteful security lamps that ran along the edge of their yard. *All the other children,* she thought, and it clicked into place: Marsha was her enemy. Little bats were dipping in and out of the funnel of light, catching insects, Cammie assumed. She watched them for a while and felt calmer.

"Look," she said, and gave her mother a cheerful smile. "Bats!"

Her parents still try to contact her. They leave messages on her old cell phone, which she'll listen to sometimes. *It's not too late for you,* they say. *You still have a choice.*

"Listen," her father says. "I have contacts that know people who are very high up in the NSA, and they are willing to cut you a deal. We can work this out, your whole life doesn't have to be ruined."

"Oh, Camilla," her mother says, pleadingly. "I . . . just want you to know I'm thinking of you. You're never out of my mind, my sweet girl."

"They sound scared," Cammie tells me, and then she's quiet. Considering. "I think they're in big trouble for losing me," she says.

"Mm," I say. The sun is setting behind me as I head east along Highway 30 through Indiana, and I like the way it feels on the back of my ponytail. I'm trying to stay in a peaceful zone. I'm trying not to think that this situation is way above my pay grade.

"Big trouble from who, though?" I say. "Kurch?"

"I don't know," she says. "Whatever cult or corporate entity or collective they were part of, I guess. That's what you're supposed to be helping me with."

"Right on," I say. I scratch the beard hairs under my chin, as I'm prone to do. *I am so screwed,* I think, as Flip and I exchange glances.

He agrees.

It was around Christmastime, Cammie remembers, when Ronnie called to tell her that he thought they'd been bugged. "I mean," he said, "that there's a fucking tracking device. Inside us. Probably in one of the bones of the wrist or ankle."

On Skype, she saw her mouth pinching a little, skeptically, and she tried to smooth out her expression. She didn't not believe him. Not exactly.

But it just seemed so extreme, so paranoid, it was hard to swallow. That was always the problem, these days—it was disconcerting to live in a time in which accepting reality required a suspension of disbelief.

He claimed he had discovered the forty-ninth of their kind—an infant living in Hong Kong whose mother worked for a well-regarded bank, 渣打銀行(香港)有限公司, and he saw, he said, that there was a pattern to the spread of the Spome Derner's seed, the Mandelbrot equation, $z_{n+1} = z_n^2 + c$, he said. "It's like . . . mold . . ." he said, and she was, like, *He's at the word salad stage of mania,* and this was also during a period when he was sending her a lot of pics of his naked body.

"Listen," she said. "I've got to go."

It was late afternoon and she was alone in the living room in a chair next to the Christmas tree, which was twinkling with pink and white LED lights in the shape of candle flames, and she signed out of Skype and set herself to invisible. She was in that old velvet wingback chair that she'd loved since she was a child, it was like something in a children's book from olden days, and she leaned her head against the wing, her laptop warm in her lap like a cat, barefoot, cross-legged, and her father was out of the country and her mother was in her studio, making sculptures out of antique doll parts.

It was snowing, and even though it was only late afternoon the room was already growing dim. She saw the spark of a blue light coming from the ceiling. A miniature CCTV camera, providing security. Watching.

She hadn't really thought about it before. There was an eye in every room and an ever-listening voice-activated AI virtual assistant that could turn on the lights or tell you the temperature or play you a song, there were cameras all along the outside walls, an eye in the driveway and on the perimeter fences. There were hundreds of hours of archived footage of empty rooms, footage of her sitting up in bed scrolling through her Instagram feed or moodily reading *Little Dorrit*, footage of her mother sewing doll's clothes in her studio, her mother quietly masturbating with a vibrator she kept in a nightstand drawer which Cammie had discovered when she was about ten and which had only deepened her burgeoning awareness of the world's sad depravity.

Never once had the security system recorded a robber or a home invader of any sort. Never once had it recorded any paranormal activity.

But as she sat there that day, she thought she could feel a humming from somewhere inside her foot. If you were very still, she thought, you could feel it—a low-level current that was communing with all those watching and listening devices.

"I don't get it," I say. "I don't think a device like that would be buzzing, would it?"

"No," she said. "I mean that it was more like a realization. Maybe more psychological than physical."

"Uh-huh," I say. I know what she means. I have the same thing, sometimes.

"So," I say. "Your mom didn't end up having the baby, I'm guessing."

"No, she did," Cammie says, reflectively. "It was a little girl. She died when she was eighteen months old, just after I turned nineteen. She was born with a neurogenerative disease. Neuronal ceroid lipofuscinosis," Cammie says.

"Well, hell," I say. "I'm sorry to hear that."

"Mm," Cammie says, and she doesn't say anything for a while.

"I think it was her punishment," Cammie says. "They told her not to try to have a baby, but she wouldn't listen."

Too Late to Put the Egg
Back in the Chicken

So it goes: back through Indiana, back down through Ohio and West Virginia—which, of all the states, has changed the least, despite the civil unrest in the rest of the country, despite the plague cities and martial law and so forth, West Virginia remains remarkably constant, for better and worse. I'm not going to bother trying to get through that military checkpoint at Big Walker Mountain Tunnel. I have to take the long way around and all in all it's going to be a good sixteen- or seventeen-hour drive.

I haven't called the number that Cammie gave me, even as I come closer to the town where Patches lives. He grew up in South Carolina, just south of Charleston, and that, apparently, is where he has returned—his Old Low Country Home, as he used to call it. *The Manse St. Germaine,* he would say, in the voice of an actor from the 1940s, and he'd recline on the couch with a glass of whiskey over ice, heavy lidded, and I found him very witty and urbane. But he couldn't have been *that* rich, I thought. Rich people didn't let their sons become doctors. That was a striver's profession.

Out of curiosity, I broke into his bank account once when we were living together and there wasn't even a thousand dollars in it. Still, he'd been very generous in helping me out when I needed money, a lot of times when he went off to school he'd just leave an envelope full of twenty-dollar bills on the table in the breakfast nook.

In the old days, when Patches and I were roommates and best friends, people always thought it was hilarious. Patches was thin, short, and severe, and had been bald since his early twenties, whereas I was six two, built like a linebacker, and very hairy—having rocked a long braid or pony-tail plus beard since a teen. I was regarded as a stoner of low ambi-tion and questionable intelligence, a drug dealer and player of hacky sack who sometimes pretended that he had been a philosophy major at Loyola, whereas Patches was driven and neurotically ambitious. Patches said, apologetically, that he was descended from "old wealth"; whereas I claimed that I had grown up in a trailer park in Alaska. And so forth. The unlikeliness of our friendship delighted our acquaintances. They said we should have our own TV show.

The truth was, most of the things that brought us close were not apparent to the people who knew us. We both had bad habits, nasty hab-its. We liked to shoplift together, for example, we were both thieves, and we both enjoyed telling lies for no reason and committing light vandalism—lighting fires in restaurant bathrooms, putting nails in the tires of cop cars, dissolving a tab of LSD into a coffeemaker in the North-western medical school dean's office.

By the time I get up the nerve to call him, I'm almost halfway through North Carolina, skirting around the Piedmont Triad and traveling qui-etly, unmolested, through Uwharrie National Forest, Flip sitting in the passenger seat in the pose of the Sphinx. He gives me a grim look. *Too late to put the egg back in the chicken,* as my mom used to say.

"I know," I say, and I reluctantly dial the number.

He picks up the phone on the first ring.

"Who's calling?" Patches says. His voice is clipped, uninterested—but I feel the hairs rise on the back of my neck, because it's definitely him. Hard to believe, but it seems that Cammie was right.

"Hey," I say. "This is . . . Davis Dowty. Not sure if you'll remember me."

He's silent, and I'm not entirely sure there's a reason he *would* remem-ber me. Twenty-five years is a long while.

Then he says, "Davey?" And he laughs in that distinct, contagious way I had almost forgotten, but the sound makes me smile involuntarily.

"Yeah," I say. I chuckle uncertainly. "It's . . . good to hear your voice."

"Likewise," says Patches. "Though the circumstances are less than ideal."

"Right on," I say. "But when would they ever not be?"

He lets out a soft breath. It sounds like he's outdoors, in some sort of public area. I can hear music and chanting, and he clears his throat.

"I can guess why you're calling," he says. "But I have to say that I didn't really think you'd get involved. I thought you had a stronger sense of self-preservation."

"I'm not involved," I say. "I'm just an interested party."

He laughs again, and I remember the thing that got me about his laughter was that it always seemed like he was laughing with you but also laughing at something you couldn't see, and at one time that was intoxicating. "Listen," he says. "I'm sorry I can't talk on the phone. I'm going to have to hang up shortly."

"Yeah," I say. "But would you meet with me in person? I'm in the area."

"Ha," he says. "Of course you are. Bless your heart."

"Where do you want to meet?" I say.

"I'm in Charleston currently," he says. "At the Bay Street Biergarten, watching the protests. I imagine I'll be here for another few hours." He pauses, and I can hear the terrible sound of a bagpipe wheezing off in the distance behind him.

"I must warn you," he says. "If you're driving, parking is going to be difficult."

Dang if he isn't right. We start to see protesters and such along the road as we get closer to Charleston. Here are some motorcycle men with helmets in the shape of the ones worn by WWI German soldiers—*Pickelhauben*, I believe they are called, with the spike on top. Here are some barefooted hippies with rainbow-colored hemp backpacks trudging together along the roadside, and some fat white men in Hawaiian shirts carrying AK-47s over their shoulders. Folks have set out lawn chairs to watch the parade and hold up signs that support their favorite team. A person dressed as a fetus is doing a dance and carrying a sign that says, WHAT ABOUT UNBORN LIVES? Others just sit on their porches with glasses of sweet tea, observing.

I check the radio to see if there's some kind of traffic station, but all I

get is a garble of various oldies hits and a couple of right-wing scream-
ers and religious ranters and so I turn off on a side street before I end
up getting stuck in a traffic jam. As I round the corner, a little cadre of
teenagers in black hoodies start calling after me—possibly in hopes that
I've got some Kickin Chickin in my possession. One of the few advan-
tages of this van is that most people, no matter what their creed, have
kindly feelings toward you. "Yo!" the young men cry, waving their arms
hopefully. "Yo!"

I find an alleyway next to a pink two-story rowhouse, put an antitheft
club on the steering wheel and lock up the van, and then we step out
into the afternoon sunlight. Even though it's late October, it's as nice as
a sunny day in late spring, seventy-five degrees or so, a lot of folks in
shorts and flip-flops, including myself. I imagine I'm a confusing specimen. Though I am a big, bearded, braided white man, I do not wear the
stomper shoes of the Norsemen. Instead, I don a pair of pink plastic sunglasses and a pair of rubber clogs, a straw hat and a Lewiston Maineiacs
T-shirt and cargo shorts, and I move along with the crowd at low speed.
I put a bland, puzzled smile on my face, soft shouldered and nonthreat-
ening, my taser and other objects of defense tucked into a fanny pack.
Flip sticks close to my heels, head low but eyes watchful.

There are more people than you'd expect. The whole mess apparently started with a group of white separatists who believed they were
descended from the Vikings and wanted to reclaim Greenland as their
ancestral homeland in the same way that the Jews claimed Palestine.
Though they are virulent anti-Semites, they like to make certain com-
parisons. WHITE HOLOCAUST! reads one sign. YOU WILL NOT
ERASE US! reads another. A group of them are bellowing off in the distance. "Greenland belongs to the Norse!" they chant. "Greenland is our
Israel!"

But these dingbats are not alone. It seems that once the Viking Defa-
mation League had a parade permit, the whole white-separatist community got stirred up and started to flow into Charleston to have parades
of their own. And the antiracist and antifascist folks showed up as
well, to counterprotest, and now the National Guardsmen and Homeland Security Forces and citizen militias have also arrived to "keep the
peace," as they say. In short, I'm surprised that the city isn't already in

flames, but so far the vibe seems relatively cheerful, more like we're at a state fair, and in fact some entrepreneurs have set up vending carts to sell bottled water and funnel cakes and chocolate-chip corn dogs and so forth. There's a cart with a rainbow-colored awning that declares JUSTICE PIZZA FREEDOM EQUALITY LOVE 4 ALL!

What's Cammie up to right now? It's been hours and hours since we spoke, and I hope that she's found herself a secure location and something to eat. Last time I talked to her, she said she was "making arrangements," and I hope that means she's serious about going into deep hiding. I'd like to think that she's in the boxcar of a train or in the trailer of a nondescript semi, curled up in a crate, on her way to one of the less densely populated regions of the country.

I told her that there was a family I knew that lived near the Salton Sea, she could potentially stay with them—and also, a collective that worked at the old copper mine in Anyox, British Columbia, might take her in, I said, if I sent them some money.

"Thanks," she said. "But I'll take care of myself."

And then we were both of us quiet, just the sound of our breaths digitized and traveling through the phones. "I get it," I said.

It makes me sad that she can't trust me, but to be honest I don't fully trust me, either. Who's to say that I won't be compelled to betray her at some point in the future? When I look deep within my heart, I can't guarantee anything.

Patches is sitting at a table on a patio outside a pub. He's wearing sunglasses and an N95 surgical mask, but I recognize him right away by his posture—his arm draped over the back of a chair, cigarette dangling loosely between his fingers, legs crossed at the knee, his foot ticking back and forth with slow amusement, like the tail of a cat that's watching a bird through a window. I raise my arm and he lifts his eyebrows, watching as I separate from the flow of the crowd and make my way up the steps toward the patio of the biergarten. In the street, heavily armed bearded men in helmets with antlers on them are marching along behind a bagpiper, some of them carrying signs with Anglo-Saxon runes, some of them carrying battle axes.

"Sir," says a young blond woman behind a lectern, and it takes me a moment to realize she's addressing me. "That section is reserved!" She brandishes a laminated menu in my direction. Her hair is astoundingly straight and silky, the color of butter. "We have additional outdoor seating around this way," she says urgently.

"Thanks," I say. "But I'm going over to talk to that fellow." I gesture toward Patches, and she gives my outfit the once-over and her face hardens and I'd guess that she's seconds away from calling for backup when Patches makes a magnanimous, kingly come-hither gesture in my direction.

"It's fine, Aria," he says to the alarmed hostess. "He's a friend."

Though it's clear she finds my appearance, and Flip, doubtful, she's a professional. "What are you having to drink, sir?" she says, suddenly honey voiced, and I tell her Tito's vodka with a lemon slice, no ice, and off she goes without a backward glance.

"Sit!" says Patches, from beneath his umbrella-ed table, and gestures at the white wrought-iron chair across from him. "Delight!" he says, which is the way he says *Hello* or *Good to see you.*

"I can't believe you're still alive," he says, as I lower myself into the chair and Flip settles, shoulders hunched, at my feet beneath the table.

"Ha ha," I say. "What gives you the impression that I'm still alive?"

As always, his laugh is dark and complicated—it's got a lot of odd minor-key notes in it, which almost express a musical phrase. It kind of sounds like he's laughing to the tune of "Rock-a-Bye Baby."

Our awkward silence is filled with the sound of the crowd—people intoning slogans at one another, and people telling jokes and laughing, and people screeching, and a helicopter off in the near distance and a grinning, baby-faced weeble drone trying to maneuver its way along the sidewalk, beeping as if to say, "Make way, please! I'm coming through!" Patches and Flip and I sit there watching for a while, and then the girl comes back with my vodka and Patches gestures at her.

"We'll have an order of the Bloomin' Onion," he says. "With an extra side of the horseradish sauce."

"Of course," the young woman says, and makes a little bow or curtsy and I lean back because it always freaks me out when people are servile. I never wanted to be part of the ruling class, that's one thing about me.

But Patches likes it. He leans back as the girl goes off on her quest and I can't even guess what he's thinking/feeling/seeing. He closes his eyes and then, after a moment, reopens them.

"So," he says. "The Sisters have gotten to you, have they?" He lifts his mask up like it's a visor and takes a sip of whiskey from his shot glass. "I hope they're paying you."

"I'm not under anybody's employ in this situation," I say. "I'm just a neutral observer who wants to be helpful. There's this young woman who says she's my biological daughter, so—I agreed to make some inquiries on her behalf. As a favor."

"You only spoke with *one* of them?" he says.

"Yeah," I say, and shift, uncertainly.

"Are you sure?" he says. "How would you know the difference?"

And I don't say anything. *Sisters,* I think. *Sisters, plural.*

I don't know whether to believe him or not—it's very likely that Patches is just yanking my chain. But still, it gives me pause. *How would I know the difference?* he asks, and I can't help but think of the times when Cammie seemed inconsistent, when I struggled to get a handle on her personality. Maybe it was because I was talking to more than one person? The idea gives me the fantods.

"How many of them are there?" I say, at last, and he smiles faintly and makes a beneficent gesture.

"Hard to say," he says. "I haven't been part of that project in a long while. But I'd venture to guess that there are more than a hundred. Of varying ages. It would be hilarious if there weren't so many dangerous people involved."

"Mm," I nod, as if I know what he's talking about. "It's kind of a mess, isn't it?"

In the distance, there's the fizzle and pop of flashbangs going off, and people along the street pause and lift their heads. Alarmed cries can be heard, followed by the voices of authorities filtered through megaphones.

Then a woman nearer to us lets out a scream, and the frozen crowd suddenly ripples. A few people turn and start running, pushing their way past moms and dads with strollers and grannies carrying small Confederate flags and drunk women in Lilly Pulitzer capri pants, and once a few people start running the whole crowd turns en masse like a bank of starlings, rushing and scattering, following the flow of new panic. The people are wailing indignantly as tear gas cannisters start to rain down on them. A man runs by with a baby strapped to his chest in a papoose contraption, and the poor infant is waving its arms and the look of terror on its face makes me stand up and clench my fists, and Patches is also standing in an instant, as the stinging stench of pepper spray begins to waft into the restaurant.

"We should leave," Patches says, and takes me by the elbow, walking fast and guiding me past the bar and into the restaurant's kitchen and toward the back door, and Flip hurries along behind us, and the last thing I see before we exit is our hostess Aria, holding our Bloomin' Onion as the tear gas begins to drift over her.

Low Country Tidings

We come into the living room of Patches's house and there is a chimpanzee sitting in a wingback chair by the fireplace, smoking a blunt. He holds the cigar tip between his thumb and index finger and takes a slow drag. His toes play with each other as he puckers his lips and blows out a smoke ring.

"Holy shit!" I say. "A monkey! That is so cute!"

Patches clears his throat uncomfortably. "Davey," he says, and places the palm of his hand on my shoulder blade, "this is Ward." Then he gestures toward the chimp, who is wearing a pair of Levi 501 jeans and a black T-shirt. "Ward," Patches says, "this is Davey."

Ward is less than impressed. He takes another grim puff from his blunt, and then makes a few elaborate gestures with his paws. Sign language, I guess, because Patches responds in kind and they have a little back-and-forth, signing at each other in an emphatic way that feels like it might be a restrained argument.

Meanwhile, my own animal companion has been excluded, left outside. I can picture Flip sitting on the columned porch of Patches's manse, shifting anxiously from foot to foot, worried, agitated.

Patches touches my arm. "Let's go out back for a moment, shall we?" he says.

We'd made our way by helicopter to Patches's estate on Kiawah Island, and admittedly I am a little dazed. Like most people of means, Patches lives in what you might call a secure compound, surrounded by a high fence of decorative concrete that looks like a quaint stone wall in Hobbiton or Scotland or something, except that the delicately woven sculpted metal curlicues at the top of the fence are actually razor wire, and there are mounted lights and cameras every ten feet or so, and even some of those four-legged scampering drones that hop along like rabbits but look like mechanical beetles. Now, as we stand outside on the back deck, I can see them gamboling through the grass, patrolling the perimeter. We look out onto a long, overgrown yard that slopes down to a dirty, tree-clogged river.

"Dude," I say, as we stand there. "When did you get the chimp? That's so exotic!"

"Listen," Patches says, "could you please not refer to him as a chimp or a monkey? That's very upsetting to him."

"Wow!" I say. "Sorry!"

"His name is Ward," Patches says. "Just call him Ward."

"Right on," I say.

Patches lights a cigarette, his hand trembling a little, and we stand there watching fireflies bobbling above the grass. "Maybe don't use the term *exotic*, either," he says. "That's problematic."

"Gotcha," I say. "Understood."

He nods. He's just a silhouette in the dark, but the tip of his cigarette glows as he breathes in and I get that shudder of almost remembering something. Down toward the river the bird they call chuck-will's-widow makes its insistent, gloomy crooning.

"I tried to help you, you know?" Patches says at last. "I mean, you just randomly showed up at my frat house and we had an . . . encounter, and then—what was it? Two years later? You come back to Chicago and I could see you needed a friend, so I made myself available. I got you a few sperm donation gigs, just because I liked you. I didn't have any ulterior motive. And I didn't have any idea that you were—what do they call it?—*on retainer?* And I wouldn't have known, either, until Tim Ribbons came to talk to me. He just paid me to look after you, that's all. But I would have done it anyway."

"Look after me?" I say, and he turns to smile with his chin down.

"Keep an eye on you," he says. "Keep you occupied. I think he thought you were my boyfriend."

"Huh," I say.

"We should go back in," Patches says. "Ward will think we're talking about him."

Ward is still sitting in the same chair looking at something on a laptop, and he glances up and does another bit of hand puppetry in Patches's direction. I have no knowledge of American Sign Language whatsoever; nevertheless, I can intuit the tenor of the exchange is still of a quarreling nature, and it kind of feels obvious that I myself am the subject of their disagreement. But I try not to be uncomfortable.

"Hey, Ward!" I say. "How's it going, buddy?" He just stares at me for what feels like a full minute before he finally lifts his paw, or maybe I should say hand, into a gesture of hello.

I'm thinking about that one time back when we were first living together and Patches took me to his medical school building to show me his research lab. It was about three in the morning, and the building itself was like a haunted castle. "The Feinberg School of Medicine—and Impenetrable Fortress!" said Patches, clowning. But he had keys, and no one stopped us as we entered and then ambled down some flights of stairs, fairly well stoned as I recall, chuckling at each other.

And then we were in a sub-basement and he opened a security door onto a long hallway that had bare pipes running along the ceiling. "Most people don't even know this exists," Patches said. The fluorescent lights mounted to the walls flickered, and I felt spooked and I stood close behind him and he took my hand and gave it a squeeze. "Don't worry," he said. "It's fine." And I remember how I really liked him. I was so surprised that he'd noticed that I was nervous. And that he would make a gesture and put his hand on my hand to calm me down, that was really insightful and impressive, I thought.

"Here we go," Patches said, and his set of keys jingled as he unlocked a windowless metal door with the number 00237 stenciled on it.

I heard the stir and scamper of them even before he turned on the light. And the smell—dense body odor and hair, almost human and almost like a pigsty.

The monkeys were in cages stacked five high, and they lined two walls of a hallway that extended down into darkness. Hundreds of little monkeys, and they all turned to stare at us. Some gripped the bird-cage bars, some hopped angrily or excitedly but their cages didn't give them much room to move around. They set up a chorus of cheeping and chittering.

"Holy shit!" I said, and I grinned because I don't think I'd ever seen a live monkey before. "Monkeys!" I said. "Are we going to rescue them?"

Because I was stoned out of my mind, I had this idea that we could let them all go. I imagined them all flowing thankfully out of their pens and down the flickering hallway and up the stairs and scattering across the city, making homes for themselves in parks and abandoned buildings and so forth, except that one of the kind of meek ones would hang back and I would pick him up and say, "Don't worry, little dude, I will take care of you," and that one would become my lifelong pet.

"*Rescue them?*" Patches said, just as I was imagining that my pet monkey would be named Trusty.

"Don't even *think* about trying to take one of these fuckers," Patches said. "Jesus! Not unless you want to spend forty years in federal prison for industrial espionage!"

"Oh," I said.

"They're not intelligent," Patches said. "They're lower in IQ than squirrels."

"Oh," I said.

"I just thought that it would be fun to come down here and mess around," Patches said. "But don't break anything or steal anything, okay?"

"Okay," I said. And he did let me hold one. I remember how its long tail wrapped around my wrist like a snake. The word *prehensile* came to me. I beamed friendly vibes down into its tiny, humanoid face, and fed it a raisin.

And now I wonder if that's maybe how Patches got Ward? If Ward was some kind of lab chimp that Patches had met and they'd hit it off and become friends—despite the situation, despite the fact that he was the scientist and Ward was the specimen—and that ultimately Patches had adopted him and brought him to live at last in a forever home.

I realize that I'm thinking about these random memories instead of trying to parse all the information that Patches has relayed to me or trying to come up with the questions that I should be following up on. But I believe strongly in the importance of free association, that our subconscious sometimes gives us messages in times of stress if we just allow ourselves to be open to chance and the arbitrary.

And that's what I'm looking for while I make a peanut-butter-and-jelly sandwich in the kitchen, and Patches and Ward are sitting on the couch in a more conciliatory mode now, signing at one another peace-. ably but sternly. I'm looking for a message.

The style of the house is very minimalist, Scandinavian I guess you'd say, with a few folksy touches here and there. There's a nice needlepoint wall hanging that portrays a boy child and a girl child underneath a cypress tree. "Low Country Tidings," it says—one of those folk art things that might be worth a lot of money, and I make a note of it. If I get a chance, I could steal it before I leave.

"Hey," I say, "do you all have any milk? I wouldn't mind a glass of milk with this sandwich."

Patches glances over. "We're a dairy-free household," he says. "But there's almond milk."

"Haw! I didn't realize almonds had titties," I say.

It's lame, but it's an attempt. I'm trying to feel my way into the situation. Back in the old days, Patches was a sucker for corny jokes and puns, but now I reckon he has more sophisticated taste. He looks at me blankly, and Ward gives me a stare of dignified disgust. He considers me a vulgar person.

"Ha ha," I say. "Joke," I say, and show my teeth in a big smile and my subconscious tweaks a little but still it won't tell me what to do.

"How about a real drink," Patches says. "Would you like a vodka and cranberry? Greyhound? Screwdriver?"

It's weird. We never slept together that I can recall, but there was a lot more physical closeness in our friendship than I've had since then, and I'm aware that I can remember what he smells like, I can remember sitting together in our underwear beneath a blanket on the couch in that Evanston apartment, watching TV or playing video games, and he would put his cold feet on my thigh to warm them up; and sometimes, drunk and stoned, we would wrestle to electronic dance music and blow pot smoke into each other's mouths, not quite kissing. I know what his breath tastes like.

This stuff is probably not important—I wouldn't even bring it up, except I recollect that there was this one time when we were tripping on mushrooms and I was giving him a scalp massage and he leaned back and was like, *Davey, what sound does a gorilla make?* And I was like, *Oo-oo-oo?* and he was like, *Keep doing that,* and I kept on rubbing his head and making my ape noises and he put his hands down the front of his pants and began stroking himself and it was slightly uncomfortable but I accepted it because I was 'shrooming and it seemed like everything in the world was good and acceptable.

And now I feel like, meeting Ward: *Hmmm. What's that about?*

None of my business, really.

We go out back again and sit in some sweet Adirondack chairs, passing a bong between us. Patches puts on some music. The weed is some kind of Indica-dominant strain, possibly related to Headband or Trainwreck—very physical, and I feel it almost immediately as we sit there, surrounded by citronella candles, surrounded by the *zuzz* of living insects and the calls of night birds and New Order's song "Blue Monday" is playing now and Patches and I both start singing at exactly the right time: *How does it feel . . .* and I glance over to him and grin and then laugh, because we're synchronized, we both know the lyrics by heart, we listened to this album so many times together, and Ward, who seems mollified, perches on the arm of Patches's chair and leans his head on Patches's shoulder as we sing.

And then when that's done and I'm exhilarated and in an elevated frame of mind the mixtape transitions into some kind of cocktail jazz bullshit and Patches sighs and leans his head back so his Adam's apple is fully exposed.

"Jesus Christ, Davis," he says. "Why are you doing this?"

"What?" I say. It's a terrible transition. I was just starting to feel comfortable, and now I have to think again. Ward stares at me steadily. He's got his arm draped over Patches's shoulders and he has placed one foot just below the line of Patches's khaki shorts, his long toes clutching Patches's bare knee, and I meet his gaze and shrug.

"The question is whether it's worth risking your life for," Patches says. "You're not indispensable to them anymore."

"I know that," I say—and I do, though it has never been spelled out so plainly in so few words. "The thing is," I say, "I think I might be on a voyage of self-discovery."

"Hah," Patches says. "That's why I can't stop loving you, Davey," he says. "You're so blissfully self-unaware."

I smile as if it's a compliment and make a hand gesture that I hope doesn't mean anything in ASL. "So that's why I'm here, right?" I say. "I'm just here to talk, aren't I? I'm assuming that you're not planning to kill me . . . or . . . ?"

"Pff," Patches says, and we smile at each other again. I like the high I'm getting off his psychedelic bong, and I sit there, feeling the sound of the frogs on the river pulse pleasantly against my skin. "Say, what's that glooping sound?" I ask, and Patches says there are schools of tadpoles in the shallows of the river. Patches says it's probably the splashing of baby alligators come to eat them.

"Alligators," I say. "That's so neat!"

"Oh, they're a nuisance," Patches says. "Our neighbor found a ten-foot-long monster in her pool last week."

"But they don't attack people, right?" I say. "I've always heard that they're more afraid of us than we are of them."

"Not really," Patches says, and I stretch my neck and peer down toward the river, hoping to get a glimpse of a baby alligator. "They're not terribly aggressive," he says, "but I wouldn't call them shy, either."

Patches takes a sip from his very strong screwdriver, which appears to be approximately seventy percent vodka. "In any case," he says, "we don't have any trouble disposing of corpses, when necessary."

"Ha ha," I say.

"Ha ha," Patches says.

Even Ward shows his sharply fanged incisors in what I guess is a grin.

* * *

Remember when I was living in Mrs. Dowty's boardinghouse and how I met Patches at the bar? That could have happened randomly, I think. The fact that he found me and told me about the clinic he worked at which would give me fifty dollars for a sample of my semen, it doesn't mean Tim Ribbons or some other entity put him up to it. *Just because I liked you,* he says, and it would be nice to believe that.

He has been hooked into any number of organizations. But he is no longer. Even a person as low as me can sense that he bears the social stench of the ostracized. He's one of those rich people that other rich people think of as expendable. He's the kind of rich man who will go to prison eventually, and it will shortly thereafter be reported that he committed suicide in his cell.

So I've got to ask the right questions.

I get out of the Adirondack chair and sit down on the floor of the deck and try to think. I'm observing as Patches exchanges gestures with Ward, it's kind of fun to watch, the way Patches pulls broad gestures and makes his fingers into precise, shadow-puppet shapes, and Ward moving his big long fingers in kind. They seem to have come to some agreement, and Ward rolls his eyes darkly and then turns to look at me. I pretend that I haven't been staring at them this whole time as if mesmerized and I nod politely as he hands me the bong and I take it and make a point of not balking that there is monkey slobber around the mouthpiece.

It could be, I think, *a game-changer . . . ? A transformative . . . ?*

I take a hit and hold it in, looking down at the river and the live oak trees and slash pines dripping with Spanish moss. There is a wind chime that is making its puzzled-xylophone sounds, and the singing of the frogs that the alligators haven't eaten yet. *So, listen,* I think. *So: listen. So . . . the question is*—I imagine myself saying it, practicing it in the theater of my mind, but it feels off. I remove my left clog and scratch my foot sole thoughtfully.

"Hey," I say, "do you all have any wasabi peas? Or snack mix of any kind? I'm having a craving."

"I'm not sure," Patches says. "Ward? Do we?" And Ward gives him that *Wait, did you just talk to me like I'm your servant?* look, and then there is body language I can read. *What? I didn't do anything!* Patches's body says, and Ward goes, *Fine,* and gets up from his chair with chilly dignity. He takes the bong out of my hand and gives it to Patches and then turns and stalks off without looking at either of us.

"Oops," I say. "I hope I didn't . . ."

"Don't," Patches says, and glances over his shoulder toward where Ward has disappeared. "Just leave it, okay?" He looks down at the bong in his hand and sniffs the lip of it. "Ugh," he says, wrinkling his nose, and he puts it down by the leg of his chair.

"You say *ugh* a lot," I observe, and Patches gives me a long look as I stretch out my legs and flex my toes.

He tips his glass back and drains it and crunches a piece of ice between his teeth.

"Ward!" he calls. "Would you mix me another drink while you're at it?" He puts a cigarette in his mouth and then feels over his pockets for a lighter.

"Here," I say. I take my own lighter out of the vest pocket of my tee and give it a flick, holding the flame out to him, and he leans over, his lips puckered, and touches the tip of his cigarette to the fire. He breathes in and then lets the smoke plume out of his nose. On his mixtape it's the Psychedelic Furs playing now.

"I love this song," I say.

"I remember," he says. We sit there, listening together for a minute or so. "The ghost in you . . ." I sing, and then I hate the sound of my voice, I am an ugly singer, and Patches stirs the last piece of ice in his glass.

"Why are you doing this?" he says. "You know I can't help you."

"For real?" I say. "Why not?"

"We're not on the same side, Davis," he says. "For one thing."

"Oh," I say. I nod wistfully. "I heard that you and Brayden Kurch were on the outs, or whatever."

"Ugh," Patches says. "Kurch is the least of my concerns."

"Do you think I should just try to contact him directly, then?" I say, and he turns his head away from me and blows out smoke.

"How would you do that?" he says. "He lives on a sea-steading somewhere between Bermuda and Puerto Rico. You can't just walk up and knock on his door."

"So maybe let me just ask you one small question, then. For old times' sake."

"Fine," says Patches. "I probably won't tell you the truth, but I'm curious."

He cocks his head in that way that always stunned me in the olden days, it's this subtle tilt that's both kindly and belittling and God, I envied it, back when I wanted to be a real person.

"All right," I say. I'm sitting on the floor with my clogs off and my hands on my knees, and I look up at him. "The question is: Why would my sperm . . . or whatever . . . ?"

But then Ward comes loping onto the deck and Patches turns his head. Ward has his long, ropey arms extended, with a drink in one large hand, and a pink candy dish in the other. He gives Ward the cocktail and thrusts the dish toward me. There are five wasabi peas in it.

"Thanks, Ward," I say, and when he looks at me, I am reminded of a news story I read about a pet chimp who literally ripped off a woman's face. They are very strong and dangerous, are chimps, and Ward perches back on the arm of Patches's chair, his inhospitable eyes upon me, and I put one of the peas into my mouth.

It's not exactly an answer to my question, but Patches decides to start holding forth about sheep-human hybrids, and pig-human hybrids. *Chimeras,* he calls them, and tries for a while to educate me about blastocysts and genome editing and technology and he goes into a long explanation of what an RNA-guided DNA endonuclease enzyme is—the upshot being, according to Patches, the technology now exists to grow human organs inside pigs or sheep, so if you wanted to, you could keep a herd of them with your DNA, growing replacement organs for yourself as needed.

"That would be ironic," I say, "if a pig was hosting the stomach that would one day digest his bacon!"

"Very ironic," Patches says. He takes a big swallow from his drink and gives Ward a sidelong look. "Eventually, there won't be a need for the things that your people do."

* * *

One of the things I've learned over the years: a discussion of what "my people" do is almost never productive. I make no apologies for my country, or my kind, or my various employers. I don't align myself with them politically or morally or emotionally: I'm neutral.

I'm still sitting there at Patches's feet with my legs crossed in a kind of half-assed lotus pose, gazing up at him like a schoolchild during story time. I scratch my ear thoughtfully. "So . . . Brayden Kurch is involved in this chimera thing, eh?" I say. "In addition to distributing all these little baby embryos that I fertilized. That's crazy!"

"Brayden Kurch is a dilettante," Patches tells me grimly. "A nothing. He's not an intellectual. He's a self-promoting con man. He pretends to be profound and he manages to sell his various schemes to the gullible, but in truth he just wants to be the spiritual leader of a death cult. That's your answer."

"Dang!" I say. "That's messed up." I shake my head and adjust my feet, which are sort of slipping off my knees and into more of a Sukhasana pose.

"But you know—" I say and grin apologetically, such a dopey ape am I. "Actually . . . my big question is more along the lines of what my part—and the part of my progeny—might be in all of this? I mean, Patches, you don't have to give me the whole story, but you could give me a nibble, right?"

"Oh, God, Davey," Patches says. "Your *progeny?* That's what I've always loved about you, you're so eloquent and sentimental about the stupidest things. Lord, I remember once when you told me this story about how your mother made you drown a baby rabbit, and these big tears were streaming down your face as you talked about it and I was fascinated because it's so common for people with PTSD to focus on these small, utterly banal moments, rather than to face the real traumas in their lives. Also common with sociopaths, apparently, just saying! But either way, I'd have thought you'd have developed at least a little more awareness with age."

"Right on," I say. "I guess I've failed in that regard."

"Progeny!" Patches says. He takes a long pull from his drink, and he and Ward glance at each other and then back at me.

"I can't believe I told you that story about the rabbit," I say.

"Pff," Patches says. "I know you better than you know yourself."

"I know myself plenty," I retort. "Though I realize there's still work to be done."

I stare down at the river, down to where the security lights are sweeping across the roots of the cypress trees, which poke up out of the water like periscopes.

"Look," I say. "This isn't even about *her*, you know. I'm curious for personal reasons, too."

I look him in the eye, and I hook it. My pupil to his pupil.

"I mean, really, Patches, why would they use *me* to make all these babies? That's what I can't figure out. Why would they want my trashy DNA? What makes me special?"

Patches leans back and looks at Ward again, and Ward makes a hand gesture that I think means *Wait*. The moment is pregnant. I just don't know what with.

"Oh, honey." Patches passes the bong to me, reaching down as if he is patting a sad child on the head. "Baby, I don't want you to think that you're not special."

"Ha," I say, and take the bong, and push my lips against the mouthpiece and strike my lighter. I blow out the smoke. "I don't think that. I'm not saying I'm special or not special. That's not of interest to me."

"Actually, you have very unusual DNA," Patches says, kindly. "You have an inordinately high number of strands that are associated with the Neanderthal genome."

"Huh," I say, and the hair on the back of my neck prickles.

"It's a minor anomaly," Patches says. "Kind of a little joke on my part. But Kurch's people loved that angle, that the babies had unique non–*Homo sapiens* DNA. But ultimately the whole thing is just a scam—a Ponzi scheme. Brayden had this whole shtick about these embryos being 'post-human,' but the ultimate selling point was that you—and your 'progeny,' as you say—had the potential to inherit an enormous multinational fortune. Getting one of these embryos was like investing in a hot stock. At one point, your semen was selling for high six figures."

"Huh," I say. "My mom used to tell me sometimes that my daddy was rich, but I never took her seriously."

"Nor should you have," Patches says. "The likelihood of you or your offspring inheriting even a paper clip is slim to none."

"But," I say, and there's that sinking feeling again, "that doesn't make any sense."

"No," Patches says. "It doesn't. Nor does the stock market. Nor does any of the hogwash that Brayden Kurch has been selling people. You haven't even read *Transhumanist Séance*, have you?"

"I picked up a copy once, but I misplaced it."

"So you don't know that we're on the verge of evolving into two new species? One will be bodiless and digital and immortal, and the other will be physical and empathic and attuned to the earth and servile. You're the latter."

"Wait," I say. "Rich people are downloading their brains to computers or something? And then they'll be served by, like, mutants with my DNA?"

"No, Davey," Patches says. He makes a little shrugging expression with his lips—a *moue*, I think it's called in French—and I observe as he rests his head against Ward's shoulder. "*Transhumanist Séance* is a bizarre mix of crackpot eugenics and creaky sci-fi tropes. It's not real. It has only a tenuous basis in science and medicine. And yet—many of the minor affluent bought into it. That's Brayden Kurch's one spark of genius: I never would have guessed that he could find so many suckers, but so it goes. Your DNA is the Eucharist of his fake religion, and your *progeny* are"—he waves his hand—"a grift."

I have all kinds of thoughts, of course. My mind is buzzing with them as I sit there cross-legged at Patches's feet, my mouth open slightly— yes, Cammie, the resting face of a simpleton can be an advantage.

How much of what he says is true? Fifty percent? Twenty-five? An eighth? I don't know. Patches is mean as dirt, no doubt, but what comes to me now are memories of times that he did me a kindness, the times when he brought me a glass of water when I was sick or woke me up when I was passed out on the floor and got me on the couch and covered me with an afghan. The many times he gave me money, just because he knew I needed it. That doesn't mean nothing, I don't think.

"So," I say, as if I am neither surprised nor unsurprised by his revelations. As if I might've known all this. Or as if I don't believe a thing he says. "So," I say. "You were an obstetrician, right?"

"Oh, Jesus," he says, and I watch as he takes a little clear plastic packet out of his pocket, and carefully shakes it out onto his fist and snorts it. "I've done that kind of work, but only in very rare cases. Mostly, only as a consultant."

"Cammie," I say. "My—Cammie, she says that you were the obstetrician."

"Ugh," Patches says. "I wouldn't say that. We were so short staffed, I might have filled in on occasion." He bends down again and snorts against the ham of his hand, and Ward makes a sharp gesture toward him, which Patches ignores.

In general I don't have a problem with people getting drunk or high as is necessary for their particular situation, people can do whatever they need to do, that's my belief, but my sense is that Ward has grown weary of it. His irritation emanates from him in waves as Patches sniffs delicately.

"This is so frustrating!" Patches exclaims. "It's like watching a blindfolded kid at a birthday party going in the opposite direction of the piñata."

He stands up and leans a wobbly elbow against the railing, and claws one hand against his chest, searching for his pack of cigarettes, and so I stand up and hand him a smoke and light it for him and he nods at me, *Thank you thank you,* and then leans back and breathes out smoke toward the October stars. Cepheus. Pegasus.

"Okay," I say. "What would you ask yourself, if you were me?"

Before he can answer, I see that Ward is signing in Patches's direction. *Stop,* is the gist of it. Possibly Ward is saying, *Shut your stupid mouth you motherfucking asshole,* but I don't know ASL so I can only guess.

"If I were you," Patches says, "I'd ask myself whether there were any more of *me.* Surely you can't think that you're an only child?"

"Wait," I say. "What?"

Meanwhile, Ward is making quick, sharp, exasperated hand gestures, and Patches spreads his palms broadly and Ward makes some more angry signals with his fingers.

"I did not," Patches says. "Lighten up." He gives Ward a big smile and signs something, but Ward doesn't sign anything back. They stare at one another.

"C'mon," Patches says. "Dance with me. I love this song."

He holds his hand out to Ward and begins to boogie. "C'mon," he says, and he's always been a good dancer, a provocative dancer, too. He and Ward gaze at each other as he grinds his hips, but their fingers do not communicate. Patches puts out his tongue and kicks off his boat shoes and prances, lithely, barefoot.

"C'mon," he says, and takes off his shirt, and does a passable shimmy of his belly. "Ward? It's time for the forgiveness dance."

But Ward is having no truck with forgiveness dancing. He sits there stonily, and so Patches turns to me, grooving his arms and swaying his hips, giving his ass a little twerk.

"Don't mind him," Patches says to me. "I hope you don't feel unwelcome." He puts his hands on my sides and tries to push me into his rhythm, and I kind of shift from foot to foot along with him a little bit but not too much because I don't want to upset Ward any further.

Have you ever seen that movie called *Who's Afraid of Virginia Woolf?* with Elizabeth Taylor in it? I feel like I'm in the *Planet of the Apes* version of that.

"Patches," I say. "Maybe we should sit down again, man. What was that crap you snorted? It's making you a little wiggly."

"No," Patches says. "You are hilarious if you think I'm going to stop dancing. Didn't you used to love to dance?"

"Well," I say. "In the right circumstances."

The song that's playing is Shannon's "Let the Music Play," but it's like a twenty-minute remixed version, and Patches, shirtless, shoeless, now takes off his shorts and bomps his ass in my direction. Then he does a hard strut toward Ward and raises his arm full length and snaps his finger and cocks his hip, very sassy.

He looks over his shoulder at me. "Ward doesn't want me to tell you this, but . . . he's also your progeny. Or more like your brother, or cousin . . ."

Patches is still grinning, still swaying to the beat of the song when Ward rises from his perch on the chair leg and in one second, he plants his enormous long-fingered paw against the side of Patches's face and *bam!* Patches is flat on the floor. I wouldn't call it an assault, exactly.

Patches hasn't been wounded, but he nevertheless is now pinned face-to-floorboard by a very powerful hominid creature.

"Whoa, whoa!" I say. I'm not sure what I should do in this situation. If Ward is, in fact, my cousin or brother or whatever, I'm super glad for him that he slapped Patches. But if he's actually more like a pet—an animal?—maybe I should intervene?

"Hey," I say. "This isn't necessary. Let's all just take a breath and center . . ."

But Ward interrupts me with a glare so fiery that my voice goes dry. He points at me sharply, and then at the sliding door into the kitchen. *You need to leave,* is the gist of what he's saying.

"It's fine," Patches says, and he rises up on his elbows and also gives me the *You need to leave* look. "Nothing to worry about," he says. His coiffed hairpiece is awry, and he looks pale, but he sits up and puts his shirt on backward. "Let's all take a moment," he says, and pulls the shirt down so that it covers his privates. "Ward and I just need to have a little alone time, and . . ."

"Sure," I say. "Of course."

I go back through the sliding doors and into the kitchen and then into the front room where I first saw Ward sitting on the wingback chair, and then I wander down a hallway until I find a bathroom.

Dang, I think. The things that Patches has told me are a lot to process, and most of it, I have to say, seems far-fetched. Chimeras and Neanderthal DNA and my sperm selling for high six figures! Plus the idea that there are more of my kind out there, and that Ward is somehow one of them. I saw a program about human-chimpanzee hybrids once on a TV show called *Unexplained!* But I never took it seriously, any more than I believed the tales of Sasquatch and so forth.

The bathroom is long and narrow, made up almost entirely of black and white marble. There is a square sink, and a toilet and a bidet and a small, tasteful hot tub at the end. Behind a Japanese shoji door, there is a shower. There is a shelf of sumptuous white towels, and a single, diamond-shaped window that looks like it's going to be tough for a man of my size to fit through.

I lock the door and sit down on the floor with my back to it.

The one thing Patches told me that I do pretty much believe is that there's more than one Cammie I've been talking to. Three or four, is my guess, tag-teaming me, and it makes me sad, to think that they played me like that.

And yet I ask myself—what choice did they have, really? And you know what? If it turns out there are multiple Cammies, I don't give a shit. Whatever debt I might owe to one, I owe to them all equally.

Do you believe in instinct? I don't really, but still, there is some magnet that pulls me when I think about her—them—my offspring, my babies, yes, it's ridiculous but it is a strangely powerful feeling and maybe it turns out that most of our emotions and longings are hardwired into us after all.

I pull my secret Cammie phone out of the thigh pocket of my cargo shorts and dial her number, sitting with the back of my head pressed hard against the door, listening to the phone ring, but also listening to hear if Patches and Ward come back into the house.

And then she picks up. "Where are you?" she says. A Cammie says.

"I'm at Patches's place," I whisper. "Where are you?"

"What do you mean, you're at Patches's place?" she says, and I try to gauge if her voice is the same or different from the last voice I heard—which seems like a long time ago. "Are you serious? You're in his *home*?"

"Where're you?" I say. "Are you safe?"

"Yeah," she says. "For now. But what's going on with you? You've talked to him?"

"You need to make your way to the Salton Sea, like I told you," I say. "From there book passage to Hawaii, as soon as you can. The people I told you about will help you."

"I'm working on it," she says. "Just tell me what's happening. Has he told you anything?"

"Well," I say. "Yes and no."

My head feels unpleasantly swimmy—not like pot, I don't think. Like something stronger. I look at the wall hanging above the hot tub, and it doubles, jiggling gelatinously. It takes me a moment to realize that it says the same thing as the wall hanging in the kitchen. *Low Country Tidings*.

And now I'm aware that the vibe here is much worse than I thought.

My subconscious has finally relayed its message, which is *You are not safe here.*

"I've got to go," I say. "I think I need to excape."

There's a tingling in my scalp that feels like it's pressing toward my brain, and my eyeballs are pulsing as strongly as my heartbeat. I sense my fingers enlarging, and I'm pretty sure I've been dosed with something. The cereal? The almond milk?

The wasabi peas!

Of course, it was the peas, I think, and my neck muscles go loose as I try to stand up, my head wobbles on its stalk as I grip a towel rack and try to make my feet touch parallel to the floor.

I'm aware now that I'm a twenty-minute helicopter ride from downtown Charlotte, and the van is parked somewhere beyond that, and the question of how to get back hasn't been considered thoroughly enough.

"Did he leave?" Patches says. I can hear his voice beyond the bathroom door, down the hallway, and I assume he's just come in from the back deck. "I think he left, which is what a person would do after witnessing . . . that kind of circumstance. I can't believe you did that."

I have made it to the sink, and I lean heavily against it. I try to breathe in and breathe out, just focusing on oxygenating my lungs as much as possible.

"Why does it matter to you?" says Patches, a little closer now even as I'm trying to crank open the diamond window. "He'll be dead within a week," Patches says. "If his own people don't kill him, Kurch's will."

I peer down from the bathroom window and Flip is sitting below, staring up at me. Even if I can squeeze through the window, it's a good thirty feet to the ground. I wish I could command Flip to bring some soft branches and such to buffer my landing.

Meanwhile, I can hear Patches and Ward, not far away now, and Patches laughs. "Oh. Oh. Oh," Patches says. There are some wet noises.

"Oh! God!" he says.

4

Need Some Love?
Take as Much as You Want!

OOF!

I land on the flower bed below Patches's bathroom window and given that it's a thirty-foot drop it's not as bad as you'd think. I do get stuck briefly and I do lose my clogs somehow in the process, but I manage to land on my feet with my knees and elbows bent and I fall back on my butt and nothing's broken.

I get up and brush myself off and the impact seems to have knocked some of the swimminess out of my head and I try to hurry as fast as my wobbly legs will carry me across the lawn and toward an elegant and quaint but garage-shaped outbuilding where I hope to find a Mini Cooper or Vespa that I can steal but all that's in there is a Segway plugged into a wall socket and so I reluctantly get on that and ride it out of Patches's front gate, which has inexplicably—or purposefully?—been left open. Then I'm out on the street with Flip following, riding along the unlit highway holding my phone out as a flashlight, pursued for a while by one of those hopping rabbit-beetle hybrid drones until finally Flip grabs the thing in his powerful pitbull jaws and I stomp on it and wince because I break its little legs and its death twitches are upsetting.

If I'm lucky, I think, I have about a week to live, just as Patches said. I figure the bounty on me has moved up to a level five or even level four assassination, especially if, as Patches said, Tim Ribbons has abandoned me. Which, given the disloyalty and disobedience I've displayed over the past few days, I guess is his right. I don't blame him.

But I don't dwell on it, either. I'm riding along the smooth paved berm at twelve and a half miles per hour, past the rustling beach grass and gnarled, beautiful marsh groves, and the wind is blowing back my hair and I can smell the sea air, and an enormous Cecropia moth brushes past my face and Flip is galloping along beside me with his tongue lolling out of his wide grinning mouth and I have to say that whatever drug they dosed me with at Manse St. Germaine, it is really quite fine and if circumstances were different I would go back to find out the substance's name and recipe.

I cross a bridge over the Kiawah River and make my way along some winding marsh roads with the full moon hanging above them and then I come at last to the beginnings of a suburban area. It seems to be a mostly abandoned shopping village—there's a boarded up BB&T Bank and an empty Aubergine Home Interiors store, and one of those high-end grocery stores called Thyme Enough at Last, which looks to be on the verge of bankruptcy and foreclosure.

But there are a trio of teenagers skateboarding in the parking lot, making use of the asphalt and the halogen lights. They've built themselves an obstacle course made out of scavenged construction materials, and they are all performing daredevil tricks, but they stop and stare as I ride up on my Segway, a longhaired, barefoot Sasquatch of a man— gaping at me as if I am some mythical creature descending into their midst, accompanied by a large, scarred, and muscular hound.

"Greetings, mortals," I say in a jokey voice, but they just look confused. They are maybe sixteen years old or so, lanky and shaggy haired, tall as men but still boys nonetheless. They take a step back from me. Sometimes I try to be exuberant and expansive with teenage people and it just scares them.

So I try my best to look casual and unthreatening. I step gingerly off the Segway and onto the asphalt in my bare feet and smooth my hair down with my hand. It must look like a fright wig, I reckon, and I also see that there's a bleeding gash on my knee that I hadn't noticed before.

"You come from the riots?" says the tallest of the three, a white kid whose lower lip is pierced with five gleaming rings, and whose upper lip is doing a passable job of growing a full mustache.

"In a way," I say. "I was down there earlier this evening but then I got sidetracked and ended up out on that island and now I'm just trying to make my way back to my van without being killed by my enemies. You know how much farther to Charlotte?"

"About twenty-five-some miles," the boy says. "But you're not going to make it on that thing."

"Right on," I say.

"You can't go up there anyhow," says the smallest of the three, a wiry Asian kid with a thick drawl. "I got some friends that were downtown and they're saying the whole city's under lockdown. They got Homeland Security storm troopers parachuting in. Tear gas and pepper spray. Roads are blockaded."

"I'll be darned," I say. "That's a fly in my ointment."

"What kind of people are trying to kill you?" says the third kid, who's black and shy and cradles his skateboard in his arms like a puppy.

"Yeah," says the tallest kid. "Who's your enemies?"

"It's hard to say," I admit. "There's one of these dogfight rings that has it out for me because I rescued Flip, here"—I gesture to where he's sitting attentively at my side—"and there are a couple of those white supremacist outfits that bear me a grudge for complicated reasons. And some corporate entities I've run afoul of." I consider. "There's actually probably a lot." It occurs to me that I've been living my life for a long time as if I'm not doomed.

"Anyhow," I say. "You lads can have this Segway if you'd like. I borrowed it from a friend, but he won't need it back."

I look around, and I'm heartened to see that every CCTV camera I can spot mounted up on the stalks of those halogen lights has been broken. There's probably two acres of parking lot, spreading out as far as the eye can see, and I try to imagine a time when some hopeful architect believed with all his heart that these hundreds of spots would one day be filled by the vehicles of eager consumers.

"I wonder," I say. "Are there any abandoned-looking cars nearby?"

They make eye contact with one another and shift their feet.

"I think there's a couple over that way," says the smallest, at last. He climbs on his skateboard. "C'mon," he says. "I'll show you."

I follow along behind them and yes, there are stickers and broken glass and jagged stones beneath my bare feet, but these boys kindly don't leave me in the dust. They roll ahead and then circle back and loop-de-loop, crouching and gliding around me as graceful as birds, and if I got to choose my offspring I would pick these boys.

I would've done a good job raising them, I think, and I remember Patches saying, *Progeny!* Saying, *You're so eloquent and sentimental about the stupidest things.*

The bugs swimming in the halos of the streetlights are as thick as if it's July—moths, giant mayflies, some winged beetles, maybe—and their shadows dapple the ground as I walk tenderly along and the skateboards sweep past, the *ker-sshunk!* as the smaller kid banks across the side of a cement planter with a dead fern in it.

We pass by a large dumpster that has been filled to overflowing with stuffed animals. Hundreds and hundreds of them in so many terrible shades of pink and purple and tangerine and swimming-pool blue, and an entire panoply of creatures—bears, yes, kitties, yes, penguins, dinosaurs, horses, unicorns, dragons, monkeys, ducks. In graffiti on the side of the dumpster, it says, *Need Some LOVE? Take as Much as You Want!*

"Say!" I say to the gliding lads. "What's this!"

"Aw," says the big homely one. "It's nothing. Some middle school girls started it and it just keeps getting bigger and bigger. Stupid!"

"I like it," I say, and I reach down and pluck an old brown rabbit off the pile, sorry, I can't help myself.

We come at last to some derelict cars that look like they are steal-able, and I pause to access the possibilities.

The best bet is a Toyota Corolla that I'm guessing is an abandoned rental car and the boys stand at a respectful distance and watch as I break into her and get her started and disable the dashboard GPS.

"Shit, man," says the Asian kid with the high-pitched Low Country accent. "You have skills!"

"Yeah," I say, and they watch with interest as I unscrew the license plate of a beat-up Chevy Camaro and transfer it to the Corolla, and I give them a modest smile. "It's nothing fancy," I say, but my heart glows at the compliment and I grin at them fondly.

"Hey, guys," I say. "Can I ask you a favor?"

"Maybe," says the tallest one. "What're we talking about?"

"I can give each one of you fifty dollars if you help me break my nose," I say.

Back when I had the *Guiding Star*, I had a drawerful of disguises. I had those five-second latex masks like the CIA spies wore back in the 1970s, I don't know what they do now, but I had some very convincing pull-overs. Male and female, all the different ethnicities, elderlies, too. They were pretty realistic.

But now I'll take whatever disguise I can get.

"Whaddya mean, break your nose?" says the tallest one, surprised.

"Well," I say, reasonably. "You see, lads, I have an urgent need to change my appearance in a fairly radical way. I think I mentioned that I'm being hunted by some bad folk, and I'm concerned that they'll be able to use these camera doodads, such as you see hanging on these light posts, to locate me."

They look up toward where a broken CCTV camera is dangling by a wire. They nod grimly—I'm guessing that these kids spent a long time breaking all those things.

"Why do you want us to do it?" says the quiet one. He looks suspicious, and more than a little frightened. "Why don't you break your own nose, man?"

"That's a good question," I say. As a black kid in Low Country South Carolina, he has no good reason to trust a strange and possibly dangerous white man. "I understand your concern," I tell him. "But the thing is, it's trickier than you'd think to do this kind of thing to yourself. Even if you have nerves of steel, there's a natural instinct to flinch at the last second and screw it up. I knew a young lady not much older than you are who had to cut her own foot off because there was a tracking device in it, but she couldn't do it on her own. She had to have a helper."

I'm aware that my gregariousness is starting to have an edge of manic babbletry, in part, I think, due to the unknown drug I was given back at

Patches and Ward's place. So I hold my breath quietly for a moment and count backward from five, then let it out evenly for a count of seven.

"Listen," I say. "Let's make it a hundred dollars each, okay?" I pull out my wallet and hand each of the boys two crisp fifties. The shy kid doesn't want to accept it, but I gently take his hand and press the bills into his palm.

"Whether you participate or not," I tell him. "But I promise you it won't be that bloody or scary, and you won't get into trouble."

Then I turn to the smallest one. "What's your name, friend?" I say, and he shrugs.

"Bing?" he says, uncertainly.

"All right, Bing," I say. "What do you weigh? About a hundred fifteen or so?"

"Yeah?" he says.

"Okay, good," I say. "I'm going to lie down here on the ground, and cover my face with my T-shirt, and you're going to stand over and me and stomp down hard on my nose. Just a strong firm smack with your foot, like you're on your skateboard and you're slapping the ground."

"Aw," says the mustached white boy. "What am *I* going to do?"

"You," I say, "are going to go over to that bin and get me a large stuffed animal to use as a pillow. Then you're going to hold my head steady while Bing stomps."

I turn to look at the worried black kid. "And you," I say, "if you don't mind, you'll keep watch for cars and so forth."

So we are agreed, and the tall boy, whose name turns out to be Tregg, brings me a panda bear the size of a newborn calf, and I lock Flip in the Corolla in case he misunderstands the situation and then I get on the ground and rest my head back on the panda and hear the crunch of the plastic beads inside it, and stare up at the sky for a moment, there's that October moon laughing down at me. I drape my T-shirt across my face, and Tregg kneels down and puts his sweaty palms on either side of my head, covering my ears. But I can still hear my own voice, as if it's coming from a tinny radio.

"Okay, Bing," I say. "Take good aim."

I close my eyes. I imagine I am asleep on an airplane, buoyed above the rush of air and velocity, on my way to an island somewhere in the Pacific. "Go ahead," I say. "You can do it," and I wait peacefully for what seems like a very long time, so that I almost believe they've left me and I almost open my eyes when Bing's tennis shoe connects. I'm surprised—not by the pain, which I expected, but by the very vivid, lightning-like, glowing tree that branches through my brain at the moment of impact, and which still remains, hovering in front of me when I open my eyes—the way a ghostly circle of light will bob in front of you if you look directly at the sun. It appears that there's a great deal of blood, and when I sit up, I see Bing hopping on one foot, saying, "Oh, man, oh, man, that hurt, Jesus!" I put my hands over my face, and rock back and forth a little, and pain water comes out of my eyes.

"Good job, boys," I croak. "I think we did it!"

In the dream—in another life—in the splices of the film that were edited out—I'm still driving but not sure which state I'm in. Then I come to.

I am in the *Guiding Star* and I say to Liandro, "I know you don't want to go to Utah, I wouldn't, either. But there's nothing you can do about it now."

"So that's it?" Liandro mutters bitterly. "You make one mistake and then your whole life is screwed forever?"

"Sometimes it's not even one mistake," I tell him. "For some people."

"Hm," he says, and I can see the steam of his emotion wavering over his head like a heat mirage. He makes his mouth small and stares out the window. I'm not sure which direction we're pointed in. What state is this?

Kansas, maybe?

There are fields of corn on both sides of the two-lane highway, no cars, though I can see the road extending far into the distance. No houses, either, not even any trees, though the horned skeletons of power line transmission towers are marching along the horizon on all sides. Flip is curled in the passenger seat and gives me a some-of-us-are-concerned-about-you sort of glance.

My brain feels heavy from whatever Ward slipped me in that wasabi pea, it's kind of like I'm wearing a stocking cap that's tightening and untightening in an unfriendly way, and I put my fingers to my face and then I notice there's a bandage over my nose. It hurts well enough to the touch. Seems like it's probably broken.

"Don't put your dirty hands on your face," says my mother. "You want to catch that virus?"

I glance over and she's sitting in the passenger seat of our old Plymouth Road Runner and I lower my hand to the steering wheel and give it a hard clutch. We've been driving down the Alaska Highway through the Tanana Valley Forest, and the trees are lined up on either side of the road like the audience of a parade—black spruce and balsam poplar and quaking aspen—

"I never even met the old man," she is telling me—or rather she is talking, whether to me or not I can't tell. "They put you up inside me with an insemination kit. Paid me in promises." She leans back, smiling dreamily, rolling her eyes, high on diazepam. She is thirty-two and I am seventeen.

"If I knew then what I know now, I never would have done it. Ha! You should be grateful that I was young and stupid and greedy."

"Yeah," I say, though I don't feel particularly grateful. The fat Alaska mayflies spatter on the windshield steadily until finally I give them a blast of cleaning fluid and turn on the wipers.

"What was his name?" I say. "The old man?"

"Rich," she says. "Rich McDollarsigns." She is holding a paper sack full of small, pocked McIntosh apples between her legs and I watch as she dips down and fishes one out, pulls it up and takes a bite tentatively, like drugged people do.

This is one of those scenes that my mind generally excludes from my repertoire of memories.

She puts her bare, dirty-soled feet on the dashboard above the glove box, curling her toes. "You'll be happier without me," she says. "We were never good for each other."

"Right on," I murmur. It's day but overcast, and the blue-gray clouds drain out of a long funnel of trees. I wonder if she knows that I'm thinking about killing her, about making my escape. Does she know that I don't hate her, despite everything?

"Why are you slowing down?" she says. "You can drive a hundred miles an hour in this state, no one gives a shit. I'd like to get to Saska-toon before we lose the deal."

"Uh-huh," I say. I don't speed up. In Saskatoon is a representative of what she calls "your new mom and dad," and sometimes she gives me an apologetic smile when she says it, *just kidding, just kidding,* she puts her long-nailed hand on my knee and gives it a little squeeze.

"Cheer up," she says. "This is a good opportunity for you, too. We all have to leave the nest sooner or later, little rabbit!"

I nod, but a trickle runs down my neck and along my spine, and the brushy pines seem to tremble along with it. It's not about opportunity, I know that much. It's not about leaving a nest, as if she ever was one. She just needs to pay a debt, and for that she will trade me to a white separatist Christian criminal syndicate who will make me cut my hair all off and try to indoctrinate me into their racist, muscle-Jesus-riding-a-Harley-Davidson religion. On the plus side, there are probably some interesting nature habitats on their compound.

"You're resourceful," my mother says. "You'll work something out," she says, and puts a half-eaten apple into the bag between her legs and takes out a fresh one.

And I look down at my leg because my phone is vibrating, and I dig around until I snag it out of the deep side pocket of my cargo shorts and hold it up to my ear.

"Oh my God," Cammie says, and lets out an anxious breath. "I can't believe you finally answered!"

I'm in a Toyota Corolla rental car that smells strongly of baby pow-der and lemon air freshener and the air conditioner is going full blast and Flip is in the passenger seat beside me curled into a fetal dog ball with his muzzle tucked between his hind legs.

"Yeah," I say to Cammie. "I've been having some challenges."

I hear her hesitating, choosing her words, maybe a little frustrated with me. Like maybe I'm a valuable but difficult-to-manage employee.

"Where are you?" she says. That's it. You'd think there might be some joy and hosannas at finding me alive, but she's all business. "The GPS on that phone I gave you isn't working right anymore."

"You don't say," I say. I look out the windshield and I'm on an interstate and I don't immediately see any distinguishing features. It's Great Plains prairieland by the looks of it, rolling yellow sod and blank, weatherless sky, the lusterless sun at about ten a.m. or two p.m., depending on whether I'm headed east or west. I'm guessing it's South Dakota or Nebraska, but it might well be Oklahoma or even north Texas.

"I'm not sure," I say. "I'm driving down the highway. What day is it? It's still October, right?"

"Yes," she says, and I wince because she can barely contain her exasperation. "It's the twenty-ninth of October," she explains. "The last time I talked to you was two days ago and you said you were at Porter St. Germaine's house in South Carolina."

"Ah," I say, and the shadow of her disappointment settles over me. I can't help but feel that she thinks that I am not a very good father. She doesn't know that my nose is broken, that my foot soles have thorns and cuts on them from walking barefoot across an abandoned parking lot, and I'm not going to tell her, either, I'm not asking for her pity.

But I wish she'd take a softer tone. If there's more than one Cammie, she's not the nicest of them. I want to say, *Be kind to your old dad, he's not long for this life,* but then again, neither is she, probably, and if her way of dealing with it is to become cold and irritable, who am I to judge?

"Sorry," I say. "I think that monkey slipped me a mickey."

"I have no idea what that means," she says. She sighs, and it is such a perfect echo of my mother's sigh that for a second I am back in the Road Runner driving through Alaska again, I can picture Cammie picking a small mottled McIntosh apple out of a bag and I wonder what I would have done if, in our alternate life together, she had turned out to be exactly like my mom was. Could I change her? Or would I have accepted it as an opportunity to have a different kind of relationship with the sort of person my mother was? I hesitate, considering the important talks we could have had, and I try to adjust the blaring air conditioner and instead turn up the volume of the radio, a blast of Backstreet Boys harmonies, before I turn it back off.

I clear my throat. "What I mean is," I say, "I got dosed with a drug by Patches's chimpanzee companion. Or—maybe a genetically altered chimp-human chimera, if you believe in that sort of thing."

"Mm," she says, and though it's probably the most neutral thing she could possibly say, it wounds me nevertheless—I can't help but feel like a failure as a fatherlike figure, as a rescuer, as someone who she hoped might save her from the forces that are coming to get her, and I glance over to Flip, whose single open eye also says "Mm."

I wish this were easier. In another life, I would love Cammie as unconditionally as I loved those skateboard boys who broke my nose for me. In another life, I would tell her everything I know, and we would work it out together as a team, dad and daughter, and we would escape hand in hand into some untraceable wilderness.

I clear my throat again. "Anyways," I say, "I've experienced some lost time and delirium." I look out at the road for some sign that will give a clue as to my actual whereabouts, but all I see is a yellow triangular road sign that says: CAUTION ICE BRIDGE, though there's no ice to be seen. It looks to be around sixty-five degrees outside.

"Hey, Cammie," I say. "Can I ask you a serious question?"

"What?" she says, and not necessarily in a hostile way but how different things would be if she'd just said, *Of course, ask me anything, Dad.*

"Are you one person?" I ask. "Or are you multiple persons?"

There's a nonplussed silence, a breath. A suspicious pause.

"I'm a person," she says, and not without a touch of annoyance. "You can't be more than one."

"Right on," I say, though that's not entirely true. I'd like to explain to her that her own grandmother could be ten or more people in a day, but I don't want to go off track again. "But Patches—Porter—says that you're part of a rogue hacker collective. He says you all call yourselves Cammie, and that there's at least a dozen of you, and you've all been catfishing me. Just pretending to be one person. He refers to you as 'the Sisters.'"

I've come upon one of those megafarms that stretches out on either side of the highway, otherworldly in its vastness. Corn on one side, soybeans on the other, as far as the eye can see, watered constantly by enormous walking sprinklers that lumber down the rows, spitting mist that arcs and gives off shimmering, metallic rainbows. The crops have the sheen and greenness of artificial houseplants; you'd think that by late October they'd be yellow, but not these piteous hybridized creatures. You can sense that they are not exactly living things, they don't have souls the way most plants do.

"Anyways," I say, because I have decided that I'm going to be as up-front about everything as I can be: what have I got to lose at this point? "I guess he also thinks that there's more than one of me—that I have siblings or whatever, and that I have some kind of unusual caveman DNA, and also that he might have spliced it with a chimpanzee DNA to create his unhappy companion. I can't be sure if any of this is true. He was in the midst of what I can only describe as a lover's spat, and he was drinking and drugging himself pretty elaborately."

"Mm," she says, and that is all for a while. The unearthly fields unscroll on either side of my Corolla, spreading unbroken to the horizon line.

"Good," she says, and her voice is lighter and more forbearing; it is, eerily, almost as if it belongs to a different person. So maybe she is like my mother in that way, too? Her moods are more than moods, they are separate beings?

"I'm glad they think that," she says. "Maybe I'm still half a step ahead of them, after all." She makes my mother's intoxicating, bitter laugh. "Unfortunately," she says, "I'm only one person. I've got a lot of online avatars, and I call them the Sisters, but it's really just me. I mean, I did have some friends who helped, but most of them are dead now, or in custody, or whatever."

"I'm sorry to hear that," I say. "It's always sad to lose a friend."

"Yeah," she says. "It is."

And I guess she is silent because she is thinking of loved ones who have passed. Maybe there was some shaggy Antifa guy she was sweet on, wiry as a spider monkey but kind and musical; maybe there was a girl pal with pink hair and scrunchy, expressive lips, so funny and loyal, she probably took a bullet for our Cammie. Maybe she thinks about poor sweaty Ronnie, who's likely sitting by a window at some private seaside lunatic asylum, slack-jawed and pumped full of clozapine.

"What else?" she says, and her voice sounds like she has faraway eyes.

"Well," I say, regretfully. It doesn't really seem right for me to cast shade on her mom and dad, but so it goes. "He says you're all a Ponzi scheme. He says your grandfather—my dad—is some old Midas and your parents invested in you because you stand to inherit a part of a fathomless fortune. But it was just a moneymaking scheme that he and

Kurch came up with, Patches says. Any claims on old Midas's estate will be in the courts for generations."

"I'm assuming he didn't give you the father's name," she says.

"No," I say. "Nor would my mother."

"It would have to be a fairly small number of men who would fit the bill."

"If true," I say ruefully. Up ahead one of those big bright yellow robot drones walks contemplatively down the median, swinging its hydraulic arms and looking down at its feet as if it's having a downhearted memory. It has a mouth like a kitten's and enormous cute eyes that take up half its face.

I reckon it's made to look like one of those Japanese mascot critters, the Pokey-men, I think they were called, kids were crazy about them once.

"Hey," I say, "did you ever collect those Pokey-men when you were a kid? Wasn't that the big fad?"

I gaze out at the robot, which must be thirty feet tall. They're so adorable, these things, you can't help but smile at them. This one has floppy rabbit ears and a plump body and stubby legs that give it a sort of waddling gait. "I've got one of those drones out here alongside the road that looks like one of those things."

"Pokémon?" says she. Now she's a little annoyed again, and it's my fault—some might question why I'd go off on a tangent when I'm supposed to be answering all the questions to the mystery, but I'd counter that my need to have a few pleasant images of Cammie's girlhood is just as urgent. Besides, the thing is mesmerizing. They do a really nice job of making these drones look like they're alive.

"Yeah," she mumbles. "Yeah, I played Pokémon Go that one summer, like everybody. But," she says, "how would Kurch and St. Germaine know you had this DNA?"

"I figure that Patches was working for Tim Ribbons, for a while at least," I say. "He probably learnt it from Tim, and then he betrayed Tim and went off to make his embryo scheme with Kurch."

"Okay," she says. And I can sense her taking all this in, calculating, recalibrating: she's a little clockwork, our Cammie, and also, emotionally, it's probably hard to realize that you're just a poker chip that can be cashed in at some future date. I can hear it sinking in.

"Too bad," she says. "I was hoping that we'd have some kind of super-power."

"Right on," I say. "But look: we are inordinately wily! And anyways, it's hard to say how much of what Patches told me is factual or believable. We may turn out to have superpowers yet, darlin'!"

"Ha ha," she says joylessly. But at least the attempt at a laugh is a kindness to me, and I will take it.

In our alternate life together, it probably would have taken years for us to grow truly comfortable with each other; no doubt there would have always been a lingering awkwardness, a shadow of wariness between us. I would have come over for dinner at her apartment, and after dessert and coffee she might have allowed me to fix some minor electrical inconvenience—a faulty ceiling lamp, maybe. I'd talk her into watching a musical from the 1950s, and we'd sit side by side on her sofa, staring at the screen together as long-dead people sang and danced.

Probably the best thing would have been to take vacations, the two of us. Like, for example, I always wanted to visit those big butterfly preserves in the cloud forest in Ecuador. I can imagine us staying in a cabin that's built in the branches of a giant ceibo tree, walking along paths that lead us to scenic views of fantastical wildlife. Later, on a camping trip in the Alaskan wilderness, I would break down and confess to her that I had killed my own mother, and in the distance a moose would stand with its antlers silhouetted by a full moon.

"I'm sorry," I say. "I'm kind of a disappointment as a dad."

"No," she says, and her voice changes again. There's a stutter as if one Cammie takes the phone away from another Cammie, and her voice goes reedy and sad.

"It's just . . ." she says. "My parents are dead."

"Oh, no," I say. And should I say sorry? They were her mortal enemies, she'd told me, that she wanted to send to prison, but I know from experience that wishing a parent not alive and finding them dead are two completely different things.

"What happened?" I say, and she swallows wetly.

"Murdered," she says. "It's on the news. They're saying I'm a person of interest."

"Dang," I say, and I try to think of some words that might be comforting.

"Where are you?" I say. "Are you safe?"

Abruptly, there is a screeching sound. It's one of those ripping twelve-tone notes such as you might have heard back in the day when you connected to a fax machine via the phone line.

"Oh! Fuck!" Cammie says, and lets out a cry of despair that I would describe as heartbreaking. "Shit!" she says, and now her voice has gone distant and tinny. "They know where we are!" she wails. "Throw your phone out the window and get off the main roads! Trash your phone, hurry!"

"Wait!" I say. "How will I get back in touch with you?"

But she has already disconnected, and I roll down the window and toss her phone out—the only thing she's ever given me. I see the shards of it bouncing and glittering in my rearview mirror.

In the distance, the robot drone has stopped, and it now appears to be looking directly at my car. Its big eyes are honeycombed with CCTV cameras, like the compound eye of a bee, and it tilts its head, recording me from multiple angles and multiple layers of close-ups.

Then it takes a step toward me. Yes, it seems that I am an object of interest, and though the phone has been tossed, the robot begins to sashay in my direction, like a plump gerbil on its hind legs, not swiftly but in a determined and relentlessly optimistic fashion.

I turn the car off the road and onto the embankment, and then I go ahead, fuck it, and plunge down the steep incline into the fields of uncanny zombie corn.

And now I am pretty clearly being pursued by a swaggering two-story drone whose every gliding movement somehow communicates joie de vivre. Still, I do not want to die under the hydraulic foot of the Pokey-man.

The Toyota Corolla hybrid is not particularly made for off-roading but it gets into a groove on either side of two rows of corn and it does its best. The corn rows flatten before us, their stalks slapping the bumper with a sound like an angry pack of playing cards being shuffled. Ears of drying field corn bounce up on the hood.

It's clear that we're not going to outrun that thing. Though we are ahead of it by a few miles, its mincing steps are bigger than you'd expect, and it won't take more than five or ten minutes for it to close the gap. For it to be upon us.

I stop the car and jump out and start running flat-footed through the stalks of corn and Flip goes galloping along ahead of me.

Behind us the poor Toyota is mewling, *Bong bong bong! Bong bong bong!*

It's sad and concerned because I've left its door open. *Please don't leave me,* it seems to be crying.

Your Kindness Will Never Be Forgotten

I'm alongside a two-lane highway on the other side of that endless field of spooky corn with my bare feet in a patch of clover. It feels nice. The soles of my feet are pretty cut up, plus caked with cornfield dirt, and I try to wipe them off on the clover like it's a doormat, hoping to get the worst of the mud off.

Then I look up and see an old Ford Ranger pickup truck coming down the road toward me. I stick out my thumb and Flip lifts one paw and cocks his head demurely and the old gray farmer slows to a stop and rolls down the window on the passenger side.

"Where you headed?" he says.

"Ah," I say. "Next town?" And I try to give him the thankful and good-hearted grin I've perfected over the years. "I'm having some car trouble, so I need to get to someplace with a pay phone."

He lifts an eyebrow at me. By the way he wears his wrinkles I'd guess him to be in the eighty-year range. He's in bib overalls and a flannel shirt and a faded green trucker cap that says *Dewdrop Inn Ladies Night, Feb. 22, 1996*. He nods.

"All right then," he says. "Get in."

It's only after I climb into the truck that I realize that I forgot to take a look at the old man's license plate, so I still don't know what state I'm in. I take a quick assessment: *glove box, beer can, sun visor, shotgun, gearshift, dashboard, a pack of Morley cigarettes*—but there's nothing that provides much intelligence.

"I guess you lost your cell phone, eh?" the old farmer says. "There aren't too many of the pay phones left, so far as I know."

"I can't tolerate cell phones," I say. "For health reasons."

"Yech," he grunts. "Those things ruined the country. I don't know how, but they convinced the people that they should spend their whole lives inside a screen the size of a playing card. I'd take a jail cell over that bullshit any time."

"Right on," I say, and give him a little fist-raise in solidarity, but his eyes just gaze at me. Then he holds out his hand. He's wearing surgical gloves.

"I'm Bill McGregor," he says, and we shake.

"Nice!" I say. "I'm a William, too. But I go by Willie. Willie Bare Jr!"

"Good enough," Farmer McGregor says, and he puts the truck in gear and Flip settles uncomfortably in the footwell beneath me, he's shivering and anxious and gives me a look like, *Now what?*

And I don't know the answer. We drive along in silence for a while and I just quietly smell the dank breath that wafts out of the truck's vents, neither heater nor air conditioner but some flavor all its own.

I'm trying to get myself centered and focused again, but it's not easy, I'm still feeling a little dazed and sore. And yes, I'm fully aware that these are my doomed final days and that I urgently need to make an effort to save Cammie and defeat our enemies and so forth, but to be blunt my brain is not burbling with freshly inspired ideas. I try closing my eyes lightly and open my mind to the wisdom of the subconscious, but all I can sense is the flickering shadows of the telephone poles passing outside the window, playing across the surface of my eyelids.

"Now isn't that something!" says Farmer McGregor, and my eyes flap open. "Would you look at that?" He gestures off to the left, where, in the distance, a giant yellow drone has gotten itself tangled up in electric transmission wires like a fly in a web. We watch as it turns its head from left to right in puzzlement, trying to move forward even though it's completely stuck. It lifts its hydraulic arms and flexes its fingers delicately, and a flock of grackles circles its head like a wreath.

"Jerry F. Christ," says McGregor with resigned exasperation. "What's that damn thing doing out in the middle of a cornfield?"

"Often they're not as intelligent as people think," I say. "They're easily confused."

"Mmph," he grunts. He reaches down and grabs a cigarette from his pack of Morleys and tucks it between his lips but doesn't light it. We keep driving and I take a glance over my shoulder to watch the robot growing smaller in the distance.

"So," I say, at last. "Are the crops good in Kansas this year?"

"I wouldn't know," he says. "Never been there."

And then we lapse into silence again, which is good—which is pleasant. I listen to the rhythm of the truck's tires against the crumbly asphalt. This highway hasn't been repaved in my lifetime, I'd guess, and it's all crackled and beginning to break up into individual puzzle pieces. I find myself thinking back to my conversation with Cammie. Maybe it was the last time I'll talk with her, I think, and now I feel embarrassed and sad. I must have sounded like a clown to her. Why couldn't I have been more solemn—reassuring—fatherly—more a person who could be of real use?

I don't know. In the other life where I didn't meet her, I'd still be driving along in the *Guiding Star,* circling around and around the Northern Hemisphere, from the Murchison Promontory all the way down to Suchiate in southern Mexico, a dreamy and cheerful henchman with my faithful hound, riding along, carrying out my various orders— transporting prisoners, delivering packages, planting explosives, spying, guarding abandoned factories, cleaning up millionaires' compounds after bloody massacres, assassinating minor people. The usual. *If only I'd stayed invisible to myself,* I think. If only I hadn't started remembering the past and considering the future, I probably would have stayed pretty satisfied.

But I must have made a choice to throw it all away at a certain point. I wonder when that was, exactly? I reach down to itch my thigh and I notice that there's a lump in my pocket and I slide my hand in and pull out that dirty old stuffed rabbit that I nabbed from a pile back in the parking lot in South Carolina. How embarrassing.

The poor thing has a kind of wet-garbage smell to it, unfortunately. It's filled with beans, I think, but they've grown soggy, and the polyester fur is worn down and the stiff hairs of it flake off when I rub its floppy ears with my thumb. But the beads of its eyes are awake nonetheless. What had Patches said about my rabbit story? *You focus on these banal, sentimental moments,* said Patches, and now I'm like: *Huh.*

I glance up and I see that gray old Farmer McGregor is watching me, his unlit cigarette still dangling on his heavy lower lip.

"You got little ones?" he says, eyeing the stuffed animal, and I nod.

"A few," I say. I touch the mouth of my bunny, which is a little thread stitching, the expression a mouth makes when it is disappointed or surprised.

"I've got a daughter who's twenty-two," I say. "She's having some trouble. That's one of my concerns."

"Uh-huh," he says. He looks thoughtfully at the rabbit I'm fingering, but that's all he says. In the distance, I can see the belfry of a grain elevator rising above the corn, so I know there must be a little town ahead.

I press my thumbs against the chest of my bunny, where its heart would be. Forgive me my sentimentality, my self-pity. How I'd wanted a life like Cammie's, I think. A real mom and dad, and a house and a room of my own where I could brew and stew as a teenager, posters that I liked staring down from the wall. The idea of being a kid in college, and not even knowing about all the human suffering that brought me there.

Poor Rosalie Signorelli, who gave the egg that was fertilized by the sperm that made Cammie, hanged on a noose in a closet in a third-floor apartment above a package liquor store on Belair Road in Baltimore. Poor Posa Penza, who birthed the egg that was fertilized by the sperm, poisoned in the back room of an Italian restaurant in Thimphu.

Poor son Ronnie, poor doomed Cammie and her sisters, poor progeny, all 167 of them, babies and toddlers and grade school kids, teenagers, I regret that I couldn't offer more than the world I'm going to leave behind.

And yes, poor banal, sentimental baby rabbit that I drowned in a toilet bowl in a motel bathroom outside State College, PA, my mom standing over me with her fists on her hips, shaking her head sadly. "Poor thing," she murmured, but her eyes had a fiery glow. "So cute," she said, "if you hadn't touched it, it might have been all right," and I closed my eyes as its tiny, clawed feet scratched and scrabbled wildly against my wrists and my mom said, "You need to learn not to get attached. It'll be your undoing."

Poor Mom. Maybe it was teaching me not to get attached that was *her* undoing. I hadn't intended to kill her—I was going to tranquilize her and then dump her off in a gas station bathroom outside of Anchorage and make a run for it in the car, but she saw the syringe before I could stick her with it and her hand shot out and grabbed my wrist. Her eyes widened and then narrowed. Sudden realization: "You dirty bastard!" she cried, and though she was extremely strong for a small woman, she knew that she wasn't strong enough to arm-wrestle a large seventeen-year-old male and so she lunged down and bit into my forearm and took a chunk out, and it was only then that I punched her in the face and started choking her. Poor Mom, she didn't know how easy it was for me to drown that rabbit because I was pretending it was her.

Poor Mom. She had given birth to me as a moneymaking scheme, not realizing that it would never pay out, not in her lifetime and probably not even in mine, but she had tried her best to make me into something that was at least useful to her. She had mothered me well enough that I could access the calm, murderous joy that allowed me to tighten and tighten my fingers around her throat. I don't remember any sounds. I don't remember her fingernails scratching my face and arms. Mostly I remember how the light was so golden over the river, on the bridge, and I felt more peaceful then, than ever since.

I put my hand down and stroke Flip's thick, solid pitbull head, and he breathes and puts his ears back and we ride along for a while this way, until the truck makes an abrupt turn into the lot of an abandoned gas station. We stop, and now I can hear the wind blowing across the prairie, I can hear the faintly creaking hinge of a sign that advertises Morley cigarettes. Old McGregor's face is expressionless, and so is the face of the gas station storefront. The windows are broken and patched with pieces of cardboard, and there is some trash, some paper cups and plastic bags and leaves and such, dancing in a ring on the oil-stained asphalt.

Old McGregor gestures with his gnarled hand. "There's a pay phone mounted to yon wall," he says. "Last I heard, it still worked."

He shrugs. "Or I could drop you off in Beck," he says, and points his chin off toward the tiny village down the road, a cluster of houses and sheds and dead trees at the foot of a grain elevator, a row of boxcars sitting on the railroad tracks. "They've got a café down there if it's open. But I can take you no further."

"That's okay," I say. It strikes me suddenly that this old fellow has taken an unexplainable risk. My clothes are beginning to smell bad, and my nose is probably black with bruises and swollen grotesquely, and my filthy bare feet are bloody. What would possess him to pick up a person such as me, I wonder.

If it had been Experanza, she would have killed him already and taken his truck. Or at the very least incapacitated him and left him on the side of the road. That would be the smart thing to do in this particular situation. I wonder if he has any notion of the kind of danger he is in.

"Thank you," I say, and I open the door and Flip and I get out. "This will be fine." I hold up my hand to him. "Thank you, sir," I say. "Your kindness will never be forgotten."

His pale eyes hold me for a moment, grim old eyes with a flicker behind them. Like me, I think, he has had many lives.

"Take care," he says.

My Tender

Nebraska. That's what the license plate says when Farmer McGregor drives off. NEBRASKA . . . THE GOOD LIFE, and I stand watching as his pickup disappears and then I face the pay phone mounted to the side of the abandoned gas station's wall.

It's in rough shape—the metal cord that connects the receiver to the box is rusted and fraying, and the backboard is dotted with petrified pieces of chewed gum and penknife graffiti you wouldn't want me to describe, but unbelievably there's a dial tone, and I dial O for operator and I'm not even sure if that's a thing anymore. But there is a series of distant bloops and an automated voice comes on the line.

"Well Come! To Teleprime!" the muffled voice exclaims, and I tell it that I would like to make a collect call and again there's a distant bleeping as it calculates.

"You'd like to: MAKE A COLLECT CALL!" it announces. "Please enter the number! Of the person! You're trying to reach!"

And I go ahead and punch in Experanza's number.

Yeah, I know it's a bad idea. Do you have a better one?

I'm remembering a time when I was eleven and Experanza was thirteen. We were staying at a motel in the desert of California, and she was dicing up an onion to put into the ramen noodles we were cooking in a hot pot and I admired her deftness with a knife. She was a good chopper.

More and more, we were being left to our own devices—our moms sometimes went off for weeks—and we'd be sitting in motel rooms bored and broke and restless, watching hours of TV, begging our fellow motel guests for spare change, stealing beer from the front office, waiting and waiting, with no end in sight. It was tiresome, and I wouldn't have minded going to school or something, I said, though Experanza told me I was crazy. She had been to school a few times, unlike me, and she said it was the lamest-ass thing she'd ever seen.

"I would like to get out of this place, though," she said.

It was a one-story courtyard motel on the edge of a half-dead town, the kind of place where people parked their cars in a spot in front of the door to their room, and we walked around looking for unlocked vehicles. Sometimes a car would be stuffed with all a person's belongings, crammed into the backseat and trunk, and Experanza knew how to go past the piles of clothes and boxes of dishes and get right to the real treasure, such as it was—the place where they'd stowed their jewelry or coin collections or so forth. She had a real knack for it.

I, on the other hand, had a talent for unlocking cars using an untwisted coat hanger. I knew how to stick it down the passenger window and wiggle it around and often I could hook the mechanism in a matter of seconds, and then Experanza would use her amazing intuition to get at whatever valuables might be waiting.

People often thought we were brother and sister—sometimes, because I had long hair and Experanza had short hair, they thought I was the sister and she was the brother, though now that my shoulders were broadening and her breasts were growing, that didn't happen as much.

It was about three in the morning on a night in early June and we had just broken into a purple El Camino. Experanza stood there smoking while I got the door unlocked and then I stepped aside and sort of blocked the view while she sat in the passenger seat and checked the glove box.

"Whoa," Experanza said. She held up a brick of weed that looked like it had been professionally cut, wrapped tight in cellophane. "Nice!" She grinned.

Later, we stood by the vending machines outside the swimming pool area and smoked some of the weed through a makeshift pipe made out of a Pepsi can. "You know what?" Experanza said. She gave me her roguish grin. "You're a good guy, you know?" She wetted her palm with her tongue and wiped her hand over my cowlick, smoothing it down. "Of all the boys I have to babysit, you're my favorite."

"Shut up!" I grinned. "I'm *your* babysitter!" And I put my arm over her shoulder and pulled her in affectionately. Even though I was eleven and she was thirteen, I was already taller than her, a big ape-faced boy, not lovable, but she leaned into my hug anyway and rested her head against me. We could see the moon and stars reflected in the chlorine-blue pool, and the neon sign for the Wile-a-Way Motel. We were so stoned and happy. Maybe it was the closest I've ever felt to a person.

"If you're ever really in trouble," she said, "I'll be there for you. I promise." And we hooked our pinkies together and she kissed my little finger and I kissed hers and go ahead and call it a banal sentimental moment but I've held onto it.

And then her voice comes on the phone. She has accepted the collect call and she says, "Billy?" She says, "Billy, what the hell?"

"I know," I say, and I smooth my hand along my hair, guiltily tightening my ponytail. "I'm sorry," I say.

"What are you thinking, baby?" she says. "Seriously. Talk to me."

"I don't know," I say. There is a small coin return slot at the bottom of the phone and I stick my index finger into it instinctively and fish around. I want to explain to her why I've lied to her and betrayed the codes of our friendship and so forth, but I don't even know if I can explain it to myself. "I guess I'm hell-bent on a voyage of self-discovery," I say, and it doesn't sound very convincing.

"Don't start rolling out your jaunty little sayings." Experanza sighs, and I can picture her sitting at the counter in her half-built McMansion with her vodka and grapefruit juice, wearing some kind of bandana over her frizzed-out brown-and-white hair. Her nail probably has glitter polish on it, and she taps it against the Formica. "This was a crazy thing to do, Billy. Are you having psychiatric issues again?"

"No," I say, though I must admit that I do feel a little otherworldly. The lot behind the gas station is full of tall weeds, thick with grasshoppers, and as I search for my cigarettes a big one lands on the breast pocket of my shirt and clings there with his barbed hands when I try to pull him off. "There's nothing wrong with my mind," I say. "It's just—you know—it's my *daughter,* Experanza."

"But why do you care? You didn't raise her! You're just a sperm donor, which makes any duty you might have to her pretty minimal in my book. Besides which, you don't even know if she's for real."

"Yeah, I do," I say. "I think I've pretty much confirmed that."

"Really?" she says, and I think of the way her dark eyes can widen when she's skeptical, it's like she can make her irises expand without even moving her face. "Confirmed how?" she says.

"I talked to someone who worked with Brayden Kurch on the whole thing."

"Who?" she says. "Porter St. Germaine?"

"Well," I say. It's a little surprising that she knows his name, kind of upsetting that news of my activities has spread so quickly. I shift awkwardly, leaning my hand against the stucco wall of the gas station. "Plus, there were other things," I say. "Let's just say I'm putting two and two together."

"Oh, brother," she says. "You got your information from this St. Germaine character and now you think you have everything confirmed? You're having one of your mental episodes, sweetie. Once you come out of it, you're going to see just how illogical you're acting."

"It wouldn't be the first time," I oblige, and for a second I think, *Maybe she's right.* But if it's all in my head, why are so many people trying to get me? Off in the distance are some yellow hills with rocky cliffs made of white pumice and they stare back at me with indifferent unfriendliness.

"So how'd you know I went to see Porter St. Germaine anyhow?" I say at last.

"Honey, I just know what I've been told—which is that you've been consorting with our competitors, and you've stirred up a bigger mess than anyone expected. Tim just wants to bring you in and get you some help, but it's very possible that others will find you first."

"Uh-huh," I say. Her voice is loving but stern, the same voice as when I was on that fainting couch and she was performing Reiki on me. The tiny village of Beck looks to be about a mile down the road. It must hold all of thirty souls, but I'm guessing there's a car or two down there that can be hot-wired.

"So . . ." I say at last. "I guess I'm worth a lot of money, is that right?"

"I don't know," she says sadly. "I doubt it," she says, but not in a mean way, and I remember how she used to lick her palm and smooth my hair down when it was kinky. "You're probably just an old investment that they don't want to let go of yet."

"Uh-huh," I say again. My lips brush against the little dotted holes in the mouthpiece of the phone. Here's that sinking feeling, that slow realization. *Oh.* She knew more about me than she ever said, she's known for a long time, and I feel myself wince. How have I gotten through this life for so long, as gullible as I am?

"So. Tim's not going to kill me, then?" I say.

"No, no," she says. "He'll probably put you back in a home for a while so you can get your head straight. But he might have *me* killed," she says. "Or at the very least I'll lose some of my pension. And that's the thing that really burns me up about all this. You can spend all this energy on this sperm baby that you haven't even met, consequences be damned, but I've been like a sister to you for practically your whole life and you haven't given a single thought to how this might affect me!"

"Why would it affect you?" I say. Honestly, this had never even occurred to me. I sink a little further now, slow realization, blushing as I go. "You didn't do anything."

"I was supposed to be tending you, dum-dum," she says. "I'm your tender. And I should have shut you down when you were in my house, but I trusted you. Shame on me. I thought you'd do the right thing."

"Oh," I say.

An obvious puzzle piece locks in and gives me a painful shock, and I start to think about all the memories of our times together that will now be recalibrated. *Dang!* All the times I thought we were just friends.

"So . . ." I say. "From, like, when we were kids?"

"Yeah," she says, low in her throat, and I know that sound, I know she is feeling sorry/not sorry, she knows she should have told me but I was an idiot not to know. "I've been stuck looking after you most of my life. You and three of your half brothers. Two of whom are in the loony bin right now."

"Where's the third one?" I say.

"With me," Experanza says. "We're about fifteen minutes away from you. Just stay where you are."

Rendezvous at the Dollar Dangle

Well, I'm a mess. *Deep-fried, freeze dried, and left to the side,* as Experanza's mom used to say. She had some cute sayings, did Jude, and I feel a little blue, remembering her, remembering my childhood. I do not like having to rejigger my recollections of the past, all the things about Experanza and her mom, with the new knowledge that even then they were hired to tend us. Spies, basically.

The fact that I didn't realize it feels bad. The fact that the good memories are now poisoned for all time feels badder still.

I've made my way down to the tiny village of Beck and I'm in the driveway of a small box house, where a dirty, moon-faced Caucasian toddler is sitting on a stoop in a swollen pink disposable diaper, watching solemnly as I hot-wire her family's car. I give her a friendly waggle of my fingers, but she only lowers her drooly lower lip mistrustfully.

I'm guessing there's a mom inside the house, asleep in front of a TV, or maybe an older sibling who's supposed to be babysitting, but is instead chatting by text on their phone, so I'm trying to keep the poor neglected infant quiet and entertained by making silly faces at her. She's young enough that she's still almost bald, and the fine silken hair that she does have stands up like whipped meringue. She puts the nipple of a baby bottle into her mouth and nurses on some bright purple liquid, watching me mug and grimace.

At the same time, I'm thinking of how much I will miss Experanza's advice. If I was ever puzzled about something, if I ever had a question, she would answer it. Sometimes not correctly, but she would always venture a helpful guess. She could draw on a broad base of knowledge—she was an LPN and a notary public, she had a real estate license and a pharmacist license and had taken the FINRA's Series 7 test to become a stockbroker, and she was well-read and a member of an online book club. And if she was stumped, she would consult the Tarot or the Yi Jing, which I don't believe in literally but as a metaphor it could often be helpful. It was a comfort, is what I'm saying.

And then the old two-door Ford Focus trembles awake beneath my ministering fingers, it sputters and coughs, phlegmy as a fifty-year-old pot smoker waking on a fall morning, but it doesn't cut out. I put it in reverse and off we go, heading away on a graded gravel road, up toward those yellow sod hills.

"Dang it," I say to Flip, who's sitting in the passenger seat. "This day is just burning my tail feathers!" He gives me a look I might describe as sardonic, then glances over his shoulder at the vanishing settlement of Beck, expecting, I guess, that someone will likely be chasing after us again shortly.

I don't know whether Experanza was just posturing when she said she was fifteen minutes away, or whether she was honestly giving me fair warning, but in any case, if experience holds true, "fifteen minutes" in Experanza time is at least an hour.

Still, it's not wise to take chances on a forked-up day like today, so I flee in earnest. Matter of fact, I'm wondering if there's some kind of cave in these rocky, cliffy hills that I could potentially hide out in, just shelter in place for a few days, I think. Maybe that's my Neanderthal genes talking. But remember: I'm supposed to be rescuing Cammie.

"What am I supposed to do?" I ask Flip. "I don't know where she is. I don't know how to get in touch with her." I fish around in my fanny pack for that joint I took from Patches and Ward's place, and my fingers tiptoe across the last of my possessions—my taser and my mother's old Beretta mouse gun, a syringe full of GHB, a roll of hundred-dollar bills, a couple of credit cards and driver's licenses, beef jerky, Swiss Army knife, chewing gum, penlight, lockpick kit, cigarettes, and—finally— one last nub of a blunt still a bit damp with monkey slobber.

I stick it in my mouth and light it, one hand loosely on the wheel, and I roll down the windows as I take a puff. Flip puts his head out and lets his ears flap in the breeze. I've got the Ford Focus up to seventy but I think that's as fast as the old dear is going to go. We're pulling a plume of dust behind us as we wind along the dirt roads that curve through miles upon miles of barren hills.

I reckon my only choice is to head up toward Anyox, British Columbia, and hope that she'll make her way there, too, like I told her to, but that doesn't really seem like much of a plan, to be frank.

Alas, as they used to say in olden times. I usually try my best to be optimistic in these situations, but an awareness of the futility of all human endeavor is steadily nagging at me, and I observe as a horsefly knocks itself around in the space between the dashboard and the windshield and ends up on its back buzzing and jittering his legs until he finally rights himself and then he crawls along gingerly, he's like, *Screw flying, I'm not going to try that shit again.*

"What's the matter, buddy?" I say. "Old and confused?"

He pauses to stare at me, rubbing his hands together in that cute mad-scientist gesture. We look at each other, he and I, and as I drive along, I notice that the tarsus of his forelegs grows still. The calypters that keep his wings vibrating slow and then stop. The thousands of images of me in his compound eye all grow dim, blurry.

"It's okay," I say to him. "It's okay."

The sun is setting when we cross over the border into South Dakota, so I'm guessing it's a little after five o'clock on a late-October afternoon. We've been driving with barely a sighting of another vehicle for more than two hours—we took scenic routes through the Oglala National Grassland, staying off the main roads, and I'm beginning to think it's possible that we've eluded Experanza for now. However she's tracking me, maybe I'm outside of satellite range. Maybe she's not even nearby, maybe she was just trying to fool me, which she's been known to do.

I wonder what other lies she's told me over the years. I keep thinking of her with my other brothers, half brothers, whatever they are. Did she tell us all the same stories, or was she a different person for each one of us? Did we all of us have a night where we tagged graffiti on an underpass with her and drank rum and Kool-Aid from a jelly jar? Did we all have uncomfortable sexual encounters with her where we realized she felt too close to being a sister? Or did we each, like in the parable of the blind men and the elephant, get a different piece of her? I imagine that she and Jude had different backstories, depending on who they were visiting, and I picture her adjusting her personality slightly from brother to brother, praising their strong points and pointing out their weaknesses, just like she did for me. I wonder if she ran her thumb along the backs of their earlobes when she was talking seriously to them. I wonder if she really did put her mom in a home, like she said. I even wonder if her name is really Experanza.

And I could go on shuffling through memories and speculation, but at this point we're in need of gas and we need to locate some more civilized area, so I slide onto Highway 71 going north, which, if memory serves, will take me into Hot Springs. It's a grim stretch of a grim state. Rickety barbed-wire fences line the long tracts of sagebrush plains, dotted occasionally with a tortured tree that some cruel pioneer planted in the sandy dirt and left there to suffer.

We manage to putter on, even though the gas gauge is below empty. As crummy as it is, this is a car that is used to running on a few dollars' worth of gas, and God bless its lion heart, it takes me all the way to the edge of Hot Springs, and there, just a few thousand feet from a Dollar Dangle Gas-N-Shop, it expires.

I pull the Focus over to the side of the road as it gasps its last, and Flip and I get out and I put my palms on the hot hood of the car and silently thank it for its service. I try to say a little prayer: that this modest but honorable vehicle will be treated with the dignity it deserves, but Flip flaps his ears impatiently. *Billy! Come!* he means to say, and I turn and follow as he trots up toward the Dollar Dangle.

I usually feel lucky when I come across a Dollar Dangle, and even in these dark moments it lifts my spirits a little to see it. In addition to being a full-service fueling station, Dollar Dangle sells an incredible variety of discount and clearance items. Would you like to buy ten cans of sardines with labels in Russian for only one dollar? How about a twenty-piece crochet hook set? An eight-ounce bottle of generic codeine-laced cough syrup? A gallon of ammonia? I'm aware that it's probably weird to be so gladdened by the prospect of a shopping experience, given my current situation, but the heart takes what joy it can, doesn't it? I hope I can steal a car that's big enough to hold all the stuff I'm likely to buy.

Problem is, there's not a soul in the parking lot. There are ten gas pumps lined up underneath a long red-and-white metal canopy, but nobody is getting gas. I note that there is a Honda Civic parked around back, I'm guessing that's the store clerk's car, but it's not really ideal. I get really claustrophobic in a coupe.

Well, somebody's going to come in for gas or provisions before too long, I figure, so I go in, thinking that I'll just browse while I'm waiting for a vehicle to appropriate. Of course, I know there will be cameras in there, but that's why I invested in a nose-breaking, isn't it?

The woman behind the counter is an older lady with iron-gray hair in braids and steel-gray eyes and the kind of crevassed wrinkles that you only find in the driest climes. She gives me a once-over, and I see her left eye twitch as she notes my bloody bare feet and my broken nose and the scarred pit bull beside me, but she doesn't say anything. She's seen worse, is my guess.

"Slow night?" I say, conversationally.

"*Comme ci, comme ça,*" she says, and I feel like there's a flicker of recognition between us. Do we know each other from somewhere?

"Say," I say. "You're not a Friend, are you?"

"Nope," she says.

Fair enough. It's not like the Friends would help me at this point, anyway. I pick up one of the plastic shopping baskets they have stacked up near the entrance. "Right on," I say. "I hope you don't mind if I browse!"

Flip and I turn and walk back toward the cavernous rows of aisles— it's like a small airplane hangar, enormous, bright white halogen lights shining down from a flat corrugated-metal roof, Christmas music playing from staticky loudspeakers, and there's a feeling of vast emptiness even though it's cluttered. Here are piles of excess inventory scraped from the floors of bankrupt warehouses, out-of-season holiday decorations and mass-produced electronics and sodas with flavors that didn't catch on, like turmeric-mint. I walk down the aisle labeled HEALTH AND

BEAUTY, and it's depressing to think that, once upon a time, I would have looked at these shelves and felt lucky, I would have seen them as heaped with treasure.

Fifteen minutes pass, and still no one has showed up with a car that I can rob them of. I'm anxious, sure, but I'm also just kind of gobsmacked. *My tender*, I keep thinking as I'm sorting dully through a bin of slippers and sandals, looking for something in my size. *She was just my babysitter,* I think, and the largest male shoe they have is a size ten shower sandal, which I suppose will have to do, even though I'm size thirteen.

Time slows down when your heart aches, there's that hovering sense of loss along with the dull throb of resentment and you start to think about *that time when* but you shut it down hard. Experanza used to call this disassociating, but I don't think that's the right word. I grab some duct tape and antibiotic crème and some bandages and a liter of hydrogen peroxide, and a backpack that has a unicorn stencil on it, and then I get distracted by a tub full of cans of Vienna sausage and I start sorting through them, looking for the ones with an expiry date that is the least far in the past.

That time at a Michigan state fair when she talked me into standing up on the top of the Ferris wheel and I did a little swaying dance, waving my arms like a hula girl and it was the scaredest I've ever been but also I believed that I couldn't fall because Experanza wouldn't let me.

That time when I was supposed to kill Mrs. Wetz and Experanza showed up out of the blue to help me and she told me how even if you are murdering someone it could be done in a gentle and loving way, like putting a baby to sleep.

That time when she was teaching me how to be a normal human and we were in Burlington, Vermont, walking down the Main Street sidewalk holding hands and every time we passed a person I had to give them a compliment. "Always compliment people when you meet them," she said. "Then they feel safe around you. And they'll probably compliment you back."

"What if I don't want a compliment?" I said. "I never know what to say."

"If you don't know what to say," Experanza told me, "just say 'Right on.' It's like agreeing with people but not."

And still, nobody is pulling into the parking lot. I'm thinking that maybe I'll have to take that Honda Civic after all, or else buy a can of gas and go down and try to revive the poor ramshackle Ford Focus. I don't have a whole lot of time to putter around. I lean impatiently against the glass of the storefront window, flipping through a rack full of back issues of *Doomsday Prepper* magazine. There looks to be some pretty interesting articles: "6 Ways to Wrap a Shemagh," and "Stock Up on Forever Foods," and "Blood Stoppers! Making Your Own Tourniquets and Trauma Kits." But I just glance at the headings.

There's a tap-tap at the window, and when I lift my head from the magazine, I see that outside, only a layer of glass away, a little pink drone is hovering nearby at face level. It's one of those Pictie-Pet AR drones, the kind that follow you around, saying affirming things in a baby-animal voice and taking pictures of you that can be posted to social media via their built-in wifi system. They're about the size of my palm, two looping figure-eights hooked together into a clover that encloses four rotor propellers, and they maneuver through the air with a kind of spastic, desperate grace, like hummingbirds. Sometimes, you'll see whole flocks of them hovering around recharger poles, waiting their turn to plug themselves in, and there's always a sad little pile of dead ones that had to wait too long, on the ground underneath the docking station.

The gimmick of these things is that they will trail their owners wherever they go, for as long as they can keep charging themselves, and so if you buy one you've basically purchased a lifetime stalker. But I reckon this one is lost. It taps against the window again. *Taptaptap.* And then again, slower. *Tap tap tap.* And then urgent again, *taptaptap!* Almost as if it is trying to send me an SOS in Morse code. I watch as its camera eye swings around and looks at me, but I pull out my penlight from my fanny pack and give it a flash right in the lens before it can take my picture, and then I turn and begin striding away. Better to pay for my goods and get out of here now, I think. Can't wait any longer. I'll have to settle for the Civic in back.

Up at the counter, I unload the items from my basket and the stoic cashier picks them up, one by one, slow and methodical and serenely uninterested in my condition. There isn't a bar-code scanner, so she has to locate a handwritten sticker on each one and manually enter the price into the cash register. I glance over my shoulder and the little stalker drone is hovering right outside the entrance, I swear it's staring right at me.

"Looks like somebody wants in," I say, and point my thumb in its direction. The lady lifts an eyebrow and shakes her head.

"Fff," she says. "Those cheap things. The GPS on them is for shit, and once they get separated they can't find their way home. The most merciful thing you can do is just knock them down and smash them with your shoe. Put them out of their misery."

"Yeah," I say, as the drone taptaptaps on the door: SOS. SOS.

"It's a perversion of love, you know?" she says. "All they care about is just being close to you. To me, it's cruel."

"Right on," I say, and we both nod pensively. "You're a kind and thoughtful person," I say, remembering to give her a compliment, and I pause for a respectful moment and then I say, "Can I also get three packs of Gray Tortoise Ultra Lights?" And she nods and turns to the cigarette rack behind her.

"Say, is that your Honda Civic parked around back?" I ask, as she rings up my smokes.

"No," she says. Her expression doesn't change, but I see her eye twitch. "That's the owner's grandson's car. He's supposed to be working tonight, but his girlfriend came by and picked him up. They go to a motel down the road."

"I see," I say, and I'm thinking I should leave her a couple hundred dollars for the inconvenience she's probably going to experience once the grandson returns.

And then, a pair of headlights. The cashier and I both turn as a black Cadillac SUV pulls up to the pumps—and for a moment I'm hoping I can forget about the Civic and just nab this beauty, which would be perfect for my needs.

But then the driver door opens and Experanza gets out. And the passenger door opens and I guess there's my younger half brother.

Protagonist

"Good Lord," Experanza says. She stands in the doorway of the Dollar Dangle and judging by her expression I guess she's genuinely shocked by my appearance. "Jesus, Billy," she says. "What happened to you?"

"I've had a rough couple of days," I say, and shrug. She herself looks pretty well put together. She's wearing those motorcycle boots that she got in Sturgis, South Dakota, at the motorcycle rally, she's always loved those boots, and she's got a leather jacket that has almost like a bolero cut to it. She even put on lipstick.

Behind her is the man who may be my half brother, and we acknowledge each other with a glance. He's shorter than me, and younger; he's got this barrel-chested weight-lifter body, like a badger—short, thick legs, long muscular arms, big hands and feet. He's even paler than me, with bright, buzz-cut ginger hair, but it's also clear from his homely face that we're related. He's holding a Smith & Wesson M&P .45 with a silencer on it, just letting it hang loosely in his hand.

And behind them is the little pink Pictie-Pet, which flew in behind them as they entered and now hovers, wavering a few feet beyond Experanza's head. Neither Experanza nor the half brother is paying it any attention.

"I thought I told you to wait for me," Experanza says to me. "We need to get you out of here. You're in danger, baby."

She beams me with one of those searching looks—very puzzled and thoughtful and trying hard to understand where I'm coming from, and it saddens me to think that all this time she was just paid to give me that look and to make me feel a certain way.

She probably wants to get close enough so she can tase me, I think.

"By the way," she says. "Billy, this is Tommy. It's a shame you guys never met before. I think under different circumstances you would have really hit it off."

"Right on," I say, though it's hard to picture another life in which that is true. He widens his lips into a sleepy, froggy grin. "And it's a shame you didn't let me know about this brother stuff earlier. It kind of puts me in a creepy situation, don't you think?"

"Tim thought it was in your best interest," Experanza says. "Sweetie, you know you have very delicate emotions. Tim didn't want you to get overwhelmed again."

"Huh," I say. "You say there's four of us?"

"Billy, Bobby, Trevor, and Tommy," she says. "You're my babies. It's my job to look after you." She does that thing with her eyes like she is looking into your soul, and your soul could potentially be handsome but it has its shirt on backward and it has a terrible haircut and needs a lot of dental work. "Look," she says. "I know you think you're doing the right thing," she says. "And I think *I'm* doing the right thing. I'm here because I think you're confused about the situation, and I'm putting myself on the line to help you, baby. Just because I'm your tender doesn't mean I don't care about you."

"Right on," I say, but when she takes a step toward me, I take a step back. I cast a glance behind me and note that the braided cashier lady has astutely assessed the situation and, ninja-like, silently backed herself away from the drama and out the side door. *Good for her,* I think, and I manage to hop the counter without injuring or humiliating myself too terribly, and I stand behind the cash register panting a little and realizing that if I am alive to wake up in the morning, my back is going to be sore.

"Right on, Experanza," I say. "I've been confused about the situation my whole life, and I don't think anything's going to change that now."

This seems to amuse my half brother—either my comment or my half-assed gymnastics—because I see him put his hand over his mouth to suppress a grin, in the same way I myself do.

But it does not amuse Experanza. She tilts her head back and then lets it fall forward, slumping her shoulders: *Exasperanza,* as I used to call her.

"Do you want to die, Billy?" she says. "Is this just one long suicidal gesture? Because if that's what you're after, I can help you out. I can take you to a nice forest glade or something and put you to sleep with some fentanyl so at least you don't have to suffer. Is that what you want?"

"No," I say. "No, I do not."

"Dammit, Billy Bonehead!" she says, and it gives me a shudder, this old nickname she used to affectionately tease me with when we were children. "Why are you doing this? If you're looking for a family, I'm your family. I'm the one who's been there for you—ever since we were kids!"

Three realizations:

First off, you should know that if there's a contest between me and Experanza, she will win. Even when we were children, rolling around and grappling, she had frightening strength in her legs, and I never beat her once in arm-wrestling. I'm aware that she's taken martial arts classes for thirty-some years, and that she is handy with a knife and a better shot than I will ever be.

And secondly, it has dawned on me that we will never be able to recover the old friendship we had. Her pinkie kisses, her advice and encouragement, her promise to be there—that was all paid for, and maybe not all of it was fake but there is enough deception that I will not be able to trust her again. There is another life where the ghosts of me and Experanza live on as the friends I thought we were, but it's not something I will ever touch again.

And third—of a sudden it comes to me: I am doing this because Cammie loves me. Or—maybe not yet, but she could possibly love me. *Has the capacity to love me.* And Experanza does not.

"You know," I say. "I think I'm going to try to handle this on my own." I smile and run my fingers through my tangled, ratty hair. "I appreciate that you're looking out for me, and I thank you for your service over the years—as, like, my tender and my friend and so forth—but I think I'm going to have to decline your offer of help."

I glance at my half brother, who's still smiling vaguely at me, but he's not really engaged in the conversation. How many times have I been in the same position, I wonder? How many times have I stood by as nego-tiating conversations were underway, alert but also bored, not really listening, thinking my own thoughts, maybe surreptitiously watching a house spider crawl up the wall behind my target? I have been where he is standing for so many years of my life.

"I quit," I say to Experanza. "I release you from whatever responsi-bility you have for me. Tell Tim that I'm proffering my resignation to pursue other opportunities."

She looks at me with sad incredulity. "Billy," she says. "You know that's not how this is going to work. You don't have a choice. If you keep galli-vanting around, trying to play the protagonist and be the rescuer of the girl and whatever else you've got in your head, you're just running into the arms of your own death."

"Then I do have a choice," I say. "I choose gallivanting. Can you respect that?"

I have an idea that I can possibly follow the example of the cashier and just back the heck out of here through the side door and I take a scis-sor step in that direction. But I also stick my hand into my fanny pack and quietly pull out the little Beretta, which is not much bigger than my palm. I'm pretty confident that Experanza doesn't have plans to kill me, or she would have done so already. But I expect that she's got a taser or a syringe gun loaded up with haloperidol or etorphine, and I'd like to provide myself with some cover in case she tries to trank me.

But I'm not subtle enough. Even before I can slip the gun out of my pack, Experanza spies it. "Oh, you are *not*," she says, with a fierce older-sister tone of command that freezes me for a second. "Billy, don't you dare ever pull a gun on me—"

And quick as a flash she takes her opportunity and up comes a stun gun, a sweet little Taser Pulse with an extended thirty-foot range—which, actually, I gave her for her birthday a couple of years ago. I take a quick sidestep and try to duck and dodge but stumble into the cigarette rack and the packs come cascading down on me and then time slows down and many things converge at once:

When Flip sees Experanza point a weapon at me he lunges at her immediately, and before she can even pull the trigger her forearm is clamped in his teeth, and she screams and drops the taser and he gives a brutal shake of his head like he's playing with a rag, and he snaps her wrist and knocks her to the floor, and she cries, "Billy! . . . Tommy! Help!" and I yell, "Flip! Stand down!"

And my half brother Tommy is startled from his daydreaming and does a double take and points his Smith & Wesson toward Flip and Experanza. "Hey!" he yells, like a kid trying to break up a schoolyard skirmish. "Hey, cut it out!" And he fires a stray shot that hits the cigarette rack above me and a few more packs tumble down on my shoulders, and I flinch and run up behind the cash register, which I can use as cover.

And Flip has Experanza on her back on the floor and she's making deep guttural struggling sounds—"No! No!" I guess she is snarling—and I cry out again, *"Flip! Stand down!"* but he's in berserker mode at this point, I don't think he even hears me as he gnashes at her flailing arms as she tries to protect her face and neck, the hand on her broken wrist bouncing like a puppet.

And I don't want Flip to kill Experanza and I don't want Experanza to kill Flip and I think the only solution is for me to tackle Flip and get him in a bear hug and knock him off her and hope that he doesn't, in his fury, maul the shit out of me; but then I also know that the next step after Experanza is safe is that she will tase me and kill my dog; or Tommy will shoot Flip and me together once I knock him off Experanza. Every scenario, every choice, seems hopeless.

"Tommy!" I bellow. "Truce! Stop shooting! Let me get that dog off her!"

But Tommy doesn't listen. He's trying to take aim at Flip but there's a lot of movement to account for, and he fires and the shot pings off the cash register I'm hiding behind, and then he fires another shot that takes off Flip's left ear and there is a spray of blood and Flip lets out a sound that rends my heart—I wouldn't call it a scream or a yelp or a howl, but something much more terrible, the deepest kind of despairing rage or raging despair and I yell, "Goddamn it, Tommy, don't you hurt my dog!"

And meanwhile, Experanza has managed to reach down with her good hand and grab her scalpel out of her pocket. I know it well—she's showed it to me a number of times, bragging on it. "A medical-grade surgical scalpel is the best close-range mêlée weapon you can have," she used to tell me. "Simple. Portable. You don't need some kind of fancy mercenary knife." She swings it up, still making those guttural, grit-teethed fighting noises, panting, and she cuts through the hide and muscle of Flip's foreleg and he lets out that shriek again, and whatever efforts I've made over the past few years to soften the memories of the fighting pits are undone. He thrashes and bites, and bites, and bites, and Experanza swings her blade wildly. And maybe I should just try to jump over the counter and try to land on top of the two of them and separate them, but Tommy can't seem to decide whether to hold his gun on me or shoot the dog, so he swings back and forth between the two of us—he fires at me as I try to get up on the counter, and then he turns and fires at Flip, and he misses both times—he's not even giving himself time to aim— and I can see by his expression of surprise that this is not at all what he expected. Experanza probably forgot to tell him about the dog.

And then, out of the blue, as he tries to take aim at Flip again, the little pink drone flutters down and taps him directly in the nose. "Ow!" he says, and swats at it, but the drone avoids his hand gracefully and circles around his head the way, in cartoons, chirping birds circle the head of a knocked-out fighter. "Hey!" Tommy cries, "What the hell?"

And I rise up from behind the cash register and shoot him in the forehead. He freezes there for a second, still holding his gun, still wavering on two feet, and then gravity takes him and he tips and flops onto the floor on his back.

And I turn with the intention of saving Flip and Experanza from each other, but I'm too late. Experanza slices another line across Flip's side, missing his belly by inches, but before she can cut him again he seizes a glimpse of her exposed throat and catches it in his jaws and I see her body, her arms thrashing and her boots kicking, and I yell out, hoarsely, "Flip! Flip! Flip! No!"

There is a geyser of blood as he opens her carotid artery and it splatters him in the face and shoots up all the way to the ceiling. I run over and yank him off her and he doesn't fight me at all. He lets himself relax into my arms and I feel him lean against my chest, shivering, he presses his bloody head against my chest as if for comfort, limp and trusting as a puppy, which is something he's never done before as long as we've known each other. "Oh," I whisper, holding him. "Oh. Oh."

Experanza is dead. Blood is still gurgling in a low fountain from her neck, and her eyes stare at me with disappointment, as if I am a minor and unwelcome character who has appeared at her deathbed as she breathes her last. But I know she can't see me, even as I take her broken-wristed hand. The heart pumps a third of a cup of blood with each beat, and so the five quarts that we have inside us can drain out in a few minutes, though the brain will be dead long before the person has been exsanguinated. This is something Experanza told me once. *Exsanguinated*: a word she taught me.

I think of the time she made me slow-dance to her favorite song. Me fifteen, maybe, her seventeen, maybe, the song "Surrender," by Suicide, playing out of a tape deck in a motel room outside Providence, Rhode Island, her hands around my neck, my arms around her waist, the two of us swaying from foot to foot—and I pull Flip closer to me, and he presses his muzzle into my underarm and I guess that maybe he is dying, too, and we kneel together in a wide-spreading pool of the blood of the only human I ever believed loved me.

And maybe she did, and maybe she didn't, and now I will never know.

I look up, and the little pink drone is fluttering above my horrifying, bloody pietà, its little propellers whirring, and it says, "Will. We need to leave."

And even though the speakers on this thing are lo-fi and tinny, I recognize the voice.

"It's me," the drone says. "It's Cammie. I hacked this thing," she says. "But I'm here. I can see you. I'm with you."

"Cammie," I say. I can feel myself crying, and the tears are hot and they hurt. Oh, I always practiced crying, I used to cry all the time for emotional hygiene reasons, but I never even knew what crying was. Weeping, I hold Flip close.

"Cammie. You've ruined my life."

"No," the drone says, and its camera light shines on my face. "No. I'm rescuing you."

A Riddle, O Traveler

I minister to Flip as best I can. I dab some antibiotic crème on his poor torn ear and the scalpel cuts on his foreleg and his side, and I wrap his wounds with gauze and I hear myself softly singing the old lullaby my mother used to sing, *Doo-lang, doo-lang, doo-lang,* I whisper and he allows all this with a stoic dignity, making tiny yelps so soft they are almost inaudible.

And the little pink drone of Cammie hovers nearby, impatiently. "We need to go," she says. "Someone could drive up at any minute."

I nod and walk back into the cavern of aisles, looking for a blanket. I'm not talking to her right now, and she seems to realize that, though she follows behind me fretfully. I can't really claim that I've lost everything, because she wouldn't think I had anything to lose, and probably she's right, but still I wish she would go plug herself into a charger and give me some space for a minute.

I find a Mylar thermal emergency blanket, pack of ten, which is not great but it will have to do. I come back and tuck it tenderly around Flip's quivering body, I guess he's in shock, and even though the thin reflective silver Mylar sheet is the sort of thing that would usually make him back away with his teeth bared, he allows himself to be covered without protest. He watches with forlorn dark eyes as I drape Mylar over Experanza's corpse, then Tommy's.

"I'm sorry," Cammie says. "About your friend. And your dog. I know you're upset, Will, but I have a safe space set up for us!" And she's flitting, jittery, near my ear. Herding me. "Not far," she says. "But we need to go soon," she says, and I grunt and grab an artificial red poinsettia bouquet off the Home and Garden shelf and stalk back and kneel down and lay it on Experanza's body.

One thing I never prepared for is that she would die before I did and I want to say some kind of eulogy but nothing comes to me. I put my palm on a soft puff of curly hair which sticks out of the blanket above her covered face.

"Right on," I whisper at last. "Right on, baby." And I think I will never say *Right on* again.

The drone of Cammie floats restlessly behind me. "We really, really need to go, Will," she says, and I nod and gather Flip's shuddering body in my arms and I try not to think that he looks like an eighty-pound pot roast wrapped in aluminum foil that I'm about to pop into the oven. The automatic doors of the Dollar Dangle slide open with a hiss and I carry Flip out to Experanza's black Cadillac SUV and lay him on the front seat and the drone of Cammie settles herself on the charging station island between the seats and I get behind the wheel. It's about nine or ten at night, I figure.

"Okay," I say hoarsely. "Where am I going?"

Cammie has a contact in Hot Springs, she says. "A dog person," she says. "Very much into pet emancipation. I'm positive they can take care of your dog. And then we can tend to your wounds and we can hopefully get out of the country. I think you're right, we need to get to Canada, first. And then out of the Northern Hemisphere altogether."

She has connected herself to the car's audio system via Bluetooth, and her voice comes out of the speakers from all sides, Cammie in stereo. Everything she says seems logical, but I'm still woozy with resentment. Herded, earnestly harried. I stick a cigarette in my mouth and light it with one hand, the other hand tight on the steering wheel.

"Is this friend of yours," I say, and clear my throat. "Is this one of the— diblings? One of my . . . ?"

"No, no," Cammie says. "It's someone I met in an anarchist chatroom online. I have a network of people I'm working with."

"Okay," I say, though the word *network* curdles my blood. I've never liked networks, or action groups or cooperatives or collectives: generally very untrustworthy, with a weak central organization and a lot of squabbling. But I don't have a better solution. I reach across and put a hand on Flip's square, muscular, bloody head, and I run my fingers as lightly as I can over the top of his skull and down his neck. It took me so long to teach him to understand what petting meant, but now he leans into my hand, soaking up the stroke hopefully. "Okay," I whisper to him. "Okay."

"They're living in a collective that took over this old abandoned tourist attraction," Cammie tells me. "The Mammoth Site, it's called. They're mostly all animal rights advocates, and there are veterinary doctors there. And medical technicians. Because I think you may need some patching up, too."

"Yes," I say, "I know the place." And that *in another life* thing hits me hard.

Experanza and I visited it once, maybe twenty years ago? I remember I thought it was amazing and Experanza thought it was boring and she was anxious to get back up to Sturgis to the big motorcycle rally where there were some white-power cults she was fleecing. But I insisted on going in, and I remember that it is a fossil bed where fifty-some young mammoth males met their end, lured into a sinkhole. They'd built a big domed museum showroom over the dig site, so you could go and see the fully excavated skeletons and also look at some dioramas of Columbian and woolly mammoths going about their daily lives and read some information about them and their habitat, and then have lunch in the café and browse the gift shop, where I bought a yellow hooded rain jacket with a mammoth skull on the breast pocket—which, I reckon, is still on a hanger in a closet in the *Guiding Star*, which is in a garage on the grounds of Experanza's old compound.

But I should not think about Experanza. I should not think about the *Guiding Star*. Chin up, eyes forward.

The place is just off the Highway 18 bypass south of town, and when we pull up I'm a little troubled to see that the parking lot of the old museum is now surrounded by a twelve-foot-high razor-wire fence and swiveling floodlights and there's a security gate at the entrance. I pull over to the berm, my heart beating suspiciously. *A network of people, a collective.* And why would they be helping Cammie? Why would they participate in my "rescue," as Cammie called it?

"Are you sure about this?" I say.

"Let's just get off the road," Cammie says. "Once we're inside, we can talk, okay?"

"Mm," I say. I'm afraid that Flip might die without medical aid. Otherwise, I would keep on driving, I wouldn't even slow down.

"The monitor is going to ask you a question," Cammie says. "And the answer is *'A riddle, O traveler.'*"

"'A riddle, O traveler'?" I repeat and shake my head dubiously. "Wait. What's the name of this outfit? Are they religious?"

"No," Cammie says. "They're just called *the Mammoth Site.* Don't worry. I've vetted them and I trust them. They're good people."

"I'm sure," I say. I'm guessing that she doesn't realize that *good people* is code for *run.* She doesn't seem to recognize that every reassuring word that comes out of her speaker only makes me more concerned.

"Good people," I say. "But who funds them? Who paid to put up that fence? Not a bunch of crusty skunk-huggers, I'd reckon."

"Mm," Cammie says thoughtfully. But confident, as if she had prepared for my question in advance. "Mostly private donors, a lot of it Patreon and GoFundMe. They have a tangential connection to the Mondegreen Collective, but it's minor."

"Let's hope so," I say, and I resign myself. I had an unpleasant encounter with some Mondegreen gun traders in Oregon a few years ago, but it hadn't turned overtly violent. So maybe it will be all right, I think, and I push the button on the speaker box and it buzzes and then a crackly voice comes out.

"Where does time reside?" the filtered voice says, and for a moment I'm given pause. It seems like it'd be an interesting question to sit down and chew the fat over, but I know how I'm supposed to answer.

"A riddle, O traveler," I say, and there's an unhealthy vibrating bleat and the jenky gate trembles and rattles open.

Inside, there's the sign I remember: THE MAMMOTH SITE spelled out on a big, monument-style wooden tablet, and behind it, a life-size cement mammoth raising its trunk in greeting. It's sad to think of the innocent old days, when people went on vacations and there were educational points of interest and kids were bused in, or old folks on a cheap tour, or bored families, or people with a strong interest in the prehistoric, or murderers on holiday.

As we pull into the parking lot, a tall woman comes out of the building with her arm raised. She's built like a basketball player, broad shouldered and long-legged, in torn skin-tight black jeans, with her hair in one of those Louise Brooks bobs, dyed green. I roll down the window and she leans down and peers at me, smiling. "You must be Will," she says, and her voice is deep but feminine. "I'm Curtis Chin."

I get out of the car and we shake hands. She's maybe three or four inches taller than me, and she gently reaches her hand to my mouth and takes the cigarette from between my lips.

"You can't smoke here," she says, and takes a long drag before dropping the cigarette to the ground and crushing it beneath the steel toe of her stomper boot. "It's totally straight-edge," she says. "No drugs, alcohol, nicotine, caffeine, refined sugar—any of that, okay?"

It sounds like my idea of hell, but I nod. "I've got a dog here," I say. "He has some pretty serious injuries. I understand you might be able to help."

I follow Curtis Chin across the parking lot toward the museum building with Flip in my arms and there's some blood leaking out of the silver Mylar blanket he's wrapped in and I'm concerned about blood loss. His breathing seems more or less normal. He's awake but sleepy, making that soft yippy sound under his breath.

Meanwhile, Cammie the drone buzzes alongside Curtis's head. "Thank you so much, this is so helpful," she's saying, and Curtis holds the door open for us and we walk through what used to be the gift shop and restaurant area and Curtis says, "You're very welcome. I hope you're in a safe place?"

"Yes," Cammie says. "For now." And I realize that I should probably have asked her that question myself, maybe. I don't know. I feel like I've been ripped out of my old life by an emergency cesarian section. Have I made a mistake? *You're confused about the situation,* Experanza said, and I'm thinking that by now, certainly, the corpses at the Dollar Dangle have been discovered and probably a sheriff or local militia chieftain has been called in to examine the crime scene. They'll take her body and cremate it and I feel Flip shivering and Curtis opens a steel security door and holds it open for me. Her long, ropey arms are covered in stick-and-poke tattoos: little cartoon dogs.

"Thank you," I hear myself say.

And then we walk into the enclosed fossil dig site, and I can't help but hesitate for a moment. Stunned. It's a space as big as a cathedral, lit by tiny LED lights under an arched dome, with a big curved skylight that reveals the stars. I cradle Flip in my arms and I feel myself draw in a breath of wonder.

It's so beautiful. A boardwalk runs around the circumference of the pit where the skeletons of the mammoths have been uncovered, but it's been turned into a kind of bazaar or community center. It's a small village down there. Groups of hippies are talking together in small clusters, eating bananas or sitting on thrift-store sofas, typing on laptops, sitting arch-backed in lawn chairs wearing virtual-reality helmets, hands fingering the air. Some children are giggling in sleeping bags among the tusked mammoth skulls and piles of delicately uncovered bones and I imagine in another life what it would be like to grow up in a place like this. I can picture me and Experanza as kids running around and getting into trouble, but here we would be tolerated, here we would be forgiven, I think—

"Will!" says Curtis, and she has opened another door at the end of the boardwalk. "This way," she says, ushering me into a subterranean office hallway.

"We have a doctor coming down," Curtis says, but she's talking to Cammie, not to me. Cammie buzzes near Curtis's head, and I follow, bearing the silvery wrapped Flip, whispering to him encouragingly, and for some reason I think of that baby I dropped off back in Vicksburg, Mississippi. How long ago was that? It feels like months, it feels like the child is probably crawling and saying his first word by this point, and I hope that he remembers me, just a little.

This underground part of the museum is basically a bunker corridor from a cheap 1970s office building, steel doors with tiny windows and slatted louver vents, fluorescent lights on the ceiling and extra-thin industrial carpeting on the floor. Curtis leads us to door number seven, which turns out to be a small room that looks like a typical veterinary office—a metal examination table and a counter with a jar of cotton balls and a stethoscope and various bottles of ointments and antiseptics and so forth. I lower Flip to the table and Curtis starts to help me unwrap him but I push her hand away. "He could bite," I say. "He doesn't like people."

"He's smart," she says. "But don't worry. Dogs know they can trust me." And to prove it she reaches down and softly strokes the top of Flip's head, and he doesn't take her hand off as I expect. He makes a low groan and half closes his eyes as she gently peels back the Mylar, which is sticky with his blood.

"Oh dear," she says, and Flip allows her to run her fingers along his face. Cammie is drifting serenely near the door, seemingly watching but keeping her distance. I take his forepaws in my hands and massage his sandpapery footpads, and we lock eyes, and thereby feed each other β-endorphin, oxytocin, dopamine.

"This is a fighting dog," Curtis says, and she shakes her head and stares at me—not accusing but grim and saddened. She touches the long scar below his left eye. "He's seen a lot of action," she says.

"Yeah," I say, and I keep softly squeezing Flip's paws. This was the first kind of touch he ever allowed—back when we first became companions and I was trying to teach him to trust me. "He's had some rough times," I say. "I rescued him from a dogfighting compound in Virginia a few years back."

"Oh really?" she says. "Which compound was that?" She keeps slowly stroking Flip's muzzle, but her dark eyes are on me. "Out of professional curiosity. I hunt dogmen."

I nod, and decide that I like her, and if I had a last will and testament I would leave some money to her organization to support their quest to exterminate those fuckers. "It was an outfit called Bandit Farm Kennels. South of Richmond."

"Oh!" she says and brightens. "The Bandit Farm Massacre? That was nicely done! Were you involved?"

"Not really," I say, made bashful by her now admiring appraisal of me. "I just did the cleanup," I tell her modestly, and I'd hate to have to tell her that the killings at Bandit Farm weren't the work of Animal Rescue Freedom Fighters, as was widely disseminated, but merely a double cross by a disgruntled investor who wanted to collect on the insurance money.

"So," she says, astonished. "This . . . this is King Philip, isn't it? Wow! He's a legend!"

"That's not his name anymore," I say. "Let's not call him that, I think it's upsetting to him." I palpate his paws like I'm pumping up a blood pressure cuff, and I whisper *ss ss ss,* and his dark eyes hold mine.

Experanza had told me that I had stolen a valuable dog, that he had been insured for two million dollars and that he was one of the top-ranked fight dogs in the country, but I had thought she was exaggerating. I knew he was special, I just didn't realize he was actually famous, a grand champion in his terrible sport.

"We don't talk about that part of his life," I tell Curtis. "We've gotten past it, and we're not looking back."

And then the doctor comes in, and she tells us to clear out, and we do, standing awkwardly in the hallway outside the closed door.

"C'mon. You should clean up," Curtis says, and touches my shoulder with her long, green-nailed fingers. "Take a shower, put on some clean clothes, and then come back and see how your buddy is doing. He's in good hands."

I allow myself to be reluctantly led down the hallway, and Curtis has her palm firmly on my lower back, guiding me along. "You just need to quickly wash up, get the grime off, and I'm going to see if I can get a nurse down here to look you over, okay? We're going to take care of you, Will, and it's all going to be fine."

We stop at a doorway with a sign that says SHOWERS and I nod. I do not think it will be fine, but I have no idea which direction the unfineness will be coming from. So I do as I'm told, I slink into the locker room and glancing over my shoulder, I see the drone of Cammie is whirring along behind me.

I turn and look into her blank, glinting camera eye. "I think this is a men's shower room," I say. "Folks may not appreciate it if they see a Pictie-Pet viewing them in the nude or whatever."

"I feel like you're mad at me," she says, and I try to imagine that somewhere beyond this propellered pink gyroscope there is a real young woman typing on a laptop in some dim basement room, and she's scared, and she's maybe surprised by the number of forces that she's managed to stir up against her. She maybe doesn't fully understand how reckless she's been, how careless of the costs to the lives of others. "I'm sorry," she says. "I handled this the best I could."

"Right on," I say, though I told myself I wasn't going to use that expression anymore. "Okay," I say. "But I'm going to be needing some privacy. I have to disrobe and take a shower and so forth."

"I'm not going to look," she says. She levitates demurely to a corner and turns her camera's eye away from me. "We need to talk," she says, as I sit down on a bench next to some lockers and peel off my blood-spattered T-shirt.

"About what?" I say and begin to unload the pockets of my cargo shorts—the keys to Experanza's SUV, a wrapper from a gauze packet, a half-smoked cigarette. Here's that damned stuffed bunny.

"I think your dog's going to be okay," Cammie says, as I unbuckle my fanny pack and tentatively step out of my shorts. I glance her way and she's still facing the wall, not looking, so I limp in my skivvies toward the showers.

"But," she says. "He's got to stay here. And we've got to go."

"No, no, no, no," I say. I step into the tiled communal stall, which is like the showers in an old-fashioned gymnasium, a bunch of spigots lined up above big drains. "That's not under discussion."

"He's got a GPS tracking chip," Cammie says. "That was how your friend found you, I think. That was how I found you, too. I mean, I noticed early on that there was a signal following you, but I didn't realize it was the dog until Curtis helped me."

"Bullshit," I say. I turn the water on, hot only, and stand there with my hand under the spray waiting for it to heat up. And now I *am* mad at her. The way she says *the dog*, as if he's not an individual. The way she says *your friend*. The way they say the waitress or *the lawn boy*, all the things that are just placeholders to them, gaps to be filled. *The embryo,* I think, though I don't say that to her.

"If he's got a microchip in him, we'll take it out," I say, and step underneath the steaming shower head and let it pour down on me. The water that runs from my hair is dirty with blood and cornfield dust and I undo the braids and let my hair hang in wet tendrils, tenting my face. "I'm not leaving my dog behind."

"The only way to get the chip out is through exploratory surgery," she says. "It's smaller than a grain of rice, and once it's been in awhile it becomes almost impossible to find, even with an X-ray. You'd have to make an incision several inches long and then carefully dissect the tissue in that area . . ."

"How do you know that?" I pour some lavender-scented liquid soap into my palm and rub it across my chest and under my arms. More filthy water circles the drain. "You're not a doctor! You're just reading shit off the internet! That's not knowledge!"

"Okay," Cammie says. "I guess we can ask the veterinarian. But I think she'll tell us the same thing."

And she says it in this way that she thinks is so slick, so reasonable and accommodating, the way my mother would talk to a patsy, the way she'd talk to an Uncle Rabbit, and I can picture myself striding out there and snatching the drone out of the air and shoving its camera eye up close to my face and holding it so tight that its plastic frame cracks in my clenched fingers.

But I am not a violent man. I've killed a lot of people, sure, but only once or twice in anger. Despite everything, I would never want Cammie to see the monster of me, the burning eyes and bared teeth, and so I stay where I am and say nothing. I lift my foot and begin to gingerly wash it with a rag. It's pretty cut up and there's a broken toenail to contend with and I wince but I am also shaking with emotion and I scrub my poor foot mercilessly. I guess I'm going to lose everything, I realize. The *Guiding Star* and Experanza and my job and Flip and then my own life. I lift my other foot and wince all over again.

Damn her for contacting me. Damn Patches for tricking me into creating her. Damn my greedy mother and the turkey baster that put me inside her.

"Besides," Cammie says. That calming, slightly reproachful voice that a therapist might use with an enraged client. "Besides," she says, and I put my hand over my eyes. "He's seriously injured. He's not going to be able to walk very well with those wounds on his legs. He's going to need time to recover. You know he's not going to walk out of here tonight. Or tomorrow."

"So we'll wait till he's healed. You said we were safe here."

"*You're* safe," she says. "I'm not actually there, remember? And I'm not going to be able to occupy this drone for very much longer. I'm in a pretty precarious situation."

"Uh," I say. I lean back and let the shower spray pour on my face and I comb my fingers through my beard, undoing the tangles.

And what if I were to choose Flip over Cammie? Would the Mondegreens still let me stay here in their safe space while my dog got better? I'm here—Flip's here—as Cammie's guest.

"You know you can't tend to him the way he needs right now," Cammie says. "They'll take good care of him here. Helping abused animals is their life's work."

She doesn't say that he'll be better off without me, but that's what she means. And I want to say that he won't survive without me, but I picture the sad contented look in his eyes as Curtis Chin stroked his muzzle, and I guess what I mean is that *I* won't survive. I think of that movie where the dying cowboy is riding off toward the horizon, slumped on his horse, and the kid cries, "Shane, come back!" and it's heartbreaking but the kid gets over it probably. Just as Flip would get over it, I imagine. He could have a long and happy life here, and he would miss me of course but he would think of me less and less as time went on. One of those kids in the sleeping bags would adopt him and love him and he would have another life. A real other life, which maybe dogs can have more often than people do.

"Maybe if we get out of this situation you can even come back for him!" Cammie says, in the bright voice that parents use to lie to their children. "It's just—you have to do what's right. For everyone. For the time being."

"I'm not going to leave my dog," I say, but I feel less conviction. Leaving him might be what's best for him. Leaving him might be the unselfish choice.

"Will?" says Curtis's voice. "Hey, man! I'm coming in, just so you know! I've got some clothes for you!"

And I open my eyes and water is running down my face and the bandage over my nose has sloughed off and I reach up and brush my fingers across my swollen nose. My new nose. My new face.

"And I have Roger! He's a nurse. He's going to take a look at you and stitch you up a bit, and I think we may even have some pain pills for you!"

"Uh," I say. I can picture how the next hour or so will proceed. I will sit on a locker room bench and the nurse will squat and sew up my cuts and dab salves and listen to my heart and put a splint and a fresh bandage over my nose and give me some antibiotics and OxyContin or something of that sort that will dull my emotions and then I will be taken to see Flip for the last time and he, also, will be sedated and the doctor will tell us about his condition and his prospects for recovery and I will put my hand on his head and kiss his mouth and stroke his short fur and his eyes will half open and he will see me saying goodbye and he will know he's being betrayed.

He will know that I tricked him into trusting a human again, and now I am leaving him, and I will see his eyes register this with a dull and eternal disappointment. What a fool he'd been, he'll see now, he'll recognize, and he'll close his eyes and won't be able to bear to look at me as I walk out the door.

"No," I say. "Don't need a nurse. We've got to go now. I guess that— Cammie and I have to get a move on."

"It won't take long," says Curtis, cheerfully unaware of the roiling in my heart, and I turn off the shower and wrap a towel around myself. "Roger will be down in five minutes, it's not a big deal."

"I—I think we have to go now," I say, and I can hear my teeth squeak as I grit them. "You'll take good care of my dog, won't you?"

Harland Jengling and the Temple of the True Science

We are heading north, me and the drone of Cammie. It's about five in the morning, and I'm clean and dogless and smelling of lavender soap, dressed in a white T-shirt and dungarees, wool socks and Birkenstocks. In addition to arranging indefinite room and board for Flip at the Mammoth Site, Cammie also negotiated an exchange of Experanza's Cadillac for a 1984 Jeep Grand Wagoneer with 190,000 miles on it, and I don't think much of either deal but I'm not in the mood to haggle over it. I just get in behind the wheel and start driving, and Cammie settles on the passenger side, nestling on the dashboard above the glove box.

"Where am I going now?" I say.

"I'm going to try to get you into Canada," she says. "There's a couple of spaces on the North Dakota–Saskatchewan border where we should be able to get you across. And then I'm pretty sure I have some people who can help."

"Pretty sure, eh?" I say.

"I'm working on it," she says. "Just keep going north on eighty-five to Fortuna."

"Alrighty," I say, but I don't have much hope left in my heart. It's an eight-hour drive, at least, and I find it highly doubtful we'll make it that far.

"How many do you think are after us?" she says.

"I don't know," I say. In the rearview mirror, a black KTM Super Duke motorcycle is approaching, and then it zooms past. The rider is wearing a silver helmet shaped like a wasp's head, and he turns to look at me as he zips by. "Could be as many as ten or fifteen different organizations," I say. "It seems like there are a lot of interested parties. Some worse than others."

"I'm really sorry," she says. Her camera swivels to look at me, then back out the window at the road. "I know I screwed this up. I just didn't realize that everything would start cascading so fast like this."

"Right," I say, but I stop myself before I say "on." I watch the Super Duke buzzing up the highway, it must be doing over a hundred, and I decide it's probably okay for me to pick up a little speed myself.

"Don't worry about it," I say. "You didn't know what you were getting into."

We both look out at the highway as the headlights of the Wagoneer illuminate a billboard for a tourist attraction called Reptile Gardens, and another advertising the fun, comfortable, and convenient Roosevelt Hotel of Keystone, located at the base of Mount Rushmore. But of course Mount Rushmore is nothing but rubble these days, and who's to say what became of Reptile Gardens? I hope the reptiles got away, that they didn't starve to death in cages and display cases.

"I feel like I manipulated you, maybe," she says. She floats above the glove box, ticking slightly up and down, up and down, her little propellers blurred with their rotation. "Like, I had the idea of emancipating you, but I didn't really—ask, did I?"

"You never forced me to do anything," I say. "I made my own decisions." It's still an hour or so before sunrise, but there's a glow around the edges of the hills and scrub pines on the horizon. *You had a choice,* I think, and I wonder, why? What made the wish for another life, for another version of myself, so strong this time? There was somehow a lot of power in that imaginary father, that imaginary daughter, however dimly possible. Did I know I was going to wreck my life? I must've, at some level.

I wish I could see her in her true human form. If such a form exists.

"Where are you now?" I say. "Are you safe?"

"I'm in the trailer of a semi, and we're in northern Wisconsin, not far from Duluth, Minnesota. I'm going to cross the border into Canada near Grand Portage."

"Describe it for me," I say. "Help me picture it."

She hesitates—she imagines there are more urgent things to discuss, I reckon. But she humors me. She says it's a refrigerated semitrailer carrying watermelons, and it's about forty-five degrees, and she's in the very back surrounded by crates and she's in a sleeping bag with her fleece coat on and a stocking cap, her computer is in her lap and she has headphones over her ears like muffs, she's got gloves on with the tips of the fingers cut off so she can type. It's pitch dark. The only light comes from her laptop, and she has a lithium battery that will last her six more hours, and she doesn't know what will happen after that. "I don't know," she says. "Maybe I should parcel it out?"

"No," I say. "Stay with me."

I glance over and she's still just floating there blankly as an ornament on a Christmas tree, unable to sit in the passenger seat though I guess as a drone she doesn't feel discomfort. Beyond the window it's a clean stretch of two-lane asphalt, barbed-wire fences enclosing rolling prairie on either side, no other vehicles on the road. Driveways, mailboxes, mile markers with glimmering reflectors.

"Tell me what you're thinking about," I say. "How are you doing with the—loss of your parents?"

". . . What?" she says, and I guess she was probably looking at something or other on the internet, texting something to some comrade or network associate, maybe she can see the condensation of her breath in the refrigerated air.

"Talk to me," I say, and I try to imagine her in her semitrailer. She's in her fleece coat and hat and her dyed hair peeks out, and she has big eyes and a small freckled nose, and I'll bet her hands are trembling. The smell of watermelon all around her. "Tell me what I don't know," I say. "Tell me what you're reading about on the internet."

She asks me if I've ever heard of a man named Harland Jengling, and I tell her I don't think so and she says she thinks he's probably my father. "I can't confirm it yet," she says. "But that's what it's looking like."

Harland Jengling, she says, was the leader of a cult called the Temple of the True Science, which was originally headquartered in southern New Mexico, but now has many branches all across North America, from Guatemala up to the Northwest Territories of Canada, little settlements that most people don't even know about.

"They just come in and take over a small town, like a virus," she says. "They buy up the real estate, and eventually they drive most of the locals out. They're very aggressive."

"Aggressive how?" I say. The light of dawn is breaking over a hill in the distance, and I check the speedometer, eighty miles per hour, and I slow a bit. The Wagoneer is not a race car.

"Litigious," she says. "They know how to bully people with lawsuits, and they have influential lobbyists and connections with some of the big corporations and banks. But they're also extremely secretive. There was a journalist who was writing a book about them? He was poisoned with a nerve agent."

"Nerve agent, eh?" I say. "Did it kill him?"

"Yes!" she says. "Plus a few of the people he had interviewed—former cult members—disappeared. There's people online who say that they kidnapped them and flew them out over the Gulf of Mexico in helicopters and pushed them out."

"Right," I say, and I once again don't say "on."

I think I know this group, I realize. I have a brief flash of memory—it must have been three or four years ago?—the last time I was in New York City, right before the big floods started hitting Manhattan. Tim had rented me out to a foundation that administered charitable funds for some billionaire or another—but I don't think their name was Jengling. Anyway, I can picture it clearly now. It was right before they declared martial law, and the streets were packed with dissidents and protesters, marching and singing and carrying umbrellas to protect themselves from the tear gas.

"What kind of nerve agent did they kill him with?" I ask. I reach down and grab a cigarette and poke it into my mouth.

"What?" she says. "I don't know. Does that matter?"

"No," I say. "Not really." I'm guessing that it was a carbamate. EA-4056,

I think it was called. "And this journalist—he died about three or four years ago?"

"Yeah," she says. "You read about him?"

"Mm," I say. I can picture myself dressed as a janitor, wearing coveralls and an N95 respirator, vacuuming the carpets in the hallway of an apartment building, and there was an atomizer with a solution of EA-4056 in my pocket.

"And it was the Dakota Apartments, right? Where he was killed? In New York City? Like, Central Park West?"

"I don't know that, either," she says. "I think he was from New York, but I'm not sure. The point is," she says, "if I'm right, I think that we—you and me and all the others—are descendants of Harland Jengling."

"Uh-huh," I say. "And that's bad?"

"Yes," she says. "Because the Temple of the True Science considers us their sacred property. And I think they're just now finding out that you had children."

We're in what used to be the Black Hills National Forest now; we pass through what remains of the small towns of Pringle and Sanator and Custer as the sun is coming up. The Ponderosa pine forest is deep on either side of the road, dotted with some blue junipers and Halloween-y bur oaks, and it seems peaceful though I know it's not. There are bandits all through this area, and we pass the skeleton of a burnt-out Ford Mustang smoldering on the side of the road, onto which someone has spray-painted ALL LIVES ARE SACRED.

And I'm thinking that it's likely that I'm the one who killed that journalist. I wonder if Tim knew that he was hiring me out to the Temple of the True Science? Probably not. My guess is that Value Standard Enterprises was keeping me for their own purposes—that I was a chit my mother had used on multiple occasions, like a dirty credit card: that she'd sold me to multiple organizations. Tim and Value Standard must have known that the Jenglings wanted me back—maybe that was my one true worth to them—so why would they have rented me out to them?

Maybe they didn't realize it was the Jenglings who were leasing me. Maybe the Jenglings used a front to hire me—not because they were impressed by my skills as an assassin, but because they were interested in finding out more about me personally. Even then, years ago, they were fishing? I don't know. Maybe that's a stretch. At this point, I'm just grasping at straws.

"So where's this Harland now?" I say. "Still in New Mexico?"

"He's dead," she says. "He died before you were born."

Strangely, this makes me feel sad, that I will never meet him, though maybe it's just a placeholder for other losses—Experanza, and Flip, and even poor half brother Tommy, whose murder I honestly haven't had time to process.

"Apparently his head is cryogenically frozen and kept in some kind of underground bunker," Cammie says. "He was a big early supporter of cryonics. Along with basically any other sort of pseudoscience there is."

"Pseudoscience," I say. I recall how disparaging Cammie was about Experanza's Reiki. I remember Experanza raking her fingers through the air above my back and the way I could feel—what?—magnetism? electricity? the movement of the particles of my aura? But I don't say anything. I just let the memory play in my mind, my skin tingling.

"He was a huge eugenicist. And of course he believed that his genetic materials were special and superior and his purpose was to seed the world with his offspring. There was like, seriously, a breeding program. Women were paid to come to this ranch, and—"

Like stalls in a stable, I remember my mother saying.

"And this is where it gets kind of apocryphal, but apparently he wanted to impregnate a woman from every different race and ethnic group—and women with different disabilities, mentally ill women, women with chromosomal disorders like Down syndrome. And according to one source, he even tried to inseminate chimpanzees and bonobos. And then many were harvested and the embryos were put in cryopreservation."

"Like the head," I say, and she says, "Yes, like the head," and I do not say, *Like you were.*

"The thing is," she says, "very few of the embryos were ever implanted, as far as I can tell. I guess they have, like, an embryo bank? With hundreds or maybe thousands of preserved specimens, dating back to the 1950s."

"Huh," I say. My guess is that my mother wasn't supposed to keep me. Maybe I was meant to be frozen like the others, but she ran off with me in her belly. She had calculated that I'd be worth more as a live baby than as a frozen embryo, and who knows how many groups I was promised to, how many different times she used me as collateral for her unpayable debts.

Outside, there are more and more dead trees—scorched-looking pines and leafless shrubs, and I guess we're coming up toward the exclusion zone, which extends in an eighteen-mile radius around the site of the Mount Rushmore bombing. Back in the *Guiding Star,* I had a Geiger counter which would have told me how much radiation was wafting over me, and I know that this can't be good for my potential prostate cancer, but what can I do? I crank the Wagoneer up to ninety, though this seriously compromises the maneuverability of the vehicle. In the distance is the jagged rock formation of Black Elk Peak, with the castle-like lookout tower atop it.

And meanwhile Cammie is going on about Harland Jengling. My father. Her grandfather. I stare out at the toothy buttes and dead ponderosas and listen. He was born in 1890, she says, in Spanish Fork, Utah. His parents were immigrants from Iceland, from Reykjavík, and they were in some fringe religious group, and Harland himself was this oddball prodigy who began delivering sermons at tent revival meetings when he was five years old and supposedly he would heal people and cast out demons and so forth. "And then he was orphaned," Cammie says. "Both his parents were murdered when he was seven, and then he was adopted by this even fringier group. It's crazy."

By the time he was in his early teens, he was the ringmaster of a sort of traveling circus. "It had a religious component," she says. "But there was also a freak show, and exotic animals, and cryptids—like, you know, a monkey and fish taxidermied and sewn together and they called it a mermaid. That kind of thing." He wrote a tract called "The Brotherhood of Men and Animals," which was one of the early texts that would become the foundation of the Temple of the True Science.

Listening to her, I am aware that Cammie, like me, can get captivated and pulled into a bed of knowledge from which she can't awaken. Never mind that both of us are probably doomed. Never mind that we should be brainstorming about avoiding our enemies, never mind that my old friend has just died, and my previously unknown half brother, and my heartbroken dog is pining in a cage in a basement room beneath the bones of mammoths who died in a sinkhole back in the Pleistocene Era, never mind that we're driving through an exclusion zone that might not be truly habitable for thousands of years and absorbing eight to thirteen kilobecquerels of radioactivity per hour, Miss Cammie is bound and determined to go down the rabbit hole of the history of Harland Jengling, and if I needed further proof that she is indeed my daughter, this would be it: I recognize that focusing and circling of the mind's eye—which is one of the things, I imagine, that both of us inherited from Harland Jengling. Hell-bent, I think. Fixed and fascinated, and more power to her, I guess, though I don't listen to everything she's saying as I push the Wagoneer toward 90 miles per hour and hurtle through the morning toward the town of Deadwood.

When we come upon another Super Duke motorcycle, I slow down. This one is cherry red, and my neck prickles when I see it. I've never liked the look of them—they've got a stylized frame like a metallic shrimp or other crustacean that's always looked a bit malevolent to me. It's not typical to see one such vehicle in a day, let alone two—especially not in this part of South Dakota, which is very firmly Harley-Davidson country.

"Hey, Cammie," I say. "Look up ahead. You see that KTM?"

She pauses from her talking and turns her camera eye to me, then back at the road.

"What's a KTM?" she says.

"Motorcycle," I say. "It's the second one I've seen today, and I don't like it."

"Okay . . ." she says. She sounds dubious, but she makes a little clicking sound as she takes a picture of it. We're on a curve, hugging a corrugated-metal guard rail with a gulch just beyond it, and I slow. "Do you want me to try to reroute you? I don't think it's a good idea to get too far off the main road, this is a tricky area."

"Might be too late," I say. I stop as we come to an intersection, with the red Super Duke in front of me. The rider is dressed in a heavy Gore-Tex one-piece coverall, wearing a helmet with a mirrored visor, and I see him turn to stare at us with his blank glassy face reflecting the sky and the asphalt. To his right, a sign tells me that we're entering Dead-wood, "resting place of Wild Bill Hickok," and a mural portrays the fabled gentleman himself, in his wide-brimmed hat and bolo tie and goatee, and the five cards of his fateful "dead man's hand" are displayed alongside him—two black aces and two black eights and a card with a bullet hole through it. "Dang," I murmur.

"What is it?" says Cammie. Her camera does a 360, scoping to the side, behind us, then back to my face. "What's wrong?"

"Nothing," I say, and I try to decide whether to pass the motorcycle—which is going about fifty miles an hour now—or whether to cruise along behind it. "Just a bad omen," I say. I figure she probably doesn't believe in omens, so I don't say any more. We're cruising through the long, winding strip of motels that line the road leading into Dead-wood, most of them derelict or abandoned. Here is a burnt-out Super 8; here is the Thunder Cove Inn, which looks like a series of semitrail-ers stacked on top of one another, with some tent-and-junk structures set up in front of it in the parking lot. A small group of people in puffy coats and baseball caps are unloading a dead deer from the back of a dune buggy, men, women, hard to tell, they're all shaped like potatoes. They lift their heads and stare as the Super Duke rolls past, trailed by our Wagoneer.

Turns out that our rider doesn't like being followed. He glances over his shoulder at me a couple of times and then slows down to forty-five, and then down to thirty as we pass through the downtown area, and when we emerge onto a four-lane highway he starts casting his left arm like he's throwing a baseball: *Go! Go around!* he's urging, and so finally I do, and I wonder whether I ought to clip him as I go past but I don't because maybe he's just an innocent motorcycle man out for a Sunday drive.

Is it Sunday? I have no idea.

"Hey, Cammie?" I say. "What day is it?" I glance over and the little drone is motionless. It has come to rest on the dashboard and its pro-pellers have stopped spinning, its camera eye does not ratchet toward me when I speak. "Hey!" I say. I wave my hand in its direction, trying to get its attention. "Hey! Wake up!"

Surprisingly, it does. It emits a little chime, *pong ping pong,* and a green light starts blinking. The propellers rev a couple of times, uncertainly, and then they start to whir, and the drone lifts up, wavery as a drunk.

"Hi!" it exclaims. Not Cammie. It has the exaggerated, childlike voice of a cartoon character, not quite male or female, and it lifts up and taps unsteadily against the windshield and then spins around and backs up with alarm. "Hi," it says, and turns to look at me. "I'm Pikti! What's your name?"

It makes the sound of a camera shutter, and a light flashes at me. "I just took a really cute pic of you!" it ejaculates. "We should post it to your social media! But first I'll need your usernames and passwords to connect!"

"No," I say. "Stop talking," I say to this being that has possessed my Cammie. "Don't! Speak!" I enunciate clearly.

"Playing the song 'Don't Speak,' by No Doubt (1995)," announces the drone, and music I don't much care for begins to burble from its speakers. We're passing a log fortress compound that has a sign that says TATANKA: STORY OF THE BISON—yet another former tourist attraction? But now snipers in guard towers stand on either side of the entrance, and the driveway is dotted with caltrops.

"Picky!" I say. "Stop the music. Quiet! Silence!" I try to think of other keywords that it might respond to, but now it appears to be unfamiliar with the English language. "Shut up!" I say. "Shut down! End!" And I would throw the thing out the window if I could reach it, except that I'm still hoping it's possible that Cammie might come back.

I'm hoping that she just lost her connection, or maybe her battery went dead, though I can't help but imagine something worse—the semi she's riding in pulled over by robbers or militia guys, Cammie huddled in her sleeping bag, trying to crouch low to the cold floor as the door hatch slides open and light pours in, and grubby bearded fat men begin unloading the watermelons.

I'd hate to think that the last thing I ever said to her was *What day is it?* I'd hate to think that our last conversation was of her reciting facts about Harland Jengling and the Temple of the True Science, which, while interesting, and maybe eventually useful to know, wasn't what was important. There was a lot of emotional and interpersonal discussion that needed to happen before we were parted. I should have told her that even though I was grouchy and yes, mad, I still cared about her, I wanted to get to know her, to talk about our memories and play each other music that we liked, to find out what kinds of jokes made her laugh, what kinds of food she most longed for, whether she liked to play cards, what animals were her favorites. *What is it? What's wrong?*: that's the last thing she said to me.

I make it a little past Spearfish before I see the motorcycles again. I'm still arguing with the drone, who has become increasingly insistent that I give it my usernames and passwords. "It's so much more fun when we can connect with our friends!" it says petulantly.

"I don't have any friends," I tell it as we leave the north end of Spearfish, out of the hills and into the treeless flatlands. We're passing a warren of brick buildings that looks like it might have been the campus of a community college and there are four Super Dukes sitting in the big empty parking lot: two reds, a black, and a blue. Waiting for us, I reckon. The helmeted heads of the riders lift as we go by and I hit the gas.

And, yes, it does seem that the motorcycles are going to be chasing me now. I can see them in the rearview mirror, the four of them moving in a little swarm behind me.

"Everybody needs friends!" says the drone. "I'll always be your friend, no matter what!"

I get the Wagoneer up to a hundred and it's a straight shot now, a two-lane highway running parallel to I-90 and I wonder maybe if I should get on the interstate but I let the entrance pass, I stick with Highway 85 like Cammie told me to, but I am not putting any distance between myself and the motorcycles. They've got themselves in a diamond formation, and they're coordinating behind me, giving each other hand signals and probably talking to each other via headsets.

"My name's Pikti! What's yours?" the drone says—I guess it's decided to start from the beginning, and I kind of wish I had that option. If I could go back to the beginning when I first spoke to her: *So . . . I think you might be my biological father?* says this young woman. *I mean,* she says, *I'm pretty sure. That you are.*

If I could go back, what would I say? I'm sitting there in the *Guiding Star*, and Flip is dozing in the passenger seat, and I could have thrown that phone away, too, I could have said nothing. Would it have changed anything if I'd said, *You need to run. Run away from me, dear one, and never look behind you.*

I push on the gas and we're going 115 now, but that's not enough to lose the little swarm of Super Dukes. They're close at my bumper, and the blue one speeds up and pulls right alongside me, only feet from my side window, and he gestures. *Pull over!* I guess he's trying to communicate.

"Mister Billingsly?" says the drone, in a staticky male voice. "Please slow down and come to a stop. You will not be harmed."

Damn this faithless, promiscuous drone! Apparently any sort of person can occupy it.

"You're in danger right now, sir. We're here to help you."

Up ahead is a side road and I make the hard turn and fishtail in the gravel and for a moment it seems like I'm going to be able to straighten and roar off into the maze of dirt roads beyond.

But instead the steering wheel bucks and jerks out of my hands and we swerve, and wouldn't you know, here's one of the few trees on the prairie, planted by pioneers a hundred years ago and waiting all this time just for me.

A Good Tombstone Epitaph

My hands are cuffed behind my back and I'm sitting sidesaddle in the passenger seat of a Ford F150 pickup and a young guy is bent down at my feet, applying manacles to my ankles. Beyond him, near the remains of the Wagoneer, three of the motorcycle men are having a cheerful conversation. The one in the blue helmet, the one who pulled me from the wreckage and checked to see that I was still breathing and then zip-tied my wrists and ankles, laughs jockishly, his feet set apart and his arms crossed, *Ho ho ho!*

"Aw, hell," I mumble, and the kid at my feet lifts his head and gives me an apologetic look. He's a skinny boy in his early twenties, black-haired and sad-eyed.

"Sorry," he says. "This is just standard protocol."

"Understood," I say.

"It's not too tight, is it?" he says, and I shake my head. The lad helps me turn to face the windshield and buckles me into my seat and slams the door shut.

I can't believe I hit a tree. I sit there, dazed, stars and cheeping birdies haloing my head, and maybe I've got a concussion or maybe I'm just mortified. Though I was able to swerve just enough that I didn't have a head-on collision, and managed to sideswipe the tree in a somewhat artful way so that I wasn't thrown through the windshield to my death,

I still feel embarrassed by my incompetence, by the realization that I've failed in my mission.

"So," says my captor as he settles into the driver's seat. He gives me a searching look, and his eyes are surprisingly kind. "My name's Cameron. Or you can call me Cam."

Cam. This gives me a nasty jolt, but maybe it's just a coincidence. I nod my head, returning politeness with politeness as my mother taught me.

"I'm Billy," I say.

"Billy!" he says. He pulls a crumpled manifest from the pocket of his hoodie and gives it a puzzled once-over. "Says here your name is Barry. Barry Billingsly, fifty-year-old white male?"

"That's a pseudonym," I explain. "I'd prefer Billy."

"Okay, that's cool," says Cam good-naturedly. "Billy! I like that. Kind of a classic. As in Billy the Kid." He shows me a big grin, some teeth capped with gold crowns.

"I've got a daughter named Cammie," I tell him.

"Nice," he says courteously. I study the shape of his face, his nose, his mouth, and wonder if maybe we're related. Is this a son? A half brother? A cousin of some kind? Or just a journeyman trying to do his job, as I once was, not that long ago.

"Anyways," he says. "We got a long drive ahead of us! So let me know if you need anything to make you more comfortable. There's some bottled water here, and I can give you an Ambien CR or a Lunesta?"

"You got any weed?" I ask.

"Naw," says Cam. "No smoking. But I have some THC gummies if you want."

"That'll do," I say, and he reaches across and opens the glove box and fishes around until he comes up with a little baggie full of gelatin chewables in the shape of marijuana leaves. He takes one in his thumb and forefinger and cautiously holds it toward my lips. He has big hands, and they're not unlike mine. He's got that shovel-shaped thumb.

"Don't bite me, okay, man?" he says.

"I won't," I say. I open my mouth wide like a baby bird and he drops the gummy in and I chew thoughtfully. I suppose I'm at the end of the line, and I ought to be coming to terms with my life and what it all means and so forth.

I lean my head against the passenger window and let my eyes droop. North of Spearfish the landscape gets monotonous, steppes so bleak that there's nothing between us and the horizon except a long string of power-line towers. I imagine that Liandro would be tickled by this karmic retribution if he knew about it, and I listen as Cam flirts on his cell phone with someone named Caroline, as he tells her that he's on his way and that it'll be twelve hours, weather permitting, and he chuckles bashfully at something she says. I eye the phone as he puts it in the cupholder of the center console between us and I remember the hungry look Liandro had when I tossed that burner phone out the window—though who could he have called? Who could I call, now, who among my network of associates would offer me aid? Maybe Experanza would if she were alive. I don't know. Part of me thinks that she was never a friend, only tender, and her advice was always meant to keep me locked in my circular, sleepwalking path. But another part of me still believes that she did love me, that she meant it when she said, *I'm your family, I'm the one who's been there for you since we were kids,* and I can see how she would feel hurt and betrayed by my allegiance to Cammie, that it would seem like a delusion to her. That's my fault, too: I could never explain why I felt so strongly, why this daughter who I've never seen, who might be imaginary, has such a powerful hold on me. I can't even explain it to myself now.

But the feeling endures. Whatever Cammie's up to, I do not believe her intent toward me is malevolent. She might even be a good person—though what that might mean in these times, it's hard to tell. I think of her huddled in her sleeping bag and stocking cap in that refrigerated semi, and I hope she's not going to die in there; I hope she makes it to where she's going, and that whatever this was all about, it was not a vain attempt—journey. I do not think we will talk again.

Cam's hand brushes across my knee as he reaches for the glove box again, and my eyes flutter open. "Sorry," Cam says. "I was just grabbing some music!" His hand scrabbles around in the recess and comes out with a homemade cassette. "Do you mind if we listen to some tunes?" He gives me his gold-tooth grin. He has big ears and large eyes and sort of reminds me of the old comic strip character Dondi, and that must be useful to him, I think, to have a face like that—just as, once upon a time, I found that acting the part of a jolly, chatty redneck was useful, not realizing that if you perform a role for long enough, it's who you are in the end. Cam plugs the cartridge into his dashboard tape deck and it's some low-key old country music, Crystal Gayle, and we listen for a while to her mournful, honeyed voice. The sky is full of little fluffy clouds, and I lean back, flexing my cuffed hands, making sure I've got good circulation.

"Where're we headed?" I say, and Cam gives me a sly sidelong glance. I'm not supposed to ask, and he's not supposed to tell, but why not?

"Compound just north of Saskatoon," he says. "It's real nice. On a pretty lake in the middle of the forest."

For the second time I get a jolt of uncomfortable connection. The place my mother was going to deliver me to—that was north of Saskatoon. Wouldn't that be a twist—if the place I'd been running from for all these years became my final resting spot? All those choices I made between then and now were just an elaborate cul-de-sac, leading me back to the inevitable.

"Church of I Am That I Am?" I say.

"I Am That I Am!" he says, raising one eyebrow with mild derision. "Ha! That's from the olden times. Those guys got cleared out a loooong time ago! Now it's the Temple of the True Science."

"Harland Jengling," I say.

"Exactly!" says Cam, and gives me a confiding squint, grinning out of one side of his mouth. "He's my father," Cam tells me.

I let this sink in. Here's the second brother I've come across in a matter of days, and it's sort of surprising that it doesn't have any kind of emotional spark. Maybe it's because I see too much of myself in them—I recognize the flunky I've always been, a born henchman, good-natured and cheerfully ruthless. I wonder what exactly we inherited from old Harland? No doubt we got a bit of his sociopathy, that ability to disconnect when it's necessary to hurt or kill a person. Maybe there's a part of him that was dreamy like us, a part whose only true joy is in being fascinated by some small, obscure piece of the world. But we weren't child prodigies like he was, nor even very smart; we weren't driven to be emperors of our own kingdoms, and I, for one, don't have any interest in such things. Cammie is my tribe, I think. I want to be the father of Cammie, not the son of Harland Jengling; not the brother of Tommy or Cam, who is now softly singing along with Crystal Gayle. "You've been talking in your sleep," he croons. Like me, he is kind of an ugly singer.

He's probably not a bad guy. I like him better than I liked Tommy. In another life, we might have been friends, but I also won't hesitate to kill him if need be.

"You know what's strange?" I say, and Cam stops singing and turns the music down a little, politely.

"What's that?"

"I just recently learned that Harland Jengling might be my father, too," I say. "Spooky coincidence, isn't it?"

"Not particularly," says Cam. He's driving one-handed, his other arm leaned back loosely on the back of the seat and we plunge along the empty highway with stubble fields on either side. "The Temple is pulling in new strays all the time," he says. "It's part of the mission this year, to bring all the lost ones back into the fold."

"Interesting," I say. I flex my fingers again, feeling around in the crack of the cushion behind me. A paper clip or a piece of wire would do. Even a little piece of metal that I could use as a shim. "And then what?"

"Well," Cam says. "They'll probably give you the opportunity to repatriate. It's a family, you know, so they welcome the prodigals."

"Uh-huh," I say. My finger digs along the dry, grainy sludge that has collected in the crack between the seat. I touch what feels like a penny. I touch a sticky lozenge—a sunflower seed shell?

"They have a lot of them in suspended animation," Cam says. "Or whatever you call it. They're preserved for the coming times. And they seem happy."

"Are they naked?" I say.

"Yep," Cam says, and leans back dreamily, drumming his fingers to some slow groove in his head. "They've got bunkers stacked up with Father's progeny. I guess they're in medically induced comas? But they're well cared for. It's the perfect temperature in there, and they're never hungry or thirsty and they have nurses who bathe them with a warm sponge and turn them so they don't get bedsores and so forth. Some people would call that heaven!"

"Some people would," I say, and now I'm peeling some of the seat upholstery looking for a wire or a small pin and from the corner of my mind Experanza says, *Give him a compliment*, and I say, "But you're not the kind to want to sleep your life away! It looks like you've been doing pretty well for yourself. I used to work as a driver and in my organization you never saw a guy as young as you with so much responsibility. You must've really impressed them."

"Well," he says modestly. "I'm a hard worker."

"Hard work and stick-to-it-iveness," I say. "You'll find yourself in a position of leadership someday." I flex my fingers. Experanza once told me about a technique where she'd dislocated the CMC joint of her thumb and slipped out of handcuffs, but she had unusually flexible hands and small fingers.

"You want to hear a joke?" I ask him.

I tell him I'm reading a book about anti-gravity, it's impossible to put down. What do you call a creature with just a nose and no body? *Nobody knows.*

It's sad, in a way, because every corny joke I can think of tickles his funny bone. Who would have guessed that a vulnerability to dumb humor was hereditary—like being susceptible to a disease? He laughs a little like I do, *Haw haw haw, snick snick snick.*

"Do you know what my grandpa said to me before he kicked the bucket?" I ask, and then put on an oldster voice. *"Sonny, watch how far I can kick this bucket."*

He lowers his chin to his chest, shaking his head. "Damn, that's bad," he chortles. "That's awful!" We've crossed into North Dakota now, and we've achieved a kind of camaraderie. I've given up on finding a pick or a shim, and now I'm focused on his body language. He doesn't smoke, but he consumes sunflower seeds and pistachios as fervently as I consume cigarettes, and he's got a fascination with the exact same piece of his chin hair that I'm always pulling on my own beard. He twists his right ankle to and fro, like he's squishing a bug, and I know exactly what that's about, too: he's got to take a whiz, but he doesn't want to stop.

We're passing the village of Bowman and to our right is a smattering of houses, a cluster of trees, and Cam's eyes turn sidelong, wistfully, as the turnoff slides away behind us. I reckon he knows of a gas station in there with a clean restroom.

"You gotta pee, right?" I say, and he gives me a squint—maybe surprised that I've read his mind.

"Eh," he says. He makes a little grimace. "I should've gone before I picked you up."

"Yeah," I say. I yawn and stretch my shoulders though my heart is beating fast. "I could probably stand to drain the radiator myself. Shake the dew off the lily," I say, "change the water on the goldfish. I wish I'd peed before I drove into a tree." He laughs and gives me that conspiratorial grin, poor thing. I don't blame him. If I was his age, I wouldn't be afraid of me, either.

"Okay," he says, and slows down as we approach a crossroad, a dirt track that leads toward a small hillock. "I lose points for doing this, but I don't think I can handle it for another ten hours."

"And I support you," I say. We turn and cross a cattle guard and head up a ways, and I can see by the way his eyebrows shift that he can't hold on much longer and he makes a decision that this is far enough away from the highway and comes to a stop. He hops out and glances over his shoulder, back at the highway, and then he comes around and opens the door for me.

We stand there awkwardly on the great expanse of prairie and he angles away from me and unzips his pants and I hear a heavy, almost horse-like spattering of liquid. "Uhhh," he says, with relief, and I clear my throat.

I'm standing beside him, in handcuffs and ankle manacles, helpless as an old man can be. "Would you mind," I say, and glance down to the fly of my Mammoth Site jeans.

Well. He would mind. I know from experience that it can be fairly uncomfortable to unzip the pants of a handcuffed man and, pretending nonchalance, take his penis out and aim it for him while he urinates. Turns out Cam does not have the fortitude for it.

"Hold on," he says, and he gets out the handcuff keys and I do my breathing exercise, 4–7–8, as he stands behind me and unlocks the cuffs and even before they are loose I make my move, I twist and grab him by the throat before he can reach his stun gun or syringe, and I chomp down on his arm just like my mother taught me.

Slow Realization

We all know that this is a fluke. This is the last time I'll be able to wriggle out and it's only a short hop and jump before I meet my doom, but I can't help feeling exhilarated as I drive toward Canada in the pickup I stole from Cam, loudly singing along with Crystal Gayle, "don't it make my brown eyes blue," I sing, and "ready for the times to get better." Cam is bound up in a tarp in the back, sedated with an injection of Lunesta. I thought about leaving him in a ditch by the side of the road but then it started snowing and I had the image of him lying there slowly freezing to death and I decided I'd take him a ways up the road until I could possibly get him situated someplace warmer.

The motorcycle men can't be far off. Surely they'll be able to trace the phone that Cam is carrying, surely there's a tracking device on the pickup or inside Cam himself—somewhere in his ankle, like it was for Cammie? Right now, the snow is powdery and fine as sand, not accumulating but coiling in snaking streams, or sticking together in light pellets of graupel. This might slow down the Super Duke boys if it starts to get slick and visibility goes to hell.

There is a strong pull of exhilaration yanking me forward, you know how it is—a kind of ecstasy of adrenaline, the desire to dance, scalp tingling, butterflies filling the stomach, driving through the gathering snow feeling the story of my life hit me like the tunnel of snowflakes that are roiling forward and peacefully drifting at the same time, *Many will perish,* says Pastor Avery, tweaking my toe, *but not Billy O Lord,* and Helen Shindle kisses my mouth and lets out her fun-house laugh. *Where are you excaped from,* she asks, and we blast down the road and the road blasts back. Simulation of a starscape. All the Barely Blurs break free and drift off like dandelion seeds: inanotherlife, inanotherlife, inanotherlife, the rumble of the truck tires beneath me—

And okay, I guess this is the end. I know it really wasn't much. I chose loneliness at every turn, that has always been my punch line, but I swear I can still change I can be a different man: *Youhadachoice, Youhadachoice,* the rumble of the tires beneath me—

I have been given this last chance, I think, and even if the hope is slim, even if I don't really know where I am going—the border crossing at Fortuna is all that I remember the drone of Cammie telling me—I drive in that direction and let myself believe that this is not a delusion, not just another one of my episodes, as Experanza called them. I wish I could have convinced her that it was real.

The snow thickens and the world begins to go to blur, the sky and the land merging together into a fog. I glance at Cam's phone which is still in the cup-holder and I keep believing that it will ring at any moment, that Cammie will work the same magic she's worked before and my skin is prickly with anticipation. I wish I'd taken better care of my teeth, and I wish I could lose twenty pounds or so before she sees me, I wish I hadn't murdered so many people. I've never been the sort of mercenary who keeps count, but part of the reason that Cam is alive and bundled like a burrito in the truck bed is that I don't want to meet Cammie with a corpse on my hands.

And also, I think, if there is a tracer on him, or on the car, I want them to think that he's still moving north to Saskatoon with his prisoner.

I know I'm going too fast but I can't bring myself to slow down. The shadow of the road fades to white about a hundred yards in front of me and then it vanishes altogether and I am driving on a cloud, a semi floats out of the mist with its red cab lights like lanterns, its wheels not visible, though it blinds me with a sheath of spray as it passes and I go forward into a world of pure haze, cloud upon cloud, like a slow realization that never does dawn on you no matter how long you wait, mystery upon mystery, a hallway that stretches a little farther every time you think that you'll come to a wall, and you enter and enter and enter and you can feel some inkling of the infinite.

And then out of the mist I see the blinking of a VMS sign by the side of the road, LED lights spelling out letters, each letter made up of a matrix of dots, dynamic message signs, they're called, and you see them rarely these days since there are few functioning departments of transportation left, but sometimes they are used by militias to issue threats to passersby or by random weirdos to advertise their cultish thoughts or religious convictions. Here it is, nevertheless—an electronic billboard on the side of the road.

NATURE BOYS TEXT
94090
FOR PRAYER REQUEST

My breath catches in my throat and I slow down, staring, and then I fumble with Cam's phone, still recklessly driving seventy-five miles an hour, and I hold the phone against the steering wheel and I text to **9 4 0 9 0** with my thick clumsy thumb and I write

> Icomjhg

By which I mean, "I'm coming," and there is a reply text almost at once.

> N 2 Fortuna

And I would like to reply back with a heart or a flower emoji but I don't have the dexterity at this time. I am so close. So close, and I pick up a little speed and let myself glide blindly forward, into the open expanse of blank white.

Escaped!

Or no—not escaped but found at last. Rescued.

The border wall at Fortuna is a high metal palisade, spike tipped, and a big robot stands sentry near the crossing point, fifty feet high with a mouthless head like a helmet and pale glowing eyes that beam out like a lighthouse, snowflakes flickering in the column of light. The wall extends to the east and west, a ragged, nasty fence made up of concertina wire and metal fencing and concrete posts, dotted along the way with land mines and needled spike strips.

I text

> HERE!

And sit there idling at a distance from the small cluster of houses and trees that makes up the tiny village of Fortuna. I hold the phone in my two palms like a scrying stone, waiting, waiting, and I see some murmuring bubbles at the bottom of my screen which means that she is typing.

> Continue 4.2 miles west on 5
>
> Air Force base historical marker on right

This is the tricky part I guess—last I remember, she was "pretty sure" she had some folks who could smuggle me across, and I have to believe that she's managed it somehow. I keep the phone in my hand, pressed against the steering wheel, watching its screen and watching the mile marker signs and speed limit signs on my right rising up out of the snowstorm like dark hitchhikers. The sound of the windshield wipers and my heart. Round bales of hay with their backs striped with a layer of ice. If it's an Air Force base, maybe she's got a helicopter waiting, and I picture taking off in a whirlybird, eluding the hand of the giant robot who runs behind us like a kid chasing a butterfly.

But I don't see any helicopters. I come to the historical plaque that announces THE FORTUNA, ND, US AIR FORCE STATION but there is nothing left of it that I can see except for a single, ruined concrete tower and some broken pieces of road. My phone pings.

> Abandon vehicle walk north follow path

I get out and start walking, leaving the truck on the side of the road. There's a rutted dirt wagon trail that seems to lead up toward the grim tower. Then, dang it, I remember that Cam is still in the bed of the pickup, and I kick the ground with my toe. But I didn't haul him all this way just to leave him to freeze to death, and so I march myself back and drag him out and trundle him into the front seat behind the steering wheel, still tied up in his tarp and unconscious. I leave the keys in the ignition, the motor running. But I keep his phone, which lets out another peep.

> **Where R U?**

"I'm coming," I say, and my words come out as a puff of steam in the cold, and I turn and start jogging alongside the road in a northerly direction.

> **500 yards ahead police cruiser**

I see it. It's a white Chevy Impala parked at the edge of some brush, and it says Border Patrol on the side. It's not running, and there's a thin sheet of snow over the body and the windshield.

Ping, ping, ping, says Cam's cell phone.

> **Ditch phone now.**
> **Trunk is open.**
> **Get in it.**

This is one of those trust exercises you always hear about, I reckon, and even a few days ago it would have been a deal breaker—unthinkable. But now I've made my choice, I believe in her, and I look over my shoulder hesitantly before dropping Cam's phone into the snowy weeds. *Sucker,* my mother whispers as I peer into the trunk, which is empty except for a couple of green wool blankets, and I clamber in awkwardly as Experanza sighs in the back of my head, brokenhearted for me, and I hunker down, curling up on my side with my legs tucked in, and I reach up and pull the trunk closed.

Darkness. Silence.

At last, I hear the crunch of quick footsteps on the gravel outside the car, and I hear the driver's door being opened, and then the engine starts and the driver puts the car into gear.

Time passes differently when you're locked in a trunk and being hauled off to an unknown destination. I can't tell how many minutes or hours are passing, how far we are driving, and I don't even try, really. I can see the red taillights come on when we slow and turn, when we come to a brief stop and there's the metallic creak of a gate opening. I feel the soothing rumble of tires over asphalt, the pleasantly sleepy smell of carbon monoxide exhaust, and I guess I am at peace. Though I am a biggish man in a small space, I am not uncomfortable—ever since I was a child I have loved being tucked in, and I used to try to find the tiniest holes to fit myself into—cabinets and dresser drawers, air vent crawl spaces, dumbwaiters, culverts.

I close my eyes. In the distance maybe brother Cam is waking up and squirming around, and his compatriots from the Jengling compound are coming to his rescue on their motorcycles, and they are disappointed to have lost me but it's not a tragedy. They have many stray children to collect, and I imagine they might already have the half brothers that Experanza mentioned, and maybe a few of Cammie's diblings have been captured, and Ward the chimpanzee.

It's strange, I suppose, that I don't feel any pull toward them; wouldn't it be logical to love all your kin equally? But it's Cammie I want to meet, and I know it sounds mystical, delusional, this idea of connection, but the prospect of seeing her, the actual physical Cammie, fills me with joy. Maybe it's as simple as that.

The car comes to a stop. The driver puts it into park and turns off the ignition and I shift and my arm comes up to cover my face as the trunk opens and the glittering, blinding light of car headlights comes down upon me.

Above me I can see three figures, backlit, stocking-capped, and I squint and hold my forearm across my eyes. I try to unfold myself and sit up.

"Cammie?" I say, and I hold out my hand, and she reaches down and we touch, her palm pressing against my palm and it fits like a puzzle piece.

And then the young woman on the left holds out her hand, and it is the same fit, and the one on the right finally offers her own hand, and our fingers entangle, and she helps me out of the trunk.

"Hi, Will," she says shyly. "I'm Cammie."

I Wake Up

In the dream I am peering out through Flip's eyes as he breaks off the leash they have him on—he could never abide a leash, for as long as he was with me—he twists his head and catches the lead in his jaws and yanks it out of the startled human hand. He holds his own leash in his mouth even though it's still attached to the collar around his neck, and he crouches and backs away from his handler and when they try to grab him he feints and dodges and then starts running up along the ramp that leads past the Mammoth excavation, toward the doors, and he's going to try to find me, and in between he will befriend a wise Siamese cat and a scrappy Chihuahua and a mischievous macaw and together they will go on an incredible journey that will lead them, eventually, to my doorstep.

I open my eyes and at first I don't know where I am. I'm asleep on the floor—or on a mat, I guess you'd call it, a mat of woven palm with mosquito nets draped over it like spider webbings, and then I remember that I'm on an island in the Solomon Sea with my daughters. I sit up and their three mats are empty, and I reckon this is the fourth day in a row that I've slept later than anyone else.

It's a one-room bamboo hut we're living in, with a palm-thatch roof, built up on stilts about six feet off the ground, and there's no furniture except for the mats and the mosquito nets. Outside, there is a bamboo-and-palm-frond awning, and a brick grill for cooking, and some low benches where the girls—the young women—sometimes sit, but they're not there now. I dip a cup into a pot of water that was boiled the night before, and brush my teeth, and then I head to the outhouse behind the hut, and then I bathe in a little stream. There's a type of frog here that sounds like a banjo being plucked, and a bird called the helmeted friarbird that makes a *woot-woot* a little like a loon, and those are the only sounds I hear. It's exactly half of my dream come true: I got to wake up on a tropical island, but sadly without amnesia.

The Cammie whose real name is Morgan found this place for us, and the itinerary was brutal—from North Dakota to British Columbia, and then by boat to Hawaii, and then Guam, and finally to a little island called Goodenough, where there are no roads or cars, no electricity or running water. Where she thinks we will be safe for a while.

Morgan is the most ruthless of the three of them, the only one who has the makings of a killer, the one who is most interested in the various tricks I picked up in my years as a mercenary, and also the one who has the least patience for my clownishness.

Meanwhile, the Cammie who will laugh most often at my jokes is a nineteen-year-old named Heidi Schlegel—her hair is red and kinky like mine, and she can also rock braids, and maybe she is the one who makes me feel most at ease. During the terrible passage to Guam on a fishing boat, she and I made up hilarious crossword puzzles for each other, and we smoked the last of her pot together and we can make each other snicker just by trading glances.

And the Cammie who is Camilla Willacy is more or less who she said she was—a melancholy rich girl from Lake Forest, Illinois, who got caught up in a mysterious conspiracy beyond her control, who got her parents killed and many of her diblings captured by a cult, and who rescued me without being asked to. The one who hoped for good discussions, the one who will be most disappointed in me in the end, which maybe means she's the one I love the most.

I stroll down toward the beach, looking for them, and I take out a braid of hard tobacco—*brucey bruce* is what they call it here—and shave off some pieces with my pocketknife and roll it up in newspaper.

Cammie is down at the shore, looking out at the tropical bay, watching a brightly painted fishing canoe with a sail made of blue plastic tarp.

"Hey," I call, and she turns and lifts her hand. Her prosthetic foot is beside her, and her stump is making a hole for itself in the sand.

"You should've woken me up," I say. "What time is it?"

She looks at her watch. "Eleven twenty," she says.

I sit down beside her, and she gives me the grimace that a depressed person thinks of as a smile. "Where's the others?" I say, and she shakes her head.

"Morgan took a dinghy to Alotau," she says. "So she can get on the internet. Heidi went up to the market to get ramen noodles and betel nuts."

I take a puff from my little hand-rolled cigarette, and she wrinkles her nose. "If I can live without cell phone service, you can live without tobacco," she says.

"Right," I say, and stub it out in the sand and we both sit looking at the waves. I can feel the heaviness of her thoughts, a doominess emanating from her.

She pulls her knees up and rests her head. "I'm sorry," she says. "I wish I could have worked this out differently."

"I'm okay with it," I say. "I like it here."

I smile and touch her shoulder, and then draw back, uncertainly. "One thing I was thinking," I say. "Next time you get on the internet, could you contact that Curtis Chin and have her send me some pictures of Flip? I'd like to see how he's doing."

"Sure," she says, and her footless left leg digs deeper into the sand.

Heidi comes down to join us, and she sits beside me and gives me a betel nut and winks, and I put it in my mouth and begin to chew it. It is a little like caffeine, and a little like cocaine, and a little like a psychedelic.

"Look!" she says, and points at a hermit crab who is waddling down the beach with a bright blue plastic laundry-detergent lid as his shell.

"That's so cute!" I say, but the girls stare after it without smiling. I reckon the crab's situation hits a little too close to home for their liking.

I scratch at the sweet spot on my beard. Having three daughters is more difficult than a person might think. Having children, period: you can't help regretting the world you've given them. The future, from their point of view, grows narrower and narrower, and by the time they are my age, huge swaths of the world will be uninhabitable, and mass extinctions and wars over remaining resources will occupy civilization's last days. Whatever they dreamed of growing up to be isn't on offer anymore, and sometimes they wonder if it's worth becoming what there is left for them to become.

And what can I say? *My apologies?*

So we sit and watch the sea.

Meanwhile, who knows what Morgan is up to, as she's out traversing the internet. Morgan thinks a war has begun. How many have they got? How many can we get? Brayden Kurch lost fourteen billion dollars when his stock tanked, and for now he's no longer one of the world's twenty-eight hundred billionaires, though the rest of them are hard at work, building citadels. The Jengling family will release the apocalypse and only those with Jengling blood will survive, and this has been predicted, Morgan says, these are the end times and we are not going to get our lives back, we are not going to ever be better.

And maybe she's right, but I think it's just as likely that the Temple of the True Science is yet another loony doomsday cult with criminal connections, which, if you read your American history, come and go like ripples on a stream, are forgotten and replaced, over and over. It's almost like we never learn.

I don't know. People are crazy, that's what I want to explain. Most people are. It's so much easier to kill you than suffer the agony of empathy, and even to the last we won't be able to help dividing into tribes, even when there's only a handful of us left. Even on our day of reckoning, we will be calculating our profits and losses, we will be humming to ourselves about what we will accumulate tomorrow.

Alas, as they used to say in the olden times. How happy the world would be if all of us, all of humanity, could wake up on an island with amnesia.

Acknowledgments

The voice and spirit of this novel owe a lot to my late father, Huck Mount.

I am indebted to my friend Lynda Barry, who walked me through the writing of this book. Without her encouragement and advice, it wouldn't exist. My son Philip Chaon, the original nature boy, made so many important comments and invaluable suggestions and helped me see the world of the story through fresh eyes. I am also deeply obliged to friends Tom Barbash, John Martin, Imad Rahman, Mike Rocheleau, Dan Riordon, Simona Mkrtschjan, Lynda Montgomery, Sylvia Watanabe, Charlotte Tate, and my sister, Sheri Lieffring, all of whom read versions of the book along the way and gave helpful advice.

Thanks also to the Civitella Ranieri Foundation. Much of the early draft of this book was written during my time at Civitella, and I'm thankful to Azar Nafisi, Igoni Barrett, and Esperanza Spalding, among others, for inspiration.

Thanks to everyone at Holt, and particularly my trio of different editors—Michael Signorelli, Barbara Jones, and Caroline Zancan—each of whom helped shape the book for the better.

Finally, thanks to my agent Renée Zuckerbrot, whose incredible efforts on my behalf I can't begin to repay. I'm so grateful.

About the Author

Dan Chaon is the author of six previous books, including *Ill Will*, a national bestseller, named one of the ten best books of 2017 by *Publishers Weekly*. Other works include the short story collection *Stay Awake* (2012), a finalist for the Story Prize; the national bestseller *Await Your Reply*; and *Among the Missing*, a finalist for the National Book Award. Chaon's fiction has appeared in Best American Short Stories, the Pushcart Prize Anthologies, and the O. Henry Prize Stories. He has been a finalist for the National Magazine Award in Fiction and the Shirley Jackson Award, and he was the recipient of an Academy Award in Literature from the American Academy of Arts and Letters. Chaon lives in Cleveland.